THE
EMPTY
CELL

THE
EMPTY
CELL

A NOVEL

PAULETTE ALDEN

RADIATOR
PRESS

Epigraph by Alexander Chee from "The Autobiography of My Novel," in his collection of essays, *How to Write an Autobiographical Novel*. Permission of the author.

Published in the United States of America

Library of Congress Cataloging in Publication Data:
Alden, Paulette, author
The Empty Cell: a novel / Paulette Alden
Greenville, S.C.: Radiator Press
Identifiers: LCCN:2020913758 | ISBN: 978-09885189-2-6 (pbk.)
978-09885189-3-3 (ebook)
Subjects: LCSH Earle, Willie—Fiction. | Lynching—South Carolina—History—Fiction. | Racism—Southern States—History—Fiction. | Greenville, S.C.—History—Fiction. | BISAC FICTION/Historical/General | FICTION / African American / Historical
Classification: LCCPS3551.L334 E47 2020 | DDC 813.6—dc23

Cover Design: Emily Mahon
Interior Design: *the*BookDesigners
Cover photo of Willie Earle, courtesy of the Greenville, S.C. Police Department

To the civil rights leaders and foot soldiers in
Greenville who led the charge for change,
and to those who are carrying it forward today.

"I made a world I knew, but *not* the world I knew,
and told a story there."

—ALEXANDER CHEE

AUTHOR'S NOTE

Just before sunrise on Monday morning, February 17, 1947, the owner of Sullivan's Funeral Home, the Negro mortuary in Greenville, South Carolina, received an anonymous call to pick up a body in the woods off Bramlett Road. The man had been beaten, stabbed, and shot. He was twenty-four years old, and his name was Willie Earle.

Growing up in Greenville, I'd never heard of Willie Earle. I only learned of him when I happened upon "Opera in Greenville" by the British author Rebecca West, whom *The New Yorker* sent to Greenville to cover the trial of his killers. I was shocked and fascinated by what had occurred in my hometown; I couldn't get it out of my mind. When I began researching the events, I found that others had covered the case extensively. But I wasn't interested in just the facts. I wanted to imagine how ordinary people in my town might have been affected by what happened to Willie Earle. This novel is that story.

The facts of the lynching and trial are historically accurate, to the best of my ability. The attorneys and the judge at the trial were actual people (except for Lawton Chastain, my fictional prosecutor), as were the named defendants (except Lee Trammell and Lily's husband, Lou Reynolds). The direct dialogue spoken by the lawyers at the trial I drew from Rebecca West's *New Yorker* reportage. The scenes about library sit-ins and lunch counter sit-ins are based on newspaper articles and interviews with some of the participants. The court cases I've referenced are real. A.J. Whittenberg, Reverend James Hall, Willie T. Smith, and Donald Sampson were actual leaders of Greenville's civil rights movement.

But this is a novel, a work of fiction. If it were nonfiction, there would be no novel. I've invented characters and scenes based on what I imagined to be true, and through interviews and research, what I believe to be true to the times. No doubt I've gotten plenty of things wrong. But I hope what I've written rings true.

I've fretted over the reactions of some to me, a white woman, trying to write the experience of Alma Stone, a Black woman. My fears were mitigated to some extent by a recent review of the novel *American Dirt* in *The New York Times*, in which Parul Sehgal wrote, "I'm of the persuasion that fiction necessarily, even rather beautifully, requires imagining an 'other' of some kind. As the novelist Hari Kunzru has argued, imagining ourselves into other lives and other subjectives is an act of ethical urgency. The caveat is to do this work of representation responsibly, and well." Whether or not I have succeeded I will leave to the reader.

I also know that some may be offended by the use of the "N-word" by various characters in the novel. As disgusting as the term is, unfortunately it was in common use in the Jim Crow South. My fictional character, Lee Trammell, for example, being part of a lynch mob in 1947, would have used that slur. It's his, not mine. I don't use the word lightly, but I believe I do use it accurately.

PART I

1

LEE TRAMMELL

WHEN I COME out the Southern Café at the depot on West Washington Street about three o'clock that Monday morning, I seen four or five drivers I knew walking towards me. George McFalls come out behind me, and Willie Bishop said to us, "You going with us?" I didn't know what he was talking about at first. I asked where they was going, and he said over to Pickens to get the nigger. I knew what he meant. I told him I hadn't thought about it, and he said well, they was going, and to meet up at the Yellow Cab office in an hour or so.

A farmer out there in the country near Liberty found one of our own, Tom Brown, bleeding in the weeds by the side of the road late Saturday night. It was Mr. Brown who got me this taxi job when I was working at Poe Mill. He was like a father to me, better'n' the one I actually had. All us boys went to see him in the hospital. It was a pitiful thing, him white as the sheet he was laying on from all the blood he lost, writhing from the pain and anguish of it all. My knees felt rubbery, like I might sink down right beside his bed in front of the other boys who was crowding around, some with tears rolling down their faces. I wanted to take his hand, beg him not to go. I had to choke back what felt like big hard rocks that might heave up out of my chest in sobs. We was all heart broke and mad as the dickens too, that a no-count nigger would do Mr. Brown that way. We couldn't stand it.

The police wasted no time arresting the nigger. They found a footprint leading to his mother's sorry house out there in Liberty not far from where Mr. Brown laid bleeding and alone. The nigger weren't at home, but it didn't take 'em long to find him, drunk as a skunk with his nigger friends out at the quarry. A Pickens cabbie came on over to Greenville after his shift to tell us the nigger was in the Pickens jail. It made sense that we go get him, do to him what he done to Mr. Brown. That's what all the boys was thinking, like all our brains was one.

I went on over to the Yellow Cab office. I checked my time sheets with Bill Shockley, and he said to me, "Let the law handle it. You're going to get yourself in a peck a' trouble." I told him you can't stop no flood. When I come on outside, there was maybe ten or twelve cabs there, not just Yellow but Blue Bird and American. One from Commercial. Lily's husband Lou Reynolds was there, and he took up a collection and went on over to the Poinsett next door and bought some whiskey. We passed it around. After a while, Woodrow Clardy told the drivers standing around which cabs to get into. Hendrix Rector climbed in my passenger seat, and Jonnie Willimon, Hubert Carter, and Jim Bob Forrester got in the back.

I was feeling good about what we was up to, excited and wondering what was going to happen. I didn't figure we might kill him, no, though I suppose I knew it. My mind only went so far, like headlights that shine ten or fifteen feet ahead in the dark. I just felt alive, sure, and righteous, like we was doing the right thing. We didn't trust the law to do it, we had to do it ourselves. That was the feeling in the car and in all the boys. We knew what needed to be done, and we was the ones to do it.

We drove in the dark on out to Parker Road and traveled on some back roads 'til we come out on the Easley Highway near Noah Smith's junkyard. Stansell's tourist camp is just across the Saluda River Bridge, and maybe four or five more cars was there when we arrived. It was about four o'clock by then. We waited 'til more cars arrived, all cabs except for one, a 1942 Ford four-door, black, shiny with a nickel-plated spotlight on the driver's side. I didn't know the driver. Not one of us.

It was pitch black except for the lights from the cabs. We was feeling like we was at the county fair or a fight, revved up. Like the current of a strong river was pulling us along. There was a lot of talk, voices in the night, about that nigger doing Brown so bad, and now he'd have to pay. When I saw Lou Reynolds strutting around like a banty hen I thought of Lily, and a big ache went up in me. Like I was a baby wanting to be held in her arms, snuggled up against her soft breasts and beginning to get hard, knowing the relief it would bring.

After a short while, we began to pull out. Clardy was driving the lead car with Fat John Joy's black '46 Nash sedan behind him. Fat Joy waved for us to pull alongside him, and he called, "Let's all keep together." So off we went in a line, forming a convoy. One cab had a flat tire at the stockade near Pickens, and the boys in that cab got in other cabs, and off we went again.

About five a.m. we arrived at the Pickens County jail. I'd passed it many a time, red brick, two-story, with rounded towers like it were trying to be a castle in that little country town. The civilian car turned its spotlight on the front door.

A Bluebird man, Roosevelt Herd, carrying a single-barrel shotgun, and Rector and Clardy went to the door. We all got out and stood around in the street, waiting to see what would happen. Duran Keenan had a double-barrel shotgun, and he moved to the front of the crowd. When the jailer opened the door, Herd called him by name, "Ed," like he knew him, and I guess he did. He said, "We come to get the nigger that stabbed Mr. Brown," and the jailer said, "I guess you boys know what you're doing, don't you?" Herd said, "I guess we do or we wouldn't be here."

Herd, Clardy, Hendrix, and several of us others went in the jail. The jailer asked for a minute to get dressed. There was a feeling in the air, like something was set in motion that wouldn't be denied. I wondered what that nigger upstairs in his cell was hearing or knowing. That was the first time my thoughts roamed to him, and I was sorry they did. I had an uneasy feeling just then, the kind of feeling a weak man might have. Herd said to the jailer when he come out, "No one's gonna hurt you." The jailer was an old man, round and short and not likely to protest much, especially against all of us and that shotgun. He went to get the jail keys, and several boys went up the stairs with him to the cells where the nigger was. I heard him point out another nigger up there, in for writing a bad check. He didn't want there to be no mistake about which one we took.

I was still downstairs when Rector started coming down the steps holding the nigger by the collar, shoving him along. He weren't handcuffed, and he didn't resist 'cause what was the point? Hubert muttered, "Goddamn nigger," and the jailer asked us not to cuss out of consideration for his wife, and after that, we minded our manners.

Things was moving along, not fast, not in a panic-like, but

with a force all their own. I looked at the nigger, and I saw his nigger eyes, the whites big and one eye off like my boy Lee Jr.'s. I never saw a face show that kinda fear before, not even a nigger face, and something in me jumped back and wanted to run away. My heart was stuttering so I feared it might play out on me, and my limbs felt froze. The crowd was moving along, and I moved with it to see what was going to happen next. Like some knowed what to do, didn't have to even think about it, and they carried us along. I got my bearings, pictured Mr. Brown in that hospital bed, and the rage made me strong again.

When they got to the lead car, Clardy shoved the nigger into the rear seat. Ernest Stokes sat on the right side of him, Jesse Sammons had Reecey Covington on his lap and Hubert Carter on his right. Mr. Herd and Red Fleming sat up front. We all piled in our cars and followed the lead again, turning left after we passed through Easley. No one in my cab was saying much. The mood had swung into something mean and nasty. All at once I felt tired all over, like I just wanted to go home and go to bed. The sun was not up yet, but it was brightening in the East. I wanted to be done with the whole thing. Bishop in back was drinking heavy, and when he passed me the bottle, I took a long slug.

We stopped near the Saluda dam, and we all piled out. A crowd was already around the nigger, punching him and asking him did he do it. Different boys took their shots, and the nigger was crying and stammering, *yesuh, yesuh,* he'd stabbed the old man, and someone was telling him how he was going to get the same. He was bleeding from the nose and mouth, and I hoped now the boys was satisfied 'cause he'd confessed. Somebody was pushing me forward, saying it was my turn. They was holding him up for my shot, and at that moment I thought how I'd whupped Lee Jr. yesterday morning, and I wanted to be done with hitting. But I cocked back and landed one on his jaw, his head kind of limp so I didn't get much purchase. I felt his hot nigger skin all slick with blood and sweat against my knuckles and there was no pleasure in it.

We piled in the cabs again, the nigger shoved back into the lead car. I didn't know who made the decision to move. Others was in charge and knew what to do. We stopped right off Bramlett Road at the slaughter pen. I saw the nigger pulled from the front car again, and that's when someone asked if anybody had a rope. I knew good and well I did, right in the trunk of my cab. But I kept my mouth shut. I'd seen enough and wanted to leave. But I didn't want the boys to think I weren't with 'em. I tried to think of Mr. Brown and how mad I'd been. But standing in the woods, I couldn't find the anger that had felt so good before.

It was cold out there near the slaughter pen, still dark, but you could feel morning coming on. Rector began beating the nigger to the ground with the butt of Clardy's shotgun. Lots of guys crowded 'round, and I heard something like the cutting of cloth or flesh. That's when the nigger said, "Lord, you done killed me!" It sent a chill through my soul. I couldn't help but think of Jesus when he said, "Forgive them, they know not what they do," when the crowd was gathered 'round him at the cross. But that was crazy thinking. That nigger weren't no Jesus. He'd stabbed Tom Brown in cold-blooded murder, and now he was getting the same medicine and deserved it.

The boys was like a pack a' dogs tearing at a weaker dog they had down, determined to rip it apart. That's when I heard a gunshot, and someone calling for more shells and then two more shots. I knew the nigger had to be dead, and

I was glad 'cause I wouldn't have to hear him say nothing else, I wouldn't have to hear his burblin' voice. I felt tingly and odd like I never felt before, and I didn't know what to make of it. I'd expected to feel good, but I felt strange, scared even, though I didn't want to show it. Everybody was milling around, congratulating each other, satisfied with the job. We all got back into our cabs and departed that place in the woods, leaving the dead nigger on the ground there.

2

ALMA STONE

THAT EARLY MONDAY morning when Willie Earle was taken, Alma dreamed of the Promised Land.

I am bound for the Promise' Land, I am bound for the Promise' Land. Oh who will come and go with me, I am bound for the Promise' Land.

They had sung that hymn at the Sunday service. Alma stood next to her short, sturdy mama Bessie, their voices harmonizing in a perfect blend of high and low. The choir members were clapping and reaching to Heaven, the congregation too, all their faces known to Alma, young and old, some light-skinned, others dark as a slave just off the boat, with every shade in between. On their feet, swaying to the music, *Promise' Land, Promise' Land! Oh who will come and go with me . . .* The joy Alma had felt then, their voices and souls joined together, lifted up in song! *In belief!*

In the dream she was weightless, soaring, flying out over the muddy waters of the Reedy River below, out beyond Main Street, the Poinsett Hotel and Court Square, past the fine homes along McDaniel Avenue (She spotted the Chastains' house on Crescent, Miz Chastain in the backyard, lifting her arms toward Alma). On past the green spine of Paris Mountain at the edge of town, out into the countryside, dense with pines and kudzu, the bottomlands lying fallow now in winter. Up over the mountains, Table Rock, Caesar's Head, Mount Pisgah. She was leaving it all behind, free and joyful in her flight. She could see in the far distance the Promised Land, more beautiful than anything she'd ever imagined. Bright and shining, gold and glitter.

Then suddenly she was plummeting toward earth and certain death. The wind whistled by her, the air turned bitter cold when before it had been balmy, and her nightgown—blue silk like Miz Chastain wore—clung to her like a heavy second skin, dragging her down. She woke right before she hit their red clay yard on Sycamore Street. But it was not relief she felt. Tears had come then, copious, soaking her flannel nightgown when her hands could not contain them.

Beside her, Huff woke with a start. He took her in his arms and leaned the two of them back against the plank wall, stroking the tears away with his knuckles. He was a big, silent man, not given to much talk. Alma felt comforted by his body's solid mass, his familiar musk.

"What's wrong, baby?" he asked, his voice disembodied in the dark. Alma could only shake her head. She didn't know, then. Just something, something . . . Already the Promised Land was fading. She longed to see it again, just one more time! She sheltered in his arms, feeling strangely bereft.

FIVE thirty, time to rise. She rubbed her hands over her face to break the spell. She asked Huff what he had going that day. There wasn't much to do in February. He did yard work for six white families. This time of year, things were slow. She wasn't sure how he spent his time, and she didn't ask. A man had to have some privacy, some dignity.

"Hawkins got some brush out back he want me to clear up," he said in his bass voice. He was getting out of bed, leaving Alma cold when he took his warmth away. When he switched on the overhead bulb, she curled around herself, wanting to burrow into bed, not face the day. The room took shape in the stark light: the stove against the north wall, Pretty's crib in the corner, a picture of Jesus on the cross on the wall by the front door, the small wood table in the middle of the room directly under the light bulb. There was a blue oilcloth on the table, aluminum salt and pepper shakers, the heavy crystal sugar bowl Miz Chastain had given her after Betsy dropped the top and broke it. She rested her eyes on these familiar objects, her things. Huff started the kettle on the woodstove to heat water to shave, poured cold water from the pitcher into the basin on the washstand. As he washed his face and armpits, Alma studied his strong back and arms, the result of manual labor all his life. *A proud man who has to keep that under wraps.* The thought materialized in her head, as if she were reading the words there.

Her mind skipped ahead. Today Miz Chastain was going to her church circle in the morning, meeting ladies for lunch, and getting a perm in the afternoon. Alma would be alone most of the day, the way she liked it. Miz Chastain would want her to vacuum and dust the whole house, make everything perfect that was already perfect. Mr. Chastain's birthday was coming up Thursday. Polish the silver, though it was never tarnished, make sure the cocktail and sherry glasses were spotless, dust the liquor cabinet, iron the white linen tablecloth and Mr. Chastain's shirts like always. If she put off ironing the sheets, maybe she could sneak a few minutes at the piano, trying to pick out more of that tune Miz Chastain was always playing, the one about moonlight.

Alma got along well enough with Miz Chastain. She was like every other white woman Alma knew, only maybe unhappier. That came out sometimes when she played the piano. She'd ask Alma to stop whatever she was doing and come listen—even though Alma was always busy. She never sat down in that house, not in the living room or den, not ever anywhere, except when she ate in the kitchen on a stool after the Chastains had eaten. But sometimes when Miz Chastain played, she'd insist Alma sit down in the living room. It felt wrong to be sitting there on a white person's velvet sofa, but Alma did as she was told. At those times, Alma saw Miz Chastain differently, not as the spoiled child she usually was, but as someone lost.

No matter what else Miz Chastain played, she always ended with the moonlight song. It reached right into Alma's heart, music as sad and serious as life itself. Miz Chastain told her a German man had written the music long ago and that he was going deaf when he wrote it. That was as sad as life too.

There was a rustling in the corner. Alma went to Pretty, uncovering her from the patchwork quilt made from green dress scraps, and lifted her out. She'd turned two in January, almost too big now for the crib. Alma breathed in her sweet and spicy smell, something indescribably Pretty that she would know anywhere. She brushed her lips across Pretty's smooth, round forehead and cupped her small head in her palm. Pretty's hair stuck out in six little braids every-which-way. She was the color of caramel, sweet as sugar candy but developing a will of her own. "Good morning, Sunshine," Alma whispered into her ear, which made Pretty bat at her. But here was something else different about the day. Alma took her into the bed for a stolen minute, something she never did. She cradled Pretty tightly against her body, as if somehow knowing.

But she couldn't linger long. She sat Pretty on the rag rug with BooBoo, her stuffed bear that was missing an arm, and gave her a pile of brightly colored wooden blocks to stack and crash. She washed her face at the basin, put on coffee to brew and a pot of grits. Huff had on his overalls now, and a blue work shirt so worn it might rip at the elbows at any moment. He gathered Pretty in his arms and sat down at the table with her on his lap.

The room was chilly, but Alma didn't want to add more wood to the stove, letting it burn out. They'd all be leaving soon, Pretty to Rosa Mae's down the block, Alma to the Chastains, and Huff—he'd go down to the barbershop to hang out with the other men until it was time to go to the Hawkins' place. Alma glanced at him, his dark face which revealed nothing, and tears welled up in her. *His life as a Negro man!* She didn't know where all those feelings were coming from today.

She and Huff held hands to say their blessing in unison. They ate in silence, gospel music on the radio in the background, Pretty singing a nonsense song to BooBoo. Alma let her mind float free, trying to capture a piece of the Promised Land. It had dissipated like the early morning fog when the sun rose in the bottomlands around the homeplace, leaving behind a longing, the same mournful note the old gospels sounded, like the slaves used to sing. Like her great-grandmother Callie still did. She spooned cool grits into Pretty's mouth.

When Huff left, she got Pretty dressed, hurrying, paying now for that extra minute when she'd taken her back to bed. But she took time to empty the coffee can she kept on the top cupboard shelf, money she was saving for Pretty's college. There was one hundred and seventy-five dollars in the can today, down five from yesterday. He never took more than five, though that was a lot, considering. When he could, he repaid it. Neither of them ever mentioned it.

A L M A opened Rosa Mae's front door without knocking. "We here," she called out. Alma paid Rosa Mae fifty cents a week to keep Pretty. They both paid five dollars a week rent to the rich white man who owned all the houses on the dirt street. Rosa Mae's shotgun shanty had a slanted porch held up by large stones, just big enough for her green vinyl glider on rails.

"Hold on," Rosa Mae called from behind the bedroom door. "Slow as molasses this morning." Alma sat down on the brown Naugahyde couch, a handoff from Rosa Mae's last white family, with one mismatched seat cushion replacing the original that their cat had preferred to the litter box. When she patted the cushion beside her, Pretty climbed up and laid her head in Alma's lap. The red, white, and blue plastic flowers had been in that same vase on the same doily covered table for the ten years Alma had known Rosa Mae. She nodded to Rosa Mae's parents and grandparents in ornate, oval gold frames on the bureau. Layers of cooking smells—mustard greens simmered with fatback, fried catfish, black-eyed peas, sweet potato pie—had embedded in the walls over the years, holding up the house as much as the pages from the Sears catalogues that lined them. There was a portrait of Jesus gazing up toward Heaven and a big, round Coca-Cola clock on the wall. 6:37.

"You hear?" Rosa Mae asked as she came into the front room, leaning heavily on her cane, her back bent like a branch that had snapped but not broken.

"Hear what?" Alma asked. A bit of the dream came back to her, haunting.

Rosa Mae reached for the rocker arm, steadied herself, settled in, and held out her arms for Pretty and her pink blankie. Alma deposited her in Rosa Mae's lap, but instead of the antic faces Rosa Mae usually made, she just kissed Pretty on the forehead. Rosa Mae's ebony face was ribbed with wrinkles and an expression Alma had never seen before.

"Hearse man over to Sullivan's got a call 'round daybreak. Go pick up a body. Beat up bad, shot up. They saying cabbies done did it." Rosa Mae clicked her tongue. Pretty was squirming in her lap, demanding, "Down! Down!" When Alma put her down, she ran over to the toy trunk and began rooting through it. Alma sat back on her heels. "Did they say who it was?"

"Don't nobody know."

She glanced at the clock again. 6:46. Rosa Mae called to Pretty, "Lookee here. I got a pretty for my Pretty," and she dangled a strand of plastic pearls for Pretty to come see. "Gentle like," Rosa Mae said when Pretty reached for them. "Like dis, just touch 'em gentle."

Alma kissed the top of Pretty's head and flew out the door and down the three steps. She ran up the dirt street in the dark chill, no streetlights, curbs, or sidewalks, the only light coming from windows of frame shanties. Breathless, she joined the other maids at the bus stop. Instead of the usual friendly greetings, one woman, Mafilia, took both of Alma's hands in hers. "Did you hear?" Alma nodded. The other women were silent. Alma heard a murmur of "Lord, Lord" and a few soft voices joining in agreement.

The bus rounded the corner and wheezed to a stop. They filed in, nodding politely to the driver who greeted them by their first names, but whom they called Mr. Morgan as they headed for the back seats. Some had to stand, though there were empty seats up front.

Alma stood hip to hip next to Synthia. She was eighteen, her skin lighter than any of the other maids, her eyes ebony, and her lips always painted a bright red. There was some-thing of the vamp about Synthia. She reminded Alma of a young horse that hadn't been broken, that might suddenly rear up and throw its rider. Her fingernails were so long, they curled over at the tips, painted the same bright red as her lips, evidence that she had not yet settled into her life as a maid. Synthia wouldn't last long in her job if the missus she worked for found her uppity or the mister too movie-star pretty. Alma had a soft spot for her but tried to be stern. She gave Synthia advice about some household tasks, how to iron the collar of a shirt or how to get red wine stains out of a white lace tablecloth, or sometimes, if Synthia asked, about boy-friend trouble, of which there was a good deal.

Today Synthia was smoldering. She stared straight ahead, her face hard and unsmiling. Alma wasn't sure what to say or even if she should try. She feared for Synthia. She'd better learn to swallow that anger before it got her in trouble. The bus driver was whistling "Dixieland," and Mafilia, hanging on to an overhead bar nearby, cast her eyes quickly at Alma.

But Alma had retreated deep inside herself. *What had happened? Who got himself killed?* The thought of a Negro man in the hands of a mob of white men made her shudder. Synthia glanced her way. Bile rose in Alma's throat.

S H E got off the bus at the corner of McDaniel and Crescent and walked the few blocks through the neighborhood of fine two-story brick and stone homes with dark-leafed magnolia trees on manicured lawns. The Chastains had a stately house, red brick, the front door painted a vibrant French blue set off by the deep green ivy that grew up the columns of the front porch. She went around the side of the house where the old red brick of the walkway was uneven and lined with camellias, buds forming now in February. The back door was unlocked as usual. In the kitchen, Mr. Chastain's breakfast dishes were in the sink. He'd already left for work, earlier than usual. Betsy would be leaving for school at eight fifteen, which meant last minute pandemonium as she looked for her books, her hairbrush, her sweater, her letter jacket. Alma, with troubled heart, rested for a moment in the silence of the house. Miz Chastain and Betsy were still upstairs. It was such a big house. So much space. So much quiet.

She set to doing the dishes, putting the everyday ones, rose-colored with an English country scene on them, into the kitchen cabinet. *Beat up and shot*, Rosa Mae had said. It could happen to any colored man if he slipped up, sassed a white man, or messed with a white woman. It could happen to Huff if he crossed the line. She pulled her mind away from thoughts of the killing. They'd use the good Wedgwood china and the Chantilly silver on Thursday night for Mr. Chastain's birthday dinner. Alma would stay late to do the dishes while Mr. and Miz Maxfield and Miz Chastain played bridge. Mr. Chastain would give Alma a ride home. *What had that man done to get himself killed? Liquor was involved, one way or another, of that she was sure.*

Betsy, a senior in high school, came into the kitchen dressed in a red plaid jumper. Her fine brown hair was plaited in a pigtail down her back. Alma thought of all the times she'd washed that hair when Betsy was little, a scrawny, naked little white child afraid of getting soap in her eyes when Alma directed her head under the bathtub faucet. She'd wrap her in a towel when they were done, and Betsy would dance on her tiptoes, going from anxiety to ecstasy in a split second.

"Betsy, do you see the time?" Miz Chastain called now from the hall. "You're going to miss carpool, and I'll have to drive you, and I won't be one bit happy about it. I have a very full day, so you better get a move on!"

"Mornin', Alma," Miz Chastain said as she came into the kitchen. "I'm off to circle after I take Betsy. Could you cut some of those camellia buds to see if they'll open by Thursday? I don't know what to make of this weather, and neither do they. I just hope we don't get a freeze."

"Almanac say clear moon, frost soon," Alma said. "What you want for breakfast?"

"I'm getting so fat, Alma, I shouldn't eat a thing. Oh I better eat a little something. How about a basted egg and just a piece of dry toast? Oh maybe a little oleo. But not too much."

Miz Chastain was a pretty woman with a soft, feminine face that was getting rounder and fuller with the passing years. She was right that she'd gained some weight, but what was wrong with some meat on your bones? You could still see the pretty child in her face, even though she was over forty now.

Her folks, Miz Beatrice and Mr. Lyman, lived in a big house on the corner, just three blocks down. In Alma's opinion, that was a little too close. She figured Mr. and Miz Chastain would be a lot better off—a lot happier—if they lived a couple of miles away from Miz Beatrice and Mr. Lyman, so Miz Chastain wouldn't be running over there all the time.

AFTER Miz Chastain left with Betsy, Alma set about dusting in the living room: the tall mahogany breakfront with glass doors; the white marble coffee table; the ornately-carved wood of the side chairs and velvet sofa; the round pie table with a hand-painted china lamp on top. Now that she was alone, her mind returned to Rosa Mae's news. What in the world could have happened to that man? He had to have known the rules! They all knew the rules, they learned them from the crib. The possibility was always there, lurking under the surface, like a rattlesnake in a dry woodpile. They'd heard enough stories— beatings, houses burned to the ground, flaming crosses in the yard. Every colored person in town knew about the Klan, what could happen. They hadn't marched down Main Street since Alma was a child, all the coloreds hiding in their houses. But that didn't mean they weren't still lurking out there in the woods and mill villages on the perimeter of town, ready to flare up like a gasoline torch lit by a match. What could that man have possibly done? How had he offended? No Negro in his right mind would cross the line and get his fool self lynched! Unless he was drunk.

She dusted the broad back of the baby grand piano, the black wood shiny and unblemished, and ran her fingers over "Baldwin" embossed in gold on the front. She lifted the keyboard cover, pulled out the piano bench, and sat down.

She touched the keys she was familiar with. They rang so bright and clear, sounding so much better than the ancient upright at church. Miz Chastain had her piano tuned every six months. The piano man would come with his box of tools. For an hour or so, he'd plunk each note; then he'd adjust and plunk them again.

Alma began picking out the notes of the moonlight song with her pointer finger, listening for when she made a mistake and correcting. *Dum . . . dum dum.* She got as far as when her finger had to reach far right to hit that high note. She'd concentrate on that part the next time Miz Chastain played the song, her ears memorizing it so her finger could pick out the right notes.

IT was after ten o'clock when the phone rang. Alma was ironing in the red room. She'd finished with the tablecloth and had just started on Mr. Chastain's shirts. The phone table was in the hall. It reminded her of the desks at Sterling High, the seat attached to a desk top and a cubbyhole underneath for the phone book. There was always a notepad and pen so Alma could write down who had called. Miz Chastain got a lot of phone calls—her lady friends from circle, bridge club, garden club—calling to gossip and make plans. They all knew Alma and called her by name.

But it was Alma's mama, Bessie. She never called Alma at work. They didn't have a phone at the homeplace. Hearing her speak her name, the way it caught in her throat, Alma stood still, knowing she was about to receive a blow. Maybe Callie had passed. Her great-grandmother was ninety-seven. She'd seemed perfectly fine on Sunday, her only trouble an arthritic knee, which she managed with a cane. Or maybe it was Daddy.

For years, her father had had a bad cough, but he wouldn't give up his pipe. Heart attacks ran in his family. Alma waited.

"Baby." Alma heard tears stuffed back down her mama's throat. "It's Li'l Willie."

"What?" Alma exclaimed. "Not Willie!"

"They snatched him last night. Kilt him out to the slaughterhouse. Dew came right out. Carried me over here to Pearle's. I wanted you to hear it from me."

Alma sat down hard on the phone bench seat. For a moment her mind went dark, and she wondered if she was going to faint. She was glad Miz Chastain wasn't home. They had always called him Li'l Willie, though he'd grown to be a big-sized man. But when he was a child, he had been so little, up 'til his teens when he gained his height and weight all at once. Alma tried to think when she'd seen him last. They weren't close and didn't keep in touch. She'd hear things occasionally from Bessie, who heard from his mama how he had seizures and had lost his trucking job, how he couldn't get employment, had taken to drink.

Willie's mama Tessie and her kids lived less than a mile from Alma's folks out near Liberty. Bessie had taken ten-year-old Alma along when she went to help Tessie with the home birth. Alma saw Willie when he was pulled from between his screaming mother's legs onto a towel on the wood floor. He was glistening with a slimy, shiny film attached to the inside of Tessie by a thick blue cord. And there was blood. The birth scared Alma, and she almost threw up. But she couldn't stop looking. As Bessie cleaned him up, the baby began struggling, shaking his skinny arms and wrinkled legs like he was having a fit, squawking like a stuck pig. But when Bessie laid him on Tessie's chest and he calmed, Alma drew near. He flexed the tiniest hands she had ever seen. Alma was smitten.

After that, every morning, she'd run over to Tessie's to see Willie. Sometimes she got to hold him, sitting on the floor. Tessie would gently place the swaddled baby in Alma's lap. She would press her nose against his taut tummy, breathing in his milky smell, and stroke his head. He'd been born with a full head of hair.

"They saying it was dem taxi drivers," her mama was saying. "Broke him out da Pickens jail. Say he kilt one of their'n and that's why they got him."

Alma wanted to shout that Li'l Willie wouldn't kill anyone! But she didn't really know him anymore.

"Dew'll bring y'all out to the house tonight. We got to go over and pay our respects to Tessie. See how we can help."

In a daze, Alma hung up the phone. Could Willie have killed a white man? She'd heard things about him, head-shaking things, how he had come to no good. Mama had told her about Willie's fits. Heard it from Tessie. How he would fall to the floor and Tessie would have to put a spoon in his mouth to keep him from swallowing his tongue.

Alma got herself up and went down to the basement, to her bathroom. Took her washcloth from the rack there and bathed her face with cold water. She was breathing hard and fast, dizzy-headed. Li'l Willie . . . Horror was creeping over her, making her weak-kneed. She fell to her knees right there on the linoleum floor, locked her hands into fists, pressed them hard against her lips. *Please, Jesus*, she prayed fervently. *Help Willie, Jesus, wherever he is. Hold him in your arms, dear Jesus. Take away his pain. Help us, Jesus, help us to bear this. Not our will but thine be done.* A heavy weight was spreading in her, such that she felt she might not be able to rise.

Alma used the sink to hoist herself to her feet. She leaned her weight against the porcelain bowl. She glanced in the tarnished mirror over the sink and saw an expression on her face that made her look away. She opened her mouth wide to unlock her jaw, took a deep breath, and drank a full glass of water. It was no different from any other glass, except that no white person would use it.

3

LEE

AFTER WE GOT back to town, I let the boys off at the cab office and went on over to the Southern Café to get a cup of coffee to settle my nerves. I had a bad feeling, worried-like about what was going to happen. I didn't think the police would arrest us for killing a murdering nigger, but I still felt afraid. It seemed a bigger fear than the law. I looked down and saw spots of blood on my pants, and I determined I'd burn 'em pants, a perfectly good pair. I didn't want the police to find that blood if they come 'round. I just had a bad feeling all over.

I come on home after that, it must of been going on seven by then. I poked my head in the boys' rooms. I had the urge to hug Lee Jr., remembering the whupping I'd give him and wanting to be forgiven. It was a mistake to wake him up, for when he saw me, there was a look in his eyes, just like that nigger's. He shrank back from me in the bed, curling up as far away against the wall as he could get. I was shocked, 'cause the boy had always loved me so.

On Sunday, I'd come on home after visiting Mr. Brown in

the hospital to find Lee Jr. playing with my shotgun. I took off my belt and taught him a lesson. I taught him you never, ever touch Daddy's gun. I use that gun for hunting squirrel out on Paris Mountain. My heart 'bout bust out of my chest when I saw him sitting cross-legged on the floor with that gun across his little lap. He might of hurt hisself or the baby. I had to make sure it would never happen again. I was like dry kindling someone struck a match to. But if it was 'cause of the gun, Mr. Brown, or that nigger, I didn't know.

In the kitchen, I looked down and saw them blood spots on my pants again. I piled some wood in the cook stove and lit it. About that time, Emylyn come into the kitchen. I was stuffing my pants into the fire that was going good, and she just stared at me goggle-eyed. I told her I'd messed my pants and for her to go on back to bed, weren't nothing to do here. She started in on how she could of washed them and what did I think I was doing, them was perfectly good pants and had I lost my mind . . . I gave her a look that shut her up.

EMYLYN and I got hitched when I was eighteen. I don't regret it, not much. A man has to get on with his life. Her folks worked at Poe Mill same as me. I'd see her at the company store, buying penny candy, wearing homemade clothes you could tell come from flour sacks. Some of 'em have right pretty patterns. She was too young for me at first, too shy to look me in the face. I took notice when she began to grow little titties.

I'd balled a couple of girls by then, sure, and I liked how it felt. Emylyn let me suck those little pink nips, 'bout drove me out of my mind. All I could think about was getting into her pants, her sweet pussy. But she was religious, raised Baptist like me, though with me, it didn't take. She took all the talk

of sin and damnation to heart. I should have paid more attention to that. Now that I think about it, jumping her bones was
most behind our getting hitched.

When Emylyn turned fifteen, we eloped to North Carolina
overnight. We lived with her folks in Poe Village when we got
back, where there weren't much privacy. Still, we was fucking
whenever we could. Sometimes the bed would creak when
I got going, and we couldn't help but giggle, her folks right
there in the next room. But she'd get mad too and push me
away. It was so exciting at first it made the hours at the mill
fly by. I think she liked it, but now I don't know, not after Lily.
Emylyn just lay there, and we always did it the same way, me
on top and her with her legs spread and kinda patting my
back. Every single time. It was all we knew. But for those first
few months it was plenty.

It weren't ten months after Emylyn and me was married
that Lee Jr. was born. Something was wrong with his eyes, I
could see that right away. One of 'em looking out the wrong
way-like. He's almost six now and wears thick glasses that
make him look lost. Like he don't know what's going on. But
he loves his daddy. He hugs my knees when I come home,
about makes me fall over he hangs on so tight. I lift him up
and throw him over my shoulder, call him a sack a' potatoes
to make him laugh. His laugh is high and sweet, like tinkling
bells. He ain't afraid to plant a big kiss on my cheek. That's
why it hurt so bad the way he shrunk from me this morning.

My other boy, Earl, is three now, sturdy as an ox, just the
opposite of Lee Jr. He's always into something, runs Emylyn
ragged and it makes her crabby. I'm trying to give my boys the
childhood I never had. They get to play all day, most with homemade toys since we can't afford no store-bought ones, or games

they make up theirselves. They're outside a lot in the yard, chasing butterflies, and in spite of his crazy eye, Lee Jr. is pretty good at catching 'em. He loves bugs of all kinds and wants a dog, but I tell Emylyn we can't afford no dog. He keeps spiders, frogs, and June bugs for pets. But there's always food on our table. I'm not saying we don't have to watch our money, and sometimes it's just beans and greens, but it's food. We can't be starving 'cause Emylyn done put on weight, maybe fifty pounds since Earl was born. Her butt is broad as a barn, and her arms have flaps hanging off. I hold her partly responsible for Lily.

One mistake my folks made was having too many kids. They was eight of us young'uns, the first 'un born when Ma was fourteen. Most times we ate pinto beans, one cent a pound, and a piece of cornbread if we was lucky. Ma saw to it that the youngest got fed first, and then on down the line, so there weren't much left by the time it got to us older 'uns. I understood that. But I hated the old man for the way he filled up his plate first. I told myself I'd never be like him, never selfish and mean like him, and on the whole I think I've kept my promise. 'Cause of his drinkin', Pa'd be fired from any job he managed to get. Liquor makes some men mellow and some mean, and Pa was the mean sort. I learned to avoid him if I could, and if I couldn't, I took my licking and tried not to cry. I'd do my best to steer clear of him or clamp down inside, so he wouldn't make me cry. The harder he beat me, the more I'd hate him, and the harder I'd go inside, denying him the pleasure of seeing me cry. But sometimes I couldn't help it.

ALL that was left of my pants now were a smoldering cuff and a smell of ash. I was sorry about that, they was good pants. I tried to think what to do. I was so tired, I wanted to lay down on the kitchen floor, but I found myself in my cab again. By now the sun was coming up, shedding light on all we done. I drove over to the Southern Café and got another cup of coffee. I couldn't eat nothing, and the coffee burned my stomach like battery acid. I just watched the clock, waiting for the time when I knew Lou Reynolds would be reporting for work, and I could go over to Lily's house after her kids left for school. It was dangerous for me to go to her place, especially in the cab, but I had to see her, that was all. I needed to put my arms around her and have her kiss me and fuck me and make me feel good again.

The thing about Lily is she knows her way 'round a man, and you can tell it ain't just her husband Lou Reynolds. Lily's thirty-five to my twenty-four, married to a hands-down alcoholic. It's amazing he can hold onto a cab job. He was the one who took up a collection when we was getting organized last night to go to Pickens. Bought some Jim Beam 'round the corner at the Poinsett Hotel basement, and all of us got into it maybe more'n we needed to. It eased the pain. But it fanned the fire too.

I know Lou Reynolds, sure, and I don't like him one bit, not just because of Lily, but because of what he is. Real short guy, his black hair puffed up on top like a woman's. A drinker and blow-hard. Trying to be a big man 'cause he ain't, acting better than the rest of us. Lily deserves something better in her life than Lou. I know I'm a better man than him. It ain't like I'm gonna quit Emylyn and the kids. But I figure I can have Lily too, on the side, nobody knowing. Lily and me both getting something we want and need. I think that's the way she sees it too.

When we was first getting started, I'd stop in for a Coke or ham sandwich at Kress. Lily works behind the soda fountain counter, and we'd flirt a little if things was slow. I'd see her in her white uniform, them big breasts bound tight, making you wonder what it would be like to free 'em, what it would be like to take the nipples in your mouth. She's got reddish-brown hair like a fox, and her narrow face even reminds me of a fox face, not a bit sweet, which is something I like about her. She has a way of narrowing her eyes, squinting at you, like she wants to see if you're telling the truth. I'd tell her tales about who I'd driven that day, Cary Grant or Myrna Loy, to pull her leg. I'd try to get the best of her, and it made for some fun times. I'd tell myself I wouldn't do it, but there I'd be at Kress, ordering a cup a' Joe at the counter. I could tell she was looking for me too. Squinting those gold-brown eyes and then a slow, knowing smile would start up in her foxy face. Like she was on to me. Probably seen it before.

When the school bus pulled away, I went around to the back door and knocked. She was surprised to see me, still in her purple robe, like royalty. That's the way she is to me, royalty, something better than me that makes me want to serve her. I didn't say a word, just swooped her up, startlin' her, and then she started smilin'. She put her hand down below to feel me. I laid her across the bed and pulled up her robe and nightgown, unbuckled and pulled my pants down in one motion not bothering to take off my boots. I could see by the look in her eyes that she understood how bad I wanted it, how much I had to have it, and how she was willing though I don't know if that woulda even mattered.

She lay back and spread her legs wide . . . and nothing. I couldn't get in. I pulled back and looked down and it was curled up like a slug. Like it'd been plunged into cold water. We both stared at it in amazement, 'cause that had never, ever happened before. It'd been Old Faithful, Mr. Reliable. I was so shocked I just sat back on the bed. Lily raised up and began to work me with her mouth, and nothing. I couldn't even feel it! I thought maybe it was 'cause we was in Lou's bed, not our place, the Dixieland Motel, and all the drinking and the crazy-ass night with that nigger and all. I didn't say a word, just pulled up my pants and left. I was shaken and worried, not knowing what it meant or if it would happen again. I told myself it never would. A one-time thing.

4

LAWTON CHASTAIN

AT SIX FIFTEEN that Monday morning, Lawton was having a cup of coffee in the breakfast room, enjoying a few quiet moments to himself when the phone startled him. He hoped it was just a wrong number, not bad news, but it was Bob Ashmore, his boss in the Greenville solicitor's office. The mutilated body of a Negro man had been found off Bramlett Road. Apparently in the predawn hours, a convoy of taxis had left from the Yellow Cab office in Greenville. Rumors were flying that a mob of cabbies had abducted the victim from the Pickens County jail. "It looks like we have a lynching on our hands," Ashmore said.

Lawton could hardly believe what he was hearing. There hadn't been a lynching in Greenville County in ten years; he'd thought those days were over. He sat for a moment after he hung up, too stunned to move, feeling the way he had when the news about Pearl Harbor came on the radio: the earth had shifted. He took a moment to call Delores, the secretary in the solicitor's office, and Thomas, their clerk, and told them they needed to come in as soon as possible. Then he ran up the stairs two at a time to get dressed.

Lydia was sound asleep, the covers pulled up to her chin, her hair in the blue satin bonnet she wore every night to keep her hairdo intact. He paused a moment to look at her and registered—nothing. He moved as quietly as he could in the semi-dark to put on his usual work clothes, a white Oxford shirt, a gray business suit, and a striped tie. He poked his head in Betsy's half-opened door, hoping not to wake her, but she raised up in bed. "Did the phone ring, Daddy?" she asked. "Is something wrong?" He went over and sat on the side of her bed. "Just work," he said. "It's early. Go back to sleep." When she lay back down, he pulled the covers up around her and kissed her on her forehead. At the door, when he turned to look back, her eyes were still on him.

The town was coming awake as he drove down Main Street to Court Square: a trolley clanked by, sparks flying off the rails, a few cabs were out, Jack the janitor was sweeping the steep marble steps that led up to the courthouse doors, and Leroy, the doorman at the Poinsett Hotel, recognized his Ford and saluted as Lawton turned down Court Street. He passed Sheriff Bearden's office on one side of the narrow street; the Yellow Cab office was directly across from it. The block, normally quiet, was crowded with squad cars parked halfway up on the sidewalk. He recognized a couple of reporters standing outside the sheriff's office. His thoughts were racing. Had Ashmore really said a convoy of cabs had left from the Yellow Cab office? Right across from Bearden's office? Could that even be possible?

DELORES was already in the office, and Lawton briefed her on what was going on. Bob Ashmore was scheduled to handle criminal cases in Pickens that morning and would be delayed in getting back to the office. Thomas hadn't come in yet but would be there shortly. Lawton told her he was going over to the sheriff's office and would be back soon. Handle any phone calls as best she could: "No comment at this time."

He walked across Court Street. Sheriff Bearden's office was in chaos. Their single dispatcher was already inundated with phone calls from the national press, and the reporters from the *Greenville News* and *Piedmont* were vying for quotes from any of the cops crowding the front office. When Bearden saw him, he motioned Lawton to follow. Lawton had known Homer for ten years; their offices worked closely together. He was over six feet tall and a good 250 pounds, red of face, nearing retirement, and perspiring heavily now. He took out a handkerchief and mopped his brow over and over as he filled Lawton in. A farmer had found a semi-conscious, profusely bleeding cab driver, Tom Brown, around ten o'clock Saturday night on the old Liberty-Pickens Road. Though he'd been stabbed, he was able to say he'd picked up a Negro man on Markley Street in Greenville and brought him to Liberty. Pickens deputies had taken twenty-four-year-old Willie Earle into custody in Liberty Sunday afternoon on suspicion of the robbery and knifing of Brown. They'd locked him up in the Pickens jail. He was too drunk to talk much, so they were planning to interview him today. But early this morning, the owner of Sullivan's Funeral Home, the Negro mortuary, had received an anonymous call to pick up a body before it was even cold.

Bearden told Lawton a deputy on duty overnight on Sunday had been alerted by a cabbie who'd walked across Court Street from the Yellow Cab office around four o'clock to tell him a lynching was about to take place. Lawton stared at Bearden. He told him he needed to talk to the man.

They went to the interview room where Bearden had asked the deputy to wait. All he would have had to do was look out the window to see that a convoy of cabs was forming. Bearden introduced Lawton to Officer Aikens, a slight man in his thirties with a balding head and a deep cleft in his chin. He didn't look up when they entered the room. He appeared defensive, wary, and petulant.

"Been a long night, huh, Aikens? Bet you'd like to go on home. I just have a few questions, and then I suspect you can leave, right, Homer?"

"Right," Bearden said brusquely.

Aikens didn't look at Lawton. He seemed to find something fascinating in his intertwined hands on the wood table.

"Just tell me what happened last night," Lawton said.

Aikens sighed heavily. Lawton wondered what being a deputy was like for him. Was it just another job? Did he have a passion for law and order? Was he afraid out on the dark streets at night?

"Not much," he said. "One of 'em boys—one of 'em cabbies—showed up. Drunk. Spinning tales, is how I figured it."

"What did he say?"

"Not much. Something about cabbies up to no good. I didn't pay it no mind."

BACK at the office, Lawton learned that the cabbie Brown was dying. The newly elected governor, Strom Thurmond, had been notified of the lynching early that morning. Thurmond issued a statement saying he wanted the world to know South Carolina would not tolerate mob violence. He

promised to exert every resource at his command to appre-
hend the persons involved in such a flagrant violation of the
law. Maybe, Lawton thought, Strom would prove progressive
on racial matters.

By then it was lunchtime. Lawton's friend John Bolt
Culbertson—"Cotton" so called for his white wispy hair—
stopped by to see if Lawton wanted to go to lunch and, of
course, to learn what he knew. Lawton had known John Bolt
since 1938 when he started his law practice in Greenville
after working for the FBI in Omaha. Flamboyant, outspoken,
voted the most popular student in his class at the University
of South Carolina, John Bolt was known around town as the
Negroes' friend. He was one of the few white people who'd
address them as Mr. or Mrs. and shake their hands. For that
Lawton admired him. But he was not so bold.

They went across the street to the Poinsett Hotel's club
room. Lawton wondered how many people in town already
knew about the lynching; there was a strange tension in the
air, almost like a vibration. Leroy, the colored doorman, wearing white cotton gloves and a uniform that reminded Lawton
of the guards at Buckingham Palace, opened the heavy revolving glass door. Greeting Lawton and John Bolt by their sur-
names, he projected a magnificent combination of regal manners and obsequiousness, not exactly looking at them straight
on but smiling broadly. What did he know at that point?
Rumors and news traveled fast in the Negro community.

They sat in red leather chairs at a corner table. Mason
Alexander, the popular manager, stopped by their table to
speak. Hating himself, Lawton asked if Sam had their table
today, and Mason said he would see to it. Sam was maybe
thirty-five, a short muscular man who looked too tough

for the elegant surroundings. His black eyes always locked onto Lawton's with a certain directness that Lawton found unnerving but irresistible.

Within a few minutes, Sam appeared in his black slacks and white dress shirt with a black vest and bowtie. "Gentlemen," he said, passing them the heavy hardbound menus they knew by heart. He was recommending the special, crab cakes, and Culbertson ordered them and sweet tea. "Mr. Chastain?" Sam looked right into Lawton's eyes. Involuntarily Lawton swallowed hard, feeling uncomfortable but also unable to resist staring back. "I have no idea," he said after too long a pause. "I'm not really sure . . ."

"Take your time," Sam said and again that knowing look. "Maybe the creamed tuna on toast? You always like that."

"He'll have the crab cakes," John Bolt said with a wave of his hand. "Now tell me what you know, Lawton."

"Crab cakes it is," Lawton said. Sam nodded, bowed slightly, and then he was gone.

Lawton began to fill Culbertson in on what he'd learned thus far. Ashmore would be going to Columbia to confer with Thurmond and the state attorney general in the afternoon. Lawton was going to Pickens to interview the jailer.

Eliza, a Negro woman dressed as a plantation mammy in a white uniform, black apron, and red-checked head scarf, brought around the famous spoon bread. Did she know that a mob of white men bent on a lynching had formed early this morning right behind the Poinsett Hotel?

Just as Sam set their crab cakes down, Ben Bolt and Tom Wofford came up to their table. "Don't get up," Ben said courteously as they started to rise. Ben was one of Greenville's aristocratic barristers, soft-spoken, with a full head of silver hair. About Tom Wofford, the quip around town was he was Greenville's best defense attorney when he was drunk and second best when he wasn't. He had a martini glass in his hand, and a canary-who-swallowed-the-cat grin on his face. Lawton considered him quite intelligent, ambitious, and a nasty bastard.

"Lawton," he said, "I'm surprised to see you have time to dawdle over crab cakes when the reputation of our fair city is at stake."

"I believe Greenville will live through my having lunch," Lawton said. "Starting a little early, aren't you?" He nodded at Tom's drink. Culbertson jumped in. "I suppose y'all will want in on the action, Tommy boy," he said to Tom. "Your chance to make a name for yourself, maybe get elected to some important office."

Bolt asked if Lawton could wager how many men were involved, but he just shook his head. "Way too early."

"The law will be all over those dispatcher logs like flies on shit," Tom grinned and speculated that the solicitor's office would never get a conviction.

"If you gentlemen will excuse me," Lawton said, standing up, "I have the city's reputation to uphold." He caught Sam's eye, and when he brought the bill, Lawton's hand shook as he signed the account.

"You haven't eaten," John Bolt pointed out.

"Not hungry," Lawton said. "Good afternoon, gentlemen."

At the door he paused to look back, but Sam was nowhere to be seen. A flush went over him. If people in town knew about him, they wouldn't lynch him. But they would crucify him just the same.

AS she often did, Lawton's daughter Betsy walked into his office around four o'clock that afternoon after getting out of school. She would browse in the department stores on Main Street or get a soda at Carpenter's Drug until he was ready to leave, and then they'd drive home together. He was always happy to see her, proud of her. She was seventeen, a senior at Greenville High and not a beautiful girl in a town where beauty was the gold standard. She didn't have the easy, flirtatious ways of some of her friends, didn't have a breezy personality that worked well in high school. She was tall, thanks to Lawton's genes, and a bit awkward because of it. The boys did not find her "cute," perhaps because she was smarter and more serious than they were. Lawton suspected she'd like to go on dates to Pete's Drive-in or one of the picture shows downtown with a boy. But since she became a teenager, her childhood friends had gotten caught up in social clubs and dating, and she was not a part of that.

Instead of her customary teasing banter, Delores just mouthed "not now" and waved Betsy back to her father's office. When Betsy asked what was going on, Lawton told her the bare facts. She'd need to call her mother or walk home because he had to go to Pickens to interview the jailer. Bright pink circles bloomed on Betsy's cheeks when she heard what had happened. She immediately asked if she could go with him. At first Lawton said no, he didn't think it would be appropriate. She stood before him in her plaid jumper, and said "Please, Daddy!" in such an urgent way that he reconsidered. He knew she was chomping at the bit to get beyond the social cliques and insular gossip that constituted Greenville Senior High, to learn about the larger world and even be a part of it. She made the point that since she already knew about the lynching, and it would be all over the newspapers tomorrow, she might as well learn something about how an interview was conducted. The truth was, Lawton wanted her company on the drive to Pickens and back.

The Pickens jail was a forty-five minute drive from Greenville. Mostly they rode in silence, both lost in their thoughts. Lawton's were in turmoil over what had transpired. He wondered if he had made a mistake to bring Betsy. But there was no way to protect her from what had happened, so maybe taking her deeper into it might help her see that the forces of good . . . the law, justice . . . were swinging into action and would counteract the lynching with all possible means.

THE jail in Pickens was a peculiar structure, a small-scale red brick castle set on a corner a few blocks off Main Street in that sleepy country town. It had two rounded towers, giving it a fanciful feel completely in contrast to its official function. Lawton rang the doorbell with Betsy shivering in her peacoat by his side. In the minutes it took the jailer, Ed Gilstrap, to respond, Lawton tried to comprehend what had transpired early that Monday morning.

He had felt, driving over to Pickens, a keen enmity toward Gilstrap, certain he had failed completely in his duty to protect a prisoner of the state. That morning, he'd been interviewed by state constables from Greenville and Pickens, and Lawton hoped that he would be charged for failing in his duty to protect his prisoner. But when he opened the door, Lawton felt his rage lose air, like a balloon whose knot has come undone.

Here was a mild-looking older man, rotund and gentle-appearing, perhaps sixty, with white hair, who reminded

Lawton of some of his country relatives. He shook Lawton's hand and invited them in, as if this were a social visit. Lawton could see that the jail was isolated. What help could Gilstrap have hoped for when angry, inebriated men, several with guns, came knocking on the door before daybreak? He showed them into the small parlor with its modest furnishings: a leggy spider plant on a spindly stand by a lace-curtained window, portraits of what Lawton took to be his parents and grandparents on the wall, a needle-pointed piety in an oval frame on an oak secretary, the too-soft cushions of the divan on which he and Betsy sank. Gilstrap told his story: When he heard the insistent knocks before daybreak, he'd opened the door to find a bright spotlight shining in his face. Shielding his eyes, he'd seen eight or ten taxis lining the street. Lawton asked how many men he saw.

"I couldn't say for sure," he said. "Twelve or fifteen. Twenty. Hard to say."

"Were they wearing masks, Mr. Gilstrap?"

"No sir, but a lot of 'em had 'em caps like cabbies wear."

"Did you know any of the men?" Lawton asked, and here Gilstrap paused. "No sir," he said, "can't say that I did."

At this point, his wife appeared and offered tea. She was wearing round spectacles and a stained apron over a muslin dress. She must have been frightened in her bed when the knocks came in the early morning. She appeared frightened now, wondering no doubt just how much trouble her husband was in. Lawton declined the tea, saying they had to get back to town soon. Wearily, reluctantly, to the extent that he wondered if he was coming down with something, he asked to see the cell where Earle had been held.

He indicated to Betsy that she should wait downstairs.

"I'm coming too!" she said with such vehemence that he looked at her. Her face was pinched, as if she was trying not to cry. Gilstrap led them up the narrow staircase. It smelled of sweat and fear. What must Earle have felt as they brought him down these stairs? How does the mind prepare for what it fears and knows is coming? He was sorry he had brought her.

The five cells were dank and filthy. They passed a cell where a colored man was curled in the fetal position on a bare bunk. He didn't look up as they passed. Gilstrap unlocked the barred door of the next to last cell. None of them spoke. Lawton glanced again at Betsy, whose face was unnaturally pale. He asked the jailer how many men had come this far: five, and one of 'em carrying a shotgun. Had Earle resisted? "No sir. They pulled him down the stairs. He said nary a word."

DRIVING home, he and Betsy didn't speak for a long while. When they came within the city limits, she said, "Did that colored man kill that white cabbie?"

"He was arrested on suspicion of the murder," Lawton said.

"Why?"

He told her the evidence thus far: Apparently the police had found tracks that matched Earle's boots leading from the site where Brown was attacked to Earle's mother's house; they found a jacket with bloodstains there, which Tessie Earle confirmed was Willie's; Earle had a big, sharp scout knife on him when he was taken into custody.

Betsy was silent. Then, "What if he did kill that cab driver? What if he was a murderer?"

"It's tragic that Brown was killed," Lawton said. "From what we're learning, he was an outstanding man, a World War I vet who got wounded and took the taxi job so he could take off time when his nerves were bad. Apparently a positive influence on the younger cabbies. The sort who wouldn't have let those young men get into such trouble." He paused as he chose his next words. "But Brown's murder is a completely separate matter from what happened to Willie Earle. Our whole civilized way of life turns on the rule of law. Whether Earle was guilty or not isn't the issue. We can't tolerate mob justice. The South has a long, sordid history of the lynching of Negroes— but I thought we had progressed beyond that here."

Again Betsy was silent, looking out the window into the dark that had overtaken them.

"I'm sorry I brought you along," he said as they neared home.

"What would you have done?" she asked. "If you were that jailer."

Lawton took his time answering. When he pulled into the garage, he said, "That fellow was in an awful position. I'm not sure what he could have done to stop a mob."

"He didn't even try!" Betsy said. "He let them have that colored man . . . Willie . . . and he knew good and well what would happen to him! He didn't have to get the keys. He could have sat down in the middle of the floor and refused to budge."

"And they would have beaten him with the butt of the shotgun. They were not in a mood to be denied."

"It's so awful!" Betsy exclaimed, and Lawton was shocked that she was crying. How could he have exposed her to the ugliness of all this! But how do you protect your daughter from what is in her town? From what is real? She slid across the seat and surprised him by burying her face in his neck, crying hot wet tears against his skin. Was Willie Earle all she was crying her heart out about? How little he knew her, and how dearly he loved her! Lawton held her as her sobs shook his own body. He patted her back, trying to soothe her like he hadn't done since she was a baby. He used to walk around the block with her at night when she was teething, hurting along with her and hurting all the more because there was nothing he could do to stop the pain. He put his cheek against her head, and he wanted to say, over and over, "It'll be all right, honey. It'll be all right."

Though how could that be?

I T was well after seven when they went in the house. Alma was still there. Lydia must have asked her to stay late to serve their dinner, though there was nothing to do but take it out of the stove. He had phoned Lydia with the news that morning and then to tell her he was taking Betsy with him that afternoon to the jail. Why make Alma stay, today of all days? He was sure she was aware of the news. There was a radio in the red room where she did the ironing, and it had surely been on the news all day. He told Lydia that he'd run Alma home before he ate and for Betsy and her to go ahead and eat without him.

Alma got her things and sat in the back seat. It seemed impossible to make small talk in light of the lynching. They rode in silence, unusual because normally they'd make a little conversation. She'd always been quiet, reserved, never offering anything on her own, but polite and pleasant whenever he'd bring up a subject. Her high cheekbones revealed her African ancestors, and her brown skin the white blood introduced into those ancestors along the way. Her face was handsome, peppered with black moles. She'd started working for them when Betsy was seven, ten years ago. Her mother Bessie had been their previous maid but had handed off the job to

Alma when her arthritis got bad. He felt in a way he'd raised Alma too, though that was absurd. He'd had nothing to do with her private life; he hardly knew her, in fact. Yet all these years she'd been their maid, come to their house, witnessed their daily life, cleaned their toilets, ironed his shirts, cooked their meals. She'd worked right up until labor and then was back to work two weeks after Pretty was born. She was married to a yard man named Huff, who did occasional work for them. In truth, she was a cipher to him.

When they reached Southernside, they bounced through the narrow, unpaved dirt streets, Lawton's Ford taking up almost the whole lane. It was dark and even chillier now. Alma thanked him for the ride and got out, carrying a paper bag. Lydia had probably given her some leftovers or maybe an article of clothing she no longer wanted. Lawton watched her pick her way in the dark, no streetlights, and climb the rickety wood steps to her front porch.

5

ALMA

THAT MONDAY EVENING, Alma's brother Dew came by in his newly purchased 1940 Plymouth sedan to carry Huff and her out to the homeplace in Liberty. Dew had a good job working for Southern Railway as a porter on the Crescent Limited that ran up the East Coast from New Orleans to New York. He'd come back from the war a different man from the boy who left in '42.

Alma bundled Pretty up in a blanket, for it had turned cold again after reaching the fifties during the day. Clutching her blankie, she fell asleep on Alma's lap in the back seat as soon as the car started moving. The two men sat up front, silent. As they cleared town, and the lights by the side of the road became infrequent, Alma felt a cold fear in her stomach. This was the same kind of deserted country road the taxi drivers would have driven to get to Pickens. She looked out the window at the dark woods flashing by, thinking of those men, liquored up, bent on evil. She knew what they were like. Some of them were in the Klan, of that she was sure, and they could be mean as junkyard dogs. Alma hugged Pretty tight, putting her cheek against her sleeping head.

A lot of the family had already gathered at the homeplace, a three-room sharecropper's cabin built at the turn of the century, not big enough to hold all the relatives who often gathered there. Tonight they were spilling out into the front yard. A lone bare bulb hung over the front porch, making a dim half circle of light on the red dirt. Some of Alma's cousins and uncles were smoking under a poplar tree beyond the dim illumination. The car lights swept them when Dew pulled into the open space in front. They turned to see who had come.

While Dew and Huff joined the other men, Alma carried Pretty up to the porch where her twin siblings Pearle and Jeremiah were sitting in caneback rockers. Pearle greeted her, but Jeremiah said not a word, staring out into the yard. Alma plunked Pretty, who was awake now and looking around wide-eyed, on Pearle's lap. She went over to Jeremiah, his face stony in the stark light. What came out as sorrow in the women came out as anger in the men. Alma meant to give him a hug but then thought better of it.

"Go on inside," Pearle said. "Mama's waiting on you."

Alma glanced out toward the poplar tree. Her uncles Stew and Wade and several of her cousins were standing around with the other men. She could see the glow from their cigarettes and hear the murmur of their voices, sonorous in the quiet night. Again she felt that fear in her stomach, hard as an oak knot. Her ears strained to hear if there were cars coming in the long drive, cars carrying white men. She knew the old stories, crosses burned in the yards, bodies hanging from a limb. She couldn't recall anyone ever telling her about those things; people didn't talk about them. Just a shaking of the head, a clicking of the tongue, and a hollow, breathless feeling in the heart. Yet Alma had breathed it all in.

Until today, she'd wanted to believe those days were over. It was 1947, after all; they had just come through a world war, Negroes serving their country same as white men, though Dew said they were just as discriminated against in the military as at home. Still, those men came home changed, having seen the larger world. Things were changing, had to change. But where was the change? Nowhere around these parts. She shook her head to clear it; she'd think about these things another time. Again she felt that heaviness that was new, or maybe she hadn't noticed it before because it was always there. She opened the front door, which always stuck, pushing it hard with her hip.

The front room was warm and full of women. The home-smell that greeted her was sweet and thick as molasses, ancient as milk and blood. Her eyes adjusted to the light from the bright overhead bulb. Everyone stopped talking when she entered, turning to see who had come. She went straight to the elders, who were sitting side by side on the old sofa: her grandmother Marie and her great-grandmother Callie, born to slaves brought from Virginia to work the South Carolina rice paddies in the low country, sold when she was thirteen to a farmer with thirty acres in Liberty. Alma knelt in front of the old women and took both their hands. They gripped hers back fiercely.

Marie cupped Alma's head with her palm, drawing her close for Callie to see. Callie's brown eyes were clouded over with a blue film. Almost blind, she lived with Marie and walked with a cane, but at ninety-seven, though she had no teeth, she still had her mind. She was as dark as Marie was light-skinned. Everyone knew the story. She was fifteen when Freedom came. The married white man who owned her kept her and their children in a little house in the colored part of Liberty. He took care of them, kept them fed, visited once a week. He was Marie's father, though she hadn't known him. "This here's Alma," Marie told Callie, "come home to see us."

Callie nodded, reaching out to touch Alma's face. Her fingers felt like bones. "Where that baby of yourn?" she asked, her fingers moving over Alma's cheekbones and closed eyelids. When a tear slipped out, Callie dried it with her thorny thumb.

"Pearle's getting her turn on the porch," Alma said. "I'll be bringing her in to see you, don't you fret." To stop the tears, she focused on the black, old-lady lace-up shoes they both wore. Alma felt like laying her head in their laps, either would do. Those old mamas. Everything they had experienced they contained in silence. "Your mama's waiting on you," Marie said.

When Alma stood up, she saw Bessie watching her from across the room. They looked into each other's eyes. "Mama," Alma's voice erupted in a low moan. Her mama, no nonsense and never had been, wearing her usual red headscarf, came quickly and put her arms around Alma, the hard mounds of her breasts and stomach pressing against her. She smelled of wood smoke and Murray's Pomade. "We got to go on over there, baby," she said, hugging Alma tighter. "Just me and you. 'Cause you loved Willie best."

No! Alma wanted to protest, no, don't put that on me! What did Mama mean, she'd loved him best? She hadn't seen Willie Earle in years! They hadn't kept in touch once her parents sent her to live with Aunt Delores and Uncle Stew in Greenville, so she could go to Sterling High. She was sixteen then, Willie six. She was becoming a young woman while he was still a child.

She got caught up in her new life in town and stopped going over to Tessie Earle's when she came home every weekend. No reason, surely, just that she was growing up.

She tried to think when she'd seen him last. Maybe two, three years ago? It was Christmas, she remembered a string of colored lights across the door frame of the grocery store in Nicholtown, festive-like. She was paying her aunt Delores and uncle Stew a Sunday visit. That day, Alma walked to the store to get her aunt a jar of Ragu spaghetti sauce for dinner. At first, she didn't recognize Willie. She hadn't seen him or even thought about him in so long. He was sitting on an over-turned crate near the door, a stranger, just another young man in a flat cap, a soiled jacket and overalls, looking down on his luck. She didn't pay him any mind. It was he who recognized her. "Ama," he exclaimed, jumping to his feet. It was what he had called her as a child.

Startled, she looked directly at him. For a moment she didn't know him, and then she did. His eyes were open wide in surprise and delight. Alma felt herself blush. A vague, uncomfortable feeling came over her. She had let him down. Abandoned him. Maybe hurt him. "Willie, can it be you?" she stuttered and couldn't help smiling and laughing. A feeling of pleasure, even love, came over her. She felt the impulse to embrace him but wasn't sure she should. But he quickly cast his eyes down, his face closed, the pleasure gone, replaced by a wary defensiveness or maybe resentment. They awkwardly exchanged some meaningless words: *How you doin'? Okay, how 'bout you? Makin' it, you know.*

He still had those long eyelashes that curled up charmingly, and the same shy brown eyes when he dared a glance at her. One eye was stray, an imperfection that had made her feel protective of him. For an instant, she saw him as sweet and innocent again, and she felt her heart rip. He had been her baby when she was just a child herself. It was her first experience of maternal love, fierce and passionate. She hadn't felt such love again until Pretty was born.

Now his skin was pocked with acne scars, and a stubble of beard gave him a bum's look. His clothes were wrinkled and soiled, as if he'd slept in them, and he smelled of liquor and something worse. She'd once called him Doodlebug.

He asked her for a dollar that day. Said he'd pay her back. Called her "Miss Ama," as if she'd risen high above him. Because she'd graduated from high school. She took two dollar bills from her pocketbook, rent money she'd miss herself. She'd have to take it from her college savings for Pretty. She knew what he'd buy with it. But how could she deny Li'l Willie?

"I don't even know him anymore," she tried to tell her mama now.

Yet as soon as she said the words, she started crying again. She cried into Bessie's neck, her strong, short, solid mama who herself never cried, who patted Alma on the back now as if she were a baby. For a moment, Alma was overwhelmed with memories of Baby Willie. Every morning when she woke as a girl, the first thing she'd think of was Willie. She couldn't wait to run over to Tessie's to see to his every need, feed him, change his diaper, play with him, take him by the hand when he was old enough to toddle beside her around the yard. She'd pull the stamens from honeysuckle blossoms so he could taste the sweet drop of nectar at the end. She taught him how to hunt doodlebugs by twirling a twig in their funnel holes in the sand, both of them squatting side by side with total absorption. Alma would recite "Doodlebug, doodlebug, your house is on fire . . ." with Willie lisping along, "Doo-bug, doo-bug," batting those curly lashes up at Alma, making her laugh. *Oh Willie!*

ALMA and Bessie went out the back door. Alma's daddy Nate was sitting in the dark on the top step, smoking his pipe, looking west over the leveled cornfield. The sweet smell of Prince Albert tobacco hung in the air. He was in his usual overalls and plaid flannel shirt, his handlebar mustache bright white against his dark face. When he started to get up, Alma pushed him back down gently. He had arthritis in his back, and getting to his feet would hurt. "Hi, baby," he said, looking up at her. "Oh Daddy," she said. "What we gonna do?"

Alma didn't even know what she meant. There was nothing to do. Carry on. Just carry on. That was always the lesson. Do the best you can with what you got.

"What they do to one of us, they do to us all," her father said, turning back to gaze into the dark field.

Alma swallowed hard, sucking in her lower lip to staunch more tears.

"We're goin' on over there," Bessie said. "We got to get on wid that."

Her daddy nodded, and Alma started off with her mama down the path past the big vegetable garden, fallow now in February. The worn path bisected the cornfield, the stalks cut down, dried leaves rustling in the cold air. They knew the way. The stars were so bright out here in the country, a whole firmament of them! Alma turned her face up, wanting to see Heaven. She went to church every Sunday morning and Wednesday night. All her life she'd believed in Jesus and salvation. This was their earthly home, but one day they'd all be delivered from their life of toil and strife. They'd sit at the right hand of God. Alma had been baptized when she was thirteen in Five Mile River. Now, walking the uneven path, she fervently wanted to believe that Willie Earle was in Heaven, no longer feeling any pain, his wounds healed.

Up ahead was Tessie Earle's house, another sharecropper's cabin. Only three cars were parked in the front yard, the place quiet, closed. There was a strange feeling in the air. How could a yard, a house, feel shock? Yet everything felt stunned somehow, knocked into silence as if from a blow. Bessie cast a determined glance at Alma in the dark at the bottom of the front porch stairs. Resolute, she climbed the steps and knocked softly on the door. Alma followed, twisting her hands together, trying not to cry, her breath trapped in her chest.

Slowly the door opened. They stared at Tessie, who nodded, holding the door wider to let them in. "I knowed y'all'd come," she said. Alma hadn't seen Tessie in years. She'd always had a hearty laugh and been fun-loving, easy where Bessie was stern. Now Tessie looked shrunk, aged. Shattered. Bessie reached out her arms, and Tessie fell against her in such a collapse that Alma grasped her elbow to steady her. They led her to the sofa and sat her down.

It was then that Alma noticed there were other people in the room, silent people like ghosts. As her eyes adjusted to the dim room, she saw a young girl and boy and two older girls sitting upright on the edge of a single bed, staring at the newcomers, their faces complete masks. Tessie's younger children. And now Alma noticed Reverend Bailey from New Hope Baptist in Liberty where her folks went. He was hovering respectfully in the background, but after they settled on the couch, he came over and took Alma's and Mama's hands and thanked them for coming. A few others hung back in the shadows, relatives or church people maybe, men Alma and Bessie didn't know. The room had such an atmosphere of shock and horror that Alma wondered if she was caught in a nightmare. She prayed she could just wake up.

Alma turned her attention back to Tessie. She wanted to say something, but what could she say? Tessie took Alma's hand and patted it. She looked ashen, her eyes glazed as if she couldn't let in what had happened. Bessie had her arm around Tessie's shoulders, holding her tight. Tears were streaming down Bessie's face, though she made not a sound. Alma couldn't recall ever seeing her cry.

"You was always so sweet to Willie," Tessie said to Alma. "You was like a little mama yo'self. Did you ever have you a child?"

Alma's throat closed.

"Alma has a baby girl," Bessie said gently. "I told you 'bout her. Name of Pretty. Priscilla."

"Is she pretty?" Tessie said vaguely.

"Yes," Alma said. It was all she could manage.

"We gonna do for you, Tessie," Bessie was saying. "Whatever you need, we take care of it."

Tessie turned her eyes from one of them to the other, bewilderment in them. The whites were bloodshot, the pupils bluish-brown, unnatural.

"Bring my Willie back," Tessie said. "That all you need do for me. They say he dead. But how can he be dead? They say he kilt a taxi man. But Willie wouldn't kill. What would he kill for? Naw. Naw!"

"Willie was a good boy," Bessie said. "He with Jesus now. Jesus loves him, and he in Heaven with Jesus now."

Alma felt that weight again, like her blood had solidified, heavy weights pulling her down. *Where was Jesus when Willie needed him?*

"He was coming home," Tessie said. "He didn't take no taxi. He didn't kill no white man. He was coming home on the bus last night. Dat all I know."

"Shhh, shhh," Bessie soothed. "Don't think about it now. You can think about it tomorrow. Tomorrow. It's late now. Let me help you to bed. I'll stay the night wid you."

"They gonna come!" Tessie said. "Looking to git me too!" She squeezed Alma's hand tight, almost crushing the bones.

Bessie and Alma looked at each other. "No, they through," Bessie said. "They done done they evil deeds. They don't want nothing more to do with it. Don't you worry none. I be here."

Tessie nodded. "But how I gonna sleep? I got to sit up and wait for Willie to come home."

ALMA walked back across the barren field alone. She paused to throw her head back. The full moon had come up, shedding a cool, strange light on the land. The broken-down corn stalks rustled all around her, and in the distance, the low ridge of mountains was black against the dark blue horizon. She pulled her sweater tighter, feeling a chill. At once her ears pricked up and her body tensed. Was there some movement in the woods on the far side of the field? Woods like where they had taken Willie. She heard twigs snapping, the crush of dried leaves as feet moved through them. Alma broke into a run, scrambling forward in her flight. She had to get away, she couldn't let them get her!

She ran until she stumbled on an embedded rock in the path, bruising her foot through her thin shoe. Breathless, she bent over with her hands on her knees to catch her breath. She straightened and listened. No footsteps gaining on her. No mob chasing her. There was nothing in the woods but squirrels or maybe a deer. A coon or possum like Daddy hunted. A feeling of shame came over her: she had run like a scared rabbit. She had let them do that to her. And then it came to her: She never felt truly safe, ever. Fear was in her blood, passed down from her ancestors. Fear, sorrow, rage—she'd had to swallow them down all her life, keep the feelings deep. But they all lived in her. Right now—standing alone in this big deserted cornfield at night—it felt like they were the most of her.

She didn't want Pretty to grow up like this!

She'd save more money somehow. She'd make sure Pretty got to college. She'd get an education, become a teacher, have respect. It wouldn't always be like it was now, Jim Crow ruling their lives. They had to endure, that was the thing. They couldn't give up, and they couldn't question God's ways. It would lead to no good. It would lead to standing in a field of broken corn stalks in the night, feeling a weight that could pull her down, under. Why did God give colored folks this load to carry? Why did He forsake them, let them be put in chains and stolen away from Africa to be slaves? So many years, Lord, to have to live under the white man's boot! Why, Lord, why! In all the pictures, Jesus was white. Did God hate coloreds as much as those men who killed Willie?

How could a loving God let Willie suffer the way he did! Reverend would say it was not her place to question God's plan. All would be revealed in the end. They had to trust in the Lord, in Jesus's salvation. Bessie said Willie was with Jesus now. What kind of talk was that? What did that mean? Was Willie being tortured and killed part of God's plan?

If it was, then Alma wanted nothing to do with Him.

6

LEE

I COME ON in to the cab office first thing Tuesday morning to see what the boys was sayin' and thinkin'.

"Lookee here," Paul Griggs said, shovin' the newspaper at me. There it was in black and white, splashed across the front page of the *Greenville News*: "No Arrests Reported as Officers Probe Lynching of Negro." Three stories told the tale, and there was even photographs of the Pickens County jail, Mr. Brown's taxicab ID picture, and one of the nigger looking like a jailbird. It called him by name, Willie Earle. I ain't never thought about no name. He was twenty-four, same age as me. When I saw what we done spread all over the paper like that, a lump rose in my throat, and spit flooded my mouth.

The boys was silent while I skimmed the stories. The jailer done ratted on us. Said some in the mob wore caps similar to what us taxicab drivers wear, and some of the cars in the . . . "entourage". . . was cabs.

"What's an 'en-tou-rage'?" I asked, sounding it out like Mrs. Tucker taught me in fifth grade.

"You ignoramus," Hendrix Rector snapped. "It's like . . . a tour group."

"It's pronounced 'ahn-tour-azh,'" Bill Shockley said. He'd tried to stop us from going that night. "You boys weren't exactly on a tour."

I was just starting to read more when Willie Bishop snatched the paper from me and tore the front page off, wadded it up, and ground it on the floor with the heel of his boot. "Making a goddamn fuss over one dead Negro!" George McFalls spat a plug of tobacco toward the ashcan and missed. Shockley said, "Wipe it up." George looked around for something to use but then took his own handkerchief out, wiped it across the filthy floor, and threw it in the trashcan. "Goddamn nigger," he muttered.

Fat John Joy was overspreading a rickety chair under a pinup girl calendar. Miss February was overspreading her bathing suit up top. I rested my eyes for minute on her boobs, and I couldn't help but think of Lily and what had transpired between us yesterday. "It'll blow over," one of the boys was saying, and for a second I thought he was talking about Lily and me. I glanced over at Lou Reynolds. He was eyeing me. Had Lily said something, maybe about my limp dick? But that was crazy. She stood as much to lose as I did.

"Ain't no one gonna care in a week about one nigger's death and a murdering one at that," Hendrix said. He'd been the one to beat the nigger with the butt of Clardy's shotgun, broke the wood. Clardy'd screamed at him to just finish it and quit getting blood all over his damn gun.

"You fucking idiot," Clardy said.

"Bearden's guys picked up the log books," Shockley said.

We all stared at him.

"Well, so what," George said. "We all fixed our gas and mileage records." He lit a cigar and puffed to get it started. I felt something cold spreading through me.

"I didn't log no fares after two that morning," Willie Bishop said.

"Me neither," Paul Griggs said, defiant-like. "I had better things to do." When he smirked, Clardy slapped him across the face.

"You're gonna get us all fried!" he said, and Griggs punched him in the face, smashing his cig into his lips.

"Goddamn!" Clardy spit out blood and ash. "Maybe that 'better thing' you do is fuck my wife!"

Griggs growled low like a dog fixin' to attack. "Somebody got to do it." They lunged at each other, but some of the boys pinned 'em back. "Not in the office," Shockley warned.

I glanced again at Lou Reynolds. He was still studying me. I stared him down 'til he looked away.

"We all in this together now," Fat John Joy said and rose like a mountain from the spindly chair. "I'm going to the Southern for some corned beef hash. Who wants to come?"

DRIVING home, I steered my mind around to the truth: What we did was justice, plain and simple, more than Mr. Brown got. Now *that* was cold-blooded murder, and anyone could see the difference. Brown innocent, nigger guilty, plain and simple. Any fool could see that, and the law would see it too. Sometimes the law didn't cover everything. Sometimes it was a personal matter that had to be dealt with.

When Mr. Brown got me on at Yellow Cab, it saved my life. I was working the third shift at Poe, fifty-five hours a week, the noise such that my ears rang for hours afterwards. Lint in my hair, clothes, lungs. It's only recently that my cough has about cleared up. 'Course smoking don't help it none. Tom Brown called me "son," something my own dad never done. I had to pull over for a few minutes. I was sniveling like a girl, sucking back sobs.

A S soon as I walked in the door and seen Emylyn, I knew she done heard the news. She searched my face like she didn't even know me. Lee Jr. and Earl was playing on the floor with paper dolls, something I didn't approve of, and Emylyn knew it. Just a few days ago, Lee Jr. would of jumped into my arms, but now he didn't even look my way. Still hadn't forgive me for that whupping. Emylyn said, "Come on, you boys, your daddy's home for his breakfast. Go on out in the yard and play."

"It's cold out there!" Lee Jr. whined. He was right, but Emylyn was already buttoning 'em into their coats and sticking stocking caps on their pointy heads. "Out y'all go," she said as she pushed them out the door. "Lee Jr., don't you dare let Earl out of your sight. No going out of the yard, y'all hear?"

Earl: same name as that nigger. Nothing I could do about that now. They'd identified him from his wallet. I didn't think they could call him from his face. Not after we got through with him.

"Mama and them called," Emylyn started. "Sounds like cabbies involved in this thing." She was getting the frying pan down from the nail on the wall. "You know anything about it?"

"Might," I said, biding my time.

She sliced some Spam and plunked some lard in the pan and began frying up the Spam, crispy like I like it. We was both silent.

"How many eggs you want?"

I was working the second shift and wouldn't get no supper 'til after ten. "Four," I said.

When she'd scrambled 'em hard the way I like 'em, she set the plate down in front of me. I tried to eat, though my appetite was off.

"You have any part in it?"

I took my time answering. It was going to come out anyway. "Bunch of us boys went to Pickens," I told her. "On account of Mr. Brown."

She was staring at me. "What you mean, bunch of us boys?"

I sighed. This was going to be harder than I thought. "That nigger Willie Earle killed Tom Brown in cold-blooded murder, and we took care of it. Same as the law would of done."

The eggs was sticking in my throat, and I felt like whimpering. I had that same feeling I had when we took Willie Earle, like I was weak. Emylyn's face was as blank as a white plate. She didn't understand what I was telling her. I felt kind of confused myself. In the light of day, it didn't seem quite as simple as it had that night we went to the Pickens jail.

7

ALMA

ON THE BUS Tuesday morning, all the maids in the back were silent. The white people in the front read newspapers or looked out the windows. The only sound was the bus driver singing "My Old Kentucky Home." Alma looked around for Synthia, but she hadn't gotten on the bus the way she always did.

Mr. Chastain had already left for work again, early. Alma figured he was involved somehow in the lynching case. He was a good man, not one of the white folks who would act nice but not mean it. In the ten years she'd worked for the Chastains, she'd come to know them well, though not from anything they told her.

Miz Chastain was in the kitchen when Alma came in the back door. "Good morning, Alma," she said brightly, the first clue. Something forced and artificially jolly in that greeting. "Morning, Miz Chastain," Alma answered, polite, like usual. She never said more than she needed to.

"I'm afraid Betsy is in a funk this morning," Miz Chastain

lamented. "She won't get out of bed, doesn't want to go to school."

"She sick?" Alma said, beginning on the dishes. Miz Chastain was leaning against the counter, holding a cup of coffee, shaking her head. "What you want for breakfast?" Alma asked.

"I shouldn't," Miz Chastain began as usual. "But honestly, I'm starving, Alma. Could you fry me a piece of that country ham? Maybe two scrambled eggs. I could eat a horse this morning."

Alma got the ham and the eggs out of the icebox. Mr. Chastain got a dozen eggs every week from his relatives up in Marietta. They were nice brown ones, with bright yellow yokes. She cracked two of them on the side of a blue bowl.

"Her father took her to Pickens with him yesterday. To the jail. I don't know what he was thinking, Alma, exposing Betsy to such ugliness!"

Alma shut her eyes for a long moment. Then she got out a skillet and set it on the stove. She stirred the eggs into some melted butter.

"Maybe you can do something with her, Alma. She likes you better than me."

"Girls her age and their mamas ain't 'posed to get along." Though that had never been true of Alma and her mama.

"I want her to go to school and stop acting like a fool!" Miz Chastain said. "I don't know what she's so upset about. She won't tell me. Some boy at school who won't give her the time of day, no doubt."

Alma carried the plate of ham and eggs into the breakfast room. "Come eat while it's hot."

Miz Chastain pulled out one of the chintz-covered chairs

and sat down, shaking out the linen napkin that Alma had ironed yesterday. "Go up and see what you can do with her, Alma. See if you can make her go on to school. I'll have time to drive her before garden club."

Alma went up the long staircase, wiping the banister with a rag she kept in her apron pocket. She swiped up the dust that had already gathered overnight along the sides of the wool runner. Betsy's door was closed. Alma stood for several minutes, gathering herself. She thought of Pretty over at Rosa Mae's. What were they doing just now? And what about Tessie? Was she still sitting on the couch, waiting for Willie to come home? Mama would still be over there, tending. The funeral was on Thursday. Alma would have to ask Miz Chastain for the day off.

She used "their knock" on Betsy's door, the special code Betsy had invented for them as a child: three taps, a pause, and then another louder knock.

Betsy came to the door, opening it slowly. "She sent you up here, didn't she?"

Alma just shrugged. Betsy stepped aside to let her in. She was still in her pajamas. She went and lay down on her bed, pulling her pink quilt over her head. It was a princess bed—at least that's how Alma thought of it—with gold brass scrolls for a headboard. Alma would like a bed like that for Pretty when she got older. Maybe the Chastains would give her this one when Betsy went away to college in the fall.

Alma glanced around Betsy's room. She picked it up every day when Betsy was at school and here it was a mess again. There were books scattered everywhere, on the floor, on her desk, all over the bed. The drawers of her white dresser were pulled out, clothes erupting from them like there had been an explosion. Her bulletin board was crammed with overlapping photos of her with her friends, school pictures, family vacations in the mountains and at the beach. Her stuffed animals observed everything from the top of the bookcase.

Alma waited.

Finally, in a shaky voice from under the quilt: "Mother says I have to go to school. But I can't, Alma. I just can't! But I don't want to stay here either."

Going over to where Betsy lay, Alma pulled back the cover and put her hand on her forehead. Her skin was cool and dry. No fever.

"You sick? Stomach ache?"

"Yes. No." Tears glistened in her eyes.

Alma studied her. She knew the child well. She took things hard, kept them inside. But whatever was bothering her today, she'd just have to put it aside and get on with things. Even Betsy would have to learn that. Whatever was troubling her, Alma couldn't help her with it. Not today.

"Best go on and go. Your mama will drive you. You won't be much late."

Betsy sat up and pulled the quilt around her shoulders like a cape, a strange expression on her face. Alma noted what she didn't notice every day—Betsy was no longer a little girl. She was halfway between a child and a young woman. She was having to grow up, and it wasn't easy.

"Mama thinks it's my period or something. She doesn't care about anything . . . important. I hate her! I'll be glad when I can leave home!"

"Don't say hate," Alma said. "When you was little, you wanted to stay in your pajamas all day. You not little now."

"Yes, and Mother always made me get dressed. You would

have let me wear my pajamas."

"Uh uh," Alma said, shaking her head. She longed to sit down. The weight was heavy. Just rest for a moment on the edge of the bed. "Person got to get dressed. First thing you know, you don't get dressed and then the next thing you be in bed all day. You gotta get up and get going."

She busied herself looking through Betsy's closet.

"I'm so sorry, Alma," Betsy said, tears in her voice. When Alma turned to look at her, to her surprise, Betsy was shivering, as if she did have a fever. "About that colored man," she said. "Daddy took me with him to Pickens yesterday when he talked to the jailer." She lowered her eyes. "I know all about what happened."

To hide her face, her quivering lip, Alma got out a purple corduroy jumper and white blouse with a Peter Pan collar from Betsy's closet. She bent to paw through the mess of shoes on the closet floor to find her saddle shoes. She got a white bra, panties and bobby socks out of her top dresser drawer. "Here," she said, laying them on the bed. "Go wash your face and brush your teeth. Hurry up, now."

"WELL?" Miz Chastain said when Alma came back into the kitchen.

"She be on down."

They were silent. Alma dried the breakfast dishes, put them in the cabinet, and sprinkled Ajax in the sink. There was a grease spot in it. She scrubbed it harder than was required.

"Did she tell you what's got her going this morning?" Miz Chastain asked.

"No m'am," Alma said. Now was as good a time as any. There was no good time. The funeral was Thursday at noon in Liberty. Normally she'd wait until time to leave to ask, but she wanted to get it settled.

"Can I have Thursday off?" she asked, not turning from the sink. "I'll take care of everything Wednesday, won't be nothing left undone."

There was a long pause. "Not Thursday, Alma. I'm sorry, but we're having company for dinner that night. You know that. It's Mr. Chastain's birthday, and I'll really need you. I'm thinking we'll have his favorites, steak and baked potatoes. I really can't do without you Thursday."

Alma was silent, scrubbing the spot. Normally she would have said that that was all right, but she didn't speak.

"There she is!" Miz Chastain exclaimed brightly when Betsy came into the kitchen. "That's more like it."

Betsy cut her eyes at her mother.

"Alma'll fix you some toast, and you can eat it in the car. With peanut butter?"

"Not hungry."

"Have it your way, but when your stomach growls, and you get a headache, don't blame me. Alma, we'll be on our way. I'm sorry about Thursday, I truly am, but a birthday dinner is special."

"What?" Betsy said. "What about Thursday?"

"You remember, honey! It's Daddy's birthday, and we're having Granddaddy and Grand Bee and Pop and Mom over for dinner. I got your daddy a new shirt and tie from you. You'll need to sign the card."

"But why are you sorry, Mother?" Betsy's voice was steely.

"It's nothing, honey. Goodness, you're a bear today! Alma asked for Thursday off. She forgot all about Daddy's birthday dinner."

Alma kept her back turned, her head down, laboring at the grease spot that no longer existed.

Betsy turned on her heel and stormed out the back door to the car.

"Goodness gracious," Miz Chastain said. "Enjoy Pretty now, Alma, before she gets to be a teenager. The moods! The rudeness. I hate to say it, but I'll be glad to see Betsy go off to college in the fall. She needs to grow up."

AFTER they'd left, before she started cleaning the bathrooms, Alma went into the living room and pulled out the heavy piano bench. She sat down and opened the dark cover. She touched a black key with her right index finger. That didn't sound right. She remembered it was the black key in the middle of three black keys. The middle one. Yes, that was it. When she'd first started trying to peck out the notes, she used her pointer finger for each key. That had sounded so jumpy. Quickly she realized that she could do like Miz Chastain, roll her whole hand over the keys. It was smoother to play like that.

Now that she had her place, she put her thumb on the correct, middle black key, her pointer finger stretching over to the raised black key, and her ring finger fell into place on the correct white key. Her hand remembered what to do, scrolling over those three notes. Black, black, white. She rolled over them slowly eight times, almost as if she could play the moonlight song. It brought her some comfort. She didn't move her left hand from her lap. All she could handle was the right. She played those three notes over and over, dreaming that she could play the whole song.

The next part involved a different white key, the second

black key from the first part, and then the same white key from the first three notes. She played it all again, the first three keys eight times, then the slight change as she shifted into the next three notes twice, and then . . . it was getting harder. She tried to find the next notes. She tested several, listening to hear if they were the right ones. She knew the piece by heart, and her ears tested for the ones that came next. When she had them, she started over again from the top, almost as if she were really playing.

"Alma," came Miz Chastain's voice. She was standing in the dining room. She must have come in the kitchen and stepped through the swinging door without Alma hearing her. She was supposed to go to . . . Alma jumped up and awkwardly pushed the piano bench back in place. She started toward the hall, but Miz Chastain called her back.

"Alma. I . . . you've . . ." She paused and then crossed and pulled out the piano bench and sat down. She was still as a statue for several long moments while Alma's heart beat double-time. Then she began to play the moonlight song. She played it through, while Alma stood there, wondering if Miz Chastain would fire her. Then, "Come, sit." Miz Chastain patted the bench. "Show me what you can play."

Alma hesitated; then she did as she was told. Miz Chastain stood up so Alma could sit in front of the middle keys. Alma studied the piano in front of her. She knew the keys she needed. Her hand knew where to find them. She played the three notes eight times, and then she hit the wrong white key when she started the next part.

"It's here," Miz Chastain said. "A." She reached over and tapped it to show Alma. "Now, from the top again."

The three notes eight times, then Alma touched the white

key called "A" and her pointer finger went to the black key. "C sharp," Miz Chastain said. Alma touched the white key she knew from the start of the song. "You have it," Miz Chastain said. "A, C sharp, E. Play that phrase two times. Good. Now all of it from the top."

Alma played with her right hand and it sounded good. It wasn't the whole thing, not like Miz Chastain played it, but it was something.

"It's beautiful, isn't it," Miz Chastain said. "It's the first movement of the *Moonlight Sonata*. So sad. So grave. Move over a bit. I'll play the left hand."

Alma slid over, and without looking at her, Miz Chastain sat next to her, hip to hip. Alma had never been that close to her, and she felt rattled, shifting slightly away so they didn't touch. "We'll start at the count of three. One. Two. Three."

Alma hit the wrong black key. She wanted to say, *I can't. I can't do this*! But then she looked at the keyboard. The three raised black keys distinguished themselves from all the others. She touched the right key. "Yes," Miz Chastain said. "That one is G sharp. One. Two. Three."

Alma began her three notes over, rolling her fingers through them eight times and then moving to the next notes two times. Miz Chastain's thumb and little finger spanned and held two black keys while Alma played, then shifted to another two keys. "Octaves," Miz Chastain said. It sounded all right. It sounded good. It wasn't perfect, but they were playing the moonlight song, at least a little of it. "Again," Miz Chastain commanded, and they started together at the count of three. Then again and again, more in sync, until Alma's right hand started shaking, and she had to put it in her lap. She fought back tears. The music called up all the pain and sorrow she felt. They sat there in silence for a long moment, letting the sounds fade away.

"I'm going to be late for garden club," Miz Chastain said, standing up. "And you have work to do." She stopped at the kitchen door. "And Alma. I won't be needing you on Thursday after all." She paused. "I'm sure Mother will let Macie help us out." She pushed through the swinging door, calling back over her shoulder, "We'll work on the next part sometime."

8

LAWTON

ON THURSDAY EVENING, Lawton's mother and father and Lydia's parents, Beatrice and Lyman, arrived for his forty-fourth birthday dinner. Alma had asked for the day off, perhaps to go to Willie Earle's funeral, though Lydia didn't say anything about that. He'd heard at the office that very few attended, probably because they were afraid and didn't want to be associated with the whole nasty business. Beatrice had "loaned" Lydia her maid, Macie, who had worked for the Maxfields for the twenty years Lawton had known them. Despite his usual unease, Lawton stepped into his roles of husband, son, father, and genial host.

His parents, country people born and raised in Marietta, had moved to Greenville in 1900 when they married. They'd never had a maid. There was no silver to polish, no cleaning to do but what his mother did herself. When Lawton was growing up, his mother would come home from teaching school every day and make supper, meat and at least three vegetables and cornbread. She took in ironing on the weekends to help pay for his college and law school. His father worked for a corner grocery in Sans Souci, which he was able to buy from the owner when he was forty. Lawton's folks believed in Jesus and education. There was never any question Lawton would go to college, something they hadn't done. He'd worked his way through Carolina waiting tables in the cafeteria and in the summer bagging groceries and making deliveries for the store.

His mother and father seemed diminished somehow whenever they had to endure—for that's the way Lawton thought of it—an evening with Beatrice and Lyman. The class differences were jarring, and this being Greenville, Lawton was keenly attuned to them. Left on their own, in their own lives, his parents were gregarious and warm, good friends and neighbors. They were members of the Exchange Club, which sometimes had costume parties, where they'd dress like gypsies or pirates, impossible to imagine the Maxfields doing. They couldn't discuss European trips with the Maxfields, and they didn't play bridge, being Southern Baptist. They wouldn't "take a drink" as his dad put it, and so the cocktail hour before dinner had a strained, awkward feel, at least to Lawton, as his folks drank their ginger ale, and Lyman mixed Manhattans at the bar.

It was Lawton's birthday, so he tried to put on a happy face, even though images of Willie Earle's body kept flashing through his head. That morning the sheriff had sent over a photograph of the body on a gurney to the solicitor's office. They'd passed the envelope around silently, pulling out the photo, glancing at it, then shoving it back in. When it came to Lawton, he thought he was prepared. But his whole body recoiled, his testicles tightened, and his eyes ached. They had cut the man's neck from ear to ear and stripped away skin, leaving only the windpipe exposed. The gunshot had destroyed his right eye; brains were visible.

They sat in the dining room at a table covered with a white linen tablecloth, bedecked with the Wedgwood china and crystal Lydia and he had gotten as wedding presents. A silver bowl filled with pink camellias sat on a round mirror in the center of the table; there were lit candles in candelabras on the buffet. The chandelier sparkled above them, Alma having polished it recently no doubt. The dinner was steaks, baked potatoes, and creamed spinach. Steaks were Lawton's favorite food. But when he saw that hunk of beef, pink in the middle and oozing red juices, he felt overheated and woozy.

Earlier that afternoon, he'd driven out to see the site where Earle was killed on old Bramlett Road, near a slaughterhouse, of all places, on a lane called Gethsemane, of all names. The slaughterhouse, which was no longer in operation, was a rickety wood structure with a high shingled roof where farmers brought their livestock to be killed and processed. It was hard, dirty, bloody work, the slaughter of those beasts on a daily basis, the stripping of their hides and then hoisting them by their hind legs on pulleys to hang from metal beams above.

The tall scrawny pines in the adjoining woods competed for whatever sun they could reach and whatever nutrients they could derive from the poor soil. Lawton parked near a deep ditch full of brown weeds and briars and jumped it to walk into the forest. The police had been all over the site initially, but now the place was totally deserted, evoking an empty, melancholy feel. They hadn't gone far into the woods, and the actual killing hadn't taken that long. But it must have been an eternity to Willie Earle, from the time he heard voices and footsteps on the jail stairs to the time he lay pulverized on the brown pine needles.

Lawton hoped no one would notice he couldn't eat the steak.

Lydia's father, however, was masticating large pieces of meat with his mouth open. He'd once been a highly-regarded litigator at Hendricks, Maxfield and Sloan, the best law firm in town. Lawton had been invited to join the firm when he finished law school, no doubt because he'd married Lydia. After a few years of being under Lyman's thumb, he joined the solicitor's office. He knew Lyman considered him a failure.

Lydia's mother Beatrice came from one of the oldest families in town, the Duprees, who started Dupree Mill back in the 1890s. She'd become round and soft in her later years, like a little hen. Beatrice adored bridge, at which she was quite sharp and competitive. She had that peculiar Southern trait of appearing feminine and sweet while being steely—if not exactly cold. She certainly loved her family, but her human kindness did not extend a great way beyond that.

Beatrice and Lyman couldn't understand why their darling daughter had married Lawton. He wondered that himself. Maybe it was his so-called promise: He was going to be a lawyer like Daddy. And he was a challenge. Lydia wanted to break down his seriousness, his cautiousness, make him more playful and fun. Lawton had a lot on his mind that summer. Lydia was like a life buoy when he was going down for the third time.

He met her the summer after he finished Carolina, before starting law school that fall. She would be a senior at Agnes Scott. Along with other entering law students, Lawton was invited to a big garden party at her parents' house. He first saw Lydia by a fountain in the backyard, one that had four fat, naked concrete cherubs dancing in a circle around the bowl. She was sitting on the edge of the fountain with her yellow polka-dot dress daringly pulled up to reveal her thighs, dangling her bare feet in the murky water and laughing. Back then she laughed a lot. The truth was, he felt lost in his own life, and she struck him as someone who had all the answers, who would never be adrift the way he was.

AFTER the grandparents had given Betsy her due, asking about school (fine), whether she was keeping up her piano (no), when she expected to hear from Agnes Scott (March), the dinner conversation turned, as Lawton knew it would, to the Willie Earle case. He filled Lyman in with a few details. His parents fell silent, uncomfortable with the subject. Their dealings with colored people had always been cordial and polite within the Southern strictures. His father was the sort who liked everyone, never met a stranger, and did not turn Negro customers away from his store, treating everyone with Christian kindness and goodwill, expecting the same in return. His mother had had little dealings with colored people, living in a mostly segregated world.

Beatrice piped up with the opinion that Willie Earle was not a victim.

"It's not as if he was some poor Nigra who got pulled off the street or even out of jail when he was innocent. He was not innocent, and he's certainly not a martyr," she drawled in a voice that was soft and absolutely certain. Her hair was perfectly coifed, her face powdered to an unnatural white, as if the sun had never touched it, with just the right touch of rouge. Her red lipstick was bleeding into the deep age lines above her upper lip.

"I really don't understand the great hullabaloo that Greenville is making over this. If he had stood trial, he would have been convicted and executed summarily—end of story. Those taxi drivers just saved the state the expense. But now that the national press has picked it up, it's just airing our dirty laundry."

Lawton glanced at Betsy, who was staring at her grand-mother. "But Grand Bee," she said in a quavering voice— it took courage to stand up to her grandmother—"we can't have mob violence. I mean, breaking into jail to snatch a man before he's had a trial." She glanced at Lawton for support. At that point, Macie came in to serve more hot rolls. They fell into an awkward silence. Lawton stole a glance at Macie's stoic face as she passed the bread. He wondered what rage she had had to hold in all her life, that all the Negroes had to con-tain. It took fortitude.

After Macie disappeared back through the swinging door into the kitchen, Lawton tried to make the point that Willie Earle's actual innocence or guilt would never be known. "He was denied his day in court. Betsy's right. Our whole society stands on whether people respect the law or feel free to take it into their own hands." Beatrice just shrugged, as if he had said something tactless.

"But really, Lawton," Lydia said, "the men who did this are not representative of Greenville. They're ignorant, brutal rednecks. In their own way, they thought they were doing the right thing. An eye for an eye. This incident is a total aber-ration, and I wish people weren't making such a commotion about it. Isn't that right, Elizabeth?" She turned to Lawton's mother next to her and put her hand on hers. His mother smiled politely and removed her hand. "Such a lovely dinner, Lydia," she said. "I wonder what Macie did to make that creamed spinach so good."

"Nutmeg," Lydia said.

Lawton looked at Lydia, her perfect makeup and beauty-parlor hair, a younger version of her mother, her face reflecting a kind of innocence that hadn't changed much in the twenty years they'd been married. He hoped he'd never have to destroy that innocence. He forced his attention back to the conversation.

"But haven't we come a long way from an eye for an eye," Betsy tried again. "Wasn't it Jesus who required us to love our enemies rather than poking out their eyes?"

"I don't give a fuck about that darky or those cracker cabbies," Lyman erupted. "I care about Greenville and what this mess is going to do to business! If we're ever going to get beyond being a dirty little mill town, we got to bring in industry, manufacturing. We can't have this fucking lynching besmirch our reputation as a modern Southern city!"

"Honestly, Lyman," Beatrice said mildly, taking the last bite of her steak. "Watch your tongue. The girl is here."

Lyman stuck his tongue out at Beatrice like a five-year-old. Then he turned back to Lawton. "Well, you'll never get a conviction," he opined, tipping back in his ladderback chair. "We may have a justice system, but it's still made up of white men, and they're not going to risk their necks sending one of their own, let alone twenty or thirty of them, to jail for killing a Nigra."

Lawton knew he was right, though he didn't want to hear it. Just two months ago in Columbia, a Negro had been convicted of a murder for which he was likely innocent. A white man had killed his wife, and then made him walk in her blood on the kitchen floor to frame him. The case was only two months old when they executed him.

DESSERT was crème de menthe parfaits. His parents made their exit, saying they had to get up early in the morning. Then came the predictable invitation for Lawton to join Beatrice, Lyman, and Lydia for a few rounds of bridge and his predictable response. They knew he'd refuse, gracefully he hoped, so why did they keep asking? Lydia held it against him that he'd never play. "He played all the time in college," she sometimes threw in, "so I don't know why he won't play now. It would be so much fun, Lawton," she'd cajole, or sometimes—in private—she'd be angry. "I ask you to do this one small thing for me, and you can't do it! It might actually be fun! Something you don't seem to remember much about."

The very things that had attracted him back when they met were now the things that made him feel distant from her. He was initially taken by her standard beauty, her ash-blonde hair in a perfect flip, her ready smile and petite size, her sorority girl personality, as if life were one big party to anticipate, enjoy, and then dissect. At twenty-one she was gay and bubbly, the way he thought girls should be. She represented the prize in femininity, a prize he felt he needed to win.

They'd settle for three-handed bridge. He didn't care. He told them he'd run Macie home. He was tired and wanted out of the house. When they walked through the backyard to the garage, he saw that it was a clear night, the moon as bright as if they were on a deserted island. It must have been like this in that dark patch of pine forest, though by the time they got down to their business, the moonlight would have faded. Macie and he conducted the obligatory small talk. She teased Lawton about not eating his steak. "My dog gonna like that fine piece of meat, Mr. Chastain. He be livin' high on the hog tonight!" Was this the way colored people always talked to white folk, keeping their real thoughts and feelings to themselves? And what about him? He could have asked her about Willie Earle, what colored folks were saying. He couldn't broach the subject. When he stopped in front of her house in Brutontown, she paused before getting out. "You a good man, Mr. Chastain," she said. "You on the right side." Then she disappeared into the dark.

H E was in bed, though not asleep, when Lydia came up to their room. He thanked her for such a nice birthday, kissed her on the cheek, and they turned away from each other in bed, as was their custom. It'd been years since they'd had sex. Neither of them ever mentioned it. That part of their lives— of their very selves—was something they'd put away, once they had a child. He thought both of them felt relief that that was over, but for different reasons.

He turned away from her, but he couldn't sleep. It had been a disturbing evening in a disturbing week. He reviewed the conversation at the dinner table. He wished he'd said what no one wanted to hear, that if Willie Earle had been white, he'd still be sitting in the Pickens jail awaiting trial. It would have been impolite, he thought bitterly, to bring up the racial lust of the cabbies. To broach how racism permeated all their lives.

But it wasn't just Negroes that got cast into the prejudicial pit. It was anyone who didn't match what society considered acceptable, approved. Something tightened in his chest. He knew the feeling well: fear.

What was he so afraid of?

Being deemed different. Being cast out.

Unbidden, his mind began roaming over the past. Like a homing pigeon, it flew to certain memories, certain feelings he'd hoped he'd laid to rest.

H E is back at Carolina. It's the spring of his senior year. He turned twenty-two in February, and in the fall he'll be starting a fifth year to earn a law degree. Tuition is fifty dollars a year. His mother has saved the money from the ironing she takes in to help pay for it. Lawton thinks law school is what he wants. It must be, though he has no sense of the law or particular interest in it. It feels more like a train he's about to board without knowing its destination. For one thing, his parents are so proud of him. His father finished tenth grade; his mother had two years of junior college and teaches at a grammar school in the Parker district. The idea that their son might become a lawyer, an occupation almost as esteemed as being a doctor, has elevated their status with their friends, given them something to brag about, and holds the promise that Lawton will not have the money worries they've suffered off and on. They assume being a lawyer assures wealth and prestige, a big step up.

He and two of his dorm mates at USC play bridge every night in the lounge, starting at about eleven o'clock and sometimes going until two or three in the morning. Their college careers are over as such; they're just coasting, realizing at some level that college is child's play compared to what comes next in life. Clem and Garret have been playing since junior high, taught by their parents. Garret is from a well-heeled Spartanburg family; bridge is his escape from the pressures he feels to measure up to his doctor dad. He's been admitted to medical school in Charleston, though he will never attend. He'll move to Paris the summer after he graduates and become an ex-pat there, writing the Great American Novel that has yet to appear. Clem is the smartest of the three; he craves the game for its intellectual challenges. He's majoring in math and will become an engineer for a construction firm in Atlanta, as well as an alcoholic.

Lawton is newer to bridge, which is a game of experience as much as skill. He learned the game his sophomore year and then just played sporadically. It's only when Clem, Garret, and he begin playing regularly their senior year that Lawton gets seriously involved in bridge. Every night they go to the lounge where there's usually someone around to fill in as the fourth hand. These intense, late-night games take his mind off his worries that maybe law school is not the right thing, that maybe he doesn't want to go into law, and that if he backs out, he'll be letting his parents down. And what else can he do for a living? He hasn't a clue.

ONE night a new player appears. His name is Harry Bumgarten. "I hear there's some serious bridge to be had here," he says that first night, standing in the lounge doorway, a cryptic smile on his lips. There's something different about him that makes the three of them pause. Something in his knowing look, his flirtatious voice, as if he's winking at them about a joke only he gets. He's handsome, with a sharp aristocratic nose, penetrating brown eyes, and his black hair is longer than any of theirs. At the time, the only way Lawton can make sense of him is to think that girls would dig him.

Girls don't dig Lawton. He's never kissed a girl nor wanted to. It's as if an exotic animal has walked into their forest of squirrels and rabbits.

And thus it began. They became a foursome. Harry liked hanging out, drinking beer, laughing in that certain way he had, always with a lit cigarette hanging out of the side of his mouth. He didn't take bridge seriously like the rest of them, though he was the best player, an intuitive player, with the kind of natural knack for cards you can't learn. They started out switching partners, as they'd done with the pick-ups who joined them, but after a short while, they settled into "couples," as it were, Garret and Clem as partners, and Harry and Lawton. Lawton was not a natural; he had to work hard to remember which cards had been played. He didn't think Harry kept track of who had played what, but they won as often, if not more, than Garret and Clem. All three of their games moved up a level.

Harry and he developed a kind of telepathy, their bids a special language where they understood each other perfectly—spades, hearts, diamonds, clubs—until they'd arrive at the perfect bid, the winning bid. Lawton would look across the table into Harry's brown eyes, which were always squinted in a smile, and he'd get him. Not just about the cards, the bids, but something about Harry that he couldn't put into words. He was fascinated by Harry in a way he hadn't been fascinated by anyone ever before. It was so curious and strange that he didn't know what to make of it. Those late-night games were the thing Lawton most looked forward to, as if the rest of his day, his whole life even, was just waiting for Harry to arrive.

They'd meet for coffee sometimes, walking beyond the

campus into downtown Columbia, to a Greek diner where none of the students went. Lawton learned Harry was rooming off-campus in a boarding house, and he was surprised he was from a small town, Inman. He didn't seem like a small-town boy. Starting in ninth grade, he'd spent the summers in New York City. No one Lawton knew had ever been there. Harry had an aunt, a single woman who had escaped Inman, as he put it, and worked for Macy's as a window designer. During his visits, she would take him to plays and musicals, museums and art galleries. He would sing lines from popular songs unabashedly as they walked down the street, with Lawton looking around self-consciously. "Yes, we have no bananas, we have no bananas today!" or "Nothing could be finer than to be in Carolina . . . in the mor-or-or-ning!" Harry had a terrible off-key voice, and Lawton couldn't help laughing. He was determined to live in "The City" one day, as if there were only one city.

He was a junior, majoring in philosophy, and when Lawton would go to his room to see if he wanted to take a walk, or just because he couldn't stay away, Harry'd be reading Nietzsche or someone else Lawton had never heard of. Lawton was majoring in government, which he considered a useful major, without knowing why. Harry would quote Aristotle to him: "He who has overcome his fears will be truly free," or "Happiness depends upon ourselves." Lawton knew Harry was telling him things he wanted Lawton to embrace, but Lawton felt a block, the words too abstract, making him uncomfortable. Sometimes they stirred such emotion in him, he was afraid he might cry. He hadn't taken any philosophy courses, thinking philosophy was for eggheads. Harry thought he might like to go on to graduate school, maybe at

Columbia or NYU. He intended to become a philosophy professor. He spent endless hours writing what he said would be
a book one day.

On one of their walks that spring, Harry stopped suddenly and turned to Lawton, his face gleeful. "Let's run
away, Chas!" Harry had decided to call Lawton "Chas"
when he first introduced himself, shaking his head at *Lawton
Chastain*, mocking it with a British accent. Lawton tried to
dub Harry "Bum," for Bumgarten, but it didn't stick. A nick-
name coming from him sounded forced.

"Run away," Lawton repeated dumbly, though his heart
suddenly kicked into a higher gear. "I'm about to graduate, in
case you've forgotten." He started walking again.

"After you graduate then," Harry said, running a bit ahead
to stand in front of him.

"I'm going to law school." Lawton commenced walking
again. Harry fell into step beside him. His silence was torture for Lawton. "Okay," he said, trying to play along. "Let's
run away." The thought was so disturbing and exciting that
Lawton almost stopped breathing.

"Good! We'll leave right after you graduate then," Harry
said. "We'll go to New York."

"New York."

"Is there an echo out here?"

"Out here?" Lawton said, causing Harry to punch him
lightly, creating a tingle in Lawton's arm. "And what, pray
tell, will we do in 'The City'? I don't know if you've noticed,
but times are hard. What will we live on? Your philosophy?"

Again Harry stopped and grabbed Lawton's arm, this
time sending a jolt through him. "You're not a sheep, Chas!"
he said.

"But I am a sheep," Lawton said, trying to joke. His voice caught. "Baaa."

"You are not a sheep," Harry said again, this time solemnly, still holding Lawton in place. "Listen to me. This is important. It's your *life*, Chas. You don't belong to your parents, you don't belong to 'the law,' and you sure as hell don't belong to Greenville, which has poured every notion of how to think and behave into that thick head of yours. There's more to you than you even know." Again that smile. "But I know."

Lawton pulled away and started down the block again. He couldn't stand the challenge in Harry's words. The truth was, he didn't know who he was.

"That's just sheep clothing you go around in all the time," Harry called to his retreating back. "The nice boy, the good boy, the boy who doesn't want to be noticed or get in trouble. No trouble! One day you'll shuck it all off, Mr. Lawton Chastain, and *voila*, there you'll be. I hope I'm around to see it."

LAWTON has gone over and over what happened next, replaying it again and again. The thrill. The dismay. He's tried to forgive his younger self for his betrayal. But regret, instead of diminishing, has only grown. It's been over twenty years since he last saw Harry. Harry Bumgarten. His name still makes Lawton's pulse quicken.

They were playing bridge as usual one night. Harry bid one heart, Garret doubled, Lawton bid two diamonds, and Clem bid three hearts. Harry came back with four clubs, Garret with four hearts, Lawton bid five clubs, and Clem passed. Things were getting interesting. Now Harry went to six clubs, and Garret, judging Harry would never make the slam given Garret's strong hand in all four suits, doubled, to achieve the maximum penalty should Harry and Lawton fall short. Garret led with a heart, the suit he and Clem had been bidding. Harry discarded his singleton diamond, and Lawton won the trick with his ace. From there they drew Garret's last trump, and it was all over but the flipping down of the cards. Harry and Lawton were smiling into each other's eyes across the card table, not even trying to contain their glee as they picked up trick after trick. They'd had a few beers, contraband, but there were ways to get them off campus. It was a few weeks until graduation, and there was something bittersweet in knowing that this time of their lives was coming to an end.

When they finished up about two o'clock, Lawton felt exhilarated. Without discussing it, he and Harry went down the back stairs and out the door, clearing their smoke-clogged lungs in the fresh night air. It was a fragrant May evening. Lawton's skin felt perfect on his body; he felt like bursting out in song himself. They began walking toward a small glade at the edge of campus where there were concrete benches. The glade was enclosed by white pines, mysterious in the dark night, secretive. Lawton's heart was beating hard. He started to sit down on one of the benches, but Harry startled him by reaching for his hand, pulling Lawton toward him. He could see Harry's eyes but dimly in the darkness, looking right at him with a new expression. Harry moved his hand up to Lawton's face, caressing his cheek. He kissed the inside of Lawton's palm, shooting waves of alarm and desire through him. This tableau took place in complete silence; they'd entered a heightened realm of touch. They began to kiss tentatively. Then Harry plunged his tongue into Lawton's mouth, and their hands swarmed all over each other's bodies. Lawton threw his head back, Harry kissed his arched throat, and all Lawton wanted was more. Harry moved his hand down to touch him, and Lawton gasped and moaned. Harry dropped to his knees, unzipping, taking Lawton in his mouth. Lawton was gone, grabbing the back of Harry's head. He had never felt anything so urgent or so good.

Something utterly unfamiliar had taken him over. It was as if he were someone he didn't know, but at the same time, he'd never felt so truly himself. Harry rose to embrace him again. They kissed, cupping each other's faces. Harry. Harry Bumgarten. Nothing had ever felt so right to Lawton.

THE next morning he woke with a hangover. He was horrified. What had happened? What had he done! He leapt from bed, his heart hammering in terror. Harry was a faggot! A fairy. A homosexual. And he'd tried to make Lawton into one. But Lawton wasn't one! He was normal, he wasn't like Harry! Harry had seduced him, and Lawton hated him for it. He hated him! He felt repelled by what had happened between them. He couldn't understand it or explain it. Harry had made him do it! Yet even as Lawton hated him, he longed for him. His misery was as intense and as profound a mystery as his joy had been the night before.

He told Garret and Clem he had to finish an incomplete in order to graduate; he wouldn't be playing bridge anymore. They looked at him questioningly, sensing something but not knowing what. He went to the library that night, sure Harry would show up for the game. He plotted how he could get through the rest of the term—only two weeks left—without seeing him. Lawton never wanted to lay eyes on Harry again.

When Harry came knocking on his dorm door, Lawton hid inside, holding his breath, waiting until he gave up and moved away. Harry shoved notes under the door, beseeching Lawton to talk to him. They twisted his heart, but he burned them. He made sure he didn't go anywhere he thought Harry might be. At graduation, his parents beaming in the audience, Lawton threw his cap up in the air with a special vehemence.

It was shortly thereafter that Lawton met Lydia at the garden party. He had gotten so far off track that she could be his salvation. She was everything he should want. She would correct his path. Her parents, Beatrice and Lyman, were confident that they knew exactly what was what in the world. They never questioned themselves, their place, or their values. Lawton fell for them as much as for Lydia—their big house on Crescent Avenue with the fountain in the English garden, the portraits of Lydia's illustrious ancestors on the dining room walls, the formal dinners served by a young Macie, the sense that if he just became one of them, life would unfold with no disturbances like Harry Bumgarten. He would take his place in the rightful order of things, with Lydia, Beatrice, and Lyman to show him the way.

He was in love with Lydia, he told himself; Lydia was everything he was supposed to want. But his thoughts would go to Harry, to images of his face, his hands, how he'd throw back his head, and his mouth would twist to the side when he laughed. He would berate himself, tell himself how disgusting Harry was. But his harsh thoughts would melt into feelings of tenderness and desire. He would remember how Harry moved his hand up to his cheek and kissed the inside of his palm. He played that moment over and over in his mind, unable to help himself.

He and Lydia moved through the years, newlyweds and then new parents. He settled down into the solicitor's office. With the financial help of Lydia's parents, they bought a house a few blocks from them on Crescent, so Lydia could be near them. Betsy became their focus, and they had, by all accounts, a good life. Lawton congratulated himself that he had righted himself, had achieved what anyone would consider success. He never told anyone about Harry. But he never forgot him either.

9

LEE

IT DIDN'T TAKE but a few days 'til twenty-seven of us fools found ourselves in the city and county jails. Twenty-seven! They was so damn many they had to spread us out between the two jails and walk us back and forth for questioning. At least they made sure we wasn't put in the same cell as those we'd fingered. Lawmen was running around like ants whose hill'd been kicked, taking turns interrogating us and taking our statements. Some held out longer than others.

Those of us being held at the city jail got fed supper in the municipal courtroom there, every night hamburgers with onions, a roll, and coffee. We was told not to discuss the case, but we managed to pass news along with the salt.

Turned out W.O. Burns, who didn't even go to Pickens with us, ratted on McFalls, Griggs, and Bishop for asking him to join us when we was getting organized. When they picked McFalls up, he spilled the beans, identified twelve of us. Rector caved next, adding eleven more names, most the police already had. Bishop and Griggs, they sang too.

Red Fleming and eight more was detained or arrested on Wednesday morning. I was at the Yellow Cab office on Wednesday afternoon about to leave on my shift when the sheriff's guys showed up. They took me, Fat Joy, Hubert Carter, and Johnny Willimon in. They'd already rounded up men from Blue Bird, American, Greenville Cab, and Commercial.

By the time it was my turn to be questioned, it was two in the morning. They took me in a room where two guys told me they was FBI men. I couldn't hardly believe it. FBI men! They looked as tired as I felt. *Where was I the morning of Feb. 17th between 3:00 a.m. and 6:00 a.m.?* Hard to believe only three days done passed 'cause it felt like a year. They named others who already done put me at the lynching. There was no hiding it. I told 'em the truth, like I'd been brought up to do. I named names, just like the others. I didn't tell 'em I hit the nigger 'cause it weren't much of a shot. They asked me who fired the fatal shots. Maybe Roosevelt Herd, but I couldn't say for sure.

"Can you write?" the younger FBI guy asked, shoving a pad and pencil at me. He played the big shot, but he put his pants on one leg at a time too. "Course I can write," I smirked, and I wrote down all the names best I could. Some fellows I didn't know, from Blue Bird or American. I numbered 'em one, two, three . . . 'til I got to twenty.

I pushed it back across the table and sighed, tired of the whole damn thing. I wanted to just lay down and go to sleep. It was going on four o'clock by then.

"Go get him a Coke," the old fatherly guy said, and the young one snapped, "You get it!" When the older guy left, I woke up fast, wondering what Big Shot had in mind. He smiled at me in a way that weren't a'tall friendly.

It was only a few minutes until the old guy came back. When he handed me a Coke bottle, I held it against my hot cheek, feeling the cool relief. I chugged it down and burped.

"How old are you, Lee?" he asked.

"Twenty-four."

"With that baby face, I took you for no more than twenty," he said. "Same age as my grand—"

"Cut the crap," Big Shot snarled. "Now if you two have had enough of this love fest, tell us again what happened that night at the Pickens jail."

He wrote it down, though I could of writ it myself, and read it back fast. I signed. All I cared about was going to bed, even if it meant the cement floor of a goddamn jail cell.

AT lunch the next day, all the boys was saying how those FBI men was the feds messing in our business, how the North was always picking on the South, trying to show us up as ignorant and stupid. The fear was there, I won't deny that. And worry. It began to cross my mind that I was in big trouble. Life in jail or even death. Emylyn came to see me, all teary-eyed to find her husband behind bars. I couldn't believe the fix I was in. I would'a kicked my own ass if I could of.

"Stop that mewing," I told Emylyn. "Go on home and see to our boys. Is your mama keeping 'em?" The fellows in the cell with me—they was six of us to a cell, with a guard stationed outside—was all watching. Some of 'em began making mewing sounds, like goddamn kittens. I cast 'em a hard look but that didn't stop the snickering.

"Mama says she always knew you was no-count."

"She sho was right!" one of the Blue Bird guys hollered.

"You asking for a knuckle sandwich," I said and spit on the floor. "Don't you listen to that shit," I said to Emylyn. "I'm your husband. Now go on home." I wanted to tell her not to worry, but no words wouldn't come.

ON Friday afternoon, the police brought in every taxi driver in the city, ninety-one some said. They wanted to make sure they got us all, so they had the twenty-seven of us who done signed statements take a good look at each and ever' one. We pointed out who was there that night in Pickens and who weren't. I did my best, wanting the cops to know I'd assist. That was the word they used. I figured my future might look brighter if I did. In the end, they was thirty-one of us, counting those already locked up.

ONE of the coppers gave us the Sunday paper. We passed it around at supper in the municipal courtroom where we was having hot dogs and baked beans. The *Greenville News* done printed all our pictures from the city's taxi licensing files. We was shocked to see our mugs on the front page. Some of the boys joshed about how ugly some of the fellows was, who was the best looking, who was most likely to get the girls. At least Sheriff Bearden was quoted as saying we prisoners had cooperated with his office. We took that to mean they'd go easy on us. Most everyone was sure they'd never convict us.

It'd only been a week since the lynching, and on Monday here come the lawyers from a fancy law firm in town, Leatherwood. They told us they was there to arrange bail, $2,500 a head. I whistled when I heard that sum. I told 'em I didn't have that kinda money, and none of the others would neither. They said Jim Bob Forrester's brother, who owned

Forrester Bail Bonds, done put up $77,500 in security to spring us.

By Tuesday us boys was out and back to driving taxi, that fast. But now it was sinking in that it weren't going to go away, the way we'd hoped, 'cause we was charged with committing murder, being accessories before and after the fact of murder, and conspiring to murder. A lot a' big trouble. I hadn't really thought of killing that nigger as murder. It was justice, plain and simple, more than Mr. Brown got. Now *that* was cold-blooded murder, and anyone could see the difference. Sometimes it was as clear to me as mountain air, and other times I'd get confused in my mind, like a big fog had moved in, and I couldn't see my way clear. When my mind was like that, I lost track of the fact that we'd done what needed to be done. My thoughts would get twisted up, like a hard problem I couldn't even understand, and a feeling would come into my guts, like they was twisted up too. I got where I had trouble on the pot, either all runny or too hard and never knowing which it'd be.

I LET some time pass before going to Kress again. I hadn't been by since that time at Lily's house, what with being arrested and all that was going on, plus I wanted to let things settle, put some distance between what had happened and what I wanted to happen again.

I couldn't wait to see the expression on her face when I sat down on my stool at the counter, just like old times. She had her back to me, making coffee or cutting pie. I feasted on her shape in her white uniform, her broad shoulders, wasp waist and big, meaty hips, which I couldn't wait to get my hands on again.

But when she turned around and saw me, she didn't look at me the way she used to, happy and excited to see me, something to pick up the boredom of her day, the way seeing her picked up mine. She avoided my eyes, had nothing to say. I wondered what it was, not that I'm stupid. She was remembering that limp dick, or maybe she didn't like what we'd done, the trouble us boys got into and all. I really didn't know, and I weren't about to ask.

It was hard to believe anything'd ever passed between her and me. She treated me like any ol' customer, a regular stranger, setting my cup of coffee down and asking me if I took cream or sugar, when she knew damn well I take it black. That feeling came over me again, of weakness. I downed the coffee and left. I ain't been back since.

10

ALMA

FEBRUARY PASSED INTO March, bringing with it the ancient rhythms of winter giving way to the promise of spring. Forsythias were in bloom, coloring the landscape with bursts of yellow. Crocus and daffodils pushed their way up to the light, wild dogwoods budded all through the woods, and azaleas and rhododendron prepared for their extravagant display of pink, white, and purple. In the countryside around Greenville, farmers began turning over their fields, whether with tractor or mule and plow, preparing for the new planting season. The days lengthened and brightened, along with people's spirits. But Alma's heart was cold. The heavy emptiness inside was new to her. It was the place where God had been. He had died for her along with Willie Earle.

She'd hoped that when the initial shock of the lynching wore off some, the strange emptiness would ease. But time passed, and nothing. She stopped going to church. She couldn't stand to hear Reverend talk about how far God had brought them and how he would see them through, winding the congregation up into an ecstasy of belief and salvation. She couldn't bear what had previously brought her hope and fortitude. She no longer wanted to sing the hymns that had always meant so much to her. She couldn't stand to see the congregation when they leapt to their feet, waving their hands, shouting "amen" or "hallelujah," sure that they were saved and would find their reward in Heaven one day—just as she used to believe. She wanted nothing to do with church or God or Jesus. She made that clear to Reverend until he stopped coming around.

There was a change in Huff too these days. He didn't come home some nights, when before he was always a homebody. Alma could tell he was in the sauce every night. Even though Huff didn't know Willie, she figured what had happened to him had shaken him, scared him, made him mad as hell, though he'd never talk about that. She wondered if he had another woman somewhere. When she asked him where he'd been those nights, he acted stone deaf. She didn't want to fight with him in front of Pretty.

He still wanted what a man wants from a woman, and Alma began to be thankful for those nights he didn't come home. She worried that he might give her the clap or one of those other diseases, even though he always used a skin. One night when he climbed in bed, he put his hand on her shoulder where she lay turned away from him.

"Come here, baby," he said, his breath rank with liquor. "I been thinking. We need us another baby." And he slid his hand down her hip and up under her gown.

"No!" Alma shouted, leaping from the bed. She had never refused him before. In her crib, Pretty began to cry. Alma went to her and lifted her out, cradling her against her shoulder. Huff pulled on his overalls and slammed out the door, making Pretty cry harder. Alma was glad he was gone. She didn't want to bring another child into the world. Not into their world.

A FEW times a week that spring, Alma and Miz Chastain sat hip to hip at the piano. Miz Chastain said *Moonlight Sonata* was too hard for now, so they would work on something easier. She opened sheet music and showed Alma how the black marks there corresponded to the piano keys. She said she wanted to teach Alma how to read music so she could play all kinds of pieces. They were working on a song for beginners that Alma knew well, "Amazing Grace." Alma had always been a good student in school, and she looked forward to each lesson. Miz Chastain was a patient teacher, knowing just how much to teach her each time, not too much and not too little, so that Alma could absorb the lesson without getting discouraged.

Miz Chastain encouraged her to practice on her own when she found the time, and she did, but only when no one else was in the house, and only after she'd finished all her work for the day. She looked forward to showing Miz Chastain how she was doing at the next lesson. They never spoke of their sessions, and it changed nothing, except in the ways in which it did, which were never spoken of either.

IN April Alma's uncle Ray and aunt Ladocia came to town. They'd moved to Harlem in '36 and came back every couple of years to the homeplace. Ladocia was Alma's mama's sister and as different from Bessie as an apple is to an orange, except for the roundness. Where Bessie was tart and a bit dry,

Ladocia was juicy and sweet. She was the darkest of Bessie's siblings and the oldest. She and Bessie shared the same small, stout figure, with big round breasts and buttocks, round faces with round chins and cheekbones. Ladocia and Ray always made a big splash when they came back, bringing with them exotic gifts from New York City, wearing clothes that no one in Greenville, let alone Liberty or Pickens, could possibly afford or even find. Ray worked as an elevator operator in one of the tall buildings in Manhattan, and Ladocia was a beautician at Rose Meta House of Beauty, a highly successful beauty salon with over twenty stylists. Ladocia, inspired by Rose Morgan's success, hoped to open her own salon someday. She and Ray had bought a brownstone on 132nd Street off Lenox in Harlem, renting out the top floors to boarders to help pay the mortgage.

Ladocia always brought Alma something special. This time it was a broad-brimmed black straw hat with a red ribbon and a red rose on the brim. "I carried that hat box on my lap on the train all the way from Penn Station," she said. "Wasn't gonna let Alma's pretty hat get a crimp in it!"

"'Course when we passed the Mason-Dixon line," Ray said, "we had to move to the colored cars. They don't take care of them cars like they do the ones for the white folks. I'm not saying it's perfect up North, but it shore is a whole hog better. No 'whites only' signs up there. And Harlem! Like nothing you ever seen! Somethin' always going on!"

"Somethin' all right," Ladocia said, raising her eyebrows.

"You and Huff gotta come for a visit," Ray said, pointing his cigar at Alma, who was holding Pretty in her lap. They were sitting on the front porch at the homeplace, taking in the pink-blooming crabapple trees.

"Where we gonna get the money?" Huff said. "We ain't rich folks can hop on the train and take us a trip."

"Well, you and Alma ought to move up North," Ladocia said. "Make more money. Mr. Jim Crow won't be chasing you around like down here. Give that child of yourn a better life up North."

"Now don't go putting no ideas in Alma's head," Bessie said.

But it didn't take Ladocia to do that. It was something Alma had thought about off and on, especially whenever Ladocia and Ray landed in town. But she'd never really believed it possible, always reining her mind back in when it wandered to the North, telling herself that she couldn't leave Mama and Daddy, Callie and Marie. Where would she and Huff live, and what would they do for jobs? What would she do with Pretty when she was at work all day? There would be no Rosa Mae. And what would Huff do? She couldn't picture him anywhere but here. It would be like pulling a plant out of the ground and expecting it to grow in soil it didn't like. He'd wither and die up North.

But lately—since Willie Earle—her thoughts had been turning more and more to the possibility. Why not go? One day on the bus, all the maids were astir with the news: Synthia had left town, gone up North! Didn't say a word to her folks, afraid they'd try to stop her. Didn't tell the white woman she worked for. Just took off with' a man on the Greyhound. Gone up North!

The news had rocketed through Alma. Synthia? Left? Just like that! If Synthia could do it, why not her? Leave here! Leave all these crackers and rebbys and KKKers. Leave where she wasn't allowed to sit at the soda fountain counter at Kress. Leave behind living in a falling-apart shack owned by a white man who acted like he was doing them a favor to let them rent it for more money than any white person would pay! Leave it all behind! Let Pretty grow up out of the Jim Crow South. Things might not be perfect up North, but they'd be a sight better than what the South shoveled out.

On the last day of Ladocia and Ray's visit, after everyone had finished a big chicken and dumpling dinner, Alma and Ladocia took a walk down the road in the warm spring evening. Alma shyly brought up that she might want to move up North, to Harlem. Would Ladocia help her?

"Honey child!" Ladocia exclaimed. "You like my own! I always figured you was the closest I would get to a daughter. I love you like one. You come on up and stay with us. We get you a good job. They lots of fancy people looking for a good maid like you. You make you more money, honey, not like the pittance they pay you down here. But Huff! I can't picture that man in Harlem. It'd eat him alive!"

"I... I don't know," Alma said, though she did. Huff would never leave.

"You got you any money?" Ladocia asked. "I be looking for you a job when you get there. But you gonna need some to tide you over. You got to get you some new clothes and shoes for work, and you gonna need a good winter coat for sure."

The heavy emptiness shifted in Alma's chest a little. Harlem. A new life. A better life, away from here. She glanced back down the road to the house—gray and weathered but home. Home! Could she really leave?

"I got some money saved up," Alma said. "For Pretty's college. But who'd keep Pretty when I'm at work?"

Ladocia stopped to think this over. "Tell you what," she

said. "You make the move first. Leave Pretty with your mama for now. Won't be long before you bring her up. You get yourself settled first, get a job and yo own place. Then bring her, and we find a good woman to keep her while you at work. We work it out."

"Leave Pretty behind!" Alma exclaimed.

"Just 'til you get yourself situated."

"I'm not sure," Alma said, her heart racing. How could she leave Pretty, even for a little while? No, she couldn't do it. She wouldn't be able to stand it.

"When you coming?" Ladocia asked.

Alma stood in the dirt road, her heart tearing in two. "I . . . don't know. I'm not sure. I got some things I have to work out."

Ladocia threw her arms around Alma. "You doing the right thing, honey!" she said. "You won't regret it."

But Alma was gazing off into the distance. She rested her eyes on the path that ran through the field to Tessie's. The new corn was just a few inches high, bright green against the dark red soil.

11

LAWTON

LAWTON KNEW THE opening day of trial, May 12, would be a circus, but he was still shocked by what he encountered. At least 250, maybe 300 whites crowded into the lower floor of the courthouse. They jammed the corridors and stairways, sitting on railings and radiators. Maybe 150 Negroes, having lined up at the side door to get in early, were already in the balcony. Some had seats while others stood packed against the walls. There were at least as many press people as defendants, seated at two separate tables up front.

When the thirty-one defendants were escorted in, they crowded onto benches at the front of the courtroom. They were a rough-looking crew. Most of them were in shirt sleeves, though a few wore coats and ties, which came off quickly as the heat mounted. A dozen or so wore service discharge buttons.

Under South Carolina law, a murder defendant was entitled to have his family beside him in the courtroom. One of the defendants was accompanied not only by the young wife who married him at thirteen, but also by most of the seven children she had borne him. Another's very pregnant wife kept her arm draped around her husband during the opening charges by Judge Martin. Roosevelt Herd, whom several defendants said fired the fatal shots—and the one most likely to be convicted—wore an impassive expression.

Lawton felt reassured, at least as much as he could be, by the judge assigned to the case, Robert Martin Jr. Only thirty-seven, he already had a reputation as a firm, fair, courteous, and decisive jurist. He quickly established the ground rules: no noise, no laughing, talking, demonstrations, sign-making, or hand communication. Violators would be held in contempt.

Bob Ashmore, Sam Watt, a crack prosecutor from Spartanburg whom Governor Thurmond had added to their team, and Lawton had worked around the clock to prepare their case. Lawton had been surprised and disappointed when his friend John Bolt Culbertson signed on for the defense. It was no surprise, however, that Tom Wofford was also on the defense team. He would be a formidable opponent. Sam and Bob would try the case, with Lawton serving as second chair, taking notes and helping with strategy as the trial progressed.

As the clerk of court read the indictments, each of the defendants came to the bar to answer to the charges. The clerk recited questions derived from ancient common law: "How say you—are you guilty as you stand indicted or not guilty?" Each defendant responded, "Not guilty," some in loud, sure voices, others so soft the answer could hardly be heard. "How will you be tried?" the clerk asked. Each responded, "By God and my country." Finally the clerk proclaimed, "May God send you a true deliverance." The trial was underway.

BY afternoon Bob Ashmore had used half of the state's peremptory juror challenges and the defense, six of its twenty. The judge eliminated an ex-sheriff, a deaf man, and a third for no stated reason. Sam Watt eliminated one potential juror because he'd been arrested in Spartanburg with a group of men wearing hoods and robes. On it went, man after man, until Lawton's team had a group of nine. When Martin asked one potential juror if he knew of any reason he could not serve, the man answered, "No sir, but I would rather not." Martin shot back, "I'd rather not try the case. Present him." It was the only moment of levity.

Lawton was not encouraged by the jury. Greenville had plenty of prosperous, educated citizens, including about twenty-five millionaires, but no one from the upper or even middle class was selected, every such candidate having been eliminated by the defense. What they got were eight textile workers, all probably favorable to the defense, a ministerial student, a National Biscuit company employee, a Craig Rush furniture salesman, and a farmer. But Lawton told himself you can't judge a man by his occupation and you can't always tell what is going on between the races. If just one of these men found the courage to convict, they might at least get a hung jury.

Early on Ashmore had determined that it would be almost impossible to win their case. In their statements to the FBI, the cabbies had admitted to being part of the mob and told exactly what had happened that night. But it was unlikely the judge would allow those statements to be used as evidence against anyone except the individual making the statement. In the thirties, in a Greenville case involving Klansmen who'd lynched a tenant farmer, the judge had ruled that a confessional statement made by a member of a mob couldn't be used against the others.

Bob Ashmore figured Judge Martin would rule the same way in this case. No defendant had confessed to firing the fatal shots. There was no direct evidence against Willie Earle's actual killer—unless the others' statements could be used against him. There was no other strong corroborating evidence. Ashmore intended to substitute public shame and exposure, believing conviction was not possible given this legal precedent. He would have the defendants' signed statements read in court, naming names, times, and places in horrifying detail. But if Martin did allow an individual's statement to be considered by the jury as evidence against others, Lawton believed they still might have a chance.

It was afternoon when Sam Watt began to read the first of the defendants' statements into the record. "Willie Eugene Bishop, 27, was arrested at 3:00 a.m. February 18, 1947, and brought to the Police Department for questioning."

Immediately Wofford rose to his feet. "Objection! These statements, Your Honor, might be legal evidence against their individual makers but not against anyone else." He asked Martin to rule now on this crucial point of law.

Judge Martin was expecting this. "I'm reserving a decision on this matter," he said. "For the moment, the statements may be admitted into evidence. Proceed, Mr. Watt."

Watt began to read again, ending with Bishop's confession: "We went to Pickens for the purpose of getting him and taking him out and killing him."

When it was late afternoon, the judge gave instructions for the evening to the bailiff. The jury, being housed next door in the Poinsett, could attend the Greenville Spinners baseball game, but they had to sit separately from the rest of the crowd. They could read newspapers from which trial-related stories had been cut out and follow baseball games. Jackie Robinson had broken the color barrier in major league baseball just a few week earlier. Sam, Bob, and Lawton went back to the office to talk things over, but their backs were up against a hard wall.

T H E next morning, as soon as Sam Watt started to read the second of the defendants' statements, Wofford again objected to its admission on the basis that a statement could be considered against only the one making it. When Martin again said that he would rule later, Wofford argued that they were entitled to have the jury instructed at the time the statement was read.

Martin was peeved. "Very well. We'll settle it now."

Using the thirties lynching trial as precedent, Martin allowed that the statements could be entered into the record but supported the defense's objections that they could not be used against other defendants on the first three counts: murder, accessory before, and accessory after the fact of murder. That left only the conspiracy charge. Martin warned Sam that he wanted evidence to support a conspiracy, not just the cabbies' statements—evidence they didn't have.

It was a devastating ruling for the prosecution.

D E S P I T E constant objections, challenges, and interruptions from the defense team, for the next several hours, Watt read statement after statement into the ears of the jurors, spectators, and the defendants themselves, who seemed fascinated to hear their stories and words out loud in a court of law.

It was Friday before Sam finished all the statements. It'd been an exhausting and tedious effort, full of repetitious questioning and constant challenges from the defense team. None of the defendants ever took the stand.

The prosecution called only two witnesses. Roy Stansell ran the tourist camp on the Pickens Highway where some of the cabs stopped as they were on their way to the Pickens jail. Yes, he was aware of a number of taxis stopping at the camp that early morning of February 17. But that didn't prove that the men went on to a jailbreak and lynching. Next up was U.G. Fowler, a taxi driver who'd been asked to join the mob but refused. It took a lot of courage for him to testify, but he couldn't identify— or said he couldn't— the voice that announced the expedition over the phone.

ON Saturday morning, court reconvened. The big news was that Dame Rebecca West, the famed British writer who'd recently covered the war crimes trial at Nuremberg, would be at the press table on Monday, reporting for *The New Yorker.* This was exciting, Lawton supposed, but he was too exhausted and worried to make much of it.

Watt moved to admit the photos of Earle's corpse since the mutilation of the body showed malice in the heart of the killers. But Wofford contended the pictures didn't prove a thing "except the nigger is dead and everybody knows that." The judge again upheld the defense's objection.

On that sour note, the solicitor's office rested its case. The defense never called a single witness.

TUESDAY morning the courtroom was again packed with spectators come to hear the closing statements. Lawton had told Betsy she could attend on this last day to see "history in the making." She sat toward the back, and Lawton took up his place at the solicitors' table.

The defense was up first.

Bradley Morrah Jr. rose to defend his cousin, John Marchant, the son of a well-known mill family. He was the man who drove the "civilian" car with the spotlight and had kept his distance from the actual scene of the crime. Morrah laid it on thick: "I can picture John surrounded by his loved ones. He stands firmly bottomed, like a ship, and if you convict him, the facts will rankle in the hearts of men throughout the state, from the rock-ribbed brow of Caesar's Head to the marshes of Fort Sumter. The ghosts of Hampton's men will rise to haunt you." Judge Martin dismissed the charges against Marchant.

Ben Bolt was up next. Bolt began his speech by making a case for racial tolerance, bringing up his old mammy, Aunt Hester, who'd helped raise him up right alongside his mother, and whose grave he often visited. "I feel when I go there, I ought to take my shoes off since it is hallowed ground." He went on to say of the FBI agents, "Why, you would have thought someone had found a new atomic bomb, but all it was, was a dead nigger boy."

Next came John Bolt Culbertson, heretofore "friend of the Negro." Lawton felt disgusted when he thickened his already considerably thick Southern accent, speaking of the defendants as "these So'th'n boys," and made much of the fact that the Truman administration had sent in the FBI to meddle in affairs that were none of their business. He whirled and pointed dramatically to the press table, insinuating that Northern papers would use the trial to insult and mock the

South. The judge attempted to rein him in, but of course, once something was said, it was let loose in the air.

John Bolt roamed back and forth in front of the jury, rising to his tiptoes when he made a point, waving his arms grandiosely, dramatizing every word with hand gestures and remonstrations. He crouched down at one point, his arms and hands spinning, and said, "Willie Earle is dead and I wish more like him was dead!" The courtroom came alive, the defendants giggling and expressing amazement and delight. A gasp came from some in the courtroom. There was silence from the gallery above. Lawton felt his stomach turn and unexpectedly, a pang of grief. He had considered John a friend.

Judge Martin hit the gavel and sternly called Culbertson to order, reminding him that he had forbade any mention of race. "You confine yourself to my ruling, or I'll stop you from arguing to the jury." Culbertson smiled coyly at the defendants, who appeared ready to leap up and hoist him on their shoulders as if he had scored the winning touchdown. "I didn't refer to Willie Earle as a Negro," he retorted. Martin told him to watch himself, but Culbertson cast another cocky glance at the defendants and replied, "There's a law against shooting a dog, but if a mad dog was loose in my community, I'd shoot the dog and let them prosecute me."

This was not the Culbertson Lawton thought he knew. Did he think this was a play, and he could just speak lines that had nothing to do with his values? He had a charge to defend his clients, but he was way outside the bounds.

Tom Wofford was the fourth defense attorney to speak. Judge Martin had made clear that Willie Earle's arrest on the suspicion of murder was not to be mentioned as an excuse for the lynching. Wofford knew this perfectly well. "Mr. Watt argues," he said, pacing slowly and thoughtfully in his fine suit in front of the jury, 'Thou shalt not kill.' I wonder if Willie Earle ever read that statement." Up jumped Watt in objection and down came Martin's gavel, but the damage was done.

Wofford took up the Lost Cause again, speaking of the Northern armies that had destroyed Columbia and much of the South in the War between the States, as if that were what this trial was about. "They refer to us as a sleepy little town. They say we are a backward state and poor—and we are. But this state is ours. To the historian, The South is the Old South. To the poet, it is the sunny South. To the prophet, it is the New South. But to us, it is *our* South. I wish to God they'd leave us alone."

S A M Watt began his closing for the state stiffly, saying, "The majesty of the law has been outraged and trampled upon." He warmed up when he talked about the site of Earle's execution. "That slaughter pen wasn't built for the purpose of killing human beings." He was sweating profusely, wiping his high forehead with his handkerchief to keep the sweat from rolling into his eyes as he tried to get through to the jury the violent nature of the lynching. "There's blood flowing between the lines of each of these statements, blood flowing from the stab wounds in the Negro's body, blood gushing from his head as they beat him with a gun butt, blood as they finally shot him! And after they murdered him, some of them went to a café to have coffee. Can you imagine!"

Whether the jurors were moved in any way, Lawton couldn't tell.

A F T E R a lunch break, Bob Ashmore made his closing statement. He started by saying he had no malice in his heart against any of the defendants and that he knew the jury had a hard job in finding the truth. Lawton didn't see what was so hard about it. He droned on for almost an hour, and whether it was from lunch or his pedestrian performance, Lawton couldn't tell, but one juror fell sound asleep. Lawton wished he could put his head down on the table and do the same.

After the judge took the jury through the complicated rules of what the law required and allowed, the jury was sequestered, and the judge left the bench. Lawton found Betsy sitting alone at the back. The room was clotted with tobacco fog, and he told her he needed to step outside for some air. Did she want to come too? "I'll wait here," she said. "I want to watch." Martin had allowed the defendants to remain with their families in the courtroom, and they were milling around, putting their arms around one another's shoulders in a show of solidarity. Observing them, Lawton thought they'd never been so much in love with one another as now, except perhaps during the lynching.

12

LEE

WE WAS INTO the tenth day of the trial, and it was about over except the jury's word. Outside the rain was coming down in buckets, but it was still hot as hell the way it'd been ever' single day. After the judge sent the jury away to decide, he told the bailiffs us defendants could stay in the courtroom and visit with our families and friends. Lots of folks stayed on. Some of 'em wanted to talk to the press, make some point for or agin' us to get in the newspapers. Others clapped us on our backs, shook our hands, and told us we'd nothing to worry about, though worry I still did. Some talked to Widow Brown, dressed all in black. Fat John Joy was keeping all spirits up.

Time dragged on with us waiting it out. I told Emylyn she might as well take the boys on home to give 'em some supper 'cause they was wore out. Some was saying the jury might not even decide that night.

By five o'clock I couldn't stand sitting there no more. One of the officers took a couple of us to the basement john for a piss and led us out the front doors for some air. It was still raining to beat the band, so we had to huddle just outside the doors under the scant eve. I'd walked by the courthouse a million times, and now here I was, a defendant in a murder trial. The palms of my hands felt prickly, like I'd picked poison ivy.

I was standing outside the far door just out of the rain when Mr. Chastain, one of the lawyers agin' us, come out that door. Before I could turn away, he caught my eye and held it. He nodded at me, set my face to flaming. There weren't no place for him to stand out of the rain except right near me. I took a cig from my pack and patted my pockets for matches, but I'd done used my last 'un. I felt Mr. Chastain watching me. "Need a light?" he asked in a calm, low voice.

I didn't want nothing to do with him. But there I was standing with an unlit butt in my hand, the rain thundering down in front of us, and no matches. He was dressed in a fine dark suit and tie, a pocket watch across the vest, and me in my white shirt and khaki pants. For a crazy moment I feared I had on 'em pants with the blood, the ones I'd burned, and that he'd see it.

There was a hot breeze accompanying the storm, blowing the rain almost to where we stood back against the building. I held out my cigarette, and Mr. Chastain cupped his hand around it and held the flame of a silver lighter to it while I took a drag. The smoke felt so good searing down into my lungs. I sighed it out like it contained all my troubles.

We stood there smoking together in silence. After a while, Mr. Chastain said, "I always love a good thunderstorm. The way it clears everything out. Makes the world fresh again."

I didn't know what to say. I took another drag and blew it out, and again it sounded like a woeful sigh. I couldn't stop myself from asking him how long he thought the jury would take. For all I knew, it could go on for days.

Just then a fella came out the door, looking for Mr. Chastain. "They just announced the judge is going out to dinner, Lawton, and won't be back until half past nine."

"Well, then," Mr. Chastain said, still looking out at the pouring rain, "we might as well break for supper. I'll be in in a moment, Thomas." But still he stood there, smoking and looking out at Main Street, like he was memorizing it. Finally he stubbed his cigarette out on the marble step.

He turned his gaze on me.

"They'll be taking you back to the jail for your supper now."

"Yes sir."

He looked out at the rain again, and then he turned back to me. "I know you're hoping for acquittal," he said. "But be careful what you wish for." He paused, holding me in his steady gaze. "Not guilty is not the same as innocent." Then he turned and went through the heavy courthouse door.

Those words struck me like a rattlesnake. Like poison began coursing through my veins, and nothing I could do to stop it. My legs felt shaky, and if it weren't raining so, I woulda sat down on the top of the courthouse steps. It occurred to me again that I'm a weak man. And like a flash of lightning, that rope coiled in my trunk appeared as clear as a photograph in my mind.

WHEN I went back in, they was gathering up the defendants to take us to the jail for our supper. Some of the boys was feeling jovial, some acted worried, and some you couldn't read. I kept my thoughts to myself. Over at the jail, they gave us ham steak and sweet potatoes, but the sight of food made my stomach turn. I didn't want to ever eat again until I knew my fate. I sat there with my arms folded across my chest, and when Fat Joy asked if he could have my ham, I just nodded. I thought about what Mr. Chastain done said, about not guilty not being the same as innocent. Why had he said that? I felt confused by the words, like he was trying to trick me. Not guilty was innocent, what was he talking about? And I believed they'd find us not guilty—innocent—because we was. What we did was righteous and above man's law. God's law. An eye for an eye. Willie Earle's death for Mr. Brown's.

Finally about eight thirty, they told us the jury done reached a decision. A wave of excitement run through us, and a few shouted out we was home free. Wofford and Culbertson done told us the less time the jury took, the more likely we'd be acquitted. It'd only been about five hours, not enough time to argue it out amongst themselves if they was inclined to find us guilty. We was feeling good. Yet I couldn't shake a deep dread as we filed back onto our benches.

Emylyn was back with the boys, and when I slid in next to her, she put her arms around my neck and burst into sobs. I put my arm around her shaking shoulders in her thin cotton dress, wet from running through the rain back to the courthouse. I could see Lee Jr. was afraid of whatever it was making his mama cry so. I ruffled his hair, and he looked up at me with fearful eyes. Pain shot through me, to know I'd hurt the boy and let him down. He couldn't understand adult things like what was going on here in the courthouse. I just hoped someday he'd understand what his daddy did and why. I saw something in his eyes, like he was judging me and finding me lacking, and that hurt and made me mad. He just stared up at me through his thick glasses with his crazy eye, and I wondered what he would think of me ten years from now, twenty, or when I was gone.

Just then the judge come back onto his seat and began to issue orders. There was a high feeling in the courtroom, like it might explode at any minute. Some folk was going to be severely disappointed. I just hoped it weren't us.

When the jury entered, I searched their faces. My stomach got tight, and I weren't sure my balls was still outside my body. I turned just then and spotted Lily sitting in the crowd of spectators. She looked right at me, and she had that same look Lee Jr. done give me, of judgment. I looked away but not before a shiver ran through my whole body. I had the thought that she'd expected better of me. Not the sex part, but the lynching part. Her husband had been there too, but I read in her eyes she'd thought I were better than that.

13

LAWTON

WHEN THE DEFENDANTS were taken back to the jail to have their dinner, Lawton and Betsy drove home for some supper too. Lawton tried to act if not upbeat, at least stoical. Still, he felt a sense of gloom that he couldn't keep from Betsy and Lydia, who were also silent through their supper of cold ham and biscuits. A little after eight thirty, he got a call from Watt that the jury had sounded its buzzer; they were ready with a verdict. No one needed to speak the obvious. With the jury deliberating only five hours, there would be an acquittal on all counts. It was predictable and inevitable. But Lawton felt something inside him die.

Back at the courthouse, he was surprised to find a sense of gloom pervading the room. It was nearly empty, with the defendants still at the jail, and most of the spectators having gone home for their own dinners. Only a few wives and parents of the accused were still there, looking distraught. Perhaps they hadn't been told or didn't trust what a quick verdict portended. Or maybe they were remembering details from all those witness statements. Left alone without the theater of the trial, maybe it was sinking in what their husbands and sons had participated in. Maybe the wives wept, as some of them were doing, for themselves, rather than their husbands, out of fear of what would become of them if their husbands were sent to jail or executed in Columbia. Up in the balcony, there was only a handful of Negroes left. Some of them leaned on the railing, looking down at the scene below.

The courtroom began filling up again as they waited for the judge. The defense attorneys returned, Tom Wofford already celebrating a big victory, glad-handing around. It was unseemly, but then most of the trial had been. The defendants filed back onto their benches, looking cocky. Their wives latched onto them in a show of support and drama.

Lawton studied the young defendant whose cigarette he'd lit outside. When he'd warned him that not guilty was not the same as innocent, a crimson flush had passed over his face. Now all the color had drained away. He tried to pull a frightened-looking boy with thick glasses onto his lap, but the child resisted, shrinking against his mother's side. The fellow couldn't be more than twenty-two or twenty-three, Lawton thought, but he had a look about him of a dog that has lost its home.

The rain outside was sluicing straight down in torrents that made it hard to hear in the room with the windows open. Martin ordered all the officers of the court to move to the aisles and be ready for anyone who reacted. The tension was palpable when the jury entered. Lawton noted that one juror was grinning. The others looked expressionless but for another fellow who hung his head.

They passed along the slips of paper on which they'd written their verdicts to the clerk of the court, who handed them up to the judge. Martin read them through to himself, his face revealing his displeasure, anger even. The clerk read the words *not guilty* aloud ninety-four times, *not guilty on all counts*, and the judge, without paying the jury the customary courtesy of thanking them, told them where they could collect their fee and left the courtroom, his silence speaking volumes.

Bedlam in the courtroom. The defendants leapt to their feet, whooped and hollered, laughed and cried, kissed their wives, embraced one another. Culbertson and Wofford shook hands all around, slapping the "boys" on their backs in victory, without the slightest bit of restraint or irony.

Lawton had his head down, but he looked up when he heard Bob Ashmore's voice. "Stay out of trouble now, boys," he was saying, and he was actually shaking hands with some of the defendants—as if the trial had been a curious piece of theater in which they'd all played their parts, all sound and fury, as they say, signifying nothing. "Behave yourselves," he was telling them. As if the brutal murder of Willie Earle had just been mischief on their parts.

As he watched Bob—how to explain it?—something cracked open in Lawton: He was the biggest actor of them all! All his life he'd played a part. He'd played the role the world had assigned him: homosexuals were bad and had nothing to do with him.

Harry Bumgarten's face came into his mind, smiling exactly as he had that time he'd asked Lawton to run away. He'd told him he wasn't a sheep. But for all these years that's exactly what he'd been. No trouble. *No trouble!*

But he hadn't despised Harry. He had loved him.

A door appeared before him. He was on one side, but he could see through to the other side. He wanted to walk through that door with his whole being, and he knew with certainty that he would.

He sat in a trance, for how long he didn't know. At some point Betsy put her hand on his arm, bringing him back to the almost empty courtroom. It was time for them to go. He gathered up his briefcase and umbrella. They looked at one another, neither saying a word. Her face told it all. His intelligent, sensitive, fragile daughter. She would never be the same. And neither would he.

14

ALMA

FINALLY, AFTER AN eternity, there was a verdict. Alma was lying on her side in bed that evening, feeling in her bones that they'd get the news soon, when Huff came home: *not guilty.* Alma reeled inside, even though she didn't move, afraid if she did she might vomit. *Not a single one. Even after they confessed.* She hadn't expected any other result, and yet emptiness howled inside her. Huff went out the door, slamming it behind him. He would go drinking with other dark men in some dark place, visit his woman if he had one. She might not see him for days.

Alma pulled herself out of bed and sat down at the table under the light bulb. She got out a piece of notebook paper from the tablet she still kept from her Sterling High days. She wrote May 21, 1947, at the top, like she'd learned in school, and then: *Dear Ladocia, if you really meant what you said, I'm coming. Dew will put me on the train. Just me. I let you know when I be getting there.* She addressed an envelope to Ladocia and Ray Williams, put the letter in it, sealed it up and put a three-cent stamp on it.

She took down the coffee can where she kept her college money for Pretty. When she last checked, she had almost one hundred and ninety dollars, fives and tens, mostly, though there were four twenties. She turned the can over on the blue oilcloth. Her eyes grew big, her fist flew to her mouth to stifle a shout. The money! There were only a few crumpled bills! She held the can upside down and shook it hard, as if more might materialize. She smoothed the bills out on the table with shaking hands. A ten and a couple of ones. She sat stunned, unbelieving. He had taken most of it. Almost all of it! How could he? For liquor and maybe that other woman. What a fool she was! To leave the money where he could get to it. Her mind went dark. But when it cleared, she was as certain as she had ever been of anything in her life: She would find a way.

ON the last Friday evening in August, Alma dawdled at the Chastains in order to miss the last bus home. She busied herself with making a peach pie, so she could be there when Mr. Chastain got home. Just as she hoped, he said he'd run her home before supper while the pie was baking. Alma's chest had felt tight and hard all afternoon, and she breathed a sigh of relief when she was in the back seat of his Ford. As they neared Southernside, the palms of her hands grew damp.

When he stopped in front of her house, he turned to her in the back to say goodnight.

"Mr. Chastain, I got to ask a favor." *Lurching heart.*

He looked surprised. "What is it, Alma?"

She glanced out the window while she tried to gather her thoughts. It was twilight, and all around them, the katydids were starting up, a frenetic summer chorus. In her mind, she'd practiced the words and how she would say them. But now she blurted out, "I got to go up North. I need money." She felt the blood rise to her face and neck, humiliation and hope pumping through her veins.

They sat in silence.

"Do you have people there?" he asked at last.

"My aunt and uncle," Alma said, unable to meet his eyes. Was it shame in having to ask or shame that she was leaving? He'd always been good to her. The Chastains had been as good as white people could be to her.

"Have you told Miz Chastain?"

"No sir."

"Are you going to tell her?"

"No sir."

"And Betsy?"

She shook her head, feeling the weight and the emptiness. Betsy would think Alma was abandoning her. She would beg Alma not to leave, at least until she left for college. But Alma couldn't wait. She had to go now, or she never would. She hoped one day, when Betsy was older, she'd understand.

He nodded, whether in understanding or just acceptance, Alma couldn't tell.

"Your aunt and uncle—they can get you a job there?"

"Yes sir."

"And Pretty?"

"My folks. 'Til I can fetch her."

"Huff?"

"No sir."

He nodded again. He didn't ask her how much she needed. She didn't know. Dew had said he'd buy her train ticket. But she'd need money when she got to Harlem until she could get a job. There was the five she would get on Friday from Miz

Chastain and what money she had managed to save since her savings went missing in May.

"I'm sorry to see you go, Alma," Mr. Chastain said. "We'll miss you." He got out his wallet. "This is what I have on me," he said as he took all the bills out and handed them to her. "I'm not sure how much is there. If you need more, ask me."

"Yes sir," Alma said, taking the money and jamming it into her purse, her mouth gone dry. "Thank you, sir."

"I wish I could do more," he said. "I don't mean the money. I mean . . ." he trailed off. "I don't blame you. I think I understand. But change will come, Alma. I know it doesn't seem so right now. But things will get better for your people."

IT was going to be a day like any other day. Alma would take Pretty over to Rosa Mae's in the morning, like she did every weekday, and then she'd rush to catch the bus. Nothing unusual there, except that it would be the last time.

On the floor by the door sat her cardboard suitcase, bound by two leather straps. Alma had packed it last night, putting in two Sunday dresses and four cotton shirtwaists, and laying out her seersucker suit and the straw hat that Ladocia had given her in April for the trip tomorrow. She'd packed the cotton shift she slept in, sleeping her last night in an old undershirt of Huff's. It had been a week since she'd seen him. If he'd come around, she would have told him her plans. She hadn't even had a chance to say goodbye.

What else should she take? What do you take when you're leaving? What will you need? She took the framed photograph of her family posed in front of the homeplace, all of them unsmiling given the seriousness of a family portrait. She looked through the snapshots of Pretty Dew had taken, unable to choose. She tucked all of them between her dresses, putting two of them in her big black pocketbook so she could look at them on the train trip. She looked around. She lifted her cast iron frying pan from its nail on the wall, its weight familiar and comforting. She said goodbye and hung it back up. She said goodbye to the blue oilcloth, the porcelain wash-basin painted with pastel flowers, the bib aprons her grand-mother had made, and the patchwork quilt Callie had sewed. She was tempted to tuck the topless crystal sugar bowl into her suitcase. But no.

She folded Pretty's things and packed them in a paper bag: her best dress, pink with ruffles, her playsuits and panties. Her Sunday shoes and socks. What about her Bible? She'd had it since she was thirteen, a gift from her parents when she was saved and baptized in the river. Its thin pages were worn from the many times she'd read it, the gold gilt of "Bible" on the black cover grown faint over the years. She put it in Pretty's sack.

Pretty was scribbling with a crayon in a coloring book on the floor, babbling to herself. Alma scooped her up, along with her pink blankie and her big black pocketbook, and half-ran down the street to Rosa Mae's. The old lady was waiting for her and took Pretty onto her lap in the rocker. When Alma told Rosa Mae her plans last week, that she was leaving, going up North, Rosa Mae had wrapped her bony arms around her. They had clung together for a long time. Now Alma knelt next to the rocker and kissed first Pretty on the cheek and then Rosa Mae, feeling her chest tighten. Then she flew down the steps and ran to catch the bus just as it was pulling up at the stop.

I T was a day like any other day at the Chastains. Mr. Chastain had already left for work, and Betsy was sleeping late. She often slept until ten or eleven o'clock. Alma wasn't sure what to make of that, if it was just growing pains or something more. Miz Chastain came down for breakfast and filled Alma in about her day: she'd be gone all morning, back at lunch with the groceries, and then out again in the afternoon to her folks. Next Wednesday, the women's guild at the church was sponsoring a speaker, a missionary back from Africa who would tell the ladies about her work there. "You can't imagine the conditions, Alma, the way the people live, how little they have. I said I'd have the meeting here. Just light refreshments, but we can decide on Monday. Maybe some finger sandwiches, chicken salad, and those cheese biscuits you make so good. I'm off now, but I'll be back by noon. Plenty of leftovers in the icebox for lunch, just heat up whatever you can find. If Betsy isn't up by ten, get her up. She can't spend the whole day in bed."

When she first came to work for the Chastains, Miz Chastain would write her a list every day of things to do. She was impressed that Alma could read and write and had graduated from high school. In a short while, she dropped the lists because Alma didn't need to be told what to do. She knew the house better than Miz Chastain, knew what needed tending to, what was daily, weekly, monthly, and yearly.

"Betsy's going swimming at the club this afternoon," Miz Chastain said. "Dotty Jenkins is picking her up at two. You can leave after you get supper cooked. Here," she said, taking her wallet out of her pocketbook, "I'll pay you now, and if everything is done, you can leave about four."

"Thank you, m'am," Alma said. She took the five-dollar bill and folded it as she put it in her apron pocket, her fingers lingering on it there for a minute. Miz Chastain could afford to pay her more. Alma had been to her folks' house down the block many a time to help Macie with parties. Miz Beatrice and Mr. Lyman were rich people, and Miz Chastain had plenty of money; she never did without a thing. Even two dollars more a week would make so much difference! They wouldn't have to scrape by quite the way they did. But Alma knew Miz Chastain would never pay her more than the other white ladies paid their maids. She'd be afraid word would get around, and then the other white ladies would scold her. Colored help came cheap, and white folks were determined to keep it that way.

After Miz Chastain left, Alma went into the living room. There would be no time for a piano lesson today or ever again. She thought about the times she and Miz Chastain had sat there hip to hip, something companionable and sisterly in it. She opened the piano and ran her hand lightly over the familiar black and white keys. She'd learned "Amazing Grace" all the way through. It hadn't come easy. But now she picked out the notes she'd learned of *Moonlight Sonata*. It suited her better today.

As she went about her work, quietly so as not to wake Betsy upstairs, she thought about how shocked Miz Chastain would be when she didn't appear on Monday. By then she would be up North, at Ladocia and Ray's. Miz Chastain would be hurt and angry. Alma could picture her soft, powdered face when she got the news. She would feel betrayed, and she wouldn't understand. Had she thought they were friends? But if they were friends, why did Miz Chastain never sit down and eat with her? All those years—ten—Alma ate in the kitchen on dishes for colored people after Miz Chastain finished lunch! She didn't want to hurt Miz Chastain, but her plans were none of her business.

At ten o'clock Alma knocked three taps, a pause, and then the louder knock on Betsy's door and opened it. Betsy was still sound asleep. Alma couldn't imagine sleeping like that for that long. She studied Betsy, remembering her as a child when she first came to work. In the fall, Betsy'd be leaving for college, and that was good. Maybe she'd do well there, a bigger pond where she could be herself more than here. Alma was sorry not to be here when she left, to see her off into the world. But Alma herself was leaving for a bigger world where she too could be more herself. They'd both have to learn who those selves were.

After she'd roused Betsy, she went back downstairs and cleaned the guest bathroom. At eleven thirty she got yesterday's leftover meatloaf and mac and cheese out of the icebox and put them in the oven to warm. She heated some cornbread. She was conscious of each and every task she did in this house today, not by rote, but with a sense of last time. She felt filled to the brim with an emotion she couldn't name.

Miz Chastain came in with the groceries, pork chops for dinner. Alma could fix some cream gravy, green beans, and she showed her the box of instant mashed potatoes she'd bought at the Dixie Home store. "You just add warm milk and butter," she exclaimed to Alma. "No peeling or boiling potatoes. What will they think of next!"

Alma served Betsy and Miz Chastain their lunch in the breakfast room. She could hear their voices as she washed the glass casserole dishes she'd used to warm the leftovers. She poured them more sweet tea and served the last of the peach pie from Monday night. Every now and then, she reached into her apron pocket and felt the five-dollar bill. With the money Mr. Chastain had given her, she had two hundred and forty dollars. He'd told her when he handed over the bills in the car to put most of it in her brassiere when she rode the train north and not to take it all in her pocketbook.

After lunch, Miz Chastain said a hasty goodbye, she'd see Alma on Monday. Alma stood in the open door and watched her walk briskly down the sidewalk toward her parents' house. She felt a painful ache in her throat, but then she turned and shut the door. She had dishes to finish up. Just before two o'clock, Betsy's friend Dotty pulled up out front in her mother's car and honked. Betsy went running out with her beach bag, calling back over her shoulder, "See you on Monday, Alma. Have a good weekend!" Alma stood at the front door and watched her go. Again, that painful ache, only it spread now to her chest, to her back. She stood there a long time, until it eased.

S H E caught the bus a little after four. At Rosa Mae's, there was another long embrace, another painful ache. Alma brought Pretty back to the house, gave her soda crackers and Ovaltine, and then she lay on the bed with her, running her fingers over Pretty's smooth brown arms and legs, gently tugging her fingers and toes, making her laugh. She memorized every perfect inch of her, she kissed every exposed bit of skin she could find, making a game of it. She explained to her that Mama loved her and would be back for her soon. Tears began streaming from Alma's eyes. Pretty began crying too, wiping Alma's face with her small hands. Alma forced a smile and gave her baby doll to her. They were going to see Mama Bess and Poppy, she told her, and Pretty would have fun there.

At five, Dew pulled up with Pearle, and they rode out to the homeplace. When she'd told her folks her plans last week, they'd stared at her wide-eyed, though they didn't try to dissuade her. It was only Daddy who wept, but he didn't ask her not to leave. Along with Callie and Marie, they all sat down now to another big fried chicken dinner, only everyone's appetite was missing. Bessie packed a shoe-box of chicken and boiled eggs for Alma to take on the train tomorrow. Right after dinner, Dew took charge, said they'd better get back to town, Alma needed to rest before her long trip. Alma embraced Callie, Marie, her mother, her father. Goodbye, goodbye. *I'll be back as soon as I can.*

Pretty held out her arms to be picked up when she saw Alma was leaving. "Mommy take." Alma picked her up, tears streaming again, and then handed her over to Bessie without a word. She could hear Pretty crying and calling, "Mommy take! Me, Mommy me!" as she went out the door and got into Dew's car. She shut the car door and buried her face in her hands. Pearle reached over from the back seat and put her hand on her sister's shoulder. They rode in silence except for Alma's weeping all the way back to town.

AT the depot the next day, Dew in his crisp white shirt and hand-some black uniform supplied by the Southern Railway bought Alma's ticket at the colored ticket window and ushered her to the colored waiting room. When Alma used the restroom, she almost got sick it was so dirty and smelly. She was dressed in her Sunday best, a blue seersucker suit, stacked heels, and her black straw hat. She carried her shoebox meal, and Dew made sure her suitcase got into the luggage car. He was helpful to all the colored people crowded on the platform, telling them what to expect and where they should sit. Once the train was under-way, he told Alma, he'd bring her some coffee when he could.

The platform conductor announced that the train was approaching: "Everyone stand back!" Its whistle sounded in short, emphatic blasts as it neared the station. Dew left to attend to his duties as the Piedmont Limited arrived, blowing smoke out like some prehistoric metal animal. Alma felt like a train herself, on a track that was going forward, going up North, no turning back. When the doors to the colored car opened, the crowd of Negroes heading north swarmed aboard, carrying Alma with them.

She found a seat by a window. Dew came through the car, checking on her, and shortly after that she heard, "Last call, all aboard!" shouted from the platform. The train started slowly as it left the station, out past Poe Mill and the smoke stack of American Spinning in the distance, then alongside Rutherford Road, where remains of World War I's Camp Sevier still lined the tracks. It moved through the mill village of Southern Bleachery, picking up speed as it cleared town, out into the countryside, heading for the North Carolina line. Alma stared out the window as the verdant, late steamy-summer green of the South passed by, cornfields, kudzu-covered banks, lazy rivers like the one she'd been baptized in, dense forests where the trees were so green and lush they looked ready to explode.

On they rode, the train shaking and swaying as it gathered speed, on past Spartanburg and the peach orchards of Gastonia, on toward Greensboro, through Danville, Lynchburg, and Manassas, on toward Washington, DC. On and on they traveled—Baltimore, Wilmington, Philadelphia . . . heading for the Promised Land.

15

BETSY CHASTAIN

BETSY'S NIGHTMARES BEGAN the night her father took her to the Pickens County jail. In the first dream, everything was exactly as she'd witnessed it that afternoon: the locked bars; the low cot; the slop bucket; the empty cell. A profound absence, and silence.

But as she peered into the cell, a strange sensation came over her. The space was deeply familiar, as if she'd run her hands over the rough brick walls time and time again. Looking closer, she saw her hairbrush with strands of her long brown hair entwined in the bristles; her baby blue cardigan sweater was wadded into a makeshift pillow on the cot; the pearls of the necklace she'd received for her sixteenth birthday were scattered across the wood floor, as if ripped from her neck.

She'd sat straight up in bed, a cry of "No!" breaking the peaceful silence of the house. She covered her face with her hands, pressing her arms against her chest to protect against whatever blow was coming. But no blow came. After a few minutes, she slowly released her hands. As her eyes adjusted to the dark, she saw that she was in her own brass bed in her own pink bedroom at home. Home: the big, safe house on Crescent Avenue where no harm could come. But harm had come.

After that she never knew when she'd be ambushed by the nightmare. Going to sleep became a fearful thing. Sometimes the objects in the cell were from her childhood (a silvery-pink music box with a ballerina on top, her Brownie sash, a bride doll dressed in white); sometimes they were from the present (her yearbook *Nautilus*, a dried corsage from last year's prom, a perfect sand dollar she'd found at the beach). Other times she sensed the items lay ahead, in her future. She'd jerk awake, her heart struggling to escape her chest, her breathing as panicked as if she were being pursued by a mob of angry men.

How could she tell anyone? Who could she tell? And what would she say? It was too strange, too—private—to try to put into words. She carried on, pretending everything was just the same. Her father was so wrapped up with the lynching trial, and her mother was irritable and distant. Winter became spring and spring became summer, and if they noticed there had been a change in Betsy, they didn't say a thing.

Alma was different too. She still came every day, she still did the things she'd always done. But after the trial, she'd drawn into herself, closed the door, leaving Betsy outside. Alma had known him growing up in Liberty, her father had told her. Alma grieved, though she said not a word, and Betsy grieved with her. *Willie!* She saw his ghost in the young colored men who hung around the corner store when she drove Alma home in her mother's Buick. She saw Willie in their wary, closed looks as she passed slowly in the big blue car that rocked in the ruts of their red dirt streets. Willie in their dusty, worn khaki pants and faded shirts, their flat caps, their nothing-to-do-ness. For the first time in her life, Betsy saw them: their dignity and despair, their poverty and pride, their hard lives. Kept down by the color of their skin. That was it. That was all. They were colored. It was everything.

ON the last Monday morning in August, Betsy came downstairs to find her mother sitting at the breakfast room table. Just sitting. The *Greenville News* was spread open in front of her, but she wasn't reading it. Betsy always slept late on those summer mornings, exhausted from the nightmares. By the time she got up, her mother was usually gone somewhere, or she might be practicing the piano. She was never just sitting.

Now, as if awakening from a trance, her mother gathered up the newspaper. "Alma didn't come to work today," she said, looking up at Betsy as if she would know why. "Did she say anything to you?"

Betsy shook her head. Usually she wouldn't have sat down with her mother, but now she pulled out the chair across from her.

"I hope nothing's wrong," her mother said.

"Like what?"

"I have no idea. It's just not like her. Not to have Rosa Mae give us a call. I hope it's not Pretty."

"It's probably nothing," Betsy said uncertainly.

"Rosa Mae's phone's been busy all morning. Maybe it's off the hook, or someone's yacking on the party line." Her mother paused. "Let's go find out." She stood up so suddenly she startled Betsy. "Come with me. Please?"

"Of course," Betsy said. She couldn't remember the last time her mother had asked her to go somewhere with her.

Her mother drove the big blue Buick to Sycamore Street.

Betsy slouched in the passenger seat, sleep-deprived, looking out the window, chewing her thumbnail. She thought of all the times her mother had driven her to her piano or ballet lessons, to Brownie Scout meetings, to skating parties at Cleveland Park, or summer day camp on Paris Mountain when she was a child. When had they become strangers? Her mother glanced over at her and for once didn't tell her she was ruining her nails. Betsy put her hand in her lap to stop herself, though she couldn't help finding a bit of dry lip to gnaw. "I wonder if she could be pregnant again," her mother said. "But with Pretty, she always made it to work. Even when she had morning sickness."

Alma was as steady as the sun coming up every day. Why hadn't she come to them today?

Her mother pulled to a stop in front of the little frame house where Alma lived. There was no sign of life, the front door shut when it was ninety-five degrees out. On the front porch was the big red-and-white striped plaster Christmas candle, four feet tall, a yard decoration Betsy's parents had given Alma when they no longer wanted it. Marigolds wilted in a washtub by the rickety stairs. Sweat was pouring down Betsy's sides under her arms in her white sleeveless blouse.

"Go see," her mother said. Betsy had never set foot in Alma's dirt yard let alone on her front porch. It felt like trespassing. There were places Negroes didn't go, and equally places where white girls didn't go. While her mother waited in the car, she nervously went up the three uneven wood steps and used the knock Alma always used on her bedroom door, three taps, a pause, and then another stronger knock. What if Alma was sick, really sick, or what if she had to take Pretty to the hospital? Where did colored folks go when they had to go to the hospital, Greenville General or St. Francis? Did they let coloreds in those hospitals? No one answered her knock.

"Rosa Mae will know," her mother said when Betsy got back in the car. They drove slowly and cautiously through the red dirt ruts that comprised the street. Betsy was embarrassed by the big Buick, feeling stares from neighbors sitting on their porches fanning or walking ahead of them in the street. An old man stepped aside to make room for the car and tipped his hat at them. But a young Negro man—*Willie!*—walking with a pretty young woman in a floral cotton dress stared sullenly at them.

Her mother pulled in front of Rosa Mae's. Since Alma didn't have a phone, whenever Lydia needed to reach her, she called Rosa Mae. Rosa Mae's middle-aged son Henry, who bagged groceries at the Better Food, paid for her phone. Her house was as rundown as all the other shotgun shanties, if not more so. Betsy winced at the sight of its peeling paint and the way it tilted to the left where one of the large foundation stones had shifted, as if someone could push it over with a good shove. The houses white people—at least the ones Betsy knew—lived in and the houses colored people lived in existed in two different worlds.

Rosa Mae's front door was open; Betsy knocked softly on the frame. "Come on in, y'all," came Rosa Mae's reedy voice. Betsy stepped out of the bright sunlight into a darkened room. The paper shades were pulled to keep out the sun; the room wasn't much cooler than the blazing furnace outside. It took her eyes a moment to adjust to the darkness. She saw Rosa Mae's small bent figure sitting in a rocker in front of a box fan.

"How you, child," she said. "Sit down yonder." She indicated the couch with a wave of her gnarled hand. It was a brown faux-leather couch, with one mismatched cushion. "Want you a Coke or somethin'?"

"Alma didn't come to work today," Betsy said, perching on the edge of the couch, biting her lip. "We went by her house, but she's not there."

"She done left," Rosa Mae said. "Gone up North."

"What?" Betsy said, dumbfounded. What did she mean, *Gone up North*? "You mean on a trip?"

"Done gone for good," Rosa Mae said. "Like so many done done. Took the train Sa'day."

"What?" Betsy said again. She wasn't sure she'd heard right. "She didn't . . . tell us."

Rosa Mae just shook her head. "Tilt that fan yo way. Sho is hot."

"But . . . What about Pretty? And Huff?"

"Baby at her mama's 'til she can fetch her."

"Oh," Betsy said. She couldn't think what to say. She stared up at Jesus on the wall. "Mama tried to call here," she said finally. "Is your phone out of order?"

"Henry late with the pay."

"Oh," Betsy said, feeling disconnected herself. She thanked Rosa Mae and stepped back out into the slap of heat and humidity. She took a moment to compose herself, pressing her knuckles against her bottom lip. It was bleeding a little where she'd bitten it. She opened the car door and got in.

"Well?" her mother said, looking anxiously at her. Betsy couldn't stand that expression on her mother's face: the knotted-up brow, the squinting eyes. It reminded her of her own face.

"Alma went up North," Betsy said slowly, disbelieving. "She took the train Saturday."

Her mother stared at Betsy for a long moment. "What do you mean, she went up North?"

"That's what Rosa Mae said. She's not coming back. She left Pretty with Bessie for now." Betsy stared back at her mother. She expected her to say it wasn't true.

A blush washed over her mother's powdered face. She leaned forward, bracing herself on the steering wheel, and buried her face in her hands. Betsy had only seen her mother cry once, when Betsy was seven and her father gave her a frying pan for Mother's Day. That time her mother had wept hard for several torturous minutes, the way she was doing now, as if some deep, unspoken disappointment had overwhelmed her. Betsy didn't know what to do then or now. She tentatively unsnapped the gold clasp of her mother's pink lattice pocketbook and took out a linen handkerchief with a crocheted border. When she handed it to her mother, she straightened up, wiped her eyes, and blew her nose in a most unladylike way. Betsy didn't realize she ever actually blew her nose in one of her fancy hankies. Her mother sighed deeply and started the car.

She didn't say another word about it, not when they got home that day, or in the days following. But Betsy knew what her mother was feeling because she was feeling the same things herself: Pain. Bewilderment. Betrayal. Anger. Loss. How could Alma just leave like that, without a word of explanation or goodbye? She'd been a part of their family for ten years. Didn't she love them—love Betsy— as much as Betsy loved her?

16

LEE

I'M A WEAK man. I know that now and I have to live with it. But one thing I don't regret and that's the rope. It's still back there in the trunk of my cab, coiled like a rattler I don't want nothing to do with. I ain't touched it since that night last February. Some was calling for a rope and I could of spoke up. But I held my tongue and of that I am proud. It's a considerable rope. I started toting it in case I got stuck in the mud on some lonesome red dirt road out in the county beyond Greenville—Pickens or Liberty—where they say that nigger was born and where I myself was born. It would of done. Now I got some old blankets throwed over it. I don't much like to see it when I have to get at the jack or put a trunk back there when I got a pickup at the depot. I been lucky too, not getting stuck, not enough where I couldn't rock the wheels out. I been real careful not to.

Liberty, South Carolina. I always liked the name of that town. *Give me liberty or give me death.* That's one of the few things I remember from school. Mrs. Tucker in fifth grade, my last year of schooling. When she said them words, *Give me liberty or give me death*, it felt like lightning done struck the top of my head. I took it to be my personal motto, and you could say it's directed my life ever since. We was all lined up for death at the trial, or life maybe. I'd choose death over that. I want my liberty, and now I have it, scot-free. A free man, that's me. The jury spoke and we walked free. *Not guilty!* But is that the same as innocent? I'm determined not to dwell on it no more.

Today I'm cruising down Main Street, enjoying my freedom. Life is good I guess you'd have to say. 'Course the niggers got their own cabs now, or they'll take a bus or trolley or walk ten miles 'fore they'll ride with us. Well, that's their business. Everybody got to do what they got to do. Most of white Greenville is still behind us anyway, it ain't hurt business all that much.

My main problem these days is Emylyn. Ever since the trial, she complains I'm never home. Says she's raising the two boys by herself, but I tell her that's her job, to take care of the house and family. Truth is I don't feel all that comfortable being home. When I'm there, it's like something's in the air that I can smell but can't see. That nigger Willie Earle messed up a lot of things, that's for sure.

Now I'm easing by Kress at the corner of Main and McBee. I slow down, trying to peer in to see if Lily's behind the soda fountain, but it's too far back in the store. Lily's another thing that nigger messed up for me. At night when I'm feeling extra lonely, I think about her home in bed, lying next to her crazy-ass husband Lou Reynolds, him snoring like a hog. She used to tell me how she'd lie awake thinkin' about beaming him with her cast iron frying pan. We'd giggle about it, snuggled up together at the Dixieland way out towards Spartanburg, my cab parked around back where no one was likely to see it. We never did sleep together. I mean where you fall asleep together peaceful-like, so she didn't never know that I snore too. That's what Emylyn says at least, and sometimes I do wake myself up, especially after a few bumps. We only had time and interest for one thing, Lily and me, and then maybe a little spooning afterwards, me curled against her back, my hands cupping her big soft breasts.

I'd pick Lily up in the alley behind Kress when she got off work, and we'd go on out to the Dixieland for not much more'n an hour. We was hardly in the door before we'd be stripping off our clothes, barely making it to the bed and me driving into her, her legs up around my waist or me bending her over the bed. She taught me what she liked, and I liked it too, and that's the way it went, maybe one or two times a week. We'd save up for those times, trying not to let it get out of hand. Not become an obsession, only in truth it were for me, and I think for her too. We carried on normal the rest of the time, going about our business, our families, our kids. We weren't about to quit 'em. What choice did we have? We never talked about it. That weren't the deal. There was just that brilliant time in the room, in each other. That's the way it comes to me now, like the brightest star come down to Earth, blinding and beautiful. So beautiful.

THINK I'll take me a spin on out towards Spartanburg but I won't go so far as the Dixieland. I try not to go out that way no more, though sometimes I do. Today I want to drive through Woodlawn and see if there's any new graves. I actually put good money down on two plots this summer, if you can believe that. For the future, the salesman told me, and how it made sense to buy now, before the prices go up. I knew he was just pitching me, hell, that's his job, but it made me feel good to know I had plots for me and Emylyn. My property is right by a crepe myrtle tree. I just hope I can keep making the payments. And if I ever get ahead, I'll put down money for two more, for Lee Jr. and Earl.

Lee Jr. still ain't forgiven me for the bad whupping I give him last February. He used to be my little man, and then he didn't care for me no more, even though I ain't laid a hand on him since that day. For a while there, I tried being extra nice to him, bringing him special treats, marbles or a new yo-yo, but I couldn't melt him. He's cold as ice to me, and that's something to see in a little boy. Earl's still just his naughty self, into everything. You can tell he prefers his mother. Emylyn's got what she wants with the two boys, and truth be told, they're mama's boys, especially Lee Jr. I'm not home that much anyway.

The clerk read the verdicts out loud: *not guilty. Not guilty on the charge of murder. Not guilty on the charge of conspiracy.* Not guilty on ever' single charge. Not guilty! That's when the judge turned his back and left. But what did we care, we busted into joy, clapping each other on the back, congratulating our lawyers who was pumping our hands and kissing our wives and babies. Our friends and relatives exploded all around us. The press was pushing to get statements, and I heard Roosevelt Herd say the truth for all of us, "Justice has been done . . . both ways." Some of the boys was crying, some laughing, some whistling. The feds and the court tried to make us into criminals and wrongdoers, but regular folks, like the fellas on the jury, understood what we done.

That was last May, and now it's September, the school kids gone back to class. There's an ache in the air, summer gone so fast. It's funny how life was one way up 'til that May day, and then afterwards it weren't the same. No not at all. We walked out of there free men, and everything looked the same. We went back to our jobs, our lives, and except for the niggers starting their own cab company, life appeared to be pretty much the same. But it weren't.

NOW I'm heading up the Poinsett Highway towards the mountains. I might get me a Moon Pie and RC cola at the filling station in Travelers Rest. Then on up through Marietta. I might even go as far as Table Rock. We used to play there when we was kids. We'd run up the trail, pretending we was Cherokees that lived there before the white man run 'em out. Hoping to find an arrowhead, though we never did. The Indians believed a giant chief sat on a nearby mountain and ate his supper off Table Rock, way up there in the sky. Ain't no more farfetched than Jesus rising from the dead.

Lily and I went on like we did for three months. Eleven weeks, to be exact. Seventeen times is all. I counted each time, like it was my treasure, gold or silver, something that precious. At the time I thought we could go on forever. Why not?

Then came that night last February, the night the boys was all fomenting about Willie Earle, milling around across from the sheriff's office on Court Street. Talking about going to Pickens, getting the nigger out of jail, making him pay. After that everything commenced, as if it were already writ. By the next morning, the deed was done, and no taking it back. In some ways the time has passed fast as a flash, and then again it feels like I've lived a hundred years and am more than ready for the grave.

Those was hard months between February and May, full of worry. We kept telling ourselves and each other we'd done right. Some of the guys turned on each other. I weren't surprised when some nasty stuff came out, who was sleeping with whose wife or girlfriend. I hoped Lily would keep her mouth shut. All I needed was Lou Reynolds in my face.

It seems to me now those hours in the Dixieland with Lily was the happiest of my life. It was just fucking, sure, but I don't know, we'd seemed so close. Closer than I'd been to anyone ever. It set up a craving in me, like the thirst for liquor. It weren't like we talked much. Weren't no need. I could tell she liked me, and I felt sweet towards her, like my heart opened wide. That's the feeling I miss. Not just the sex, though I do miss that. But that feeling. It's like I can see the other side of a river I can't get across no more.

I'M passing through Pumpkintown now, the big mountain with the bare rock rearing up and pulling me towards it. I know I'm on the right road, the road I should be on today. Freedom Road. Last May during the trial, I didn't know if I'd be sitting in the penitentiary the rest of my life. But I'm a free man. *Give me liberty or give me death*. No cars much on this country road, I have it to myself. There's a solemn, silent feel in the air. The deep woods. I haven't been up this way for so long. It feels like a homecoming.

I done arrived at the east gate of Table Rock State Park. I start up the mountain road the CCC boys put in, taking it slow on account of the hairpin curves. I'm in no hurry. No one around, just me and the deep woods. I turn into the parking lot of the lodge, deserted this afternoon, not even a ranger truck around. Those CCC boys built the lodge from old growth trees they logged up here, used boulders for the walls, hand-quarried the steps from local blue granite. Amazing what man can do if he sets his mind and body to it. I go down the steps and around back to the stone patio. From here the lake stretches out to the sandy beach on the far side, the mountain with its rock face rising above it. I hoist myself up on the stone wall and dangle my feet over the other side. It's a mild day, sixties I'd say, but the sun is weak. It's getting on towards three o'clock. Already dark shadows are overtaking the patio. So quiet. Silent except for a squirrel rattling some dry leaves below.

The old me, the me before all this mess, might seek a little relief out here on the patio with not a soul around. But I just don't have those feelings anymore. Like a damn gelding. I have to figure it will come back, but so far it ain't. It's part of my being weak. I never try to get it on with Emylyn anymore, and she's just as glad. And even when I do get a little urge and try to do it to myself, I feel that nigger's hot, wet skin when my fist came up against his face. The mind is a terrible thing. The way those things are connected in my brain now, like wires crossed.

I GET back in the car and drive on around the park road to the lake. The parking lot there is deserted too, the swimming area closed since Labor Day. I park in a spot that overlooks the sandy beach with its two lifeguard towers. The lake looks so calm today, sufficient unto itself, like it's relieved to be through with all them splashing young'uns and bathing beauties.

It's come to me now why I come up here to Table Rock today. To climb the mountain. It's a right steep long hike, but I intend to get to the top. I want to rest my mind on the view from up there. Everything so peaceful and far away, the lake the size of a pond below, green pines spread as far as the eye can see. Like the Indians saw it before the white man come.

There's a foul odor when I open the trunk, maybe from them old blankets. The rope's still coiled there, like it's been waiting for me. I take it out and loop it over my arm. I cross the road to the trailhead and start up. At first the path follows a clear mountain stream, and with the sun so far down behind the mountain, there's nothing but shadows. I'm shivering a little.

Give me liberty or give me death. I was just a kid, and yet those words went in strong. I think now that was the happiest time of my life. Not Lily, not the verdict, but being in school and Mrs. Tucker so nice to me. She said she saw potential in me. I didn't even know what the word meant. When I looked at her in a questioning way, she explained it meant I could make something of myself in life. I got a feeling like someone passed a kind hand over me, the way you pet a cat or dog to make 'em feel good. Then I had to quit school and go to picking cotton, and such fine thoughts and words was behind me.

The water is rushing faster now over the rocks and stones, crystal clear and pure. I'm passing Sliding Rock, what we used to slide down when we was boys. Could of broke our heads open. I leave it behind, climbing higher, the trail rougher through the woods now. My heart's beating hard, but it ain't stuttering. It's steady and sure. My legs feel both heavy and light, and I'm running some, slipping now and then where there's mud. My breathing's fast and hard in my chest and it feels good.

I used to think liberty meant you wasn't in jail. You wasn't locked up. You could go wherever you liked and do whatever you wanted. You was free. So in that sense I'm a free man, I have my liberty. Only it don't feel like it. I'm locked up inside, something is binding me and holding me that I can't break free of. I don't even know what it is. But it holds me like a vise.

Why ain't not guilty the same as innocent? And if it ain't, then I'm not guilty, like the jury said, but I ain't innocent either. Mr. Chastain won't let me have my innocence, he took it from me. I try to tell myself I don't care, what does it matter to me, I'm a free man walking around not guilty and the whole world knows it. But I'm just lying to myself. Because I'm bound. I'm locked up.

Those words that nigger said. *Lord, you done killed me.* I can't get that out of my head. What would it feel like to know you'd been kilt before you was even dead? To say those words. To know it's too late, that it's happening. That must of been what poor Mr. Brown felt. He was kilt, and he knew it. I'd give anything to take it all back. To have Mr. Brown walking around talking to us boys about church and oil changes and doing good with our lives. I'd give anything to have that nigger alive, so at least I wouldn't have to hear his voice saying those words, like something out of the Bible. That's what it seems like, something bigger than us, what we did, something writ down a long time ago that didn't even have to do with us or what we was up to. Killin'. It's been going on since Cain slayed Abel, and it ain't likely to stop anytime soon.

Give me liberty or give me death. I'd like to see what becomes of my boys. But that seems far away, like the valley below the mountain. I can't get there from here. I'm going to the top of the mountain, that is all. *Not the same as innocent.* I think I understand that now, though it's taken these months of it pounding around in my head. I can't go back to where I was before all this started. I can't help but think of Lily, and I know now that I loved her. Whatever love is. The way she made me feel. I lost that and I can never get it back.

His face was slick with blood and sweat and spit. It was warm and his skin gave under my fist and the bone resisted, soft and hard. I saw his eyes. He looked right at me in the dawning light of those piney woods, maybe pleading, maybe not. For just an instant, I paused, the blink of an eye, we paused together there for an eternity, me with my fist balled and ready to strike, him held up by the boys. In that instant I made a choice. I was afraid. I was weak. I chose, and I thought I was right when I put the white skin of my fist against the black skin of his face. I felt his head snap a little, though it weren't even a hard blow. Blood spattered on my pants. He sagged down until they couldn't hardly hold him up for the next man.

This here is a right good tree, with a big strong limb. A red oak, been growing here since the Indians roamed. High up on the mountain top, with a good view of the valley far below.

It won't take long.

PART II

17

ALMA

WHEN THE CONDUCTOR announced they had arrived at Penn Station, the audacity of what Alma was doing hit her full force. The conductor, coming back through after the car had emptied, found her still sitting in her seat, unable to move. "Everybody off," he said brusquely. "Last stop, everybody off the train!"

Afraid he would reprimand her further, Alma gathered her big black pocketbook and walked on trembly legs to the train door. She stepped down into a cacophonous world like none she'd ever seen or even imagined before. The vast terminal was filled with the screeching and clanking of wheels and brakes, the air stunk of diesel fuel, and it was so hot on the platform, she worried she might faint. But that thought was so terrifying—for who would know or help her? She bucked up, took a deep breath, squared her shoulders in her wilted seersucker suit, mopped her face with a hankie, and looked around. She was shocked to see her suitcase sitting by itself next to the luggage car where the porter had unloaded it, where anyone could steal it. Where were Ladocia and Ray! She grabbed her suitcase and was pushed along by the crowd of passengers rushing toward the station doors, her black straw hat slipping off her head and trampled underfoot in the melee.

She stumbled into the main hall, stopping dead in her tracks, oblivious to the rude comments from people bumping into her from behind. She couldn't have imagined such a magnificent space! The concourse was as long as four city blocks in Greenville. The cavernous ceiling was filled with filigree metal arches crisscrossing high above. A gigantic clock hung from the ceiling, "Timed by Benrus." The walls and floor were a lustrous white marble with enormous columns lining the sides of the lobby. Dew had told her about cathedrals he'd seen in Italy during the war. She was sure this was what they were like. Looking up, she felt her spirit expand and soar. This was New York City! But when she lowered her eyes and glanced around, she felt like a bug that could be crushed at any moment. A melodious female voice was echoing importantly through the space, announcing departing trains and their destinations. All around her people were rushing with confidence and determination, knowing exactly where they were headed. Alma was lost.

She made her way to a bench and waited to be found. She was exhausted from sitting upright during the long trip, exhausted from the battle of emotions that had fought tooth and nail in her as each mile moved her farther away from everything and everyone she knew and loved. She had almost gotten off the train when it stopped in Washington. She wanted to go home! She kept picturing Pretty's bewildered face, how it crumpled when she realized her mother was leaving without her. She kept hearing her call out "Mommy! Mommy!" as she got in the car with Pearle and Dew and closed the door against her daughter's pleas.

Yet now, alone and afraid in Penn Station, Alma didn't cry. She forced her mind to remember why she had left. She couldn't stay in the South for one more day. The fear and rage that had been tamped down her whole life had boiled over in that fallow cornfield the night Willie Earle was lynched and could no longer be denied.

She had one thing to live for: she would give Pretty a better life. She couldn't do that staying in the South. No matter what Alma did, Pretty would always be treated as less there. It was in the water she drank from the fountain placed lower than the white fountain, even though it was the same water. *Just so you coloreds don't forget: Lower. Lesser.* It was in the run-down, ill-furnished colored schools, the shabby rental house where they had to live, the menial jobs that were all they could get. It was in the wages and opportunities withheld because of the color of their skin, keeping them in perpetual poverty. It was lynchings where the murderers confessed and went free.

Alma would get settled here, get a job, and make more money than she ever could in Greenville. There were more opportunities here, that's what Ladocia said. There were no "whites only" signs. In a little while, once she got settled, she'd bring Pretty up North too. She'd find a good woman to keep her during the day. She would do whatever she had to do. It would just be a matter of weeks or a few months at most.

LADOCIA and Ray found her on the bench looking as lost and determined as she felt. They hustled her onto the subway,

terrifying, the doors shutting with no way out, the train swaying, speeding, and clanking through dark passages underground, only to burst into lighted stations with shiny white-
tiled walls. They hustled her out the door, through the turnstile,
and up steep stairs that stank of urine, greasy with filthy trash.
Up into daylight, as if they were moles. Alma looked around
her, stunned. They had come up onto a busy street where taxis
and cars sped bumper to bumper, walled in by such tall buildings that Alma could see only a small patch of sky above. They
hustled her down more subway steps, back onto the lurching
underground monster, more jostling and darkness, and then
back up, this time to emerge on to a wide, bright boulevard.

Dark-skinned people everywhere! And wonder of won-
ders, a *Negro* policeman standing in the middle of the inter-
section, directing traffic! They began walking down a wide
avenue—Seventh, Ladocia announced—bustling with fried
chicken joints, pawn shops, pool halls, store-front churches,
nightclubs, barber shops, and beauty shops where women in
pink smocks were ironing colored women's hair. Past curb
vendors pedaling cheap bags and jewelry from carts, men
selling slices of watermelon, a grocery store with wilted collard greens and bruised tomatoes in crates out front. An
angry-looking man so black he must be straight from Africa
stood on a stepladder and shook a tattered Bible in the air,
shouting hell-fire and damnation at the women in tight wrap
dresses and the men in summer suits who streamed past,
paying him no mind. Old worn women like Rosa Mae in broken-down shoes and cotton dresses faded from endless wash-
ings pushed wobbly grocery carts down the block.

A few straggly trees—nothing like the shade trees at
home—were growing out of a narrow strip of dirt down the

center of the boulevard, the only nod to nature here. How were they managing to live in this concrete world? Alma determined to be like them: to survive somehow amidst the endless cars and masses of strangers.

They turned down a side street, passing women with children sitting on the front steps of red brick tenements in the stifling heat, some calling out greetings in lilting accents—from the islands Ladocia informed her, imitating their melodic cadences perfectly—though Alma didn't know what islands she meant. A block farther, boys were running in and out of water spewing from an open fire hydrant. Two old men were playing chess on an upside-down grocery crate; a wino clutching an empty bottle slumped in a doorway. Horns blew, trucks and cars rumbled by, a siren screamed, and there was a strange roar in the air that Alma had never heard before: The City. The apartment buildings all had metal ladders zigzagging down the front. When Alma asked, Ladocia laughed and said those metal ladders were fire escapes. Alma wondered if the whole neighborhood might combust at any moment. It felt hot enough to.

Ray and Ladocia lived on the bottom floor of one of the brownstones. While Ray carried Alma's suitcase up the high steps to the heavy oak front door, Ladocia and Alma paused on the sidewalk, catching their breath. Sweat was rolling down Alma's chest and back. She was used to Southern heat, but this was worse; this was city heat, held in by all the brick and concrete.

Their apartment was not what Alma had expected, though she didn't know what she had expected. She had never been in an apartment, let alone one in Harlem. It had fancy woodwork everywhere, paneling on the walls, crown molding around the ceiling, an ornate mantel over the fire-place, a built-in oak buffet in the dining room—nothing like the unadorned homeplace or the shabby shanty where she and Huff lived. The mantel was crammed with vases, family pictures in elaborate brass frames, porcelain figurines. The wood floors were scarred, and the walls must have been white once but were now a dingy gray from years of soot coming in the open windows. The living room held a massive sofa with claw feet, two matching armchairs, and a white oval mar-ble-top table like the one the Chastains had. An oak chest was crowded with more framed photographs, and a large phonograph console with the lid open sat in the corner. The whole place looked strange and foreign to Alma, nothing familiar, nothing like home.

When Ladocia showed Alma to her room, Alma sat down on a single spool bed covered with a patchwork quilt. She rec-ognized the scraps of material used for the wedding ring pat-tern. Her great-grandmother Callie had made that quilt. It came from home. Alma started shaking. She shook until her teeth rattled in her head. She shook like she had been caught in a blizzard instead of the ninety-degree heat of the apart-ment. Her hands and legs shook, and moans escaped from her lips. She had her eyes clamped tight, as if to block every-thing out: leaving her baby behind; the long hard train ride; the terror and grandeur of Penn Station; the roar of Harlem out the open window. She clutched Callie's quilt in both hands, the way Pretty clutched her pink blankie.

Uncle Ray was kneeling beside her, holding out a jelly jar with amber liquid in it. He put his hand on her knee, covered by her seersucker skirt wrinkled and half turned around her hips. "Take you a sip," he coaxed her.

"What is it?" Alma asked in alarm, smelling something sharp when he brought it to her lips.

"It's just a little medicine," Ladocia said soothingly. "It'll ease you, child."

"It's whiskey!" Alma said. She recognized the smell from Huff's breath.

"It is, and good Irish whiskey at that," Ray laughed. "It'll relax you, girl. You in some kinda state."

She put her hand on his as he directed the glass to her mouth. A startling heat seared down her throat, making her choke and cough. She didn't even like the taste, then. Again Ray poured, and again she drank. After a little while, she felt her nerves settle like nesting hens. She lay back, pulling the quilt up to her chin despite the heat. Her eyelids fluttered once, twice, then no more.

THAT first week, while Ladocia and Ray were at their jobs, Alma ventured warily into the neighborhood near their apartment. No one paid her any mind. Walking along the busy streets, she was flooded with images of home, of her own Southernside neighborhood and the corner grocery where Moses always saved her some turnips and collards before he sold out. Now, at a busy A&P, she bought some dried beans and collards that were limp and yellowing, some ham hocks for forty-three cents a pound, and a dozen eggs for seventy-three cents. Everything was twice as expensive as back home.

When she started back to the apartment, instead of seeing the tenements around her, she was seeing her folks' big vegetable garden behind the homeplace. Now, in early September, her father would have tied the tomato plants onto stakes with strips of his old undershirts, so laden with heavy red tomatoes they'd be. The half-runner beans, yellow squash, potatoes, onions, okra, three kinds of peppers—bell, hot, and banana—and sweet corn would all be ready for her mother to can. Oh! She had forgotten to put Pretty's barnyard barrettes in the sack of things she'd given her mother. What were Bessie and Pretty doing at this very moment? Had Pretty already forgotten her? What had Huff thought when he came home and found her gone? She hadn't known where to reach him. He would have been out to her folks by now and . . .

She looked around, disoriented. All the tenements looked the same. She fished out Ladocia's address on a slip of paper from her pocketbook. Afraid to approach a stranger on the street, she chose to ask an old woman chewing tobacco and wearing a kerchief like her mother wore. The woman was sitting on a stoop, fanning herself with a newspaper. Her speech was so strange that Alma couldn't understand her. One of the islanders? She spouted out a stream of directions, pointing this way and that until Alma feared she had no mind. But when she saw that Alma was blinking back tears, she stood and took her by the hand, as if she were a child, and led her around this corner and that, back to the place Alma was trying to call home.

ON Sunday morning, Alma stood in the doorway of Ladocia and Ray's bedroom in her newly washed and ironed seersucker suit. Whenever they came home to South Carolina, Ladocia and Ray always went with the family to the New Hope Baptist Church in Liberty. Alma's were church-going people. She had never known anyone—except herself—who had stopped going to church. No one who'd stopped believing. Out of respect and gratitude, she figured she would go to church with Ladocia and Ray. She would keep to herself that she'd fallen away.

She was actually looking forward to the service. She wanted to sit in a sanctuary with believers, even if she no longer was one, and hear the oh-so-familiar cadences of the preacher, the call and response, *Huh? Huh? Can I get an amen?* In this strange and foreign Northern city, she wanted to be surrounded by people who believed as she had once believed, to see their pink palms raised toward the pulpit, to have them stand and sway as the spirit moved them. She missed Jesus, even if she couldn't forgive Him for all His sins, starting with slavery and coming right on up to the present when she'd had to leave the Jim Crow South to prepare a better life for her baby.

"You go on and go if you want to," Ladocia said from their mahogany bed with its pineapple finials. "We done got enough religion to last us the rest of our lives," Ray explained from behind the *Amsterdam News*. "Up here's not like down home. Preacher won't be coming around tomorrow to see where you was at on Sunday!" He gave a hearty laugh. Alma was shocked. She'd seen all kinds of churches in the neighborhood, from the large fortress-like Abyssinian Baptist to dozens of storefront churches with names like St. Ann's Spiritualist Church, Glad Tidings Tabernacle, Covenant Word Church; religion was alive and well in Harlem. But Ladocia and Ray no longer had any use for church.

"Up here you free, child," Ladocia said.

But this was a freedom Alma hadn't expected and wasn't sure she wanted.

WHEN Ladocia came home from the House of Beauty every evening, she'd kick off her shoes and stretch out on the sofa to tell Alma tales from the shop that day: One of her ladies had run off with her lover; another woman's husband hit the numbers and was taking her out for a steak dinner; a high-class couple was going on vacation to Oak Bluffs on the Vineyard.

One night after Ladocia got her second wind, she went in the bedroom and came back carrying what looked to Alma like a rainbow of satin across her arms: light blue, bright yellow, a deep lavender, ruby red. She held up the fancy dresses one by one. Ladocia, dark as a piece of coal, shorter by a foot than Alma and round as a dumpling, laughed and explained: "Pick you out one, girl! We going out on the town tonight!"

Alma began shaking her head. "Oh, Ladocia, I don't think so. Not me, I . . ."

Ladocia would have none of it. "It's time you had some Harlem fun, niece. We gonna show you a good time. Now let's see which of these you can fit yo-self into. I know I got some tailoring to do."

Alma had never set foot in one of the juke joints back home. It was not what she and her family did, not the way she'd been raised. Ladocia hadn't been raised that way either. But she had changed, living up North. Alma figured she might have to change too, if she was going to make it here. She slipped on the lavender dress, which was held up by two small straps, leaving her shoulders bare. How could she go out in public in such a thing? What would her mama say! And it was short on her, coming just above her knees when on Ladocia it would be halfway down her calves.

Ladocia got to work, down on her knees, straight pins in her mouth, busily taking in the dress so it fit snug in the bodice and hips, letting down the hem, then altering it on her

Singer sewing machine. When Ladocia steered her over to the oval floor mirror in the bedroom, Alma saw herself as she never had before. She turned this way and that, fascinated by her own image.

THEY walked the few blocks to the Savoy. All along Lenox Avenue, folks were strolling by, women in fur coats and expensive evening clothes, others in homemade dresses and gabardine coats, still others in hand-me-downs from their rich Fifth Avenue employers. Some of the men wore suits with wide trousers belted high and double-breasted jackets, overcoats or military-issue peacoats, others in jeans or cut-rate slacks, some sporting apparel most likely stolen by clever "entrepreneurs" from midtown department stores. Prosperous pimps and numbers runners cruised by in convertible Studebakers and Hudson limousines. Smells of asphalt and ash, perfume and piss, pomade and beer wafted through the air.

A long line of excited people waited to get in, the bright lights of the marquee shouting SAVOY, the name surrounded by music notes that looked as if they were swinging. A ripple of something unfamiliar ran through Alma— the same excitement the crowd was feeling. Her feet hurt in Ladocia's high heels, but she forgot the pain as she moved with the throng toward the doors.

Inside was a spacious lobby with a crystal chandelier hanging above a magnificent marble staircase that led up to the dance floor. The hall was two hundred feet by fifty feet of polished maple and mahogany. With two stages, one band picked up the beat just as the other was ending, so the music never stopped. The room was crowded with couples, both colored and white, cutting the rug, a frenetic kaleidoscope of moving bodies. So this was the North, Alma thought, where Negroes weren't under Jim Crow's boot! Where people could be free! The place pulsed with the blare of trumpets. Some men were actually throwing women over their backs and pulling them between their legs, the women's skirts exposing bare thighs and sometimes more! The men in the band, black and white together, wore tuxedos, and when they stood to play their horns, turning left and right in unison, the crowd went wild.

Ray found a table where they could sit down. He ordered them all drinks—a sidecar for Alma. At first she demurred, but she didn't want to offend Ray; it couldn't hurt to sip just a little of it. She was surprised in a short while to find she'd drunk the whole sweet-sour thing. It was like nothing she'd ever had before and made her feel—she wasn't sure what. Different. Ray ordered a second round. Alma found herself laughing along with Ladocia at the antics on the dance floor. When Ray ordered another round, she didn't mind one bit.

Ray asked if she'd like to dance. She'd never danced in her life. She didn't dance, play cards, or go to clubs like this. But she wasn't down home anymore; she was in Harlem having fun. The loud horns filled her up with sound, blotting out all her reserve and hesitation. Ray showed her a few steps, how to move to the beat, and she caught on quickly, until he was twirling her out and back, not like the lindy-hoppers, but at least swinging. She couldn't believe the fool she was being. Around midnight she stumbled home with Ray and Ladocia, who were laughing and teasing her, and fell into bed on top of Callie's wedding ring quilt without even taking off the lavender dress.

18

BETSY

IN SEPTEMBER THE Chastains drove over to Decatur in the big Buick, with Betsy's things for college filling up the trunk and half the back seat. The times she'd been to Agnes Scott with her mother and grandmother for their class reunions, Betsy had loved the college—its Gothic stone buildings that looked straight out of romantic England, the broad green quads, the magnificent dining hall with its stained glass windows and vaulted ceiling, the bright good looks of the girls in their field hockey uniforms, a different color for each class. It was everything a college campus should look like. But now Betsy was afraid of being left there, alone. Her hands shook as she helped her mother make up her single bed in Inman Hall, only a few feet away from where her roommate—a stranger—would be sleeping. She was desperate for her parents to leave, but at the moment when she had to say goodbye, she couldn't stand to see them go. Standing in front of her dorm, watching the familiar Buick pull slowly away, she felt as if it were dragging her heart behind it.

That night she dreamed of the jail again. She'd believed the nightmares would stop for good when she got to college. But once again, she recognized the dreadful cell. Only now it was also her dorm room, with the curled back of a stranger on the opposite bed. Her own bed—a single cot—was empty. The familiar feeling of alarm spread through her, waking her with a jolt. She hoped she hadn't cried out, for indeed, in the faint darkness, she saw that there actually was another person in the bed across from her: her roommate, Martha, a jolly, friendly girl from Nashville she'd met that afternoon.

The college had plenty of activities planned to help the new students get oriented and keep them occupied as they made the adjustment to their new lives on campus. But Betsy felt like a sleepwalker, a dreamer, going through the motions, unable to wake up. Her French class met at eight in the morning, and she couldn't get up in time to make it. She never knew when the nightmare of the jail cell would wake her in the night. She sensed the dream was trying to tell her something in a language she didn't know.

Her grades at midterm were abysmal. Her faculty advisor told her sternly there was a good chance she'd flunk out if she didn't apply herself. That frightened her into staying up late, drinking Coke 'til all hours, trying to "apply" herself. But the words on the page of her psychology text blurred, the French verb conjugations departed her mind like blackbirds startled into flight, and she couldn't keep straight who begat whom in her Bible class. She was afraid to turn on her Bunsen burner in chemistry, worried it might explode.

It was only in her English class that she escaped her anxieties. Walt Whitman and Emily Dickenson felt like kindred spirits, unlike the girls around her, who seemed untroubled, confident about themselves and life. The only comfort she found was scribbling in her notebook, writing character sketches and fragments of stories she didn't intend to ever show anyone.

When she got back her first English paper, she was shocked to see a C written in red ink on the last page, with a note from the professor to see her in her office. Betsy had never gotten anything other than an A on her papers. She'd written a paper on *Huckleberry Finn* in high school and had turned in a slightly revised version of that essay. Her professor, Miss Evans—only the male professors were called "doctor," even though the women had doctoral degrees too—was a middle-aged single woman whom Betsy was intimidated by and in awe of. She wore her steel gray hair in a chignon that released wispy strands framing her long horse face and giving her an ethereal look. She was never without a cardigan sweater, a long dark A-line skirt, clunky shoes, and a handkerchief stuffed in the cuff of her long-sleeved white blouse with a high ruffled collar. Her class was the one thing in Betsy's life she looked forward to.

Miss Evans directed Betsy to the chair beside her massive rolltop desk in her office on the top floor of Buttrick Hall. She started with a little small talk, asking where Betsy was from, how she liked college so far. Betsy wanted to answer but couldn't.

"What's wrong?" Miss Evans asked after they sat in silence for several excruciating minutes. "It's not *that* bad a paper."

"It's just . . ." Betsy said, fighting to maintain some composure. "It just that . . ." Her voice faded into nothing.

"Your classes?" Miss Evans asked. "You're obviously an intelligent young woman. What exactly is the problem?"

Betsy shook her head. She didn't know.

Miz Evans picked up Betsy's *Huckleberry Finn* paper, which Betsy had laid on the corner of the desk, wishing it would combust. "Your writing is grammatically correct. Your usage is fine. But you had nothing to say. Do you understand?"

She might as well have stabbed Betsy in the heart with the brass letter opener on her desk.

"I don't understand . . . anything," Betsy said.

"Well, let's just start with *Huckleberry Finn* for now," Miss Evans said. "Are there scenes or images that sparked something in you?"

Betsy shook her head, unable to remember one thing from the book. Then suddenly she burst out, "I wish I could be like Huck!"

Miss Evans looked surprised and then chuckled. "I know what you mean," she said, smiling. "He does have a rather high time. But tell me why you'd like to be like him."

Feeling her face turn red, Betsy said, "Because he's free! He doesn't care what people think or what society says he should do."

"Go on."

"He follows his heart." Her own felt like a horse galloping.

"That's true," Miss Evans said. "But hasn't he inculcated society's racial prejudices? Doesn't he wrestle with himself about helping a slave escape?"

"Yes," Betsy said slowly, "but he cares about Jim, person to person, way over what he's been raised to think about a slave. He sees Jim as a fellow human being, not just something to be bought and sold. He does everything he can to help Jim escape, and he isn't one bit sorry for it."

Then without expecting it, Betsy poured out the story of

the lynching and trial and how Alma had left without saying goodbye. Words rushed out of her. Miss Evans listened without speaking until the flood petered to a trickle. She pulled out her handkerchief from her sleeve and handed it to Betsy. Maybe Betsy should try writing a short story about what happened, she suggested gently. But Betsy, horrified, shook her head, *no!*

"Well, I'm going to give you a chance to rewrite your *Huckleberry Finn* paper," Miss Evans said. "I think you've hit on your theme here today: the conflict between Huck's affection and respect for Jim and what society has taught him to think and feel. See what you can do."

When Betsy got her revised paper back, she turned to the last page with trembling hands. Miss Evans had written, "You have succeeded on your own very original terms. You have a gift for expression that transcends mere critical analysis. This is an engaged and even passionate discussion of how Huck overcomes, at least at times, the racism that society has instilled in him. Excellent supporting passages. A+

"P.S. I'd like to review your papers, not just in my course but in all your courses."

19

LAWTON

LAWTON HAD KNOWN with certainty the last day of the
trial that he would no longer live a lie. It was as simple as it
was profound. He was a homosexual. All his life he'd denied
it. He'd pretended the "incident" with Harry at Carolina had
been a strange aberration that had nothing to do with the real
him. Now he saw the truth, and he was determined to live it.

But months had gone by after the trial as he struggled
with himself. Was he really willing to tear up his whole life?
And cause Lydia and Betsy pain and anger? For the nebulous
possibility of becoming his "true self"? A self he didn't even
know and could only sense.

He knew what he'd have to do to walk through that
door. He'd need to separate and eventually divorce Lydia. A
staggering thought. They'd been married twenty years. Was
such a drastic change really necessary? It wasn't as if their
marriage was a complete sham. There were still important things they shared. They'd raised a daughter together
whom they loved dearly. Lydia was a good person, kind

and well-meaning. But he knew he shouldn't be married to her—or any woman. He was attracted to men. That was his nature. There was no turning back.

He was under no illusions about how Lydia would react to the idea of a divorce. She, as had he, assumed that marriages never ended—at least not for people like them. She would be bewildered, hurt, angry, and humiliated. Divorce would be blow enough. He couldn't imagine telling her, on top of that, that he was a homosexual. He couldn't, wouldn't. He didn't want anyone to know he was queer, least of all Lydia.

And Betsy? When she was home from Scott at Christmas, she'd kept mostly to herself, responding to their gentle prodding with monosyllabic answers. Did she like Scott: "It's okay." How were her courses going: "Okay." Had she made any friends: "Not really." When her fall grade report arrived, he and Lydia were shocked to see how poorly she'd done. But Betsy assured them she'd do a lot better next term; a professor had taken a special interest in her and would review her papers. They reasoned she'd had normal adjustment problems that fall. Lydia recounted how she'd been homesick her first term at Scott, crying every night into her pillow, almost flunking out, and then how she'd had a 3.5 average in the spring. Given Betsy's difficulties, Lawton decided he'd have to wait to broach even a separation with Lydia. Betsy needed time to find her footing, he told himself, though he knew it wasn't just Betsy he wanted to spare.

FOR so many years, he'd suppressed any thoughts of desiring other men. But now he began to remember things he'd put out of his mind. He recalled the time Lydia and he were parking on Paris Mountain when they were first dating. There was a large flat open space at the top of the mountain where young couples went to make out. That night maybe five or six cars were there, with enough space between them to provide some privacy. Lawton didn't think anything of it when a new car pulled up until suddenly a bright spotlight, the kind police use, began sweeping over the parked cars. In the harsh glare he saw two men caught in an embrace turn their startled faces toward the light. Lawton hurriedly started the car, as did others, and they left. Driving home, he felt more shaken than he should have—shaken and aroused. He hadn't thought of that incident for many years, but now he played it over in his mind. The image of that embrace, buried so deep for so long, stirred him anew.

He thought about the "womanless wedding" he'd been to at least ten years ago. It was a fundraiser for a community organization and featured some of the town fathers and ministers dressed up as women. His own father-in-law, Lyman Maxfield, had played one of the bridesmaids, dressed in a floor-length gown, wearing a ridiculous hat and high heels, and carrying a bouquet. The "bride" was Lenny Berger, a Liberty Life executive who was big, fat, ugly, and obviously pregnant—with a pillow. Even at the time, the whole thing struck Lawton as tasteless. It made him uncomfortable in a way he didn't understand. But now he pondered all the laughter and ribaldry involved in the spectacle of men dressing and acting like women. What was that about? Was it that real men were so far removed from any sexual ambiguity that they could risk playing at being women? Or get a thrill from it?

He'd been so bent on passing, he'd worn blinders. But now he began to notice men. Some men. Not all of them, that was for sure, but a beguiling few. These were strangers, men he'd see on the street or at a ballgame. He might notice a certain set of shoulders or a pair of hairy legs in Bermuda shorts. Lips. Hands. When he learned that Sam, the waiter with the knowing eyes at the Poinsett, was no longer working there, he felt a pain deep in his groin.

AT least he could give notice at the solicitor's office. It was the first step in changing his life. Besides, once he and Lydia separated, it would be difficult to continue in his public position. He gave notice and explained his departure by saying he wanted to open his own practice, which, as it happened, was true.

On his own, he'd be, if not poor, then certainly in reduced circumstances. He welcomed that. Their wealth had come from Lydia's family; she'd be just fine. The idea of a small apartment, no bigger than eight hundred square feet, appealed to him. He didn't want or need all the accoutrements and upkeep that went with living in their big Georgian house on Crescent Avenue. That had been someone else's idea—Beatrice's and Lyman's, he now saw, as much as his and Lydia's.

He needed to rent an office and knew just where he wanted it to be: the Chamber of Commerce Building on Court Square. It had fallen on hard times in the Depression, and an insurance company had taken over the top floors, renting out a few offices on the lower levels. There was a large vertical sign in front proclaiming "LIBERTY" with a smaller horizontal "Life" at the bottom, visible up and down Main Street. Lawton hoped those words might prove prophetic for him.

Despite its more recent insurance name, it would always be the Chamber of Commerce Building to him. He was twenty-two when the ten-story narrow red brick building was erected in 1925. It had seemed very handsome to him then with its cornice and tall, arched windows on the top floor, and it still did. The lobby was long and narrow, with white marble walls, deep ceiling arches with glass lantern chandeliers, and a black-and-white checkered marble floor.

He knew what he wanted: a front office facing Main Street. Two offices were available, and he had no doubt which one he'd take—almost as if it already had his name on the door. It was on the fifth floor, and it faced Court Square.

Flanking the square on the right was the Poinsett Hotel, another of the first skyscrapers constructed in Greenville during a building boom in the twenties. It was twelve stories high, red brick with white terracotta detailing and tall arched windows spanning the second and third stories. When it opened in 1925, the Poinsett was said, at least by Greenvillians, to be one of the most beautiful hotels in the country. It was the Grand Dame of downtown.

Lawton had to admit that the Greenville County Courthouse, situated right next to the Poinsett across narrow Court Street, and being so much shorter, resembled a squat little brother. Ornately carved and decorated, with massive Ionic columns and cream-colored tiles, its appearance was one of weight and heft. Greenvillians had been insulted when Rebecca West described it as singularly hideous. But to Lawton it had a solemnity that was appropriate for a courthouse—where law and justice are taken seriously, or ought to be.

H E needed some office furniture. The front room off the hall would be a reception area where clients could wait, with a desk for a receptionist/secretary, if he ever got one. His office would be the back room with its tall window facing Court Square. He'd need two desks, some chairs, lamps, and a filing cabinet.

Harper Brothers had an office furniture store in town, and now something came back to him. When it first opened, Lawton was having lunch with his father-in-law and some of Lyman's colleagues. The conversation turned to the new store and the modern furniture it carried. One of the men told how the company had brought in an interior decorator from New York to help customers make selections. "A limp-wrist fellow," he said, dropping his hand in a fey way and tilting his head like a coy girl. "Harper's fairy," someone quipped, and they all laughed. Lawton had put the incident—like so much else—out of his mind, but now it pushed its way to the forefront. He determined to make a visit to the office furniture store—and not just for furniture.

When he entered the store, he was approached by a man who had to be Harper's fairy: an obvious homosexual in his early thirties. How did Lawton know he was queer? He had the limp-wrist effect Lawton's father-in-law and his colleagues had joked about. He introduced himself as Donny Sanders, and Lawton explained about his new office and what he needed. Donny had a slight swish to his hips as he led Lawton around the store, showing him various desks and credenzas, which Lawton couldn't concentrate on. He could hardly take his eyes off Donny. Not because he was attracted to him. But because he was—what he was.

Friendly and effusive, Donny tried to coax out Lawton's tastes in office chairs, but Lawton had no opinions. Aside from Harry Bumgarten, Donny was the first homosexual he'd met—that he knew of, at least. He wondered if he could ever ask Donny to have a drink sometime.

But Lawton wasn't ready for that.

20

ALMA

SHORTLY AFTER ALMA arrived, Ladocia told her about an employment agency on Amsterdam Avenue that would get her a job as a maid. Maids were referred to here as "kitchen mechanics" or "pot wrestlers"—by the maids themselves, Ladocia laughed. Alma was afraid to take the bus even though she rode it at home, and she certainly wasn't going on the subway. She walked the twenty blocks to the address and applied for domestic work. Within a week, the agency had lined her up for a job on Central Park West. Ladocia gave a low whistle when she heard the address. On Wednesday she took the bus with Alma to show her how to get there. The following Monday morning, her stomach in turmoil, Alma, in a new white uniform with a black apron, rode to the address she'd been given. She stood for a long moment gaping at the elegant gray stone apartment building with a uniformed doorman out front.

Mr. Stern, a short, thin man with a neatly trimmed beard, showed her around the apartment. Alma had never imagined such elegance and opulence. She had thought the Chastains had a fancy home, but this was of a whole different order. There was a marble foyer, which opened to a formal living room with nine-foot ceilings, high arched windows, and a Steinway piano larger than Miz Chastain's Baldwin; the library was lined with ancient-looking books on shelves and had a rolling ladder to reach the high ones; and there were three bedrooms, one of which Mr. Stern used as his office, and two baths. Apparently there was no Mrs. Stern. He explained that he had a cook, so Alma was to do only the cleaning. Her job was to mop the front hall, dust everything carefully, especially the chandeliers, go over the books in the library with an ostrich feather duster, vacuum the Oriental rugs, wash the bed linens, clean the bathrooms until the white and black tiles gleamed, and shake out the floor-length curtains and sheer liners on the living room windows so they remained free of dust.

It took only a few days for Alma to settle into the job. Mr. Stern worked in his office in the mornings, but in the afternoons, he came out and followed her around, telling her stories. In his German accent, he told how his uncle had started in the shirt business in the 1880s, selling flannel shirts his wife made from a pushcart on the Lower East Side. "He sold three hundred dollars in shirts that first year," he told her, raising his bushy eyebrows. In the twenties, the company won a patent for a new style of men's collars that revolutionized the shirt business. Two years later, the company was trading publicly on the New York Stock Exchange. "At least in the *schmatte* business," he said, "there wasn't a ceiling for Jews."

Often, after she finished shaking out the heavy brocade curtains, she pulled the liners aside to see the park across the street. Right in the midst of New York City was a large expanse of woods and rock formations, almost as if the city didn't exist. All that land for a park, right in the midst of skyscrapers! She rested her city-weary eyes on the leaves of the trees there, which were turning yellow gold and tawny brown. But she quickly got back to work. She was making more money here than she ever had in Greenville. She didn't want to lose this job.

NIGHTS that first fall were the worst. Alma would cry into Callie's quilt as she lay in the spool bed, stifling the sounds so Ray and Ladocia wouldn't hear. Her body ached for the warm, solid feel of Pretty curled next to her. Her eyes felt scorched by the thwarted desire to look upon her daughter's face. Her ears strained in the dark to hear what wasn't there: Pretty's voice singing nonsensical songs to herself. Alma missed her mother, she missed her father, she missed them all, even Huff. Sometimes especially Huff. She wondered if he missed her. Could he ever forgive her for leaving like she did? Would he take her back if she came home? She felt as if she couldn't live another day in the North.

But then she would remind herself why she had left.

EVEN though it was expensive and required patience to get through the various long-distance operators, that first Christmas Ladocia placed a call to the homeplace. Thanks to Dew, Alma's folks now had a phone, something they'd never had before. What with Pretty living there, Dew didn't want them to be out in the country without one.

Alma's hand was shaking when she took the black receiver. She'd been gone for four long, painful, homesick months. Her mother came on the phone. "Alma, how you gettin' on?"— her voice staticky and faint across so many miles. "You gettin' my letters?" Alma shouted back. She wrote home every day, telling whatever little news she had, but mainly telling Pretty she loved and missed her. "Oh we gettin' 'em all right," Bessie called as if across a field. "Wish you could be here for Christmas. We gonna miss you. When you comin' home?"

"We have to wait on that. I got a good job I got to keep."

"What dat you say?" The line crackled with white noise. Then, "Huff come 'round asking after you, Alma. He real good with Pretty. Here, yo daddy want to say something."

"Hi, Daddy," Alma said, and now tears came. "Hi, baby," he said in a wavery voice. There was a roar of silence. "Well, sho good to hear you," he said, and he turned the phone back to Bessie. Alma knew why: He was too choked up to talk to her, and he was worried about the expense of the call. She heard her mother coaxing Pretty in the background, "Here yo mama on the phone. Tell her you love her." Then Pretty's voice came on, sounding far away and small. "Wuve you," she said so softly Alma could barely hear her. She wasn't sure Pretty even knew who she was. "I got two kitties!" Pretty giggled. "A black 'un and a . . . " A clatter, and the phone went dead. Without a word, Alma went to her room and shut the door. Ladocia had the good sense to let her be.

WINTER was long and hard that first year. Pretty's third birthday came and went in January. The snow piled up, turning dirty gray on the streets, and unlike down home, it didn't melt until spring. The cold city matched the landscape of Alma's heart. Shivering in her wool coat, she rode the bus to Mr. Stern's every weekday. She tried to help Ladocia and Ray out by cooking dinner, she wrote letters home, she marked the days off on her calendar, looking toward the new year, when she hoped she would have enough money saved to bring Pretty up North.

But she was beginning to wonder how she could manage. She would have to get a place of her own. It wouldn't work for Ladocia and Ray to have a young child living with them. Who would keep Pretty while she was at work? And what about Huff? Did he miss her enough to move to Harlem? Could he forgive her for leaving without telling him? But he had taken Pretty's college money and turned to drink and women! Could she forgive him?

FINALLY there was the first warm day, and all of Harlem suddenly appeared outside, shaking out rugs, setting up checkers games, calling out to friends and strangers alike as the ecstasy of spring cast aside all woes, if only momentarily. Walking along 148th Street, Alma heard someone scatting with such pizazz it made her laugh out loud. Overnight, Central Park greened up, the trees across Fifth Avenue from Mr. Stern's apartment bursting with tender new leaves. Down the block, Alma saw other maids without so much as sweaters walking their employers' fancy dogs. Her spirits lifted. This would be the year she'd be reunited with her daughter and maybe even her husband.

ONE night that summer, Ladocia came in with news about an upcoming party for Josh White. Known as "Mr. Folk Music," Josh White was a big star, and he was from Greenville. Ladocia did his wife Carol's hair at House of Beauty. His hit, "One Meat Ball," was on all the jukeboxes, the radio—and even in a movie. The song was about a man who could afford only one meatball. Not even a piece of bread came with it. Alma could relate to that song. She never seemed able to get ahead. According to Ladocia, his wife reported that Josh had been getting five hundred dollars weekly at the Café Society, plus all he made from concerts, radio, and recordings. "Josh sure has all the meatballs he can eat now," Ladocia laughed.

Alma was making more money at Mr. Stern's than she'd ever made at the Chastains. But she had to pay some of it to the agency that had gotten her the job, she was contributing groceries to the household, and she had to buy clothes and necessities, along with a round of drinks when she went out with Ladocia and Ray to the Savoy. She tried to save five dollars a week for the future, but she wasn't always able to. Somehow the money just went. Everything was so expensive in Harlem. On 125th, the main shopping street, people were picketing Blumstein's, Grant's, and Koch's department stores, protesting that the goods in Harlem were not only more expensive, but also inferior to the goods sold in other parts of the city. Ray explained why property and rentals were so high in Harlem. Whites, he said, jacked up the prices, knowing Negroes had little choice about where to live. Why? Because whites wouldn't rent or sell to them in most parts of the city. In many ways, both subtle and blunt, Alma was learning the North was not so different from the South.

Whenever Josh and Carol White attended a Harlem party, it always included Greenville folks who'd migrated to New York. Colored Greenvillians followed White's music and career with enormous pride; he was from home, someone like them, who came from little but had made it big.

The party was in a lavish apartment on Edgecombe, crowded and smoky, people spilling out onto the street in the warm June air. Ladocia knew a lot of people and began introducing Alma around, making down-home connections for her. Just as she was shaking hands with someone who knew her uncle Stew back home, Alma spotted a familiar face across the room: Synthia! Alma hadn't seen or heard anything about her since that last time she saw her on the bus the morning Willie Earle was killed. Synthia had left for the North not long after that, and no one had heard from her. Alma had missed her and often wondered how she was faring. Synthia's movie-star face lit up at the sight of Alma. They hugged each other fiercely, laughing with joy and surprise at the reunion.

"What in the world you doing here?" Synthia asked. She looked glamorous in a sleek red dress with a high neck and a slit down the front, revealing a seductive swell of breasts. Her hair had been ironed and fell across one eye in a smooth jet-black wave. She wore her signature red lipstick. She was so young, not even twenty yet, but she looked far older and more sophisticated than she had in her maid's uniform on the bus in Greenville. Maybe up North had been good to her. "You here for a visit?"

Alma shook her head. She explained that she had moved North too.

"But it's not exactly what I expected," Alma said. "I thought . . . I don't know. I guess things are better here than at home. Everything is just so different—I thought it would be . . ." She was at a loss for words.

"Easier?" Synthia said. "White folks same in the North as the South."

"I thought there would be more opportunities . . . more

money. I'm still cleaning for white people. I can't seem to save up anything."

"That's all white folks let you do!" Synthia said with the same feistiness Alma remembered from their bus rides.

"What job you got?" Alma asked.

"Chambermaid," Synthia said. "Hotel midtown. Still cleaning up white folks' shit."

Alma snorted. "Where you living?"

Synthia explained that she was living with the man she'd come to New York with. "But I'm thinking of leaving him," she said. She showed Alma a large dark bruise on her upper arm. "Thing is I can stay with him for free. Didn't want to leave when it was cold. Now it's hot, and I'm still there. Figure it's better than some rat-infested boarding house." She looked away. "Where you at?"

Alma told her about staying with Ladocia and Ray. She found herself pouring out how she missed her daughter and how she hadn't been able to save enough money to get a place of her own, and how it wouldn't do to bring Pretty to Ladocia and Ray's. And who would keep Pretty while she was at work? "Things aren't working out the way I thought they would."

"They never do," Synthia said and took a deep drag on her cigarette.

21

LAWTON

IT WAS CHRISTMAS again, and Lawton still hadn't broached the subject of divorce with Lydia. To his great relief, when Betsy was home over the summer, she'd seemed more relaxed, not depressed as she'd been the previous year. The teacher who'd taken a special interest in her must have turned the tide. At the end of fall term, Betsy had made the dean's list.

On the night before she'd be driving back to school with another Scott girl, he and Lydia had a special celebratory dinner to congratulate her on her grades. Over dessert, Betsy said she had something to tell them: She wanted to transfer to Barnard College for her junior and senior years.

"Miss Evans went there," Betsy explained. "She thinks Barnard would be a much better fit for me. She'll write a strong letter of recommendation. They have regional quotas, so that should help." She didn't quite look at them.

"But honey," Lawton said. "I thought you liked Scott."

"It's not that," she said. "I'm just ready for a change. A bigger pond. Please, Daddy?"

"I don't think New York is safe for a young girl like you," Lawton said. He glanced at Lydia. She could help him out here.

"Miss Evans says it's safe if you know where to go and where not to."

"But honey, why don't you just finish at Scott? There'll be plenty of time after you graduate to go to New York. Maybe we can take a family trip there for your graduation present." He glanced at Lydia for support.

Lydia rose and began clearing the cake plates while Lawton and Betsy sat in silence. When she came back to the dining room, she looked at Betsy for a long moment. Then she tilted her head. "I think it's a good idea, Betsy," she said. "You'll be fine. I have confidence in you."

EVERY day that winter, the pressure built for Lawton to act. But he couldn't imagine how to tell Lydia he had to get out of their marriage. The thought of anger and tears, bewilderment, blaming and shaming stopped him. But he also knew if he didn't do it soon, he never would.

One chilly February afternoon after church, he and Lydia were sitting in the living room reading the newspaper. Lydia was playing one of her favorite records, *Clair de Lune*. Outside there was a freezing rain; the trees were glistening with a heavy coating of ice that would break limbs and possibly cause a power outage. Lawton thought about gathering flashlights and candles. But he didn't move.

He looked over at Lydia. She was sitting in her red-plaid armchair, the counterpart to his own—a matched set, as he and Lydia were supposed to be. Her ash-blonde hair was perfectly coiffed—thanks to that satin contraption she slept in that made her look like Grandma Moses. He realized he hardly ever looked at her. She was still an attractive woman, he thought. He didn't really know. Suddenly he was snuffling, making embarrassing sounds he tried to squelch.

Lydia turned to look at him, resting her open paper in her lap. A look of astonishment came over her face. "Lawton!" she exclaimed. "Whatever is the matter? Is that crying?" She'd never seen him cry. He hadn't cried since he was seven years old, when he learned that boys don't cry.

He got up and kneeled awkwardly by her chair. He wanted to put his head on her lap, be comforted, even though it was he who was about to inflict pain. "Lydia," he gasped. "I'm so sorry."

"You're having an affair!"

He almost laughed. It was so outside the realm of possibility—at least with a woman. "No, no. It's not that."

"What then?"

He couldn't speak. A branch outside cracked and broke, startling them both. The lights flickered and then went out. *Clair de Lune* came to an abrupt halt. They sat in a darkened room.

"What's wrong with you?" she asked, her voice a mixture of bewilderment and impatience. "Are you sick?"

"Lydia," he said, shaking his head, trying to gather words. He wanted to take her hand but didn't dare.

She stiffened and sat up straighter in her chair.

"Lydia, I can't be married. I'm sorry, but I can't. I just can't. I need to leave. We have to separate." His words smacked as if he'd eaten glue. "And eventually divorce."

There was a moment of stunned silence. "Have you lost your mind!"

"I've felt it for a long time," he said, desperate to make her understand. "Surely you must have felt it too. We're ... I'm ..."

"Are you in love with someone else? It's Polly Renwick, isn't it!"

"No! For Christ sake no! I just feel...wrong. In my life. In our marriage. It's not you, Lydia. It's me."

"Oh for Pete's sake," she said quickly, as if to dispel what he'd just said. "You're being a fool! This is marriage, Lawton! This is what it's like. You're just having a bad moment. Like a bad dream. You'll get over it."

"I'll move out," he said, getting to his feet. "After a year of living apart, we can legally get a divorce."

"You can't be serious." In the dim light, he saw her face. Broken, she looked.

She stood up, letting the newspaper fall to the floor. At the doorway, she paused and turned to look back at him with what he thought was pity. "Just let me know when you've come to your senses. I'm going to get a flashlight and candles. The power may be out for a long time."

LAWTON moved into the guest room. Lydia didn't speak to him for several weeks. Her way of dealing with what was happening was to act like Lawton was invisible. It was uncomfortable for both of them, but he had no place else to go. He'd rented a one-bedroom furnished apartment in The Davenport across from Christ Church, but it wasn't available until the first of May. He held off telling her about the apartment, afraid of upsetting her. They lived like housemates who mostly avoided one another. He was usually out of the house by seven thirty and didn't return until after dark, having stopped somewhere for supper so he wouldn't have to occupy the kitchen.

By April, Lydia was still angry, still hurt, but she began

speaking to him again, mostly about household maintenance: the guest bathroom sink had stopped up; could he put
up the screens this Saturday? She handed them up to him on
the ladder, a team effort they'd done together every spring for
all the years they'd owned the house. "I think it's that one,"
Lawton pointed out the kitchen window screen, "under that
big dining room one." While Lydia sorted through the heavy
wood frames he'd brought up from the basement, he rested
one hand against the warm brick wall of the house. This was
his house, their house, and in a month, he'd be deserting it, as
indeed, he was deserting her. He let the pain course through
him until it passed.

ONE evening when he came in, Lydia met him at the back
door. "There's some leftover cube steak if you're hungry," she
said, following him into the kitchen. "And some cream gravy
and rice." He *was* hungry, but mostly he was cautious about
what was to come. He took the meat and congealed gravy out
of the icebox, but he wasn't sure how to heat it. "Here," she
said. "Put a little oil in this frying pan. To keep it from sticking. I'll do it."

"Thank you, Lydia," he said. For the millionth time, he felt
the need to apologize, for his very self. She put the plate in
front of him on the breakfast room table, handed him silver-
ware, and sat down across from him.

"It's good, isn't it?" she said. "Ophelia will never be the
cook Alma was, but she'll do."

The steak was tough, but he ate gratefully. "I wonder
what's become of Alma."

"Bessie says she's got a good job, working for a rich man.
She hasn't been home."

Lawton nodded. He figured now was as good a time as any to tell her about the apartment.

"I've rented a place in The Davenport," he waded in. Then, unnecessarily, because she knew the building perfectly well, "across from Christ Church." He paused, hoping he could finish. "I'll be moving out in May." When he glanced at her, she looked as if he'd struck her. Tears filled her eyes. He realized she'd been holding out some hope of reconciliation.

"So you're really serious."

"Yes."

He wanted to tell her how he'd felt at the end of the trial—how for his whole life, he'd been playing a part and had to step off the stage—or die. He wanted to tell her about Harry Bumgarten, to make her understand. How for the first time in his life he felt free. But he couldn't tell her these things. His throat closed, and he was afraid he'd choke on the meat in his mouth. He took it out and put it on the side of his plate.

"What should we do about Betsy?" she asked.

He'd been thinking about that. She was going to be a camp counselor during the summer at Camp Pinnacle, the same camp she'd gone to as a girl. She'd been accepted at Barnard and would be leaving for New York in the fall. "I don't know," he said.

"She'll only be home for two weeks," Lydia said. "Will you please pretend that you're still living here? Pretend you haven't..."

"Of course," Lawton said quickly. "Of course. Whatever you want. You're right. No use to burden her."

"It's a lie, of course," Lydia said. "I know that. But sometimes a lie is the best course."

22

BETSY

IN SEPTEMBER, WEARING a houndstooth suit with a cropped jacket, pencil skirt, and black cloche hat, Betsy took the shiny, sylvan-green Crescent north. With its bullet nose and silver-white stripes, the Crescent looked like the future itself. Her trunk was crammed with pastel sweater sets, plaid skirts, white blouses, Bermuda shorts, jeans, panty girdles, stockings and bras, a new pair of saddle shoes, plenty of white bobby socks, a cocktail dress with dyed-to-match heels, and white gloves short and long. As the train barreled along the tracks, the South retreating rapidly behind her, Betsy wondered if Alma had taken this very train when she left two years ago. Probably not, since it had only Pullman cars. Most likely she took the Piedmont, which had coach. Betsy wondered if she could find Alma in New York. But she had left them without a word, and Betsy hadn't forgiven her.

She got a taxi from Penn Station, as she'd been instructed to do. The cabbie drove her up 8th Avenue. The marquees off Times Square announced plays and musicals in dazzling lights, horse-drawn buggies awaited tourists at Columbus Circle, and along the West Side, handsome apartment buildings flanked Central Park. Betsy had read a little about New York, but she'd never imagined such a beautiful city.

Barnard was on top of a hill opposite Columbia University. The driver unloaded her trunk in front of a tall, wrought iron gate with a dancing bear on it. Another junior who'd been assigned to show her around "the jungle"—so named because the campus had a total of twelve trees—helped her lug the trunk to her room. The academic buildings, red brick and stately, composed one square city block. They passed a tennis court where girls in short white skirts were playing doubles in the September heat. Betsy had expected to be nervous, but once she was actually on campus, a feeling of rightness came over her. No one knew her here. She was anonymous and could start anew.

She had a single room, though she hadn't requested one. When she opened the window, she could hear the heavy traffic on Broadway. She introduced herself as Elizabeth when she met girls in the dining room downstairs that first evening. They told her helpful tips, like how to take the IRT line for a dime to and from the local stop at 116th and Broadway near campus.

She was one of only a few Southern girls and the only one from South Carolina. Some girls mocked her accent, some were curious about the South, and some made it clear that she was from a backwater.

A S she was going up the steps to her classics course in Milbank Hall one day early in the term, a small, serious-looking girl with glasses and dark brown hair in a pageboy complimented

Betsy on her comment about the *Iliad* in the previous class. It was the only time Betsy had made a peep. She'd noticed that this girl wasn't afraid to ask questions. Late, they hurried in, slipping into their seats as unobtrusively as possible. After class Betsy waited to walk out with her.

"Thank you for what you said," Betsy said. "I was afraid I made a fool of myself."

"I figure that's the price of an education," the girl said. She was wearing a gray pleated skirt and matching cotton cardigan sweater.

"I'm Betsy," she said, forgetting that she was Elizabeth now.

"Zora Newman." Betsy fell into step beside her. "I'm sorry to rush," she apologized, "but I don't want to miss my bus."

"I've never known a Zora," Betsy said, hurrying to keep up. "Is it Greek?"

"I'm named for Zora Neal Hurston. Did you ever hear of her? The writer?" They were passing the tennis courts on the way to the front gate.

Betsy admitted she had not. Just another of the many things she'd never heard of.

"You've got to read *Their Eyes Were Watching God*," Zora said. "She was the first Negro to attend Barnard, back in the twenties. I'm named for her."

"Wow! You're named for a Negro!"

"I am a Negro."

"What! No you're not. You're white!"

"Light. A light *Negro. You're* white." She glanced at Betsy, not breaking stride. "But I won't hold it against you."

"Oh," Betsy said, taken aback.

"Unless you're prejudiced," Zora said, a little breathlessly from the pace. "Which I'm sure you are. I don't mean it personally. All white people are." They had arrived at the bus stop. "I am too. Only I'm prejudiced against white people." She laughed lightly.

"Oh," was all Betsy could come up with again. Now that she knew, she thought there *was* something a little colored about Zora. Her skin was the kind of tan Betsy longed for in the summers when she lay out in the sun, only to turn pink. Her nose was broader than those of the girls Betsy knew, and her hair was thicker. It must be true. She was a Negro. Here she was talking with a Negro girl her own age, something she'd never done in her life.

"Do people know?"

"The college certainly knows," Zora said, stepping off the curb to look down the street. The bus was two blocks away. "There's just a few of us. Two are obviously Negro. The rest of us are light-skinned. We're all smart, attractive, pleasant, and from good families." She stepped back on the sidewalk and curtseyed. "And we have impeccable manners."

"I'm sorry. I didn't mean to offend."

"You didn't," Zora said.

"Do the other girls know?"

"Well, some of them have asked me what country I'm from."

"What do you say?"

"I tell them I'm from the country of the United States of America."

The bus was pulling up to the stop. As Zora stepped aboard, she called back, "See you on Thursday," as if nothing unusual had transpired.

BETSY couldn't stop thinking about Zora. She wasn't like the Negroes back home, not that Betsy knew many of them. She was so curious about her. She made sure to get to class early to sit next to her. After class she asked if she could walk to the bus stop with her again.

"You don't really need my permission," Zora said. "Just pick up your pace." As they strode briskly along, she asked how Betsy liked Barnard so far. "I know you're a transfer. This is my third year on the hill, so I know the ropes. Ask me if you have any questions." She wanted to know where Betsy was from and Betsy told her. She explained she'd gone her first two years of college in Georgia.

"Why'd you transfer?"

"One of my professors critiqued my papers and advised me on all kinds of things. She graduated from Barnard and thought I'd be happier here. And that it would do me good to get out of the South."

"My grandparents on my mom's side live in Montgomery," Zora said. "I visit them every summer for a couple of weeks. Nice place to visit, but I wouldn't want to live there." She gave Betsy a big wink.

The bus was just pulling up. Betsy had to hurry her question: "Why did you tell me?"

"That I'm a Negro? I don't try to hide it. As soon as I heard your drawl, I knew you were from the South. Some of the girls here will look down on you—the way they do me. Besides, I could tell you were nice."

OVER the next several walks to the bus stop, Betsy learned that Zora was majoring in sociology and planned to be a social worker. Her family lived in Ansonia, Connecticut, near New

Haven, where her father was pastor at a large Negro National Baptist Church. She'd been one of ten other Negro students at her high school and valedictorian of her class. She was on a full scholarship at Barnard. Girls Betsy knew, including herself, had been raised to be modest, self-effacing—and certainly never to brag. Zora was confident and direct. When Betsy asked her which dorm she lived in, she said she didn't live on campus. Negroes weren't allowed to. She lived with her cousin in the Bronx. That explained why she caught the bus every day.

Zora took it upon herself to introduce Betsy to the city that fall. They went to plays or musicals where they could get in on student prices, concerts at Carnegie Hall, operas at Amato Opera, dinner at Grand Ticino in Greenwich Village where they could get a bottle of wine and dinner for less than five dollars. They saw Ethel Merman in *Call Me Madam* and rode the Staten Island Ferry, reciting Vachel Lindsay's poetry to each other in exaggerated Southern accents on the deck. They drank coffee at Chock full o'Nuts and hung out at King's Kitchen.

When Betsy confided to Zora that she wanted to be a writer, Zora asked to read one of her stories. Being Zora, she said it was clumsy in parts but that Betsy had the heart of a real writer. Zora was toying with the idea of law school. She felt social work was where she could do the most good to help people, but maybe having a law degree meant she could make a bigger difference.

One time when they were bumming around in the Garment District, a clerk in a fancy hat store stopped them as they were coming in the door. "Are you a Negro?" she asked Zora. "If you can't tell," Zora shot back, "what difference does it make?"

Betsy was mortified. She'd gotten so accustomed to Zora

that sometimes she forgot about her race. Then other times, she would marvel that she had a friend who was colored. She asked Zora how she could stand all the inequities and unfairness Negroes had to endure.

Zora said she'd been raised to believe that Negroes were making progress and that things would continue to get better. She intended to make a contribution in that direction. "I don't let little things like that shop clerk bother me."

"What's it like to be a Negro and look so white?"

"Some of my ancestors passed," Zora said.

"Passed what?"

"Passed as white people," Zora laughed. She found Betsy's naïveté humorous. She called her a *tabula rasa*. "I could pass if I wanted to," Zora said. "I have an aunt who's married to a white man, and he doesn't even know it. Or if he does, he pretends he doesn't. She's turned her back on our whole family. I'd never do that." She explained that her maternal great-great-grandmother was a white, blue-eyed woman who'd emigrated from Ireland. She married a former slave who was light-skinned himself. Her paternal great-greats were slaves. "We come in all colors in my family."

"Do you mind me asking you these things?" Betsy asked. "Where I was raised, it's considered rude to talk about race."

"It's actually refreshing," Zora said. "None of the girls here would dare talk to me about my race. They believe in manners over curiosity or honesty."

Being around Zora gave Betsy plenty to think about. If people knew she was a Negro, they'd respond to her differently—yet she would be exactly the same person. If her skin was darker, she wouldn't be welcome in some restaurants or hotels, for, as Zora explained, New York was still segregated emotionally and psychologically, and sometimes physically. Were there any other characteristics besides her skin tone that made her different from white girls?

Only the way society saw her.

O N E afternoon when they were taking a study break, Betsy told Zora about the Willie Earle lynching in Greenville.

"I know all about it," Zora said. "It was big news in the Negro press."

"My father was one of the prosecutors," Betsy said. "We had a maid who knew Willie Earle when he was a child. She moved up here to New York a few months after the trial. She actually left her baby behind with her mother. She didn't even tell us she was going! Can you believe that?"

Zora snorted Coca-Cola through her nose. "She didn't figure it was white folks' business what she did! She had her own things to think about—like leaving that baby of hers behind!" She paused, looking Betsy right in the eye, raising her eyebrows. "Which of yo doors did she come in? Which of yo plates did she eat off of? Which end of the bus did she ride in? Did she have to bend low to drink out of the colored water fountain?" Zora was fired up. "She didn't think y'all would understand, and you wouldn't have!"

"I guess not," Betsy said weakly.

"It ain't your fault," Zora said more gently. "No matter how hard you try, you cain't walk in colored folks' shoes. You cain't walk that walk unless you done walked it yo whole life."

It was the only time Betsy had heard Zora talk Colored.

S O M E T I M E S one of the girls in Betsy's dorm would ask her if she wanted to double date. But the boys she wanted to date again didn't ask, and the ones she didn't want did. At least these dates provided fodder to entertain Zora. Sometimes a Barnard girl would ask Zora if she wanted to go on a date. Zora wasn't interested in dating white boys. She liked dark-skinned boys. Barnard didn't want those boys coming on to campus, she explained. "Too afraid of all that black virility. That's the main reason we have to live off-campus." That wink again.

At the end of spring term, Betsy hated to say goodbye to Zora. They hugged, promised to write, and Zora teased Betsy about her counselor job at Camp Pinnacle: "You're going to be spending your summer telling little girls not to stand up in a canoe, showing them how to make baskets out of popsicle sticks, and singing 'Kumbaya' around a campfire?" She waited a beat. "By the way, 'Kumbaya' is a Gullah song."

Damn! Just one more thing Betsy didn't know.

"I can see you don't know Gullah from gullible. Gullahs were slaves down on the sea islands of your state. Some of their descendants still speak that language, left over from Africa."

Zora had what she described as an "equally challenging summer job" lined up at the Southern New England Telephone Company in New Haven.

EVERY week that summer, they wrote letters, telling each other everything they'd done or thought or felt. But right before Betsy was to return to school, she got an unexpected letter.

Dear Betsy,

I'm sorry to tell you this, but I've decided not to come back to Barnard in the fall. I know this will come as a shock—I'm still in shock myself. But being home, around "my people," has made me realize that at Barnard I was a token. I've been so happy all

summer being with my family and back in my church communi-
ty—a happiness I never felt at Barnard. I thought I fit in there,
but how could I really? Remember how you thought when you first
met me that I was white? Well, at Barnard I almost became white.
No one asked or knew about me as a Negro. They didn't want to
know. There were no Negro professors or any acknowledgement
that Negroes even exist. You were the only one curious about what
it was like for me. You weren't like the other girls, who were too
polite or maybe prejudiced to get to really know me. I never knew
what they thought or felt, not just about me but about anything.

I hope you understand. I'm sorry to desert you. I'll miss you
so much. I won't forget you, dear Tabula Rasa! *I know life will*
be scribbling all kind of good things on your slate. Keep writing
your stories!

Love,

Zora

W H E N Betsy returned to Barnard that fall, she missed Zora
terribly. But their letters flew back and forth, and in those letters, she could hear Zora's voice as if she were actually there,
listening, asking, and teasing.

Betsy had declared an English major, and now she threw
herself into her studies. She loved her literature courses, especially 20th Century British and American Poetry, Russian Lit,
and 19th Century Women Writers. She joined the staff of *Focus*,
the campus literary magazine. On the weekends, she walked the
city for hours, lost in the sensory overload of New York streets.
Poems and stories unfurled in her head and in her notebooks.

She'd never felt so right in herself or in the world.

And without her noticing when, the nightmares had
stopped.

23

ALMA

ALMA HAD WORKED for Mr. Stern for over a year now. He was always around, rearranging the books in the library or studying his stamp collection through a magnifying glass. Not too long after Alma had started working there, he'd told her how his parents had led a comfortable life in Berlin. When Hitler began his rise to power, his uncle in America had begged the family to emigrate. Mr. Stern had gotten out through Amsterdam, but his parents were reluctant to leave. "They believed no one would touch their constitutional rights. The Nazis would burn out." He was silent for so long that Alma, who'd been dusting the old books in his office, stopped moving. A feeling of dread came over her. She'd heard about the camps.

"By the time they tried to leave," Mr. Stern said in a voice so low she had trouble hearing him, "they were unable to attain the necessary papers. They died in Buchenwald." Another long silence. "Like dogs!" he suddenly exclaimed, waving his arms in the air, frightening her. He began to weep, putting his head down on the black leather surface of his writing desk. Alma slipped away, shaken, leaving him to his grief.

After that, Mr. Stern would often tell her that his parents had died at Buchenwald. When he got to the "Like dogs!" part, he would break down. Alma's eyes would fill with tears too. She was tempted sometimes to pat him on the back as he sobbed into his handkerchief, but she knew better than to touch a white man.

Now, after all this time, she'd grown accustomed to Mr. Stern and to the story. But one day when he started in, weeping as always when he got to the part about his parents, Alma did pat him gently on the back. At her touch, Mr. Stern suddenly sprang up from his chair, grabbed her around the waist and pulled her against him, shoving his pelvis hard against hers. He pinched her nipple so hard through her uniform she cried out. She wrenched away from him, grabbed her black pocketbook, and fled down the service stairs and out the building. She never went back, even though Mr. Stern owed her almost a month's pay.

When she told the woman at the agency what had happened, the woman said Mr. Stern had called and accused Alma of stealing a piece of his mother's jewelry. Alma stared at her, deeply embarrassed, feeling guilty, though she would never steal anything in her life! She was stunned that Mr. Stern would turn on her like that. "It's a lie," Alma stuttered, but the woman said she couldn't find Alma another job, not with a report like that on her record. Alma turned and left.

Ladocia just shrugged when Alma told her the story. Such things happened. It wouldn't take long for Alma to get another job. She'd ask some of her customers at the House of Beauty if they knew of anyone who needed a maid. But a month passed, and then another, and yet another, and Alma was out of work. After the post-war prosperity, by 1949, the country found itself in a recession. Unemployment at almost 8 percent was hitting Harlem hard.

Alma's meager savings were dwindling. One of the neighbors told her where maids were getting work, at the corner of 167th Street and Westchester Avenue in the Bronx. Alma walked to save the bus fare. When she got there, she was surprised to see ten or twelve colored women, old and young, some nicely dressed and some looking destitute, standing in a loose line on the sidewalk, holding paper bundles. Alma slipped in next to an older woman wearing a plaid coat and head scarf who hadn't exactly smiled at Alma when she arrived but at least hadn't scowled at her like some of the others. "Where's the agency?" Alma asked. "Is this where I can get a job?"

"Dis here's the Slave Market!" the woman said brusquely. She was such an unadulterated black, she couldn't have one drop of white blood in her. "Didn't nobody tell you?" Her accent was deep South, maybe Mississippi or Alabama.

"What!" Alma exclaimed. "What you mean, 'slave market'?"

"Dat about what it come down to," the woman said. "Been going on since dat big depression. Hard times done livened it up again."

"I don't understand," Alma said. "What's in all those paper bags?"

The woman held her own bag up. "Dis here our work clothes," she said. "Look dare, here come one to look us'uns over and get her a slave for the day."

A white woman pulled over to the curb in a Chrysler Town and Country wagon, got out, and began walking up and down the line. Alma shrank back, averting her eyes. She didn't want to be anyone's slave. She felt relief when one of the younger women was chosen and got in the back seat of the car. Even though she was shivering from the cold, Alma felt sweat breaking out in her armpits.

"What they pay?" she asked the woman next to her.

"Seventy-five cent an hour," she said sternly. "Don't take no less than that, or dey think dey can get away with sixty! Some of dem work you to death. Last week I had to hang out the sill and wash dem windows on the outside. Hanging on for dear life, hoping the frame don't bust loose. Dey inspect after you all the time, make sure you don't miss no speck 'a dust in the corner, make sure you starch dey husband's shirts right. Don't let dem set the clock back and say you done started at nine when it were eight. Be careful dey ain't some dirty old man waiting for the missus to leave so he can put his thang in you!"

EVERY day Alma went to the Slave Market. Some days she got work and some days not. It was always hard work, sometimes cleaning apartments that hadn't been cleaned in a year if ever. One white woman who came to the slave market asked to see Alma's knees. After taking a look, she passed Alma by. Alma asked Black Bertha, the woman she'd met the first day, what the woman was looking for.

"See if yo knees calloused. That way she know you used to scrubbing floors."

ONE of Ladocia's boarders told Alma that she might get a government job if she took a civil service test and passed. Alma had been a good student at Sterling, graduating near the top of her class. She began studying at night for the test, but by evening, she was so tired she could hardly concentrate. The material was hard and dull, she hadn't studied since high school, and it was difficult to keep her mind on the questions.

Another Christmas came and went; another phone call to Pretty. Another year of her daughter's life missed. Alma was filled with anxiety about the future, she was exhausted from the slave labor, and she would find herself staring into space, wondering if she had made a mistake to come up North. But how could she give up now? Her mama always said Alma was stubborn as a mule. How could she admit defeat? No, she'd pass that test, she'd get her a government job, a desk job with good money. She'd get on her feet, she'd bring Pretty up North so she wouldn't have to grow up in the South—a South where they killed Li'l Willie in the woods by a slaughterhouse. Like a dog.

SHE began drinking in her room. Not a lot, at least not at first. Just enough to help her sleep. She'd buy a pint of Jim Beam at the corner store and hide it in her big black pocketbook. After cleaning up the supper dishes, she'd retire to her room, saying she had to study. She'd study for half an hour or so, but soon all the material ran together. She'd get the bottle from her bag and sip from it until her mind quieted down. When the bottle was empty, she'd carry it back out in her pocketbook and deposit it in a trash bin on her way to the Slave Market. She never missed showing up there, but some mornings she had such a fierce headache she could hardly think. She did the work, no matter how humiliating or unfair, which made her look forward all the more to going to her room after supper, shutting the door, and easing into feeling she was floating in some amber cloud where nothing mattered because everything was just fine.

ONE day Alma ran into Synthia on the street when she was dragging home from one of her jobs. When she told her what had happened and about the work she was doing, Synthia said there was an opening at the hotel where she worked. After eleven months, the economy had picked up again. "Come downtown tomorrow," she said, "and I'll help you get the job."

Cleaning hotel rooms wasn't easy work either, but it was steady, and once Alma got the hang of it, it wasn't so bad. She liked the other girls who worked there: Marbel, big and strong as a man; Daisy Mae, who wasn't five feet tall and was the fastest of them, able to clean two rooms to their one; Delia, who had a wicked tongue; Ella, who muttered to herself all the time; and Hazel, who was seventy-five if a day. Whenever Alma and Synthia got to clean together, the day went faster and the work was lighter. She got to know the colored porters, who flirted with the women, teasing them and commiserating when they needed sympathy.

She quickly learned that the small white woman with scars on her face who came to the basement of the hotel every day was a numbers runner. Ray bet on the numbers, sometimes big money. He and Ladocia had warned Alma away from placing even small bets, telling her to save her money. But Synthia played the numbers, and sometimes she won as much as fifty dollars—a lot of money. One day Daisy Mae won enough to buy an RCA TV. Everyone was excited and happy for her. And envious. Alma began putting a little money on the numbers. She always used the same ones, 126, the number of the house back on Sycamore Street in Greenville where she and Huff had lived. At first it was a dime every other day, then fifty cents on Friday, and then it became a dollar or two or three sometimes. Winning seemed her best chance to get ahead. Whenever she won a few dollars, she'd put them back on the numbers. She knew she was being a fool, but the dream of winning big kept her betting. After all, some people won. Why not her?

AFTER Alma started working at the hotel, she and Synthia saw a lot of each other. She encouraged Alma when she was feeling down, poked fun at her as well as at herself, and was always full of drama—some new fling or adventure. Synthia wore stylish clothes, tightly-fitted skirts, jackets with padded shoulders that made her waist look small. She even had her hair cut short like Dinah Washington's. She would model her newest fashions for Alma at the two-room apartment she was renting off St. Nicholas. Alma didn't see how Synthia could afford all the shoes, bags, and outfits she bought. She must have been hitting the numbers more than she let on— or maybe she was shoplifting. Sometimes when Alma went to her place, Synthia would be smoking a reefer. She'd offer Alma a hit. But Alma wasn't about to smoke weed. She'd never even smoked a cigarette, which resulted in a lot of ribbing from Synthia.

They began going out together to the clubs and shows on the weekends, Minton's Playhouse on 118th to hear jazz, Small's Paradise, and the Apollo, where on Amateur Night, "the executioner" would sweep the performers off the stage with a broom when the audience booed. One night she and Synthia met two nattily-dressed men at the Savoy and had a good time dancing with them. The one who liked Alma was called Catfish, and the one who liked Synthia was Randall. It was a natural pairing. Catfish was tall, over six feet. He'd gone to Howard University School of Law and worked for the NAACP Legal Defense and Educational Fund. He told her about an anti-lynching law the NAACP was trying to pass, but opposition by the Southern Democrats was making it impossible. They were also strategizing ways to end segregation in schools. Never happen, she thought but she kept that to herself.

At work he used his real name, Henry, but his friends called him Catfish because he loved fried catfish so much. He was from Boston, and sometimes he sounded just like a white man, but other times, when he had had a few drinks and was relaxing, he liked to talk like "a down-home nigger." He always had a wallet full of cash and treated Alma like she'd never been treated before: special. Huff wasn't suave like Catfish; she couldn't help comparing.

She and Synthia began meeting Catfish and Randall to drink and dance every Saturday night. One night they all went back to Catfish's apartment in a red brick row house. They sat around drinking and listening to music. Alma began feeling loose, though a part of her stood back and watched the stranger she'd become, the laughing, flirtatious, carefree woman who was the exact opposite of her sad, anxious, burdened self. At some point, Synthia and Randall disappeared into the bedroom. Alma knew what was coming, though she wouldn't let herself exactly think about it. Catfish put on Billie Holiday singing "You're My Thrill." Alma had read in the *Amsterdam News* how Billie had gotten out of jail after being in on a drug charge and was making a comeback.

Catfish told how he'd gone to her concert at Carnegie Hall ten days after her release. "I hope she can stay off the white stuff," he mused to Alma, shaking his head doubtfully. "Otherwise I don't think she'll be around long."

Catfish held out his hand for Alma to dance. She hesitated but took his hand and slipped into his arms. It felt good to sway with him to the music. It felt good to be pressed against a man again. He was warm and smelled of something good. "Ummm," she murmured, "what's that you got on?"

"Old Spice." He nuzzled into her neck. "That's me all right. Old Spice."

But when he began running his hands all over her body, she pushed him away.

"What?" he said.

"I'm married," Alma said. The thought of betraying Huff gave her a full-body shudder. "I cain't. I'm a married woman."

Catfish stepped back and nodded, taking in this information. "I see," he said. "Well, I can't say I'm not disappointed."

Alma didn't know what to say. She was ashamed for leading him on. He called a taxi for her, gave the driver a ten-dollar bill, and wrote his phone number on a slip of paper, telling her if she ever changed her mind . . . He was a gentleman, and Alma felt a deep ache, a longing to be with him. To be saved by him.

LADOCIA was waiting up for her. It was nearly two in the morning. Alma was drunk.

"Where you been?" Ladocia said, her dark eyes burning. "I didn't take you in for you to go whoring! What am I 'pose to tell Bessie? You better get on back to where you come from, niece, and straighten out your ways!"

"I can't go back," Alma said. "Please don't make me." She needed to go lie down. "I'm sorry, Aunt Ladocia," she slurred her words, even though she tried not to. "It won' happen again."

In the light of day, Alma couldn't believe what she'd done. She'd gone to a man's apartment and danced with him. She'd almost betrayed her husband! What had gotten into her? She was so abashed and ashamed. She could hardly look Ladocia in the eyes. Even Ray, who was normally so easygoing, seemed to turn on her.

She determined to mend her ways. She had to stop drinking. She told Synthia she wouldn't be going to the clubs anymore. She gritted her teeth and stayed away from the corner liquor store. She rode the bus downtown and changed sheets and cleaned bathrooms at the hotel. When Synthia told her Catfish had been asking about her, Alma shook her head and went about her work.

24

LAWTON

AS MUCH AS Lawton had wanted out of his marriage, he missed Lydia and their home life. He was very lonely. He spent as little time in his furnished apartment as possible, feeling that someone else lived there, and he'd walked in by mistake. He preferred to keep company with his new office furniture in the Chamber of Commerce Building ("Liberty! Life!").

Now that he and Lydia had lived apart for a year, they could legally divorce. It had been a hard year. His parents were shocked and mystified by the separation. As for Lyman and Beatrice, Lyman had become senile, and Beatrice behaved as if Lawton were dead. Word had gotten out around town, and when Lawton ran into friends or even acquaintances, he felt a certain censure, whether real or imagined, he couldn't tell. Lydia, a more social creature than he to begin with, had fared better, buoyed by her women friends. She'd started giving piano lessons to children at the house. He was happy for her and a little envious of how she'd moved on.

They still hadn't told Betsy they'd separated. She spent a week in Greenville over the Christmas holidays, eager to return to New York and Barnard. It was easy to carry on the charade that everything at home was the same, though Lawton wondered if she sensed the sea change. But she seemed so happy. She loved Barnard, had friends there, told them she was dating, though there was no one special, and she was doing well academically. They were reluctant to interrupt her senior year. There was no good time, no good way to break the news. The best thing, they agreed, uncertainly, would be to tell her together when they were in New York for her graduation in May.

AT the formal signing of the divorce documents, Lydia surprised Lawton by being relatively upbeat while he felt a penetrating sadness. She even invited him to go for a drink afterward. They sat at the bar at Charlie's, a place they'd once frequented as a couple, and ordered martinis. Lawton noticed a few raised eyebrows from people they knew, but no one came over to speak.

They talked first, as they always did, about Betsy.

"I think it's natural and good," Lydia speculated, "that she's growing up and away from us. She's caught up in her own life now, not ours. We're just the old boring parents."

They talked to her once a week on the phone. "We'd know if she was in trouble," Lawton said, and Lydia agreed. They moved on.

Lydia told him how Bessie had stopped by the house with Pretty a few weeks ago. "The child wandered into the living room, plopped down on the piano bench, and began 'playing,'" Lydia said. "I showed her how to play 'Twinkle, Twinkle

Little Star.' She's missing one of her two front teeth. She told me she put it under her pillow, and the tooth fairy left her two dimes. The next night, she put a heart-shaped rock under her pillow but . . . nothing!" She grinned. "Now Bessie brings her for a piano lesson every week."

"Did Bessie say anything about Alma?"

"Seems they don't know much, and I didn't push her on it. But this week out of the blue, Pretty told me how her mother had gone up North. When she was a baby."

"What did you say?"

"I told her I knew that and that I knew her mother. She said her mama had gone up North to get a good job. And someday she was going up North and get her a good job too. So she can live with dignity." She looked right at Lawton, a bemused expression on her face. "Can you imagine a young child saying something like that?"

"Sounds like Bessie's doing a good job with the girl."

Lydia cocked her head to the side. "So I 'can live with dignity,'" she repeated softly, more to herself than to Lawton.

NOW that he was officially divorced, Lawton found himself thinking about what the future might hold. For so many years, for all his married life, he'd been so bent on passing that he'd erected a wall between himself and any verboten feelings he might have. But now he felt free to admit that men were a turn-on—at least a few of them. He didn't actually know any men he was sexually attracted to, not since Poinsett Sam. But occasionally on the street, he'd see something—a forearm covered in dark fur or the way some stranger's open-collared shirt revealed a sunburned muscular neck. The handsome clerk at Better Food became a star in a movie in his mind, taking him places he'd never been—except once.

He hadn't forgotten Donny Sanders, Harper's fairy, though he hadn't followed through with seeing him again. But increasingly he thought about dropping by the store. It wasn't that he was attracted to Donny. It was that Donny was the only person Lawton was aware of who might actually understand him. If it involved buying yet another piece of office furniture that he didn't need, so be it. He'd try to get up the nerve to ask if Donny would like to have a drink after work. Somewhere discreet, because he wouldn't want anyone to see him in Donny's company.

Donny greeted him warmly when he arrived. "Mr. Chastain," he exclaimed, remembering his name, gripping his hand in both of his. Lawton wondered how Donny got away with all his girlish mannerisms. He was a good salesman, Lawton could attest to that, and there were a lot of new offices in town to furnish. People enjoyed this kind of effusive attention—as long as no lines were crossed. Donny with his small frame and bubbly persona was innocuous. But he must have to be very careful on the streets at night.

"How do you like your splendid oak desk?" he warbled. "Very handsome, and that oak desk chair? I worried that it might be too hard on your bottom." Donny seemed genuinely concerned. Lawton said it was fine. Donny asked what he could help him with today. If only he knew.

"Let me look around a bit," Lawton said. He glanced at another salesman in the back, absorbed in some paperwork. "Show me what's new. I had a little time on my hands and thought I'd—"

"Delighted! Follow me. We've just gotten in a Kofod-Larsen chair. Airy and modern." Donny pressed his fingertips together and tipped his head in a coquettish way. "I think it's 'you'!"

With Donny chattering away about the sculptural lines of the chair, how its curved back embraces the sitter, how Kofod-Larsen is Danish and the Danes have the *best* sense of design, Lawton found himself perched in the most uncomfortable chair he'd ever had the misfortune to light on. "I don't think so," he said, feigning some reluctance. "Maybe I need to think about what I really need."

"Ah!" Donny said. "I know exactly what you need!"

Lawton looked at him in surprise. "What?" he said dumbly.

"An ear," Donny said. "Let me get my coat. I could really use a drink."

LAWTON thought it would be too risky to be seen in a car with Donny. He said he'd prefer to meet him. Donny gave him the address of Hurley's, a bar in the west end of town, unknown territory for Lawton. He drove by first to check it out, a nondescript hole-in-the-wall on a side street near the ice plant. Lawton parked a couple of blocks away and feeling exposed and nervous, he pulled open the heavy door.

It was a Friday night, and the place was crowded and noisy with people stopping by after work. Donny was standing by the bar, and he motioned to Lawton to follow him. They pushed their way through the crowd, and Donny opened a door in the back that led to another world. There Lawton saw what he could never have imagined: a room full of men, some of them dancing together to the jukebox, others with their arms draped around each other at the bar. The place exuded flirtation, sexuality, and freedom. He hadn't known such a place existed, could exist, in Greenville.

"How did you know?" he asked Donny when they were settled at the bar.

"That you're a three-dollar bill? I just know. A sixth sense. A talent, really," Donny said modestly.

Donny was easy to talk to, and over Manhattans, Lawton found himself telling him all about Harry Bumgarten. Donny said he'd had his first sex at sixteen, with a theater teacher in a summer program his parents had enrolled him in, "because I had such a 'theatrical flair.'" He went through all his crushes since, a considerable number. Lawton laughed at Donny's dramatic sighs as one lover after another fell like bowling pins. He felt a bond with Donny that he'd never felt with another man—except Harry.

Donny knew everything about being a homosexual, and he knew everything about queers in Greenville, of which there were more than a few. That in itself was a surprise. Lawton had had no idea there was a whole world—hidden, covertly thriving, often persecuted—that lay beyond the door he'd walked through.

Donny took his role as professor seriously. Over the course of several more drinks, he told Lawton the things he needed to know: cruising went on unchallenged in the men's bathroom in the basement of the Otteray Hotel; the police in Atlanta had used a one-way mirror to observe patrons in the Atlanta Public Library restroom and arrested twenty men for having homosexual encounters, ruining their lives. Lawton had to be careful. But if he was discreet, he'd be okay. Donny said the police would probably try to blackmail someone like him if he got caught. If he didn't pay up, his name would be in the paper.

Lawton was absorbed in Donny's tales when suddenly he felt a firm hand on his shoulder. He turned and looked right into the dark eyes of Sam, the waiter from the Poinsett Hotel. Sam smiled, but it was not the deferential smile he'd used at the Poinsett. This smile was cocky, even predatory. Lawton felt a wave of excitement and warning course through him.

"What took you so long?" Sam said, and he leaned in and kissed Lawton on the mouth, inserting his tongue like a quick snake before Lawton could push him away.

"I see you two have met," Donny said dryly.

Lawton was wiping his mouth with the back of his hand.

"Donny, my man," Sam said, and he started to put his arm around Donny's shoulders.

"Don't touch me," Donny pulled away. "If you lay one finger on me . . ."

"You should be so lucky, Donny boy."

Lawton was staring at Sam in the smoky dim light. It was almost as if he had conjured him up. He'd dreamed of him many times, romantic fantasies that quickly became erotic, culminating in guilty orgasms. Tonight Sam wasn't the pressed and polished waiter Lawton had been attracted to. His upper arms in his tight white T-shirt were muscular and covered in tattoos. At the Poinsett he'd seemed so tame. Now he resembled a jungle cat.

"Gotta pen?" Sam addressed the two of them. Lawton, flustered, shook his head. Donny ignored the question.

"Joey," Sam called to the bartender. "Gimme a pen, will ya?"

Joey, a man built like a cube, his width appearing about the same as his height, slid Sam a nubby pencil. "I want it back," he called down the bar. "I got your number, Sammy."

"Everybody's got Sam's number," Donny muttered.

Sam was writing on a cheap paper napkin. "Now you do too," he said to Lawton, handing him the napkin. "Call me sometime." He melted into the crowd without returning the pencil.

25

BETSY

WHEN BETSY'S PARENTS came for her graduation in June, they made it clear they couldn't be prouder of her. She was graduating with honors, had won a prize for her poetry from the campus literary magazine, and with the help of the Barnard Career Club, she'd lined up a job in a small theatrical agency on West 54th Street in the Theater District. She would answer the phone, file, do errands, and get takeout for the two agents there. She'd be making fifty dollars a week, supplemented by a check Grand Bee sent every month, so she "wouldn't have to do without."

Her parents helped her move out of the dorm and into a studio apartment at 10 Carmine Street in the Village. From the first time she set foot in Greenwich Village, she'd dreamed of living there. She recognized it as the place where people felt free to be themselves, away from the square world of their hometowns. When she found the apartment on Carmine, the superintendent, Mr. Lastrada, asked her suspiciously if she was one of those hipsters, 'cause he didn't want no hipsters in the building. In her best ladylike Southern accent, Betsy answered, "Oh no, Mr. Lastrada," though that was exactly what she hoped to become.

On the night before they were to fly back to Greenville, her parents took her to dinner at Tavern on the Green. She'd showed them the famous sights, the Empire State Building, the Statue of Liberty from the Staten Island Ferry, and Central Park where they rode in one of the horse-drawn carriages. But as they walked back to Betsy's apartment from the subway stop that evening, her parents fell silent.

They sat down next to one another on Betsy's single bed. The apartment was spare, barely furnished, but Betsy loved it. It was where she hoped to become a real writer. There was a tiny sink and hot plate in the closet-sized kitchen, the single bed, a rickety dresser painted white, the drawers of which were meant for a different dresser, and shelves on the walls that Betsy planned to fill with books. Someone had painted a round coffee table bright red, and there was an armless chair that looked very modern and was very uncomfortable. A yellow Formica drop-leaf table and two wood chairs painted yellow sat in the middle of the room.

"You tell her," her mother said. She had an expression on her face Betsy had never seen.

"Betsy," her father said in a strange, kind voice, "your mother and I have had a good marriage. But . . ." he paused. Betsy stared at him and then at her mother. She had an out-of-body feeling, as if she were viewing the scene from above, but it couldn't touch her.

"But what . . ." she said harshly, squinting to stare more fiercely from one of them to the other.

"Betsy," he said, "your mother and I—"

"We've divorced," her mother said flatly.

There was a moment of stunned, awkward silence. Betsy burst out with, "I don't believe it!" Even though she did. She did, and she didn't. Nervous laughter bubbled up inside her. An actual giggle escaped. She was afraid of what might follow, gales of raucous laughter or uncontrollable weeping. She went to stare out the dirty window that looked onto an airshaft. When she turned back to them, they looked like two guilty children. She'd never noticed how small their faces were.

"Betsy," her mother beseeched. "We don't mean to upset you. Please sit down so we can talk."

"Not upset me!"

"Betsy," her father said, again in that strange, kind voice that made her want to slap him, "I know this is hard to hear. But it isn't the end of the world."

"It is of my world," she said and burst into tears. She was reduced to a five-year-old, not the sophisticated, independent college graduate she'd been an hour ago.

When she'd calmed, she asked, "Why didn't you tell me!"

"We wanted to let you finish your senior year. We thought it best to wait," her mother said.

"I'm sorry, Betsy," her father said. "But we were afraid. You seemed so happy, and you were doing so well. We—"

"But why? Why!"

Her father spoke first, telling her how over the years he and her mother had grown apart. Then he said a strange thing: at the Willie Earle trial, he'd come to feel that his whole life was wrong. "A lie, actually." He let this sink in. "I knew then that I would be making some changes. Major changes. Difficult changes for us all. Your mother and I wanted to give you time to finish your senior year before such a disruption."

What was he talking about, "a lie"? How could someone's whole life be a lie?

Her father must be having an affair! How could he do this to her mother?

"Mother?"

When her mother looked directly at Betsy, she saw what she'd forgotten: her mother's eyes were a bruised blue-gray.

"I've known for some time," she said. "At first I was hurt and angry. Well, I still am, but it's gotten better." She gave a little snort. "You know how people talk. You know Greenville. I knew I'd be the object of gossip, and worse, pity. But I'm just holding my head high and going forward." She paused. "I don't blame your father. Not anymore. We were so young when we got married. And we did make a good life together. The best part has been you."

"But . . . what will you do?" Betsy turned to search their faces. A profound feeling of incomprehension had come over her. She was hearing words but not understanding them.

"I've rented an apartment at The Davenport," her father said. "Your mother's keeping the house. You'll always have a home to come back to."

They sat in silence.

"I thought you were happy . . . happy enough . . . together," Betsy finally said. But as soon as she spoke, she knew it wasn't true. Had she ever really thought about her parents' happiness? They were her parents, and their lives, their feelings, were not something she knew much about. They had kept their unhappiness to themselves.

SHE started work at Silverman and Jacobs Theatrical Agency the first Monday in June. It was a welcome relief to have to get up, get dressed, catch the subway, and have something to do. Her job was screening phone calls and drop-ins, mostly young people wanting to be actors or actresses, hoping Bernard Silverman or Isabel Jacobs would represent them. The office was on the seventh floor of the Bingham Building, and Betsy's desk was in the entry hall. Bernard and Isabel's offices were a few steps away, and since they never shut their doors, their voices carried all over the small space. Betsy learned how to hand-hold current clients who'd had auditions but not gotten the parts. She grew adept at doling out sympathetic, optimistic encouragement; that seemed about 80 percent of what Bernard and Isabel did. She picked up dry cleaning for them, got them Chinese takeout or pizza for lunch, and made a confused and futile attempt at filing the mountains of playbills that were piled on every surface. She fed the goldfish and cleaned its bowl.

She liked the two of them, but they were busy, and much older than she, her parents' ages at least. She didn't confide in them. The only person she told about her parents' divorce was Zora, who was living in Montgomery now, taking care of her grandparents. Betsy didn't tell anyone else about her folks; she couldn't talk about something she didn't understand herself. She saw less of her friends from college that summer. Many of them had left New York or were caught up with new friends in their post-college lives. Besides, she didn't feel like socializing. Back home in her apartment every evening, she felt a familiar weight descend. She began having nightmares again.

The scene was still the Pickens jail cell, but somehow it was also her Village studio. In the dreams, she was sitting on the dismal cot, which was also her single bed on Carmine

Street. Time passed as she waited. And waited. Hours, perhaps days, passed. No one came. She rose and wrapped her hands around the bars, straining to see down the short, dark hall. "Hello?" she called, her voice echoing off the walls. "Is anyone there?" She called again and again, "Can someone come? Someone! Please!"

Silence.

SHE was so busy at work during the week that she didn't have time to think of anything except getting through the day. But on the weekends in her apartment, she was alone, alone-oh. Her parents divorcing felt like a difficult math problem. Mother + Daddy = Divorce. She couldn't understand the equation or how her parents had come up with this answer. It was beyond her skills, as if she had leapt from simple subtraction to complex algebra.

To get out, she began going to Chumley's, a tavern on Bedford Street, to write on Saturday afternoons. It was a cozy place with a beveled glass door, a beautiful wood bar with a dazzling array of liquor bottles doubled by the mirror behind them, and overstuffed couches and scarred wood tables and chairs scattered about. At night it was packed with the hip crowd of Greenwich Villagers—writers, artists, young people like Betsy who'd escaped the hinterlands, hipsters and musicians, intellectuals, or those posing as such, all smoking, arguing, laughing, talking, and drinking 'til all hours.

But on Saturday afternoons, there were mainly people stopping in for a coffee or beer, whiling away time with friends. The owner, a large Irishman named Mickey, made Betsy feel welcome. She would buy a cup of coffee and a Scotch egg and settle at a table under a yellow sconce light to write in her speckled notebook. She was writing stories based on some face or incident she'd seen on the street, letting the story unfurl quite apart from her own disturbed life, following along wherever the words led her. For those hours when she was writing, she was relieved of the anxiety and depression that had descended on her again after her parents' visit.

THERE was another regular on Saturday afternoons, a Negro man who also came there to write. He sat far back in the corner, near the swinging doors to the restrooms. He always had his head down, scribbling furiously with a pencil, sometimes erasing just as furiously. He never acknowledged anyone else; she could tell he wanted to be left alone. It wasn't too unusual to see a Negro in the Village. Still, at first it made Betsy uneasy. She was afraid something bad would happen to him—what, she didn't know. Back home, a colored man wouldn't have been allowed in an establishment like this.

One afternoon in September when Betsy passed by the man on her way to the restroom, he looked up at her. "What is it you're writing all the time?" he asked. A slight smile played across his face. She was taken by surprise, flustered. "Just stories," she stuttered. She was sure he was a real writer and knew she was a fake. She tried to determine in the low light how old he was. She'd thought, when he had his head down over his writing, that he was much older than she, but now she saw he was in his late twenties or early thirties. His skin was a rich dark brown that made her think of mahogany. He had curious, amused eyes in an alert, intelligent face. She was embarrassed to speak, reluctant to give herself away by her accent.

"Just stories."

"About . . . ?"

She didn't want to talk about her little efforts. But she didn't want to be rude either or for him to think she was prejudiced. "People I see. Out there," she said, nodding toward the street outside the tavern. She knew she was blushing deeply.

"Good," he said, and again that slight smile. Then he went back to his rushing pencil. When she went in the restroom, Betsy's heart was thumping wildly.

She had never spoken to a Negro man before. Of course she'd spoken to Huff when he picked Alma up, and she'd always been overly polite to the Negroes who filled the car and performed various services such as delivering coal to the house. But this was different. It wasn't the same as having a Negro, cream-colored Barnard girlfriend. This was a young, dark-skinned Negro man—the very thing Zora said Barnard wouldn't want on campus. He'd spoken to her as if she were just another person. The sky had not fallen.

After that, sometimes he'd say a few words whenever she made the trip to the ladies' room. One afternoon she got up the nerve to ask him what he was writing. He told her a novel about growing up in Harlem.

"I've never been to Harlem," Betsy said. Students from Barnard and Columbia had gone on dates to the white-owned clubs there, but she never had. When he nodded, she felt an impulse to reach out and touch his face. The low sconce above his table made his dark skin looked burnished. There was something about him that drew her.

"I'll take you sometime," he said. Then he started writing again.

Again the wildly beating heart.

NOTHING in her background had prepared her for Jerome Jackman—for they had introduced themselves at some point. Now her Saturdays took on shape and purpose. She looked forward to going to the tavern, to seeing Jerome and maybe having a few words with him: *How's it going? Not too bad. You? I'm lost!* she'd exclaim. From the way he cut his eyes, she could tell he anticipated her walking past him. But sometimes he wouldn't say anything, just raise his pencil briefly in greeting. Betsy would feel disappointed then, and when she sat back down at her table, she'd chew her bottom lip, finding it hard to concentrate.

It was just that she was so lonely, not just on the weekends but all the time. She wished Jerome would take her to Harlem. But he never mentioned it again. Where did he go when he left the tavern? He always left precisely at five o'clock. Maybe he had a wife, or if not, certainly a girlfriend. He radiated masculinity, a quality she hadn't found in the boys she'd dated in college. He usually wore a white T-shirt, even when it was cold outside, or a blue work shirt with the sleeves rolled to the elbows. His smooth, hairless forearms stirred something in her. His brown leather bombardier jacket hung on the back of his chair.

One Friday in July, her boss Bernard gave her two comp tickets to a play at a small theater in the East Village. Did she dare ask Jerome to go? It made her face burn to even think of it. Girls weren't supposed to ask boys out. And he was a Negro. A Negro man. Unthinkable.

Besides, when he laughed derisively, she'd have to stop going to the tavern. She'd be too embarrassed to face him again.

Still, she knew she would ask him. She couldn't stop herself. She'd make it casual, though. She practiced in front of her cloudy bathroom mirror, her blurry face looking young and scared, the opposite of confident and cool. *Oh, by the way, Jerome, I've got two free tickets to this play. If you'd like to go. With me, I mean. You're probably busy. I just thought . . .* But even practicing various lines in the privacy of her bathroom unnerved her.

Saturday came, and there he was, sitting in the back at his usual table, scribbling away. Betsy lived in fear that one day he wouldn't be there. He would have finished his novel or found another place to write. She tried to concentrate on her own writing but gave in to the impulse to doodle. She was so nervous. All she could think about was Jerome and how she was about to humiliate herself. But maybe, just maybe, she'd get to walk beside him down the street and sit next to him at the play. The thought of him sitting beside her, their arms casually touching, made her light-headed. What would they talk about? They'd never said more than a few words. Yet somehow she felt it would be all right. But how could that be? She might be reading it all wrong. Oh she just didn't know!

She waited an hour and then got up to go back to the restroom. She wished passing his table didn't always involve going to the ladies' room. He probably associated her with peeing. The weird white girl who always has to pee. Okay, not all the time, but still. Oh stop it, she told herself, putting on the brakes at his table. "Hi," she said nervously.

"Oh," he said, looking up with what she feared might be irritation. "Hi." He squinted his eyes in a way that made her wonder if he was angry at being disturbed. Maybe he was writing a crucial scene—maybe even the climax to his whole novel—and she had broken the spell.

"Hi," she repeated idiotically. There was nothing to do

but plunge ahead. "I don't guess you'd want to go to a play tonight. I have free tickets. I mean . . . with me." She blurted it so fast, she wondered if he could understand her. The roots of her hair tingled.

He chuckled a little, as if he found her amusing. Betsy was afraid of him, afraid of what he'd think of her, what a fool she was. He was so inscrutable, so male, so *Negro*. She squelched the desire to touch his wiry hair. She was a shy, inexperienced, young white female with limp brown hair in a ponytail, bangs that needed a trim, and a telltale accent. What was she doing asking Jerome Jackman out? It didn't make sense. She didn't know who he was, but even more importantly, she didn't know who she was. She was no longer the Southern girl in preppy clothes who'd left home for Barnard, nor was she one of the hip-looking women who strode the streets of Greenwich Village in their black berets, black turtlenecks, and short black skirts. Her conversations with Jerome had consisted of only a few words about nothing personal. He never asked her to sit down or came over to where she sat. She realized she didn't even know how tall he was. For all she knew, he was a foot shorter than she.

"Hmm, that's very nice of you," he said, tilting his head. She couldn't read his tone. Was he teasing her? She thought maybe so. Flirting? She couldn't believe it. He smiled that smile, which she now realized was not only sweet, but sexy. One front tooth slightly overlapped the other. She felt a strange spasm between her legs.

"What exactly is this play about?"

"I have no idea," she said. She couldn't stop the ridiculous grin that spread across her face.

He chuckled, at her she knew. "Tonight," he said, "won't

work." He seemed to find the whole thing amusing. Was there something in the way he looked at her? Some interest, attraction even? Oh that was just wishful thinking! Her heart was banging so hard, she was afraid he'd hear it.

"Okay," she managed to choke out and fled into the ladies' room. She stood over the sink, bracing herself against it, weak-kneed. In the mirror, she looked younger than her twenty-two years. She had asked Jerome Jackman to go out with her. Her pale face was splotchy red. What would people think, people back home in Greenville? Thank goodness he had the sense to say no. Because it could lead to . . . Again she felt that strange sensation between her legs.

If she could have stayed in that restroom forever, she would have. But she couldn't spend the night in there. When she passed by Jerome's table, he reached out and took hold of her wrist, lightly, stopping her. His warm fingers encircled her arm, and he held on just a beat longer than he needed to. Her legs felt wobbly, and her skin quivered where he touched her. "Maybe we could take that trip to Harlem," he said. Again that teasing smile. "I'll show you how my people live."

"Okay," Betsy said, breathlessly.

He suggested they meet tomorrow at noon in front of the tavern.

Betsy could only nod her assent, afraid her voice would quiver. When she got back to her table, she gathered her papers with shaking hands and hurried out the door.

26

ALMA

ONE EVENING AFTER supper when she was feeling particularly lonely, Alma walked the eight blocks to Synthia's apartment. She'd stopped drinking, but it left a deep hole in her that was always demanding to be filled. Tonight the need was extra strong. She'd taken out the last picture of Pretty she'd received. She was a skinny little girl now, toothpick arms and legs, wearing a purple crinoline dress and a big bow on top of her head. Alma wondered if she'd even recognize her own daughter in a group of little girls. Seeing Synthia would take her mind off her hurt. Synthia always picked her up.

When she knocked on her door, there was no answer. She was just turning away when Synthia slowly opened the door. She had on a black silk robe open in front, revealing her slender naked body. Her eyes were glassy in the dim hall light. A voice sounded from the bedroom: "Get your tail back in here! I ain't paying you to answer no door."

How could Alma have been so dumb! Synthia was using! And tricking! That's how she bought her fine clothes on her chambermaid's salary. That's why some days she was unable to focus, making stupid mistakes in rooms she cleaned. Alma had passed it off, thinking Synthia had a bad hangover or hadn't been able to sleep, something Alma was familiar with herself. They stared at each other for a long, hopeless moment. Then Synthia sank down in a heap right at Alma's feet.

Alma's heart clutched for one stunned moment, then she pushed open the door and screamed to the man inside, "Help me!" She tried to lift Synthia, but she was floppy deadweight. A heavy-set man came out of the bedroom, naked, angry. He had that same vacant look that Synthia had had. He disappeared back into the bedroom and almost knocked Alma over as he ran past her out the door, pulling on his pants and shirt as he went. "Come back!" Alma screamed after him, but he was scrambling down the stairs.

To Alma's horror, Synthia's eyes rolled back in her head. Alma cradled her head in her lap, slapping her cheeks, trying to revive her. "Help! Help!" she screamed into the hall, but no one opened a door. Alma ran down the dim hallway, beating on every door until finally a man cautiously cracked his a bit. Alma gasped, "Overdose! Call an ambulance!" The man was impassive, but he said he would and shut the door in her face.

Shaking all over, Alma rushed back to Synthia. She'd vomited, a putrid liquid and bits of undigested food staining her chin and neck. Alma turned her head to the side and reached into Synthia's mouth to try to clear the vomit. Synthia lay in Alma's arms, ragdoll limp, while Alma tried to pray some life back into her. After an eternity, she heard a siren pulling up in front of the building. Now a few people poked their heads out their doors or came out on the upper landings. Alma screamed for someone to go downstairs and tell the medics where to come. "Go! Go! Go!" she yelled, furious with anger and terror. Was Synthia dead or alive? Alma couldn't tell. She began sobbing as the medics took over, carrying Synthia out on a stretcher. Two white policeman appeared and told Alma they were taking her to the station.

"No! No!" Alma begged, crying harder, trembling all over. "I have to go with her!"

But they didn't care. They wanted to know about the heroin, about who had been with Synthia. It was after one o'clock in the morning before they finished questioning her. She still had the slip of paper Catfish had given her with his phone number in her pocketbook. She called him from the desk phone at the 135th Street station. In ten minutes he pulled up in front, and Alma went running out to his car, frantic to get to the hospital. He drove her to Bellevue, and there they learned that Synthia had died.

Too stunned to cry, Alma leaned into Catfish's chest. He held her tightly, resting his chin on the top of her head. How could Synthia be dead? Not Synthia! Why couldn't she have saved her?

CATFISH drove them to his apartment. Alma stood shivering on the front stoop while he parked the car. She remembered the night when Catfish, Randall, Synthia, and she had come here after drinking and dancing at a club. Synthia had playfully tapped out a little rhythm with the brass knocker on the door, intoxicated and full of life! Now Catfish opened the front door, took her by the arm, steered her into the living room, and turned on a table lamp. Alma expected to see Synthia come out of the bedroom, laughing, flirting, teasing Alma for being such a square, putting her arm around her, giving her a squeeze.

Something stunk: Synthia's vomit on her coat. Catfish directed her to the bathroom. She dabbed at the stains with a towel, feeling sick to her stomach. She avoided looking in the mirror. Her head felt hollow.

When she came back into the living room, Catfish took her by the elbow as if she might stumble and helped her to the sofa. He handed her a big goblet with a little dark liquid shimmering in the bottom. "Cognac," he said. "It'll help." He went to the stereo and put on Coltrane. They sat in silence for what might have been an hour, until Catfish finally held out his hand.

Alma put her cold hand in his large warm one and stood up. He gently folded her against him. They barely moved, just swaying to the music. Alma felt his strong body against hers, his arms supporting her. Tears filled her eyes and flowed down her cheeks, wetting his shirt.

"We're both very tired," he finally said, his mouth against her hair. "And I have to work tomorrow. We need to get some rest."

He led her into the bedroom, the same one that Synthia and Randall had used. The covers were flung back; he must have been asleep when she called from the police station. She was hesitant to lie down. "It's all right," Catfish said. "I won't unless you want to." She sat on the edge of the bed, looking at him. He was such a decent man. "I still love my husband," she said, and as soon as she spoke the words, she knew they were true. "I'm sorry."

She lay down and curled on her side, drawing her knees up. He went around to the other side of the bed and got in, his weight shifting the mattress. He lay against her back, wrapping his arms around her. "Hush little baby, don't say a word," he sang softly into her ear. "Mama's gonna buy you a mockingbird." He held her, nuzzling her hair as he hummed the lullaby, his hands locked protectively around hers where she had them clenched against her chest.

They lay together like that until daylight broke through the slats of the blinds.

WHEN she arrived back at the apartment, it was almost six in the morning. Ladocia was waiting for her.

"This here is the last straw, Alma Stone! I can't have the aggravation of you around here. My nerves cain't take it! I didn't bring you up here to cat around."

Alma just nodded. She didn't try to tell Ladocia what had happened. Ladocia had never approved of Synthia.

SHE packed her suitcase and carried it to the hotel where she could store it for the day. All the girls already knew about Synthia. There was a pall in the staff room. Alma asked Marbel where she might find a place. After work she carried the suitcase over to 140th Street and knocked on the door of a run-down tenement with a "Rooms to Let" sign out front. All she could afford was a room in a cold water flat with a bathroom at the end of the hall.

She kept to herself at work. But she came back every evening to the bleak room to meet her old lover, Mr. Jim Beam. At night, alone, she'd tip the bottle until she drifted into a daze in which nothing hurt, nothing, that is, until the sun hit her east-facing window, and then everything hurt.

Sometimes she'd walk past Abyssinian Baptist Church and think about going in. But then she'd keep walking. Without her "medicine"—the same medicine Ray had given her that first night in Harlem—she couldn't sleep. She'd lie awake and think about all she wanted to forget. 'Round about midnight, she'd hum the moonlight song.

27

BETSY

WHEN BETSY APPROACHED the tavern on Sunday, there was Jerome, wearing his bombardier jacket and leaning against the brick wall, smoking a cigarette. It was shocking to see him outside the tavern. He wasn't too tall, but tall enough; an inch or two taller than she, even wearing her recently acquired wedge sandals with slingback straps. It was too chilly for sandals. Still, they made her legs look long and shapely; she did have good legs, her best asset. She had on a blazer over her shirt-waist dress, but still she was shivering, whether from the brisk October weather or excitement, she didn't know. "Hi!" she said too exuberantly. "So you came," he said. "I wondered . . ." His teeth shone white in the light of day. She wanted to drink him in now that they were out of the dark tavern. Instead she made herself stare up Bedford Street, as if it were of great interest to her. "Aren't the trees beautiful," she said, though she was so rattled she didn't even know if there were trees. He just laughed and directed her to come along.

They fell into step, walking to the subway. "Hope you got

on your walking shoes." He peered down skeptically at her wedgies. They were squeezing her toes.

On the subway she thought people were staring at them: the white girl and the Negro man. She detected disapproval from a couple of them. Jerome ignored any looks, keeping his eyes on some indeterminate space. Betsy thought of her parents. She missed them. She wondered when, if ever, she would be finished punishing them. She hadn't gone home all summer, pretending she was too busy to talk on the phone very often. She didn't let on that she was sad and lonely, keeping their conversations short and superficial. What would they think of her going out with Jerome? She put that out of her mind.

She didn't know what to say to him. What could they possibly have in common? She let the clanking of the subway fill the silence. He didn't seem to mind. They caught the A train and got off at 116th Street and Seventh Avenue. When they came up onto the street, they entered a different world: a Negro world. Here, Negroes owned the universe. Betsy was dazzled and frightened by all the dark people milling about: families with baby carriages and little children; women dressed to the nines in their Sunday suits and lavish hats; men whom Jerome pointed out as pimps or numbers bankers; a soapbox orator preaching on the street corner; shoeshine boys calling out, "Shine, shine!" Cadillacs radiating money cruised slowly by. Shady-looking men eyed her lecherously. Dark-skinned women called out greetings in Spanish or familiar, colored Southern drawls. Betsy felt very white and very out of place. She'd never seen so much human activity, a beehive of blackness.

Jerome showed her the huge Graham Court apartment building, which had been commissioned at the turn of the century by William Waldorf Astor, and the Regent Theater, a magnificent movie palace. They walked to 125th Street, past the Hotel Theresa, where Jerome said they might see Sugar Ray pull up in his pink Cadillac. The streets were crowded and dirty, so many people in too little space. Yet the atmosphere was exciting and alive.

Jerome wanted to show her where the Tree of Hope had been on Seventh Avenue. They stopped in front of a building that was now a church but had once been The Lafayette Theater.

"Bessie Smith, Louis Armstrong, and Duke Ellington. They all played the Lafayette. Do you know these names?" He didn't wait for her to answer. "It was the first of the major Harlem theaters to desegregate. Back in the twenties, this street was called the Boulevard of Dreams. A lone elm grew here." He pointed to a square of cement. "Folks would rub its bark to give them luck. My mama used to bring me here all the time. Woman 'bout rubbed the bark off that tree. They cut it down the year I turned ten."

"Was your mother a performer?" Betsy asked.

Jerome let out a dry laugh. "In a manner of speaking."

All along the street, he called out to people he knew. They walked past tenements where children were playing on fire escapes and boys were batting rubber balls with broom handles. Smells of savory food—the Southern food Alma had cooked—mixed with exotic spices and the stench of spoiled garbage from overflowing cans in the alleys; jazz played on radios behind open windows, Charlie Parker, Dizzy Gillespie. As they walked, Jerome told her stories from his childhood, some happy, some sad, some bitter. He pointed out his grammar school, the storefront church he'd attended growing up, and the tenement where he was born. He didn't show her where he lived now, and something stopped her from asking.

I T was dark by the time they got back to the Village. Betsy assumed they'd part ways, but Jerome led her to a dive down a short stairwell. They sat in a corner booth, right next to each other, his thigh touching hers every now and then. Was that by accident? What would she like, he asked politely. She had no idea, no appetite, too stirred up by the day to consider food. He ordered them beer and chicken sandwiches. He talked about how he hadn't gotten much of an education, the schools in Harlem were so bad. But it didn't matter, because all the time he was reading anything he could get his hands on. *Uncle Tom's Cabin*, *Reader's Digest*, *Life* magazine. He'd read the Bible backward and forward and *The New Yorker* at the 125th Street library. He'd read Richard Wright, Langston Hughes, Zora Neal Hurston. Steinbeck and Faulkner. And he was always writing. Writing was what saved his life, he said. She could feel his leg jumping next to hers.

He worked as a reporter for the *Amsterdam News*, a Negro newspaper she'd probably never heard of, right? "There's not a murder, rape, fight, suicide, or salacious affair—especially if it involves a prominent Negro that we don't blast on the front page," he said wearily. "And believe me, there's plenty of violence to go around, the more sensational the better. People love to read about stabbings and scandals. It sells newspapers." Had she heard of James Baldwin? He was writing a brilliant novel, *Go Tell It on the Mountain*. Jimmy was a friend, Jerome said, dragging harder on his cigarette, his leg next to hers jumping faster. He'd take her to meet Jimmy where he was staying in the Village some evening.

She asked him why he came to the Village to write. He blew smoke up toward the ceiling. "Have you ever wanted to just escape to another world," he asked her, "if only for a little while?" He turned to study her. "No, probably not."

"You're wrong," she said. "I know that feeling very well."

He walked her back to her apartment building on Carmine. He was going back to Harlem. She wondered where exactly he was going there. When they got to her building, she wanted to say, "See you next Saturday?" but she wasn't sure he would even be at the tavern again. He hadn't asked her a single thing about herself. But she was used to that from the Columbia boys she'd dated.

HE was there the next Saturday afternoon, bent over his notebook, scribbling. Every so often he glanced up, and she knew he was looking for her. As she was pulling out her usual chair to sit down, he lifted his pencil to her in greeting. She put off going to the restroom as long as she could. When she passed by his table, he looked up and said, "There you are. I thought you might not come back. I wondered if I said or did anything to offend you."

"No," she said, shaking her head hard.

"Next time I'll take you to one of my places." Again that sexy smile.

THIS time they stayed in the Village. They went to the Five Spot, a jazz club where he knew the musicians, some Negro, some white. It was so crowded they had trouble getting in the door. Dark and smoky, the Five Spot was packed with hip-looking white people, cool-looking Negroes, many of whom Jerome knew, and amazing jazz that sounded to her like the spirit of the Village itself. It didn't matter who or what you were in the Village. You could be anyone. She'd told her parents their getting divorced was the end of her world. Well, this was the world she wanted now.

Jerome ordered her a martini and left her sitting at the bar. She watched him as he moved around the packed room, greeting people. He was poised and graceful, laughing with his white teeth flashing in his dark face. What did he see in her? Was he playing with her? She was dazzled by him, amazed that she was dating a colored man. It didn't seem possible. He brought over a couple of his friends and introduced her over the din. When he sat back down beside her, she felt something electric pass between them. She sensed he felt it too.

THEY began going out on the weekends, visiting different clubs and bars, always ending up at the Five Spot. One night when they left the club, it was snowing, the flakes large and sloppy wet. It was early December, the first snow of the year, one that wouldn't last. Instead of going the few blocks back to her apartment, they began walking through the twisted streets of the Village. Impulsively she slipped her arm through his, and he hugged her to him. At Washington Square, he took off his jacket and tented it over her head. They stopped at the fountain, dry, it never worked, and in the snow there, he put his soft lips against hers, holding her gently by both arms. Without a word, they walked on. They said goodbye hurriedly at her building's door.

Climbing the stairs to the fourth floor, Betsy realized that this strange feeling she had was happiness. Pure happiness. She'd never felt it before.

28

LAWTON

LAWTON CARRIED AROUND the napkin with Poinsett Sam's number in his wallet, but he had no intention of calling. Sometimes he'd take it out and carefully smooth it. After a while, the penciled number began to fade into the cheap paper, so he copied it in ink in his calendar. Donny had told him to stay away from Sam. When Lawton asked him why, Donny shrugged. "He's a type. And not yours." He left it at that, and Lawton didn't push him, not wanting to hear. But sometimes Sam would visit him in his dreams, his tattooed arms pulling Lawton to his chest.

He hadn't intended to go back to the bar near the ice plant, but late one fall night he found himself opening the door to the back room. It was the same scene—crowded, smoky, men drinking and paired off, in some cases, kissing. A lot of the men who came there had been in the war, Donny had explained in one of his lectures as a professional homosexual, where they'd discovered the pleasures of other men. Lawton sat at the end of the bar and observed the scene. Some of the men were clearly effeminate. Others looked normal, Lawton thought, the way he hoped he looked; no one would guess they were "different." Quite a few were muscle men, brawny, tough types. Sam was nowhere in sight, which was a relief.

He'd been there a couple of hours, had one too many drinks, and was just about to leave when he heard a voice saying to the guy on the stool next to his, "Do you mind?" in a way that left little choice. He turned to look Sam right in the face. "Scotch," Sam said to Joey behind the bar, and Lawton, whose glass was almost empty, held his up for a refill.

The bartender poured scotch into two glasses and set them in front of them. "Pay up," he said to Sam. "You know the rules."

"Put his on my tab," Lawton said.

"In that case, make mine a double." Grinning, Sam held out his glass for an extra shot.

They drank in silence for several long minutes. Lawton found the silence uncomfortable, but he couldn't think of a thing to say, and Sam offered nothing. It had been so easy to talk to Donny that first night he had come here. They'd told each other their queer histories, cutting to the chase, getting right to the heart of the matter. It was worth a try.

"Tell me," he said to Sam, feeling boozy and a little shaky, "when did you first know?"

"That you were a fag?"

Lawton grimaced. "That you were."

Sam snorted and drained his glass. "I was eleven," he said. "A couple of the neighborhood boys—Beany Alexander and Jack Rogers—caught me down by the creek. They were older—thirteen and fourteen." He gave a mirthless laugh. "They knew about me before I did!" He held up his glass to

Joey, who filled it again when Lawton nodded to him. "Of course I was frightened. Of course it hurt." Another swig. "But the funny thing was," and here he paused for effect, "I went looking for them the next day."

Lawton felt dizzy, whether from the scotch or the story, he wasn't sure.

"Did you ever tell anyone?"

"Yes," Sam said. "You. You're the first." He gave it a beat. Then he laughed and slapped Lawton on the back. "You came looking for me tonight, didn't you?"

"I came for a drink," Lawton said. "And I think I've had enough. More than enough."

"You sure as hell didn't come looking for that fairy Donny."

Lawton was motioning to Joey for his tab when suddenly there was a loud pounding at the backroom door. "Raid!" someone screamed. Men began stampeding for an exit in a back hall. The police were pounding on the door, trying to break it in. Lawton froze, the implications of being caught here washing over him.

Sam grabbed him by the upper arm and pulled him toward the bathroom. The door was locked, but Sam drew back and broke the lock with one massive kick. Two men inside shrank back. Sam pushed them aside roughly, reared back again and kicked out the frame of the filthy window. Glass shattered on the gravel below. "Go, go!" he said to Lawton, giving him a boost up. Lawton slithered through the opening, falling face down on the gritty dirt below, pieces of glass cutting his cheek. Sam landed on top of him, and they scrambled up and ran down the alley in the opposite direction from the other fleeing men, cutting through beside an industrial warehouse. They ran through dark streets and alleys Lawton didn't know existed, running until he feared his heart would explode. They ended up in Southernside, the colored neighborhood Lawton recognized from taking Alma home. They collapsed on a patch of dry grass in a vacant lot, unable to speak.

After they'd caught their breath, Sam sneered, "Did you see how those fags scattered like cockroaches!" He laughed to himself. Then, "You okay?"

"I think so," Lawton said, putting his fingers up to his face in the dark. He took out his handkerchief and dabbed gingerly at the places where cinders and glass had cut it. "You saved my life," he said to Sam.

"Yes I did," Sam said. "Or at least your ass."

"How did you know what to do?" It was a clear night, and Lawton's eyes were adjusting to the dark. A harvest moon cast a strange, spooky light on the sleeping shanties. A couple of stray dogs came sniffing, and Sam kicked at them, sending them scurrying.

"Marines," Sam said. "Sixth Division."

"God! If I'd been arrested—"

"Well, you weren't," Sam said, slapping him on the back again. "I could use a beer."

They'd passed a small store several blocks back. Ten or twelve Negro men were hanging around outside, drinking and laughing. They'd gone silent as Lawton and Sam ran past. Now Sam headed in that direction. Lawton wondered if he'd ever see him again, but in a few minutes he was back with two six-packs. "Niggers take white money as good as colored," he said jovially. "Let's go to my place and have us a party."

THEY took back streets in case the police were out prowling. As they walked, they drank. Lawton hadn't realized how

parched his throat was. He learned that Sam was now working at the warehouse they'd run past, driving a forklift. "It
suits me better," he said, "than sucking up to rich guys like
you." He chortled about backing over a nigger there, breaking his leg. He slapped Lawton on the back yet again, a little
harder than was necessary. Lawton was feeling winded and
weak. He knew he should just go home. But he followed Sam
to a row of three-story weathered boarding houses near the
depot, an area Lawton would normally avoid. Sam led him up
the back stairs to his room on the top floor. "Welcome to my
castle," he said, unlocking the door.

There was a daybed with clothes spread all over it, laundry hanging from a makeshift clothesline across one side of
the room, dirty dishes piled in the sink, ashtrays full of old
butts, and empty beer bottles everywhere. "If you think this
is nice," Sam said, "you gotta see the bedroom." He motioned
Lawton into another equally chaotic room, with an unmade
double bed, the covers tangled on the floor as if its occupant
had wrestled with the devil during the night. Sam switched
on a small lamp on the floor by the bed; the lampshade had a
hole burned in it.

Sam flopped down on the bed, punching a flat pillow up
and wadding it under his head.

"Bring us them brews."

Lawton got one of the six-packs from what passed for a
counter and brought it into the bedroom. Sam was propped
up in bed, smoking. Lawton handed him a beer and took one
for himself. There was nowhere to sit except on the bed. He
perched on the end of it, near Sam's feet, feeling both uneasy
and excited.

They drank in silence. Then Sam lay back and shut his eyes.

"Maybe I should go," Lawton said.

"You don't really want to," Sam said without opening his eyes.

Lawton didn't answer. He felt exhausted and inebriated. He lay down next to Sam.

"I thought so. That's more like it." Sam reached down and cupped his hand on Lawton's crotch. "Which way do you like it?"

Lawton sat up. "I'm going."

"Like hell you are," Sam said. "You didn't come here to go, you came here to come."

"No, I mean it. I have to leave." He started to get up, but his legs felt wobbly.

"Christ!" Sam said. "I should have known. You're just a goddamn cock tease!" He leaned across the bed suddenly and hit Lawton in the face.

Pain exploded in his skull, like a bomb had gone off there. It took a moment to regain his senses. Blood flowed into his mouth. He struggled to his feet.

"Hand it over."

Lawton tilted his head back, squeezing his nose with his handkerchief to try to stop the bleeding. "What!"

"'What!'" Sam mocked in a high girly voice. "You fucking cocksucker. I saved your fucking life, remember?" He was leaning up on one elbow now, glaring at Lawton.

Lawton fumbled for his wallet and took out all his cash.

He left Sam counting it and ran down the back stairs two at a time. He began running down Lloyd Street, afraid Sam was coming after him. But after a few blocks, he stopped. He was alone in a deserted area near some railroad tracks. The sky was just brightening in the East. He walked until he came to the bridge over the Reedy River on South Main Street, and from there he made his way back to The Davenport. He'd leave his car for now. He didn't want to go anywhere near Hurley's.

He hated himself with a burning fervor.

29

BETSY

IN COLLEGE SHE hadn't understood about love. Most of the girls—at least the popular, pretty ones—were obsessing over fiancées and future husbands with the same obsession she now felt for Jerome. She'd dated a fair share. She'd made out, let a few boys get to second base, one to third. She'd squirmed and faked heavy breathing. She'd touched a few hard bulges in khaki pants. But she'd never been in love, until now.

Before long, kissing in the shadows was not enough. But Jerome never asked to come up to her apartment. He treated her with diffidence. Because she was a white girl? Once, much later, when they were thoroughly intimate, she asked if he'd had any other white girls. He had laughed, ambiguously she thought. "No, Bets, you're my first." *And your last?* she wanted to ask, but by then she was afraid of what he might say.

One night as they stood across from her building in one of the dark shadows, lingering as usual, reluctant to say goodnight, she could stand it no longer. She asked if he'd like to come up. His eyebrows raised in surprise. A complex expression crossed his face, resolving in an enigmatic smile.

Betsy started up the four flights to her apartment alone, in case Mr. Lastrada popped out of his door. Jerome would follow stealthily ten minutes later. She worried that if her super knew about him, he might evict her. Mr. Lastrada had feelings about Negroes.

On the second flight of stairs, knowing what was about to happen (it was she, after all, who'd invited him up), a part of Betsy stood back, amazed. She was about to lose her virginity. She was not going to save herself for marriage. Not only was she going to have sex out of wedlock, she was going to do it with a Negro! She was about to throw overboard all she had been raised to hold dear. She thought of her mother. She swallowed hard. And Grand Bee and Grandfather Lyman! She was about to commit miscegenation. She wasn't sure what miscegenation actually was. At the third story landing, she stopped to make sure. Then ran up the last flight of stairs.

She didn't know how these things worked. She'd expected him to take her in his arms, kiss her passionately the way he did on the street. But he was off script. He looked around the studio, examined her hat collection hanging on the wall as if it were of great interest. Betsy, lost at sea, told him she'd just be a moment. Was that what she was supposed to say? In the bathroom, she hurriedly took off all her clothes (before she lost her nerve) and put on her pink chiffon robe. When she came out, Jerome was sitting at the yellow Formica table. She had no idea how to proceed. Awkwardly she put her arms around him from behind and kissed his neck. He sat still as a stone.

Didn't he want her? Wasn't that what they were here to do? Finally, when she slipped between the covers, he stood up. In the light cast from the half-open bathroom door, she watched him as he began to take off his jeans, his white T-shirt, and finally, heart-stoppingly, his white underwear. His body was muscular and lean, his skin such a delicious shade of brown she wanted to lick him all over. She avoided looking at his penis. She'd never seen one before and was afraid to look. Besides, it seemed impolite.

They lay in bed and began to kiss. But it wasn't like when they kissed in the shadows on the street. Now it felt as if they were play-acting a love scene. Betsy tried to regain the feeling of intense desire she always had around him, but she felt stiff with anxiety and uncertainty.

Finally, when it seemed the actual moment was near, she had to whisper in his neck, "I don't . . . really know what to do."

He froze in midair above her. There was a moment of silence as he stared down at her. Then he emitted an incredulous sound halfway between a laugh and cry. "I've never met anyone as innocent as you, Bets!" he exclaimed. She detected what she thought was affection rather than exasperation in his voice. Then he resumed kissing her, running his hand lightly back and forth between her legs. It was the first time she had seen a condom, though by no means the last.

AFTER that first time, their evenings at bars culminated not just in kisses in the shadows, but separate trips up the four flights of stairs. Going ahead of him, Betsy had just enough time to brush her teeth, pee, undress, and don the pink robe, trembling with the thought that soon, Jerome would remove it.

She couldn't tell if Jerome knew she was frigid, a condition she'd read about in a women's magazine. He loved sex so much himself, wanting her all the time, he must have assumed she was enjoying what they did as much as he. It built her confidence. Gradually, over the next few weeks, his desire made her feel desirable, possibly even sexy, a new experience. Sexy was not something her upbringing had encouraged. She began to catch on, becoming relaxed, playful, creative in ways to please him. Sometimes when he was in her, rising up above her, he would tell her she was beautiful, his brown eyes looking right into hers. She had to shut her own eyes against such intensity.

Finally when "it" happened, she felt like a boat being pulled toward a dam by an irresistible current. Over she went!

That first time, she blurted out, "I love you, Jerome!"

"I love you too, Bets."

A perfect moment.

CHRISTMAS came and went, and Betsy didn't even consider going home. She didn't want to miss any time with Jerome, and she didn't want to face her parents. She'd begun talking to them separately once a week on the phone, but she kept those calls short. She told them she was dating lots of boys, and the agency needed her during the busy time. Besides, staying in New York, not going home for the holidays, meant she was an adult with an independent life of her own.

One night she told Jerome about how her folks had gotten a divorce. "It's like they lost their minds!" she exclaimed. "I mean, why? I don't get it!" She fought back tears, but when she broke down, Jerome held her until she cried it out. "Maybe their love ran out," Jerome said into her hair.

She pulled back from him. "What do you mean? You make it sound so simple! Love doesn't just 'run out.'" Now she was mad at him, as well as her folks. "These are my parents, Jerome. They're ... they're ... good people," she finished lamely. But who were they, really, these parents? She thought of them like a salt and pepper set. There couldn't be one without the other.

"Maybe one of them's having an affair."

She scoffed. "You don't know my parents."

"Do you?"

"Of course I do. I mean. I did . . . I thought. Oh I don't want to talk about it anymore!"

THEY were both working on their writing. They'd sit across from each other at her yellow table, scribbling away. Sometimes they'd read each other a passage. She could see the future: She and Jerome would be writers together, leading a Bohemian life in the Village—their friends other writers, musicians, and artists. Maybe they'd travel to Paris or Rome, live abroad. How her mother and father—and his mother, who lived in Harlem but whom he hadn't introduced Betsy to—fit into this picture, she couldn't fathom. She put it out of her mind. She and Jerome were living for today.

ALL day every day that winter Jerome Jackman lived in her. He was always there, a secret, obsessive presence. She thought about sex all the time, of when she could be with him again, and what they would do. She asked one of the actresses she knew from work where she could get a diaphragm, afraid to trust the weird Trojans. She directed her to a doctor on the Upper East Side. Getting pregnant—especially with Jerome!— too horrible to even think about.

Sometimes Jerome would tease her about her accent, mocking it. He would play that he was a slave on her plantation, saying "Mistress Liza" could do with him what she would, tussling with her before sex. She couldn't help laughing, though it made her uncomfortable. He had never been below the Mason-Dixon line, and he made it clear that was somewhere he didn't care to go.

One evening he started kidding her about being a Mississippi cracker—as if he thought all Southerners were from Mississippi. She reminded him she was from South Carolina. "Greenville," she added.

His mood changed completely. He pulled away from her and sat up in bed.

Alarm coursed through her. She put a hand on his shoulder, tried to pull him back down next to her. "What's wrong?"

"That's where y'all lynched that nigger," he said, getting up and going to sit at the yellow table. "We carried that story. All the papers—the *Pittsburgh Courier, The New York Times*— all the rags carried it. They tried to cut his heart out while he was still alive." He paused to let this sink in. "I guess that's the way you treat niggers down in Greenville, South Carolina." He spat the name, emphasizing "South."

He'd turned away from her, his jaw locked.

She got out of bed and sat down across from him. When they were alone, in bed, the outside world didn't exist. In bed, the only reality was theirs. Now other realities made themselves known.

"My father was one of the prosecutors," she said. "He wanted a conviction." She took his hand in hers. "Willie Earle has nothing to do with you! With us!"

Finally his face softened. He turned to look at her, contrite. "No, you're right, Bets," he said, nodding his head. "I'm sorry. Sometimes . . . it all just gets to me."

She didn't ask what got to him. He withdrew his brown

hand from her white one.

He began pulling on his khakis and T-shirt. "Are you going!"

"Got a busy week ahead. Catch you in a few days." He kissed her on the lips. Then he was gone.

SHE hadn't dreamed of the empty cell in a long time. But after Jerome left that night she dreamed of it again, the same wretched cell she'd seen when she and her father went to Pickens. Only now she saw herself sitting on the cot, her hands clasped between her knees. She'd been arrested for committing a crime. She didn't even know what she'd done. Only that she was guilty.

SHE didn't hear from Jerome for a week—a week of agony for her—but then he was back. They resumed, without saying a word about what had happened or where he'd been.

Sometimes as they lay in bed after sex, he'd tell her stories about growing up in Harlem: a knife fight he'd witnessed where a friend of his was stabbed and died on the street before an ambulance came; young mothers he knew who prostituted themselves because they couldn't feed their children; boys getting hooked at twelve, thirteen; the insults and abuse he had faced in the army from white soldiers; the way some people still called him "boy." She would listen silently, curled against his back, holding him, trying to transmit through his skin how much she loved him.

HE took her to the apartment where Jimmy Baldwin was staying. There were twelve or fifteen people of both races sitting on the floor. The place was sparsely furnished, with bare hardwood floors, a hi-fi, and long windows with floor-length curtains. Baldwin was seated in a high-backed green brocade armchair, smoking and holding forth to the group. He had a striking, sculpted face, bulging hooded eyes, and a wide, feminine mouth. His eyes were penetrating, his fingers delicate. Betsy realized he was a homosexual. It was in the way he held his cigarette, how he kissed some of the male guests on the lips, the whole androgynous look of him. She'd never known any homosexuals personally, though she'd seen pairs of men—queers or fairies they were called—in the Village. Here was a man who loved other men, who had sex with other men! Yet everyone here revered Baldwin—a Negro homosexual intellectual.

At some point in the evening, Baldwin began saying how Negro servants had been stealing from their white employers for generations. "And the white folk are delighted to have them do it," he said, "because it confirms that whites are morally superior." He spoke in beautifully cadenced sentences, as if he were reading, so perfect was his diction and thought. "And yet it's the whites who have robbed the Negro of his liberty and who profit constantly by this theft." She felt her pale face turn red. She sensed how the other whites around her on the floor were chastised too. "The whites consider themselves Christians, but the virtues they preach but don't practice are in fact another way of subjugating the Negro." She saw Jerome nodding in agreement.

Walking home, Betsy told Jerome that Baldwin had it wrong. "Alma would never have taken anything from our house," she said. "Bessie and Macie would never *steal*!" They'd been raised as she'd been, not to steal—*Thou shalt not steal*. The Negroes Baldwin was talking about were not the

Negroes she knew. The whites were not the whites she knew.

"Don't your folks accept that Negroes should come in the back door?" Jerome said in a strangely quiet voice. "Don't they accept that Negroes sit in the back of the bus, eat on separate dishes, use only colored restrooms, aren't allowed to stay in white motels or get good jobs?" These were not really questions. "Don't they approve of Negro children attending schools that they know are second-rate, if that?" He paused. "Don't they let lynchers go free?"

"It's not that simple!" she cried. "Why are you doing this!"

They walked home in silence. Jerome didn't come up that night. She didn't hear from him for two excruciating weeks. Then he was back, reaching for her, pulling her down on her single bed.

JEROME never spent the night; this became a point of contention. He always said he needed to get back to his place to finish up whatever story he was working on for the paper. She asked if she could see his room, but he said there wasn't much to see. She didn't even know his address, and he said he didn't have a phone, always calling her from the office.

Sometimes he'd disappear for a week or two without calling. She knew she risked ruining things by wanting him too much. She lived in fear he was seeing someone else. Or maybe he'd only wanted a white girlfriend, and now the novelty had worn off. But then she reasoned that he was busy; newspaper reporting was demanding. Still, she didn't understand why he couldn't at least call. When she tried to chide him, mildly, he didn't understand—perhaps because he didn't want to. Too many days with no word from him tortured her. Once, after they'd had one of their arguments, he said to her, "Don't you know by now that I want you, and I will always want you?" She was thrilled. But when he left later that night after another round of lovemaking, she lay alone in bed wondering when she would see him next. Was "want" the same as "love"?

A YEAR had passed since that first kiss. It was December again, a cold wind whipping through the twisted streets of the Village, howling down the corridors between the skyscrapers in Midtown and through the interstices of Betsy's heart. She worried that she was losing Jerome. She didn't know when, but he'd stopped calling her "Bets."

She was dreaming of the empty cell again. Most of the time, the images faded, leaving only amorphous feelings of loss. But one night when Jerome hadn't called in a week, she dreamed she saw a shadowy naked black man pressed against the bars, violently shaking the locked cell door. She knew that back, those muscular shoulders and arms. *Jerome!* The anguish of it jolted her awake. Alone in her single bed, she began sobbing.

She decided to tell Jerome about the dream. He might even comfort her. She'd feel less alone. For at some point, she'd begun to feel alone.

She tried to pick the right moment, when he was softened and receptive, curled against her back after sex. "Can I tell you something?"

"Of course."

She was silent, gathering herself, speaking quietly in the dark.

"My father took me with him when he went to interview the jailer at the jail where Willie Earle had been. I was seventeen. We saw the cell they took him from. After that I began to have nightmares." She waited for some word from him. After a long moment he said, "Go on, baby."

"At first in the dreams, the cell contained my things. Sometimes there were things I didn't quite recognize, but I knew they were mine. The cell was always empty. It was me who'd been taken." He gathered her tighter against him.

"Then the nightmares changed. Now it was me locked in the cell. I was the prisoner." When he said nothing, she wondered if she should go on.

"A few nights ago, I dreamed about the cell again. Only this time, it was you in the cell, Jerome."

She felt his breath catch. He loosened his hands from hers.

A cold dread came over her. "I'm sorry," she said, trying to turn over to face him. "I didn't mean . . ."

But he was unwrapping himself from her. When he got out of bed, cold air rushed in, chilling her.

Naked, he crossed to the fridge and took out a beer. He switched on the overhead light, shocking in its harshness, and sat down at the table without a word, half-turned away from her.

Shaken, she studied Jerome in the unforgiving light—his strong bare arms that had embraced her, his closed, unreadable face, the arc of his back—the same back she'd seen in the dream. At that moment, she hated him for never telling her what he was thinking and feeling. For being so . . . male. So . . . Negro.

Now he turned to face her. "Maybe you're only sleeping with me because I'm a nigger."

He might as well have slapped her. "Are you crazy!"

"White girls love black cock," he said coldly.

"That's disgusting, Jerome! I *love* you!"

When he was silent, she did the only thing she knew to

do. She went to him, put her arms around him, began kissing his neck, running her hands up and down his hairless chest. Soon enough, he followed her over to her narrow bed pushed against the wall, where there was only room for them to lie together, entwined.

When he left that night, he said he'd see her soon.

Then he was gone.

AT first she thought he would be back in a week or two, as he'd done before. By the third week when she didn't hear from him, it began to occur to her that he might not be coming back. Her mind was obsessed with what had gone wrong: It was just a dream! A mistake to tell him, she saw that now, but couldn't they talk it out? Maybe he had just grown tired of her.

After a month, she was still in a state of disbelief. It couldn't be that he would just stop— without a word of explanation or goodbye! She was filled with the same wrenching pain she'd felt when Alma left: bewilderment, betrayal, longing, anger, grief. After all that had passed between them, how could he leave without a word?

SHE quit her job at Silverman and Jacobs. She told Bernard and Isabel that she was going home for the holidays, and then after Christmas to Italy for a few months on a lark. A bald-faced lie, one she felt bad about, given how good they'd been to her. But she didn't want them to try to call her or be worried about her. She wrote Zora, feeling wretched, telling her the same lie. She'd never told Zora about Jerome, worried about what she'd say. She told the lie to the few friends who called, so they wouldn't call again. It was easy in New York to lose touch if you wanted to. The city was so big it provided privacy. People would leave you alone; you could disappear if you liked. And she wanted to disappear.

In the weeks after she quit her job, she must have eaten; she must have taken a bath at some point. All she could remember was walking the streets of New York until her feet ached, searching for Jerome, though she knew it was fool's work. What were the chances of running into him on 5th Avenue or in Chinatown or even in the Village for that matter? And what would she say? She knew he was alive; his byline appeared in the *Amsterdam News* every few days. She didn't dare go to any of the bars in the Village, afraid she'd run into him with a new woman. He was growing more distant every day, like a ship pulling out to sea. Growing smaller and smaller. While the ache inside her was growing bigger and bigger.

She thought about trying to contact him at the paper. But if he could just leave like he did, what was there to say?

Finally she stopped going out. She ate what was in the apartment, cans of beans, a box of crackers. She boiled a pot dry when she forgot about some noodles, so she didn't turn on the hot plate again. Had she gone to Balducci's on Sixth where she always shopped for groceries? She must have gotten takeout from the Chinese restaurant down the block; there were several empty cartons. She couldn't remember. Her mind was too obsessed, replaying words Jerome had said, remembering little scenes between them—trying to figure out what went wrong. Her phone rang and rang, but she knew it wasn't him. Finally it stopped ringing. She took to her bed.

30

ALMA

ONE EVENING THAT fall, Ladocia came to Alma's room. The only other times Ladocia had been to her place were when she came to tell Alma her great-grandmother Callie had passed in her sleep, and again last spring, to tell her the homeplace had burned to the ground. Now Ladocia looked around in disgust. The room was so bare, with just a single bed, an old dresser, and a stained, worn green armchair. There was a hot plate and an old yellow refrigerator. The room of a drinker.

"Yo mama called," Ladocia said gruffly. "It's yo daddy, Alma. He passed yesterday. Sudden." She paused, then more gently. "Didn't suffer none."

Daddy? Gone? Alma sat down on the bed, unable to absorb the news. *Would she never see him again? How could that be possible?*

"You got to go home for the funeral," Ladocia said. "You ain't been home in all this time." She shook her head. "You got you any money?"

Alma nodded, though she didn't. She spent her little extra on liquor and the numbers. *Daddy? Gone?*

"I cain't," Alma said.

Ladocia looked like she was going to spit. "Come 'round this evening and call your mama. Tell her you comin'. She need you."

But later that night, Alma went to the Savoy to dance and drink. She was too dry inside to make tears. Alcohol was the only lubrication she knew that could ease the pain.

Her partner on the packed dance floor swung her out and gathered her back in, his ebony face aglow under the spinning colored lights. "We done arrived in the Promise' Land!" he shouted in her ear as the band ripped into "Take the A Train." He was dressed nattily in a bright red zoot and crazy tie, and he could dance. But what he said caused her to freeze.

"Hey!" the man shouted over the music, still jiving to the beat, only doing so alone now. "What's wid you?"

The Promised Land? It was true the Savoy Ballroom was all glittery and gold. No one was judged by the color of their skin here (colored or white)—only how well they could dance. Like this fella, who'd sought her out as she sat on one of the settees resting between dances. But was this the Promised Land?

"I gotta go!" she leaned close to shout in his ear. She turned and pushed her way through the gyrating bodies. She'd had three rum and Cokes, compliments of her partner, and she was loaded. She went down the staircase to the first floor, twisting her ankle at the bottom. She passed the haughty hostesses in elegant gowns, light-skinned Sugar Hill beauties who added class to the joint. A bouncer with a flattened nose—probably an ex-prizefighter— held the door open for her.

Alma stopped a moment to get her bearings. She thought about taking off her heels, tipsy as she was. But she might ruin her stockings, maybe step on a piece of broken glass.

What was she doing dancing and drinking at the Savoy? How could emptiness feel so heavy? She'd given up so much! For what? The Promised Land of the Savoy Ballroom?

A man sidled up to her on the street, liquor on his breath, his brown face lascivious, a small pencil mustache over his thick lips, which he was smacking in a disgusting way. "How 'bout it, baby? Got some special bush. Lemme show you a good time." When he reached for her arm, Alma pulled away and wobbled quickly on down Lenox, everything around her a blur.

Suddenly she froze again, right on the sidewalk jammed with the Saturday night crowd. The dream! She'd forgotten it until this moment (she'd had to forget so much!). But those words on the dance floor had forced it back up through all that had buried it deep. *The Promised Land, the Promised Land . . .*

The night Willie Earle was taken she'd dreamed of the Promised Land. She'd felt so free then, flying through the air, the Promised Land in the distance. Then suddenly she was plummeting toward the red dirt yard of their house on Sycamore Street. She woke just before she hit. Huff had taken her in his arms and wiped away her tears without saying a word. Where was he tonight? What would he think if he could see her now?

A couple, laughing and intoxicated, careened into her. She began walking again. A man sitting on a stoop gave a low whistle, and a siren sounded close by. But she was seeing the homeplace deep in the night, a full moon sailing in and out of clouds, the only sounds the wind in the poplar tree and a whippoorwill chanting mournfully deep in the woods.

Mama would be asleep, Pretty asleep, Willie Earle sleeping in his grave, and soon her father would be lowered into the ground. Dead, dead and gone.

EARLY one December morning, Ladocia came back over. When Alma opened the door, she figured it was news of another death.

"Well?" Alma said, her head pounding from a hangover, her heart lurching erratically.

Ladocia looked at her and grimaced. "You look like the devil own you for sure, Alma Stone," she said. "I'm sorry I ever brung you up here."

"Who!" Alma said forcefully. "Who this time!"

"Mr. Chastain called," Ladocia sighed. "Thinks his daughter in trouble. Wants you to go see 'bout her. I got to get to work. Here her address." Ladocia handed over a slip of paper. "I remember you and your mama talking about that white girl. Kind of skittish like a colt. What her name?"

"Betsy."

WITH the super beside her, Alma knocked on Betsy's door on Carmine Street. No answer. She and Mr. Lastrada exchanged a worried glance. Alma knocked again. When there was still no response, she used their special knock: three beats, a pause, and then a louder rap. Nothing.

"I hope she ain't dead in there," Mr. Lastrada fretted. He selected a key from his ring of keys and opened Betsy's door.

"Elizabeth, you okay?" he called from the doorway into the dark room.

There came a faint response from the bundle on the bed: "Oh yes, Mr. Lastrada . . . I'm just . . . so . . . tired."

"I knew when she got mixed up with that colored fellow no good would come of it," Mr. Lastrada whispered to Alma.

"Thank you, sir," Alma said. "I got her now." She eased him out the door and shut it behind him.

She switched on the overhead light and went over to the bundle. "What's got into you, child?"

"Alma!" Betsy started to sit up but collapsed back down.

"At least you alive," Alma said. What was that awful smell? The room stank of spoiled banana peels, sour garbage, stale air, and something human and foul.

Alma put her arm around Betsy and helped her sit up on the side of the bed. She sat down next to her hip to hip to hold her steady. Betsy turned to stare at her. She stroked Alma's cheek with her knuckles. "Alma," she said. "You came back!" She tried to lie back down, but Alma held her firm.

"You got to get up. Eat you something. You got to get you some strength. I got to get you cleaned up. Phew-ee." Betsy's hair was matted and greasy, her nightgown twisted around her tight as a tourniquet.

"I'm so sorry, Alma," Betsy said. "I'm so, so sorry." She began weeping. "Alma," she gasped through her tears, "help me!"

Alma squeezed her closer. "You gonna be okay."

"What? How did you know?"

"Your daddy. They so worried about you. You never call, never answer your phone."

"Then you know about them!"

"They be time for all that later. Right now we gonna wash you and get you into something decent. You foul, child. How long you been lying in dat bed?"

Alma half-lifted her and helped her walk to the bathroom, as if Betsy were an old, frail woman. Bath towels were wadded on the scarred wood floor, along with a compact with a cracked mirror open like a clamshell, and one fuzzy green bedroom slipper. A can of hairspray, a hairbrush and comb, an open bottle of foundation, and a flattened tube of tooth-paste lay scattered across the tank top of the commode. There were old Kotex wrapped in toilet paper in the trash can.

"Looks like you ain't changed much," Alma observed. "Still don't know how to pick up and put up. Raise your arms now and help me out." Betsy did as she was told. Alma pulled the sticky nightgown over her head. She pushed Betsy down gently on the toilet seat. Shivering and naked, Betsy didn't attempt to cover herself. Alma hadn't seen her naked since she was a child. She was a grown woman now, her breasts small and high, the nipples hard in the cold air that came through the leaks around the bathroom window, her pelvic bones jutting out of her thin torso.

Alma filled the claw foot tub, the water making the old pipes knock. She made Betsy stand, holding her forearms firmly as she helped her step over the high rim. Betsy sank down shakily, stretching her legs out and leaning against the porcelain back to rest her head on the tub's rim. Alma handed her a washcloth and the remnants of a bar of Ivory. Betsy soaped under her arms, between her legs, all over her body, legs, arms, and concave stomach. Alma took over and washed her back. Betsy crouched down to stick her head under the faucet so Alma could lather the green Prell into her hair and then rinse all the suds out, just as she did when Betsy was little.

There wasn't a clean bath towel to be found, but Alma found a hand towel that had to do. Betsy stood naked and shivering while Alma dried her. "'Member how you always perched on your tippy toes after your bath," she said, bringing a small smile to Betsy's lips. "You gonna be all right. Lot of folks get down, way down, but they come through. That's what you gonna do." Betsy sat on the toilet seat in her chiffon bathrobe while Alma rummaged for clean clothes, coming up with the least soiled underwear, white slacks with mustard stains on one leg, and a wrinkled jersey turtleneck.

She sat Betsy down on one of the chairs at the table. She got cans of Campbell's soup out of her black bag, tomato and chicken noodle. She rinsed a small saucepan and bowl, heated the soup on the hot plate, set a steaming bowl of the chicken noodle in front of Betsy, and handed her a spoon. "Eat," she commanded, just as she had when Betsy was little. No nonsense, no fooling around. Eat. And Betsy did. With each spoonful, she didn't take her eyes off Alma. Alma watched her with consternation. When Betsy finished the bowl, she brought the saucepan over and started to pour her more.

"No," Betsy said, putting her hand on Alma's to stop her. "You eat too."

Alma hesitated, then rinsed another of the dirty bowls in the sink. She pulled out the chair opposite Betsy, sat down, and studied on the situation.

She'd have to call the Chastains to come get her. She couldn't leave Betsy here alone. But an idea began to swell in her. She would take Betsy home. She didn't know how to go home herself. Not that she didn't know about trains and buses and how to get there. But she no longer knew how to go home. She did know how to take Betsy home though. They could be prodigals together.

"You're not eating," Betsy pointed out.

"We goin' home," Alma said.

"Home!" Betsy exclaimed. "I can't."

"We got to," Alma said. "I can't leave you here."

"Don't you have a job, Alma? Won't you lose it?"

"Time for me to go home too."

She began gathering up Betsy's clothes that were strewn around the room. "We gonna have to do some washin' when we get there," she said, clucking her tongue. "But it'll wait."

Betsy had lain back down on the bed, too enervated to sit up any longer. She put her head on the pillow and closed her eyes.

Alma stood with her hands on her hips, eyeing Betsy where she lay curled in bed.

"I got to go out now and take care of some things," she said. "But I be back. Bring you some supper. We're gonna catch the train tomorrow. Think you can make it?"

"I don't know," Betsy said hesitantly.

"Never mind," Alma said. "We make it."

ALMA went back to her room and pulled her suitcase from under the bed. She packed her everyday dresses, a couple of wool sweaters, panties, and bras. The party dresses she had worn to the clubs she stuffed along with her high heels into a brown grocery bag. The girls at the hotel would want them. She carefully folded her church dress, a long-sleeved, dark purple jersey, though she still hadn't been to church. All the while, her mind was spinning.

She put on her best maid's uniform, black with a white apron, from when she worked for Mr. Stern. She packed the photos of her family and Pretty, and that was about it. Before she closed the door, she looked back to see if she'd left anything. It was as if no one had lived there.

At the hotel, she made a collect call to the number Ladocia had given her. When Mr. Chastain answered she said, "We takin' the train tomorrow." There was a shocked silence on the other end. "You mean . . . you and Betsy? What's going on? Is she all right?"

"I got her," Alma said.

"Oh," Mr. Chastain said, "I see," as if he didn't see at all but knew better than to ask. "I'll wire money to Western Union within the hour. We'll be at the station to meet you. And Alma—thank you."

That evening she returned to Betsy's, carrying her suitcase and her big black pocketbook, from which she produced six eggs tied in a bandana. She boiled them on the hotplate. Alma ate three, and Betsy ate one, all her stomach could handle. She folded back into bed, but every so often, she'd sit up and look to see if Alma was still there. Alma sat in the armless chair, keeping watch. Every now and then, she pulled a bottle from her black pocketbook and drank from it.

The next morning, Alma half-lifted Betsy until she stood, unsteadily. Her legs were weak, and she'd lost weight. "How long you been holed up in here?"

"What day is it?"

"Thursday. December 17th. Well, you up now," Alma said. She helped Betsy don the same clothes from yesterday, along with a wool cardigan. She stuffed her feet into her boots as Betsy leaned on her for balance. "I got most of your clothes packed in these two suitcases," Alma indicated the two Samsonites on the floor. "What else you wanna take?"

"Oh!" Betsy exclaimed. "Those notebooks!" They filled one shelf of the bookcase. Her stories.

"How we gonna carry those?" Alma asked. "We got our hands full with these 'uns."

"No, no!" Betsy cried. "I can't leave them. Put them in my

leather bag. Please, Alma. I'll carry them."

Alma shook her head. "No sir," she said, "we gonna be drug down!" But she put the notebooks in the leather shoulder bag. She directed Betsy's arms into the sleeves of her trench coat and wrapped a scarf around her head. "It's New York winter out there," she said. "Not Car'lina."

When they reached the street level, Alma told Betsy her father had wired her money for her rent and their train fare. She knocked on Mr. Lastrada's door, and when he answered, she handed him some cash. He carefully counted it and gave some back. He and his wife came out on the sidewalk to say goodbye. Both wore fretful expressions. "She be all right now. I got her," Alma reassured them. Mr. Lastrada flagged a taxi and helped load their luggage into the trunk. Betsy turned to wave goodbye to them as they stood watching in front of her apartment building. "They were so nice to me," she said as they disappeared from sight.

THEY rode in the back seat of the cab through the streets of New York without speaking. When they got to Penn Station, Alma bought hotdogs at a concession stand. "You got to get some meat on you," she said, studying Betsy's gaunt face. "You skin and bones." When she saw how Betsy gobbled hers like a starving dog, she got her two more.

"When you been home last?" Alma asked as they sat on a wood bench waiting for their train to be called.

Betsy shook her head. "Two years," she said. "When were you?"

Now it was Alma's turn to shake her head.

"You haven't been home in all this time?" Betsy asked in astonishment.

Alma was silent. Finally she said, "What happened to you, child?" She turned to Betsy, searching her face. "To wash up on that bed like near to die."

Betsy sighed. Around them people were hurrying, the big board flashing the names and numbers of trains departing on various tracks, the din of the station enveloping them. But Alma and Betsy were locked in their own private moment.

"I guess my heart got broken," Betsy said. "Plain and simple as that."

Alma was silent for such a long time that Betsy turned to look at her. "Alma?"

But Alma was staring into the far distance. "Everybody heart broke," she said at last.

PART III

31

ALMA

AS THE SLEEK green Crescent Limited neared the Southern Depot, its wheels slowed their rhythmic clacking, the horn blasted its imminent arrival, and it came to a halt with an exhausted sigh. Alma busied herself getting their things together from the Pullman sleeper she and Betsy had shared for fifteen hours. In spite of how hectic and hurried the last day in New York had been, she'd had the good sense to wear her maid's uniform for the trip. The ticketmaster at Penn Station might need some convincing that she had to accompany the young white woman all the way to South Carolina in a sleeper compartment. Negro and white together would become an issue once they crossed the Mason-Dixon line. But not if Alma was Betsy's nursemaid.

Betsy looked so pale and weak, the agent not only issued the sleeper car tickets, but also called for a porter to help them onto the platform with their suitcases. Alma was lugging Betsy's notebooks in the leather bag, along with her own heavy black pocketbook. Both she and Betsy slept for most of the trip, Alma aided by an occasional nip. But now they were wide awake, looking each other in the eye anxiously. They were home.

Alma waited until most of the car had cleared, and a porter who'd befriended them collected their luggage. He sometimes worked the line with Alma's brother Dew and was taking special care of them. He steered them through the narrow aisles to the coach door and set their bags down on the concrete platform. Alma felt her legs might fold as she started down the metal steps. She turned to take both of Betsy's hands as Betsy made her own shaky descent.

As soon as they stepped onto the platform, Mr. and Miz Chastain came rushing toward them. Alma, the luggage at her feet, was supporting Betsy around the waist. Betsy gave a sharp cry when she saw them, whether from joy or pain Alma couldn't tell. She fell into her mother's arms but shrugged her father off when he tried to hug her. Betsy had told her about how her father had divorced her mother. She hadn't forgiven him. Mr. Chastain looked at Alma, grimaced, and mouthed the words *thank you*, standing aside by himself.

Behind them Alma saw a short, bulbous woman in a red kerchief—her own mama—hanging back a few yards. She had her hands on the shoulder of a young girl who searched Alma's face with wide-eyed curiosity. The girl, dressed in a Sunday best blue dress with white polka dots, lace anklet socks, and shiny black patent leather Mary Jane shoes, came up to Alma, stopping just short of touching her. Alma was stunned. When she left, Pretty was not yet three years old. She'd be turning eight this January!

"Pleased to meet you," Pretty said, two dimples blossoming in her cheeks, and extended her hand.

"That's yo mama!" Bessie fussed. "I done told you. Give her a hug 'round de neck."

Pretty looked up at Bessie with a worried look.

Alma was taken aback. But what did she expect?

"Can I have a hug, Pretty?" Alma asked, her voice trembling. "I'm your mama all right, come home at last."

Pretty stepped up to Alma and wrapped her arms around her waist. Alma knelt down to embrace her, tears filling her eyes. "Don't cry," Pretty said, patting her back.

Alma looked over Pretty's head into the eyes of her own mama. Bessie was nodding at the sight of the two of them. "She's turning out mighty pretty, ain't she?" Bessie said. "You called her right."

"Mama!" Alma moaned, hanging her head.

"Well, you home now," Bessie said matter-of-factly. "You sure home now."

Mr. Chastain stepped over to tell them he'd take care of the luggage. They should go to the car with Miz Chastain, and he'd be along shortly. Lydia had her arm firmly around Betsy's waist. When Alma met her eyes, Lydia's face turned a rosy pink. "Thank you, Alma. What would we have done without you! Should we take her straight to the doctor's?"

"Just give her some home cooking and good rest. She be all right. Soft scramble eggs, maybe some cinnamon toast like she likes."

Lydia nodded, two new deep wrinkles across her forehead.

Pretty stepped up to Lydia and said politely, "Can I meet Miss Betsy, Miz Chas?"

"Pretty takes her piano from Miz Chastain," Bessie told Alma. "You got a lot of catching up to do."

Betsy was studying the young girl.

"Betsy," Lydia prompted, "you remember Pretty? You should hear the way she can play the piano!"

"I'm not that good," Pretty shrugged. "Mama Bess," she turned to her grandmother, "do I have to go to school tomorrow?"

"You goin'," Bessie said. "No ifs, ands, or buts about it."

Suddenly recognition lit up Betsy's face. "Priscilla! Oh my God! Pretty! I knew you when you were knee-high to a grasshopper!" The amazement in her voice made everyone laugh.

The first hard moments were over.

FIVE years Alma had been gone! Looking around as they walked through the depot, she saw some things were just the same—"White Waiting Room," "Colored Waiting Room," the "colored" water fountain right next to the "whites only" one. When Mr. Chastain drove them through town, Greenville looked just the same: the large red brick houses that anyone would know were for whites only, then farther up the hill behind the park through Nicholtown, the small brick houses and wood shanties with tin roofs that anyone would know were for Negroes.

But so much had changed! It wasn't as if she didn't know. Ladocia had kept Alma informed, even when Alma couldn't call home herself. She knew. *She knew.* Her father had died of a heart attack. The homeplace was no more. It had burned to the ground not long after Great-Grandmother Callie had died in her sleep. Bessie, Pretty, and Granma Marie were living in Nicholtown now with Alma's aunt Delores and uncle Stew.

Riding in the back of Miz Chastain's big Buick, Alma felt she was dreaming. She had only to wake for all to be restored.

Huff would be waiting to take her in his arms, hug her close, and tell her "Welcome home, baby." Dew would drive them out to the homeplace in Liberty in his Plymouth. Her father would be waiting for them, sitting on the front porch in his overalls, smoking a pipe, his white handlebar mustache tickling her face when he kissed her cheek. "Welcome home, daughter. Where you been so long?" He'd be older, but that was all right. She could take that. Callie would be there on the couch, more wrinkled and shrunken than ever. But that was all right. Alma would go lie down on the pallet in the back room where she and Pearle had slept as girls, and when she awoke, all would be . . .

Ashes. So many ashes.

MR. CHASTAIN drove them to Delores and Stew's. They lived in a two-story frame house on Glenn Road. Four rooms upstairs and four down. Stew had built it himself; he could build anything. He had a good job at Daniel Construction. Delores worked the night shift as a wrapper at Claussen's Bakery, the big commercial bakery on Augusta Street. Two of their children were out of the house, a married daughter who lived in Charleston and a son serving in the Pacific. Two were still at home, Jimmy, a tall, athletic boy who would graduate from Sterling High in the spring, and Mae, a sophomore at Sterling.

When Alma, Bessie, and Pretty got out, Lydia rolled down the car window. "Alma, come on over when y'all get situated. I know Betsy would love some of your chicken and dumplings." There was something beseeching in her voice. Alma had wondered if she'd hold a grudge. But she knew genteel Southern white women like Miz Chastain. One thing you could count on them for was manners. Maybe Miz Chastain actually forgave her for leaving like she did. But could she ever understand why? Alma doubted it.

Pretty called out. "I cain't wait to show Miss Betsy how I can play!"

"We'll see to that," Lydia smiled.

Betsy leaned across her mother to call out the window, "Alma, thank you, thank you, I can't . . ."

"I be on over," Alma said. "You get you some rest now. Eat, you hear!"

Mr. Chastain carried her suitcase across the stepping stones to the front door. He set it down and turned to her. "Betsy looks so . . ." He searched her eyes.

"She be all right," Alma said. "She just needs some time. And love."

"She'll get plenty of that!" His voice broke, and his eyes glistened with tears. When he regained his composure, he said, "All right then. Don't be a stranger, Alma. You're welcome anytime. And thank you. Thank you!"

Alma nodded. She tried to take Pretty's hand, but Pretty ran ahead. Alma turned to walk into what was now home.

THAT night they all sat down to a big homecoming supper: Granma Marie, Bessie, Pretty, Alma's brother Jeremiah, his girlfriend Nina, sister Pearle, Stew and Delores, and their kids Jimmy and Mae. Dew was working somewhere up the Piedmont line. She wasn't ready to ask about Huff. He might have another woman or maybe had even moved out of town, having given up on her.

There was ham and grits, white half-runners canned from Delores's garden last summer, lima beans, cornbread, and store-bought margarine. Bread and butter pickles. Sweet potato pie for dessert. It was a cold winter night, but the kitchen was toasty, and delicious smells were coming from all the cooking. A brightly lit Christmas tree glowed in the front room. There were stories, teasing, tales, and gossip. Alma was grateful no one questioned her about why she'd stayed away so long or what had become of her in New York—at least not yet. It was a happy time, except for being so sad.

The others had buried their dead, mourned, and grown accustomed to the absences at the table. But Alma kept looking up from her plate, expecting to see her father and great-grandmother. She was deeply ashamed that she had not come home for their funerals. She wondered if the family was looking at her with malice in their hearts, even as they seemed so welcoming. Her mama kept urging Alma to eat more, as if she could catch up on all the home cooking she'd missed. But Alma knew she'd eventually have more to say. Pretty was watching her with curiosity but averted her eyes shyly whenever Alma looked at her. Jimmy was excited about his plans to join the Navy after graduation; he was just sorry he'd missed the war. Stew clucked his tongue and shook his finger at him. "Be glad you not buried in some foreign grave like so many," he said. After dinner Bessie washed the dishes while Alma and Pearle dried, rolling the flour sack towels to snap each other's rears, just as they'd done when they were girls.

After Bessie had seen Pretty to bed next to Granma Marie, Jimmy and Mae had retired to their rooms, Delores had gone off to the bakery for the night shift, and the sounds of Stew's snoring drifted down the hall, Alma and Bessie sat down in the parlor. It was late, but neither of them could have slept.

"Tell me about Daddy," Alma said, breathlessly.

Her mama took her own deep breath. "We was up early that day to see to them vegetables we was going to take to town to sell." She paused to rub her eyes. "Telling brings it all back." She collected herself for a few moments. "It was so hot, Lord, I can feel it still, one of them August days when no breeze stirs. I didn't want to heat up the house even more than it was. I cut us some cornbread and honey, even though he always loved grits and fried meat in the morning." She paused again to compose herself. Alma's heart hurt like someone was striking it. "When I went back in there to call him to the table, he was just sittin' in the rocker, head down, like he was prayin'. I knew right away he'd passed. Already in Heaven with Jesus."

Alma wiped her eyes with an old Kleenex she found in her sweater pocket.

"He was wore out," her mother said. "Worked hard all his life. The way they done Li'l Willie took something outta him. And then you goin' off like you done. Not callin' or writin'. If it wadn't for Ladocia, we woulda thought you was dead!" Her mother gave her a stern look. "Why you stay away so long?"

Alma could hardly answer. "I wanted . . . I thought . . . I wanted a better life for Pretty. For us all. Up North."

"You think we don't have a good enough life here?" Bessie demanded. "We givin' Pretty a good life! What make you think you better than us?"

"I don't!" Alma said. "But . . . you know what I'm talking about, Mama! The way they done Willie. The way they do us all."

"And what you find out up North?"

Alma was silent.

"You don't solve no problems by running away. Guess you found that out."

"I...I..." Alma stammered. "The devil found his way into my heart, Mama."

Bessie was silent.

"He tempted me. And I ... succumbed."

Her mother didn't speak for a long time. "All right then," she said decisively. "We gonna pray on it. Ain't no one but Jesus can make it right."

Alma knelt beside her mother on the wood floor in front of the couch. They braced their elbows on the cushions, clutching their hands in prayer. "Dear Jesus," her mother began. "Thank you for bringing our Alma home. But please, Lord Jesus! Hear our prayers! Help her in her time of need. Heal her heart of wickedness and evil. Take away her sins!" Her mother prayed fiercely. "Drive the devil from her and show her your mercy and love! Please, dear Jesus, hear our prayers."

Her mother prayed on and on. But after a while, Alma stopped listening. She was wondering if there was still a little "medicine" left in the bottle she'd carried in her big black pocketbook all the way from New York. She'd taken a slug now and then when she woke on the train—had to. She'd minded to nurse it during the trip. Please let there be some left!

That was what Alma prayed.

THE next morning Alma was in the kitchen making pancakes when she heard a deep, familiar voice calling, "Y'all home?" from the front room. Busy at the stove, she froze as if she'd heard a ghost announce his presence.

"Daddy!" Pretty bolted from the kitchen. When Alma, wiping her hands on her apron, went into the parlor, she saw Pretty with her arms wrapped around Huff. He lifted her up and slung her over his shoulder, moaning that she was getting too big for such horseplay. Alma had forgotten how huge and dark he was. He had on khaki pants and a white dress shirt instead of the overalls he'd always worn. "I thought yo grandma was raising you to act proper," he teased, "and here you actin' the rascal." When he set her down, his eyes met Alma's with an expression she couldn't read.

"Huff . . ." Alma's voice caught.

"Been a long time," he said.

She nodded. "Sho has."

Just then Bessie came in from the kitchen. "You just in time for breakfast, Huff. Alma cooking us some sausage and pancakes." And to Pretty, "You hustle up, you don't want to keep Deely waiting." Deely was Pretty's best friend; they'd walk to Nicholtown School together.

Alma, feeling as if her feet weren't quite touching the floor, followed the others back into the kitchen. She was glad she had cooking to do. They all sat down at the pine table, and Bessie began telling Huff about the big Christmas turkey she'd get from a farmer out near Pelham and all the pies they'd make. Dew would be home, and they'd make a pecan pie for him with nuts from the pecan tree out back. Busying herself at the stove, Alma was trying to sort out how she felt about seeing Huff. Her thoughts and feelings were going every-which-way.

"Thought you might like to drive out to the homeplace, Alma," Huff said. "Visit yo daddy's and Miss Callie's graves out yonder. Ain't nothin' left of the house," he shook his head. "Them fields still the same though."

Alma turned from the stove. "You got you a car, Huff?"

"Pickup truck. Job too. Baggage assistant out to the airport. Don't have to be to work 'til 2:00 today."

"Can I go out to the homeplace too, Daddy?" Pretty asked. Her hair was parted and plaited into two pigtails tied with blue ribbons.

"What you thinkin', child!" Bessie said. "This here a school day. They carry you another time—if you make an A on that math test today."

Alma was jealous that Pretty hadn't asked her permission.

SITTING high up on the worn truck seat, they drove out the highway toward Liberty. It was December, and the weather was mild, but it was a winter landscape, browns and grays, leafless trees except for evergreens here and there in the woods. Alma looked over at Huff. She thought of how they'd been young once and courting, everything ahead of them. It seemed another lifetime ago.

"What you think of Pretty?" he said at last, glancing over at Alma. "Ain't she growed up?"

Alma, her throat aching, nodded her head.

"I go by there a lot," Huff said. "'Specially since they moved to town. Your mama and grandma doing a good job with her. She smart as a whip. Nice too. She know how to do."

"I wonder where that expression come from," Alma said. "No whip smart I know of."

As they cleared the city limits, they settled into silence, Alma looking out the window at the familiar landscape: unpainted country stores with shot-up Coca-Cola and Lucky Strike signs, an occasional auto repair shop on the side of the highway, pasture land where black and white cows were poking at the stubble grass, woods framing the fields.

Her heart began skipping beats as they passed under the railroad bridge on the way into Liberty.

"It all look the same," Alma said.

"It just look that way," Huff said. "But it ain't." They drove slowly down Main Street and out of town toward the homeplace. "Five years a long time."

Alma looked out the window and didn't speak.

They turned down the dirt road that led to the homeplace. Alma turned her head away. She didn't want to see.

It was gone, all but the brick chimney. A few charred beams were scattered here and there, the large stones of the foundation, the potbelly cast iron stove, and there in the middle of the ashes was the metal bedstead her parents had slept in, scorched black. When Huff stopped the truck, Alma got out and fell to her knees on the red dirt, burying her face in her hands. Huff leaned against the truck, looking off into the brown fields, letting her be. "We had many a good time out here," he said when her sobs had calmed. "I can just see your daddy sittin' on that porch, looking for us to arrive. That white mustache about to take over his face. Why he want that thing?"

Alma laughed and cried at that, wiping her eyes, getting to her feet. "I don't know." Huff handed her his handkerchief, and she blew her nose. "Why any of us want what we want?"

"At least that old poplar tree still here," Huff said. "Didn't get caught up in the conflagration. All of 'em got out though. That's the blessing."

They walked around back, where the garden lay scorched and bare. Alma looked across the field toward Tessie Earle's house. She remembered the night she and her mother had walked there in the dark, in shock and disbelief. How when she'd started back alone, fear and anger overtook her in the stubble of the cornfield. That February night, she began leaving without yet knowing it, though it took her until August to go.

THEY drove farther out in the country to the little white frame Baptist church at the top of a hill where Alma's dead were buried. Off in the distance was a ridge of smoky-blue mountains. Some of the oldest graves, said to be those of slaves, had only rock slabs to mark the resting places. Alma's father's and Callie's graves had no headstones, just typed faded cards with their names and death dates in metal frames covered by plastic. Bessie had sent along red plastic poinsettias to replace the faded flowers from last summer. Alma carried them over to a pile of discarded arrangements at the far corner of the cemetery. She and Huff secured the new flowers on the graves with coat hangers that Huff bent with his strong hands.

"Your daddy was a good man. Always was good to me," Huff said. "He sho loved all you kids. They raised you young'uns right, taught you right from wrong."

Alma felt shame rise up in her. She saw herself carrying on at the clubs, drinking and flinging her body around the dance floor.

"You home now," Huff said. "I'm glad you come back."

Alma took a long time to speak. "I ain't the same, Huff," she said at last. "I've changed."

Huff didn't hesitate. "We all changed, Alma. You ain't the only one."

When Alma didn't speak, Huff said, "I don't blame you for leavin' like you did. I know why you went. We was all tore up over Willie, just in different ways. The way I was drinkin' and cattin' around. I don't do that no more, Alma." He rubbed his big hands together. "I been missin' you all this time."

"The money," Alma said bitterly, turning to him. "The money I was savin' for Pretty's college."

Huff hung his head. "Don't know what got into me. I was 'tending to put it back, and then you was gone. But I got the money now. I been savin' it up. I got it all."

"Don't matter now, Huff. Some things can't be made right." Alma turned and started walking back to the truck.

"You ain't never made a mistake, Alma Stone?" Huff called after her. "You may be perfect, but most of us'uns ain't."

When Alma reached the truck, her legs buckled, and she leaned against the hood to support herself. How had she gotten so hard and mean? Was that what being up North had done to her? Or maybe it was the devil, who had shoved Jesus out of her heart.

She straightened and turned to look at Huff. She saw that he was suffering—suffering from her hard-hearted meanness. *You ain't never made a mistake?* "I done made mistakes, Huff," she said. "Plenty. Up North I made about every mistake in the book."

"Don't matter now," he said. "You home where you belong. Where folks love you."

"Not if they knew." She cast her eyes down.

"That's over," Huff said brusquely. "We don't need to talk about it none. We lookin' to the future." He paused. Something else was coming. "I been goin' to meetings, Alma," he said, looking at her intently. "With A.J. from the gas station and other fellas."

She stared at him. "What kind of meetings?"

"N. double A. C. P."

"Huff, you be careful! You get yourself in trouble. White folks won't like it one bit if they know you goin' to them meetings. Why you want to get involved in that?"

"You askin' me why. I tell you why, Alma Stone. Willie

Earle, that's why, what they done to him. And all of 'em walkin' around free. Willie turned our minds. We figured we have to do something, have to start somewhere. For our kids."

Alma had never heard him say such a thing.

"You better watch yourself," she said, rattled.

They rode home in silence.

32

BETSY

THAT FIRST MORNING home, Betsy woke to the faces of two strangers peering at her from beside her bed: Mother and Daddy. She hadn't seen them since her graduation. They were so familiar and yet . . . different. Why did they look so worried? She couldn't remember how she'd gotten into bed the night before.

She sat up and looked around. Her pink room had been painted yellow; the brass bed was gone, replaced by two single beds with yellow and green spreads. She asked what time it was. "You've slept for ten hours straight," her mother said.

Daddy leaned near. "What happened to you in New York, honey?" His voice cracked with emotion. All Betsy wanted was to escape back to unconsciousness. She shook her head, unable to answer. But as soon as she started to lie back, they each took an arm and lifted her to standing. Her mother helped her to the bathroom, and then they steered her down the stairs to the kitchen. Lydia soft-scrambled some eggs, and Lawton poured her coffee. He asked that question again:

What happened to you in New York?

"Boy trouble," Betsy mumbled.

They exchanged a look.

"Did he hurt you?" her mother asked. "You need to tell us, Betsy." Betsy was shocked to see tears fill her mother's eyes. "Did he—do you need to see a doctor?"

"No, no, nothing like that!" Betsy exclaimed, but suddenly tears flooded her own eyes. The next thing she knew she was sobbing.

"He stopped," she was finally able to hiccup.

"Stopped?" her father said. "Stopped what?"

"Loving me." Another onslaught of tears.

"Then it's his damn loss!" he said so adamantly and indignantly Betsy looked at him in surprise. What was he doing here? He'd moved out. He and Mother were divorced. He lived somewhere else. She frowned, confused.

"He's been here all night," her mother said. "We were so worried we didn't want to leave you alone."

"Both of you? Together?"

"Of course."

"We're still your parents," her father said. "Divorce didn't change that."

"But aren't you mad at him?" Betsy asked her mother.

"No," Lydia shook her head. "I'm not. And you shouldn't be either."

"I was only mad at him for your sake!" More tears.

When the snuffling was under control, she looked from one of them to the other. Mother. Daddy. Who were they, now? Life had gone on here, without her. She hadn't paid attention to them. Thinking she was separate from them. Wanting to be.

"You're home now," her father said, his face lined with new wrinkles. "We'll take care of you. Until you're stronger. And you will be."

All Betsy could do was nod.

CHRISTMAS was a week away. Thank God her mother told the grandparents that yes, she was home, but she had the flu. She and Lydia had the house to themselves, though her father came over every evening for a little visit. She had expected her mother to be crushed, but she actually seemed happier than Betsy could remember her being. Over canned tomato soup and grilled cheese sandwiches for lunch every day, she told Betsy how much she enjoyed her piano students. She was especially fond of Pretty. Sometimes Betsy heard her mother singing to herself, puttering around the house. It wasn't at all what she'd expected.

Mostly Betsy lay on the chaise lounge in the sunroom in her pajamas and robe, studying the way the new leaves on the philodendrons were so tightly wound. She was trying to puzzle something out: How love ended. Not hers. His. Last Christmas she and Jerome had gone to Rockefeller Plaza. They watched the ice skaters and ooh-ed and ahh-ed over the lighting of the Christmas tree. They were just beginning then. She hadn't realized it would ever end.

One night she sat at her old school desk and wrote a letter:

Dear Jerome,

I had a breakdown and had to come home—you don't even know that. Alma—I told you about her—came to my apartment after Daddy called her, and we took the train back to Greenville. I keep hoping you'll contact me. You probably won't, but I can't help feeling that you will. That you miss me as much as I miss you.

Jerome, I read about veterans who lost a limb in the war. They feel pain in their missing leg or arm even though it's no longer there. You're my missing limb. There's no cure—just a stiff upper lip. That's what I'm trying to do here at home—keep a stiff upper lip and not let Mother and Daddy know that the part of me that was you hurts all the time.

Well, you don't want to hear all this, not that you will. You never gave me your address. I could write you in care of the Amsterdam News. But I won't. If you want to be in touch, it's up to you.

She tore the letter into tiny pieces and flushed them down the toilet.

T H E day before Christmas Bessie called and said that she, along with Alma and Pretty, wanted to come over for a little visit. Her mother helped Betsy wash her hair and get dressed in a soft wool dress the color of a fawn still hanging in her closet—a ghost of her former self.

They came in the kitchen door bearing gifts: a fruitcake Bessie had soaked in rum, which she would never touch herself; a jar of homemade bread and butter pickles; and a holiday tin of Christmas cookies. As soon as she saw Alma, Betsy opened her arms. "Thank you, Alma," she hugged her close, "thank you."

"I made these cookies myself," Pretty was saying excitedly, opening the tin to show them. "Look here, Miss Betsy." The cookies were cut into crooked stars and wreaths, decorated with colored sugar.

"We gotta fatten you up," Alma said to Betsy, clicking her tongue. "I'm gonna cook you some chicken and dumplin'."

"Would you teach me to cook, Alma? I mean real food,

like you cook. Mother isn't interested in cooking, and I'm not sure she knows how," she grinned. "We eat mainly canned food and frozen TV dinners." After Ophelia got a job at a café downtown, Lydia had decided she only needed someone to clean every two weeks. "We eat a lot of Spam," Betsy added for emphasis.

"There's a lot you can do with a can of Spam," her mother countered.

"Uh-uh!" Alma shook her head vigorously. "The way to a man's heart is not through no tin of Spam!"

"Well," Lydia said, "no one here is looking for a man!"

Pretty asked if she could play the piano now, but Lydia told her that the grown-ups wanted to have a little visit first. She ushered them all into the living room. Betsy couldn't get over how everything looked just as it had every Christmas—the decorated Balsam tree in the front bay window, boughs of fresh holly and white pine laid on the mantel, prancing white plastic reindeer pulling a red plastic sleigh across the white marble coffee table—but so much had changed! Her father no longer lived here; her mother was on her own now, a divorced woman! She and Alma had gone out into the big world and lost their ways.

Alma perched gingerly on the edge of the blue velvet sofa, but Bessie sat dignified and at ease, with Pretty, in a Sunday dress, between them. Bessie complimented Lydia on how nice the house looked and they chattered away. But Betsy was only half-listening, thinking about how strange and normal it all was, colored and white together, sitting in the living room, talking like the old friends they were, and weren't.

Finally Lydia told Pretty she could play the piano now. They all stood around the Baldwin while Pretty played a lively "Oh! Susanna" from memory. When she hit a wrong note, she just corrected and went on, undaunted. When she finished they all applauded while she stood and took a bow, her cheeks dimpling.

"Now you play something," Pretty said to Lydia.

"Only if your mother will."

"I done forgot everything you taught me," Alma said. When had her mother given Alma piano lessons, Betsy wondered. There were surprises at home.

"Come on," Lydia coaxed. "You can do it, Alma."

"Play, Mama, play!"

Alma shook her head, but she sat down and positioned her hands on the keys. Lydia stood beside her and touched middle C. "It'll come back to you."

Tentatively, slowly, Alma began playing "Amazing Grace." Unlike Pretty, when she hit a wrong note, she grimaced, but when she got through the piece, she covered her mouth with her hands, hiding a grin. "Bravo!" Lydia said.

"Now you," Alma said, moving off the piano bench.

Lydia sat down. She tilted her head. She looked at Alma. Then she lifted her hands to the keyboard and struck the opening notes of *Moonlight Sonata*.

THAT night Betsy wrote Jerome again.

Jerome, I have so much to say to you! To tell you. When we were together, I was always talking to you in my head. Always telling you everything. I still am.

I'm just missing you terribly tonight. I'm so angry at you! I still can't believe you left the way you did. I'll never understand it. I can't believe it's over for you. I can't imagine it ever will be for me.

BY mid-February, Betsy had gained six pounds. On Saturdays Alma taught her how to make biscuits, pork chops and cream gravy, showed her how to fry okra, and cook collard greens with fatback. Her mother was busy giving piano lessons and going to various meetings, and Betsy was trying to write, but nothing was coming. She was beginning to feel like a philodendron herself. One evening when her father took her out to dinner, he told her he could really use some help at the office. What would she think about being his assistant?

She'd been to her father's apartment in The Davenport but she hadn't been to his office. She was curious to see it, and the idea of getting out of the house, having somewhere to go and something to do, appealed to her.

He was renting space in the Chamber of Commerce Building downtown. Her father showed her the small outer office, with two straight-backed chairs where clients could wait, a four-drawer filing cabinet, and what would be her desk, an expensive-looking oak one with a matching chair. When she sat down, the chair seat was way too hard. "I'll get you a cushion," her father said, grinning.

He took her into his office. It had a tall window that looked out at the courthouse directly across Court Square. She stood for a moment looking at it. Over five years had passed since the Willie Earle trial. Was that when her father started to change? He'd seemed like a stranger to her that final day, sitting alone at the counsel table after the courtroom had almost cleared. He was still that familiar stranger, someone just out of reach.

Her father suggested she start by learning the filing system; then she could file some old cases. After that she could find good forms for pleadings, motions, and contracts and make copies for the form file. After a few days she got the hang of things. She typed (and retyped—she made a lot of mistakes) documents and letters. She answered the phone, which in truth didn't ring that much. Mostly her job was to keep her father company. She knew he thought of it as therapy for her, and she thought of it as therapy for him.

One day Betsy was in his office, sitting across from Lawton in one of the two chairs for clients. He was tilted back in his padded Sears chair.

"Daddy, can I ask you something?"

"I've been expecting this," Lawton said. "Go ahead. Shoot."

"Didn't you love Mother anymore? Is that why you wanted a divorce?"

He took a long time to answer.

"I take it you now know yourself that love is not a simple thing, Betsy. Is that right?"

She nodded her head.

"It isn't black and white, yes or no, love or no love. People aren't like that."

"But why?"

He sighed. "I felt wrong," he said after a long pause. "I shouldn't have been married to your mother. Or any woman."

What was he saying? She must have misheard!

"Oh," she said stupidly. "Okay!" Panic was rising in her chest. "You both seem happier. At least she does."

"I think that's right."

"Well good, then!" she said, her mind scrambled. "Is there any new filing you want me to do?"

"Honey," he said. "I—"

"I've been meaning to retype the Owens summary judgment motion."

"That would be fine," he said, his eyes so sad she had to turn away.

THAT evening she asked her mother what it was like with Daddy when they were first getting together. Lydia said she couldn't remember, she was so young. She didn't have the maturity then to know what love is. But she was only a little younger than Betsy was now! Betsy felt sure she knew what love was: something wonderful and terrible.

Dear Jerome,

Are love and sex the same thing? I thought they were. Sometimes at night I touch myself and you're with me again. When it's over I cry. I had no idea of the power of sex. Or love. With you I couldn't separate them. I don't think you could either, at first. Remember when I said, "I love you," and you immediately answered, "I love you too." That couldn't have been false!

FEBRUARY turned into March, the weather up and down, seventy degrees one day, thirty-five the next, just like Betsy's moods.

Her father was giving her an ongoing education in the law: contracts and consideration; common and statutory law; criminal versus civil procedure. One day when they had nothing to do, he told her about a Clarendon County case called *Briggs v. Elliot.* He'd driven down to Charleston for the hearing.

He explained how some brave Negroes in Clarendon County—Joseph Delaine, Mr. and Mrs. Briggs—had petitioned the school board for school buses. There were no school buses for over six thousand Negro students but thirty buses for two thousand white kids. In Scott's Branch, some children walked nine miles to schools heated by woodstoves, lighted by kerosene lamps, with no indoor plumbing or running water. When approached with the school bus request, R.M. Elliott, the chair of the school board, responded, "We ain't got no money to buy a bus for your nigger children."

"That's so awful!"

"Now *Briggs* is one of five cases combined in *Brown v. the Board of Education*, which the Supreme Court will be ruling on," her father said. "You've heard about it, I'm sure. *Brown* could overturn *Plessy v. Ferguson*, an 1896 case which holds that segregation is legal as long as public facilities like schools are equal in quality. Separate but equal. The doctrine segregation rests on."

"Could the Supreme Court actually rule to desegregate schools?" Betsy asked.

"I don't know, honey," her father said. "Our governor and legislators are pouring money into improving Negro schools, so they can claim that separate *is* equal. So they won't have to integrate. But separate can never be equal. Thurgood Marshall and his team have been building toward this for years. We'll just have to wait and see."

SOME of her father's clients were Negroes. He'd settled a personal injury case for over $1,000 for a Negro man who'd gotten his leg broken at a warehouse where the forklift operator backed over him, a result that apparently gave Lawton great satisfaction. Much to Betsy's surprise, John Bolt Culbertson sometimes referred cases to her father.

"You're friends with him again? How can you forget all the things he said at the trial!"

"Calm down," her father said, "and I'll explain." He told

how he'd avoided Culbertson for months after the trial. He'd cross the street if he saw him coming, pretending he didn't see him when they were at the same restaurants. "I wanted nothing to do with him. But one day at the courthouse I heard Tom Wofford joking that after the trial, John Bolt started talking like Thurgood Marshall and acting like Walter White." He gave a little laugh.

"I walked over to Culbertson's office in the Goldsmith Building. You should see the place. It's crammed full of civil rights flyers, union bulletins, stacks of newspapers everywhere. Portraits of John Henry and John Brown on the wall."

Her father explained how he'd missed John Bolt: his backslapping friendliness, his impeccable manners, his forthrightness. He wanted to hear what John Bolt had to say about his conduct at the trial.

Over lunch Culbertson told him how he'd taken the case because the leader of the local textile union had two daughters married to husbands in the mob. John Bolt was Greenville's only labor lawyer, and he felt a duty to the union members.

"That hardly explains or forgives the way he acted at the trial," Betsy said.

"No," Lawton nodded. "And we didn't agree about the case. He said Willie Earle would have ended up dead anyway—he was a criminal. I said it wasn't about Willie Earle, it was about the rule of law."

"And?"

"He said he got carried away. Wanted to do whatever he could to defend his clients. He told me the trial was the only time he's been ashamed of his conduct as a lawyer." Her father got up from his desk and went to stand at the tall window overlooking Court Square.

"He told me how one day not long after the trial, he walked up to a group of smiling, happy Negro children and said hello. When they recognized him, the smiles vanished. At that moment he determined to do whatever he could to help Negroes achieve equality and justice. He's been true to his word ever since."

BETSY got so interested in her father's cases he asked her if she'd like to go to law school. But she wanted to be a writer.

She and Jerome were going to be writers together.

Late one night she started writing about the afternoon when she'd accompanied her father to the Pickens jail. It felt different from anything she'd ever written. When she stopped at three in the morning, she knew she'd found a path that had been obscured to her before. She thought maybe she'd begun a novel.

SHE was reading a lot, trying to figure out how to write:

Dear Jerome,

I just finished reading Go Tell It on the Mountain*! It's a brilliant book, just like you said. An amazing book! And to think I actually got to go to Baldwin's apartment and shake his hand!*

I know (because you told me so many times) that white people can't ever truly understand what it's like to be a Negro. But this novel put me as close as maybe I can get. It's heartbreaking in so many ways. Like how Deborah is raped by those white men. It's so horrible how Richard is arrested by the police, just because he was on the same subway platform as those Negro boys the cops were after. Just because he's a Negro, the police feel free—in fact, they relish—beating him at The Tombs. And there's no recourse, no justice—because he's a Negro. I think I'm beginning to understand. Maybe that's why you got so upset when I dreamed you were in jail. You're too close to being a Richard yourself.

THAT night after she wrote him, she dreamed about the empty cell again. This time the cell's interior was obscured in dark shadows. She detected a figure. At first she thought it was Willie Earle. Then she thought it was Jerome. But then she saw there were other black men in the cell. Lots of them. Negro women too. The whole Negro race.

ONE day that fall, her father arrived at the office as excited as she'd ever seen him. "Remember when Chief Justice Vinson died of a heart attack a few weeks ago! What luck!"

"Huh?" Betsy said.

He explained that Earl Warren would now be taking over as new chief justice of the Supreme Court. The plaintiffs' prospects in *Brown v. Board* had just greatly improved.

"For those of us who want to see *Plessy* overturned," her father said gleefully, "the timing of Vinson's death is an indication that there really is a God."

HER mother wanted to arrange a date for Betsy, but Betsy told her no. He was the son of one of the women Lydia knew at church, a Clemson graduate who was selling real estate and doing quite well at it. The kind of normal boy, or man, Betsy corrected herself, she was supposed to marry. Her mother got angry at her when she refused. Betsy pointed out that Lydia hadn't been on a date herself since the divorce. Her mother countered that she was middle-aged. Betsy said it didn't matter. They went their separate ways, each to think things over.

What Betsy wanted to tell her mother was that she was already married. What could be more ridiculous! But that's the way she felt. It was beyond stupid, and Betsy knew it, but there it was. She did grasp with her mind that she and Jerome were over. But another part of her, quite oblivious to reality, had its own emotions. Loving Jerome, feeling bonded to him. Being married to him.

33

LAWTON

BETSY HELPING HIM at the office was the best thing that could have happened to Lawton. Before she started working with him, he'd led a solitary life, going to work alone, coming back to the apartment, alone. He looked forward to her company every day, relishing telling her about cases and the law and just being with her again. How he wished he could reveal more of himself to her. He'd come close one time when she'd asked about the divorce, and he'd tried to explain that he shouldn't be married to any woman. He saw her expression; she didn't want to hear it. He would keep his nature to himself.

Thanks to Lydia, he enjoyed classical music. He'd started going to music programs, sometimes with Betsy, sometimes alone. One evening in late winter, he went to a piano concert at Furman University. According to the program, the guest pianist had gotten his music degree at Furman, studied piano at Juilliard, earned a medical degree and completed a residency at Columbia Presbyterian in New York. He'd recently moved to Greenville to practice cardiology. Impressive, Lawton thought.

When he came on stage, Frank Thompson looked to be in his early forties. He was of average height and build, with black hair and a mustache. There was nothing particularly striking about him, but his face was kind, his bearing gentle, the polar opposite of Poinsett Sam. No *prima donna*, he smiled warmly at the audience before taking his place on the piano bench. He played *Un Sospiro*, a lyric piece by Liszt with mesmerizing sensitivity and technical skill. There was complete silence when he finished, as if the audience needed another moment before re-entering the real world. Then the applause was loud and long.

Lawton lingered in the lobby after the concert, hoping Dr. Thompson would come out that way. He was drawn to say something to him. He noticed his heart was thumping more than the situation called for. Suddenly he came through the auditorium door, striding swiftly toward the outer doors. Across the lobby Lawton called to him, "Dr. Thompson!" He turned and perused Lawton. "Let me introduce myself," Lawton hurried over to him. "I'm Lawton Chastain. I just wanted to tell you how . . . beautifully you played."

"Oh, please call me Frank. Thank you so much. Could you tell how nervous I was? It's been ages since I performed here—not since I was an undergraduate. They only asked me because they needed to fill out the program."

"I doubt that," Lawton said emphatically.

They walked out together. A chilly March wind assaulted them, but they paused on the top step of the music building.

"Do you play?" Frank asked.

"No, I'm simply . . ." Frank's eyes were unexpectedly blue. Lawton's mind went blank. "An appreciator. Is that a word?"

Frank laughed. "It works for me."

Grasping at anything to extend the conversation, Lawton told him his former wife was a pianist and piano teacher.

"Well then, I'm sure she brought beautiful music into your life," Frank said. "Thank you for your kind words." With that he was gone.

LAWTON looked up Dr. Frank Thompson in the phone book. His office was located on Vardry Street. Were the palpitations he felt when he saw Frank's name reason enough to visit a cardiologist? Lawton drove by the building, feeling like a fool. A hopeless teenager. He thought of Harry Bumgarten and that rightness almost thirty years ago that he'd denied. He bought a recording of Liszt's *Un Sospiro* ("The Sigh," he read in the liner notes) and played it over and over, picturing Frank Thompson's face as he played. He longed to see that expression again, only with Frank in his arms.

He couldn't imagine how to meet Frank again. He thought about waiting in the parking lot of his office building. But what would he say and what would Frank think? Wouldn't it be obvious why Lawton was there? He pictured Frank's pretty wife and his lovely children. It was unthinkable.

And yet Lawton thought he saw something about Frank that he recognized. Maybe his body knew more than his mind. But he could be wrong. Very wrong. There was no way to know. It was too big a risk to contact him. Lawton resigned himself.

IT was five months later, at an organ concert at Christ Church, that he saw Frank Thompson again. It was August by then, the heat and humidity oppressive, especially in the sanctuary. The air conditioning had broken down but hopefully would be restarted shortly. They were both sitting on the right side, not many pews apart, fanning with their programs as they waited for the maintenance man to restart the AC. Frank, turning to survey the audience, recognized Lawton and stood, motioning with a tilt of his head to join him outside. No pretty wife, no lovely children. Lawton's heart halted in mid-beat. He wondered if Frank would have to resuscitate him.

Standing in the courtyard, they made small talk about the difference in temperature a few months could make. Then by mutual agreement, they decided to forget the concert and go get something cool to drink. They went to Howard Johnson's across from Woodlawn Cemetery and sat across from each other in a booth. They ordered fried clams, picking them up with their fingers. As naturally as if they'd known each other for years, they began telling their life stories while they drank sweet tea.

At one point, Frank looked Lawton in the eye and said he'd never been married. Not his cup of tea. Lawton stared at Frank in wonder. "Not mine either," he said. He pressed his hand over his heart to try to calm it, heat rising to his face.

"I thought so," Frank said, smiling.

34

BETSY

THE MONTHS WERE sliding past without her quite registering them. Betsy wondered if this would always be her life, living at home with her mother in Greenville, working at the law office with her father, writing a novel in isolation without any sense of whether what she wrote was good or bad. Even though she subscribed to *The New Yorker*, she rarely opened it. It brought back too many memories. She couldn't imagine ever returning to New York. It was hard to believe it actually existed.

Nor could she imagine ever being in love or having a boyfriend again. Even her mother had a boyfriend! Lydia was smitten with a widower, Perry Bowen, a gynecologist, which made Betsy feel a little squeamish—all those women with their feet up in stirrups. From what she could tell, everything in Greenville happened over a bridge game. One of her mother's friends had invited Lydia and Perry over to make a foursome. Now her mother was as giddy as a young girl in love. Betsy's own heart felt like an old crone's.

Dear Jerome,

I reread my copy of The Great Gatsby. *When I read it in college, it didn't mean much to me. That was before you. Now I understand Jay Gatsby in a way I couldn't then: he fell so in love with Daisy he spent the rest of his life believing that they would be together someday. His love for her was infinite—if delusional. She didn't love him the way he loved her—how could she? But Gatsby was true to his love for her. That I understand.*

O N E Saturday afternoon Huff stopped by to pick Alma up after the cooking lesson (Betsy had learned to make pineapple upside-down cake that day). He came around to the back door and knocked, and Alma took off her apron and let him in. Betsy had forgotten how big he was, a large Negro man, grinning broadly when he saw her, but deferential too, the way Negro men had to be to white girls like her. "Huff," she said too enthusiastically, as if to make up for it. She shook his big hand, which was calloused and warm. They exchanged small talk, Betsy bragging on Pretty's piano playing and Huff teasing Betsy over her reputation as the best biscuit maker in South Carolina. "If you don't mind eating pucks," she deadpanned. She walked them to Huff's truck, wondering how things were going between them. When she'd asked Alma one time, all she said was, "He comes 'round." Did that mean they were just friends now or husband and wife again?

After they left, Betsy lingered in the backyard. The red roses were in full bloom. In a pensive mood, she picked off a few spent blossoms. She was remembering something: When she was thirteen or fourteen, Huff would come over on Saturdays to do yard work. If she was home alone, she didn't want him to know she was in the house. She'd sneak around and lock all the doors. What had she been thinking? That he would break in and rape her? Simply because he was a Negro man? Even at the time she knew she was just play-acting.

Now she understood it was she who was violating Huff.

ONE evening that fall Betsy stopped by her father's apartment, walking in as usual without knocking. A handsome man with thick black hair, bushy eyebrows, and a mustache was sitting on the couch next to her father. They were having a drink. Nothing more. But the look on their faces!

Daddy had a guest, that was all. But it was weird how electric the air felt. He introduced the man, Dr. Thompson, who stood up and shook Betsy's hand. Told her to call him Frank. She stared at Frank. Her father offered her a drink. Dr. Thompson—Frank—said he was just leaving—though his drink was half full. They all experienced a frozen moment like when a movie film breaks.

Finally Betsy came to. "Oh please—don't go. I can't stay. I told Mother I'd be home before dark."

She didn't want to look at her father. She hurried out the door.

All the way down the stairs, a line kept drumming in her head: "Daddy has a boyfriend! Daddy has a boyfriend!"

She knew Greenwich Village had homosexuals—but not Greenville! And not her own father!

And yet . . . No. She couldn't even think about it.

SHE didn't know what to say to her father at work the next day. She didn't know whether to bring up Dr. Thompson— Frank—or what. She wanted to pretend it had never happened, that there wasn't a handsome man with a mustache having a drink with Daddy in his apartment. She tried to carry on with their usual routine. She went in her father's office and asked what he wanted her to do that day. He shuffled some papers on his desk and then went to stand at the window overlooking Court Square with his back to her. She waited for him to speak, but after what seemed like an eternity, she couldn't stand it any longer. She blurted out nervously, "Dr. Thompson seems nice. I . . ."

"He's a cardiologist," her father said, still looking out his window. "He moved from New York to practice here. He's originally from Virginia. He's a wonderful pianist."

"Oh," Betsy said. "How did you meet him? I mean . . ."

"He gave a concert at Furman," her father said, and now he turned and looked at her.

"Oh," she said again.

She waited for him to say more. But he just handed her some letters to retype. "You're making a lot fewer mistakes," he said, smiling in a way she couldn't read.

SHE could hardly wait to tell her mother about the man in her father's apartment. Telling about it would make it real. She pictured her mother's face when Betsy described how they'd looked: caught! She and her mother could be incredulous, hurt, and furious together. Now it all fell into place: why her father had wanted a divorce. He hadn't been able to tell Lydia the truth. Well, she would!

When she got home, her mother was upstairs getting dressed. She and Perry went out nearly every night now. She came down the stairs like Loretta Young, in a pale blue satin sheath, her face radiant. She did a twirl for Betsy in the kitchen. "We're going to the Medical Association ball at the Poinsett," she announced. "Perry's picking me up in a few minutes."

"You look beautiful," Betsy said. She couldn't give her mother the news right before they went out. She'd have to wait until she got home.

But her mother didn't come home that night. She called at eleven to tell Betsy she was staying over at Perry's. "Oh, okay," Betsy said, dazed. Were they having sex? Her mother? It didn't seem possible. But that might explain how happy her mother seemed these days.

Betsy sat in the dark living room alone, brooding. Her father was a homosexual. All these years, living a lie! How could he do this to her mother and to her? But she loved her father. He wasn't a bad person. He was about the best person she knew. Could you love and hate a person at the same time?

She'd had some experience with *that*.

And her mother! She was in love. And shacking up! With Perry. He was okay, nice enough. But—he was still Perry.

It was all very confusing.

35

ALMA

BESSIE WANTED ALMA to go to church on Sundays with the family, and Alma was willing. She figured it might help her in her struggle with the devil, who was proving a mighty adversary. When she'd finished the whiskey she brought from up North, she'd thrown the bottle as far as she could into the swirling brown water of the Reedy River. But now whenever she passed an ABC store, she couldn't resist the pull to go in. The devil tempted her every night in her room, telling her it wouldn't hurt to have a little nip. Take the edge off. That nip always led to another and then another, until she was drowsing in a hazy fog.

But Bessie was fighting the devil too, and her mama was a powerful warrior for Jesus. She knelt down with Alma every night and prayed to Him to give Alma strength. Alma prayed too, though she couldn't feel the Lord. Where once He had been a close, reliable presence to whom she told her troubles, now there was absence.

Every Sunday that winter and spring, wearing a suit, heels

that hurt her bunions, a large-brimmed hat with netting swirled around the crown and white gloves, Alma settled in the pew with Pretty on one side and Bessie on the other. She let the singing and sermons pour over her. She had thirst but couldn't drink. Still, it felt good to be surrounded by men and women who'd helped raise her in the community, who had praised and encouraged her, and who'd welcomed her home.

Reverend Albertson always started out slow, and then got rolling, calling out to the congregants, who answered back his calls for "Can I get a witness?" or "Do I hear an amen?" as he drew them in. Alma thought he had an uncanny way of speaking directly to her: *The devil knows your address, he knows your phone number, he knows what to bait your hook with . . . Through trials and tribulations, even the strongest Christian gets weak . . . Our attitude angry, our hearts hopeless, our minds miserable . . . When we look we can only see the now—but God sees the beginning through to the end . . . Grace is when you get what you do not deserve . . . Put your faith and comfort in the Lord.*

SHE was working at Carolina Blouse as a presser. Every day she rode the bus to River Street downtown. She liked pressing the beautiful Macshore Classic blouses they made. There wasn't anything hard to it, she'd been ironing all her life. She liked being in the big upstairs room with the other women. For the eight hours she was there, paying close attention to the collars and sleeves so there were no wrinkles kept her mind off her failings. She was getting a regular paycheck, not as much as what she'd made working for Mr. Stern, but more than she'd ever made before in Greenville. She was through being a maid.

WHEN school began again that fall, every evening she sat with Pretty at the kitchen table while she worked on her homework. Her math book was used, previous pupils' names written in and crossed out, the penciled-in answers erased so many times the cheap paper was torn in places. Pretty couldn't bring her Reader home because they didn't have enough for all the colored children.

The women at Carolina Blouse talked about what might be coming when the Supreme Court ruled. Some of them were for integration of the schools; some were against, saying it would just lead to more trouble, maybe even violence. Huff thought getting new school books for Negroes and building them a swimming pool and community center the way Greenville was doing wasn't enough. The NAACP wanted to go for broke, desegregation or nothing, he said. They wanted the same rights as whites, in everything. Alma didn't argue with him, but all of that was impossible. White people would never allow it.

Huff had a room on Spring Street, but he spent a lot of time over at Delores and Stew's in the evenings, courting, as Delores teased him. He wanted to rent a house, so Alma, Pretty, and he could live as a family again. Huff *had* changed. He'd stopped drinking and he went to church now, something he never did when they lived together. But Alma wasn't sure. She wasn't ready.

"What would make you ready?" Huff asked one night, turning her arm over, running his finger along the soft skin there, sending a shiver down her. "Would this make you ready?"

Alma felt long-ago feelings stir in her, something sweet and heavy in her womb. But she pulled her arm back. How could she move in with Huff? She already had a lover, whom she kept a secret from everyone. She waited until Huff left every night, and everyone was in bed. Then she'd meet Mr. Jim Beam alone up in her room. She knew she couldn't have Huff and Jim too.

HUFF was badgering her to register to vote. Bessie wanted to register, but she couldn't read and write. Pretty was teaching her to write her name. All these new ideas scared Alma. Pushing things might bring more trouble to coloreds. They didn't need that.

Huff told her about a white lawyer, John Bolt Culbertson, the very same one who'd defended the cab drivers at the Willie Earle trial. He was driving all over the state to get Negroes to join the NAACP and register people to vote. "Ol' Cotton got the registration board to paint footprints going into their office to show where to go," Huff chuckled. "You know if a white man done that, you got to do *your* part!" Alma was hesitant. She'd heard stories of Negroes being beaten or fired for registering. She kept putting him off. "'Soon' ain't soon enough!" Huff said. "Now we got the right, we got to vote. You say you want a better life for Pretty? It start with the ballot box. If you voteless you hopeless."

"I will, soon," she said, not meeting his eyes.

ALMA was pleased with how well Pretty was doing. When she went to the teacher conference, Miss Smith bragged on her. "She's a pleasure to teach," Miss Smith said. "She's quick to learn, but she also works hard. She wants to do well."

"Miss Smith said some mighty good things about you," Alma told Pretty that night when they were going over her arithmetic homework.

"She's nice to all the kids," Pretty said. "Even Hiram who can't stay in his seat. She turns her back for one second and he jumps up and pulls Deely's hair or pokes Billy with his pencil."

"What does Miss Smith do then?"

"Makes him stand in the corner."

"Do you ever have to stand in the corner?"

"One time I did. It's boring in the corner!" Pretty giggled. "Miss Smith said there's scholarships to go to college. That's how she got to college. I'm gonna get me a scholarship and be a teacher like Miss Smith."

"That a long way off," Alma said. "We see when the time come. You got to keep learning your lessons now."

"I'm gonna go to the University of South Carolina," Pretty announced proudly.

Alma was silent. The University of South Carolina was whites only.

"Well," Alma said, feeling unsettled. "College a long way off. You got to do good on this test tomorrow."

When Alma told Huff what Pretty said about going to USC, he reared back. They were sitting in the hanging swing out back of Delores and Stew's. "How she even know about the University of South Carolina?"

"She pick up everything," Alma said. "I told her don't go thinking about college, be thinking about her learning now. I figure she'll go to the colored college in Orangeburg. Delores say the legislature givin' them lots of money to build new buildings."

"So they won't have to integrate the university!" Huff said hotly. "They gonna do everything they can to keep us separate. To keep us down. Ain't nothing gonna change 'til we make 'em change."

Now Alma was silent. How could Negroes make white people change? Huff was foolish to think anything could change them.

ONE Sunday morning when Huff came by to go to church with them, he told them the police had broken into his room on Spring Street the previous night, didn't even knock, just busted down the door. Tore the place up.

"Lord, Lord," Bessie exclaimed. "What they do that for?"

"NAACP," Alma said. "Po-lice leaving their message." Bitterness flared in her. "Everybody know they treat us any way they want to."

"That's why we got to get people to vote!" Huff exclaimed. "We cain't change nothin' if we don't elect folks who take our side. Once them politicians get holt of the power of Negro voters, they change their tune."

The next week Alma told Huff she wanted to register to vote. That Sunday after church, A.J. Whittenberg came over to Stew and Delores's with a voter registration application. Alma filled in her name, gender, race, and address, her weight and height, and the color of her eyes and hair. A.J. told her where to go to register. He read her the rules: she'd have to swear under oath that she was not an idiot, insane, a pauper supported at public expense, or confined to a public prison. She'd have to demonstrate to the registration board that she could read and write a section of the Constitution of South Carolina.

"They won't fool with no Constitution," A.J. said. "It'll be the Bible."

"That won't be a problem."

"She graduated near the top of her class at Sterling," Huff bragged. "Oh go on," Alma said, punching him in the shoulder.

A. J. slowly read the last registration question aloud: "I (a) have never been convicted of any of the following crimes: burglary, arson, obtaining goods or money under false pretenses, perjury, forgery, robbery, bribery, adultery, bigamy, wife beating, housebreaking, receiving stolen goods, breach of trust with fraudulent intent, fornication, sodomy, incest, assault with intent to ravish, miscegenation, larceny, or crimes against the election laws; or (b) been legally pardoned for such conviction."

"Whoa," Huff said. "Ain't nobody that good!"

"I don't know what some of them crimes is," Alma said, "but even if I done 'em, I'm checking the box that I ain't."

Huff put his arm around her and gave her a big squeeze. "You stop that now, Huff Stone. I'm a married woman!" But she didn't push him away.

"Voteless people is hopeless people," A.J. was saying. "We done with being hopeless people."

THE voter registration office would be open on Tuesday. On Monday Alma told her supervisor that she'd be late to work the next day. Mrs. Reynolds looked at her with a worried expression. They'd always gotten along well. "What you got to do, Alma?" she asked. "You got to go to the doctor?"

Alma was silent. Mrs. Reynolds was white, and she didn't want to tell her about registering to vote.

But then she raised her eyes and heard herself saying, "I got to register to vote."

Mrs. Reynolds's eyebrows shot up in surprise. They stared at each other for a suspended moment. Then Mrs. Reynolds said, "Take the whole day off if you need to, Alma."

Was she being fired?

"You're my best presser. And your people—well, it's time. Past time."

The next morning Huff drove Alma downtown to the registration office. She'd dressed in her best clothes, a dark-blue skirt and jacket set. She was nervous, but she felt well prepared. When she handed her application back to the clerk, he told her to put her hand on the Bible and he'd swear her in. He pointed to the lines at the bottom on the form. "Is that it?" Alma said. "I don't get to read from the Bible?" "Not necessary," the clerk said. "I can tell who can read and write." She signed her name, *Alma Stone*, and the clerk circled "found qualified" and signed his name below hers.

Alma felt a strange sensation roar through her. Maybe this was what it felt like when the Holy Spirit moved through you.

But it wasn't the Holy Spirit. It was the wind of change.

36

LAWTON

IN THE BEGINNING Lawton and Frank Thompson met for dinner, varying the restaurants so as not to draw too much attention to themselves. They told each other their stories, keeping their voices low. Frank had known from the time he was six that he was different. He picked up signals, subtle and otherwise, that it was wrong for him to play with his sisters' dolls and that pink could not be his favorite color. When he was older, he was teased mercilessly when he asked the neighbor boy to hold hands as they walked to school. His parents put him in Boy Scouts, sent him to summer camp to "make a man out of him," and signed him up for football, where he was more interested in the other boys showering in the locker room than in learning the plays. He had his first sexual experience at Juilliard the year after college and fell in love, only to have his heart broken. He'd had a couple of tumultuous relationships in the service, but having been burned, he hadn't looked for opportunities for romance when he was in medical school and during his residency. He considered it a miracle that he'd found Lawton.

Lawton told Frank about Harry Bumgarten and how he'd married Lydia to escape the feelings he'd had for him. He told Frank about Willie Earle and the trial. He told him about the Open Door. "If anyone had suggested that you would be waiting on the other side," he told Frank, shaking his head in wonder, "I wouldn't have believed it."

Lawton was intimidated that Frank had had more experience. Lawton's experience consisted of a few minutes of ecstasy when he was twenty-two, followed by years of denial, guilt, and shame. But the first time with Frank wasn't as hard as Lawton had imagined—or rather it was. Very hard! And the loving touch of another human being, another man, was such a release and so satisfying it brought tears to his eyes. *Un Sospiro* indeed!

THROUGHOUT that fall Lawton and Betsy maintained their working relationship, settling back into their routine with no mention of Frank. At work they were able to pretend they didn't have unspoken business between them. But Betsy declined Lawton's invitations to have lunch or supper. Underneath her facade of politeness, he felt she regarded him with distrust and maybe even rancor.

A new development: with Christmas approaching, Lydia invited Lawton to the open house she and Perry were hosting on Christmas Eve.

The invitation caused Lawton both a pang and a dilemma. He and Lydia used to host open houses every Christmas Eve. They'd invite everyone they knew—friends, neighbors, relatives, law colleagues; it had been a favorite tradition. A pang, because if he went, he'd be a guest in his former house at a party he used to host.

A dilemma, because he didn't want to go. It would be embarrassing for all concerned. He figured he was still a blackguard to most people who'd known Lydia and him as a couple. He tried to beg off, but Lydia would have none of it. She'd moved on, she said, and wanted him to do the same. She even had a boyfriend now, a doctor named Perry Bowen. But Betsy, without saying so outright, had made it clear she wanted little to do with him. She wouldn't want him at the party.

Frank gave him good counsel: Lawton should stop feeling like a criminal. Go and hold his head up. Lawton should be gracious to Lydia since she was being gracious to him. As for Betsy, from what Lawton had told him about her, she'd come around. She'd had a shock, but she loved Lawton, Frank was sure of it. She'd eventually accept him for who he was.

"All right!" he finally said. "I'll go. Geez, you sound like my mother."

How he wished he could bring Frank with him! But of course that was out of the question.

WITH the wretched Christmas Eve open house looming on the horizon and Betsy still cool to him, something had to be done.

They went about their business on the Wednesday before Christmas, Betsy reading through a deposition for an insurance case and Lawton behind his closed door fidgeting and nervous over the plan he'd hatched.

At eleven he came out of his hidey-hole and told Betsy to get her pocketbook and coat; they were going for a ride. She looked up in alarm. "Where?"

"Just get your coat," Lawton said. "You'll see."

Neither of them spoke as they rode down in the elevator.

Lawton wondered if it would break down, and they'd be trapped in silence forever. When it reached ground floor and still without a word, they pushed through the revolving door onto Main Street.

"Where are we going?" she asked again, and again he told her she'd see. At least she didn't protest or resist. He was still her father, and she'd grown up obeying him.

He'd parked the Ford behind the Poinsett; they walked to it down Court Street in silence. It was in the fifties, a sunny mild day. "No white Christmas this year," Lawton said inanely, and Betsy shot him a petulant look.

More silence in the car. He drove up North Main, his stomach churning acid. Betsy stared out the passenger window, occasionally chewing on a thumbnail.

When he started up Paris Mountain, she said, "Are you kidnapping me, Daddy?" He wasn't sure if it was a joke or not. But at least she'd spoken.

"I'm not sure you can kidnap your own kid," he said. After a moment he said, "Do you remember how we'd take Sunday drives over Paris Mountain when you were a kid? All those scary turns. You'd have to sit in the front seat to keep from getting carsick."

"You liked to torture me then just like you're torturing me now," she said. But this time he caught a touch of sarcastic humor in her voice.

"Remember how we'd drive up to Marietta," he said. "We'd visit the country relatives. They'd always give us their hand-churned butter. You'd run down the path to the barn to visit the mule."

"I loved that mule. Where are we going, Daddy?"

"To Frank's," Lawton said. "He's making lunch for us." He

was squeezing the steering wheel more than was necessary. He slowed for the first hairpin curve.

"Why?"

"Why is he making lunch or why are we going?"

"Is he your boyfriend now?"

Lawton gave a little snort. "I hadn't thought of it like that," he said. "But yes, Betsy. That's one way of putting it. He's my boyfriend."

"But why?"

"Because . . ." He didn't know how to explain. "Have you ever been in love? I mean deeply in love?"

She was silent for a long while, staring out the window.

"You're not feeling carsick, are you?"

"I've been in love," she said at last. "I know about love, Daddy. I know all about it."

"Is that what happened to you in New York?"

"Yes."

"It ended badly."

"Badly," she said.

"I'm so sorry, honey."

"It's okay. Is this Frank's?"

They had pulled into the narrow parking space in front of Frank's house, which was down a steep grade. It was a white modern house that clung to the mountainside, like a lot of the houses on Paris Mountain.

"Before we go in," he said, "I want you to know something. I've told Frank this, but it's not his decision." He gathered himself. "If you want me to give Frank up, I will. It won't change who I am. I know that now. I didn't know or accept it, I guess you could say, for most of my life. All through my marriage to your mother. But if it makes you so unhappy . . ."

Betsy turned a serious, troubled face to him. "Daddy," she said, "I'm not sure I want to do this." She looked down toward the house. "But let's not keep Frank waiting."

THEY walked down the steep steps to the front door and rang the bell. Frank, wearing a smile and a chef's black apron, ushered them in. Lawton knew he could at least count on Betsy for manners. She'd been raised by Lydia, after all.

"Oh my," she said as they stepped down three shiny wood steps into the living room, a bright open area with a large picture window across the far side.

"There's a better view out on the deck," Frank said. "Don't take off your coat quite yet."

Lawton and he cut their eyes at each other behind her as they followed Betsy out the door to the deck, which seemed suspended in mid-air. It was a brisk, clear day. Far below was a rural valley where the few farmhouses and barns looked like toys one could hold in one hand. Beyond were the gray-blue mountains. "Is that Table Rock?" Betsy asked. Far to the right they could just see its bald rock face.

"I was so lucky to get this place," Frank explained. He told how it had just come on the market when he came to Greenville to interview for the cardiology position at the hospital. "As soon as I walked in, I had to have it. I put an offer on the house that night, even before I had the job. It was all a little nerve-wracking, but it's worked out."

"I can see why you wanted this view," Betsy said. Again Frank and Lawton met eyes behind her back, hopeful. To Lawton, watching Frank as he pointed out various landmarks below, he was perfect: his kind face, his warm hospitality without being fawning, his apparent ease in what couldn't have been an easy situation. How could he have even imagined offering to give Frank up?

"Let me take your coat," Frank said when they went back inside. "What would you like to drink? Tea? Hot or cold? Coffee? White wine? A Coke, maybe?"

"Sweet tea would be fine if you have it," Betsy said. "Oh what a beautiful piano!" She went over to the baby grand that was off to the left side of the large room. Frank had it positioned so he could see the mountains while he played. Betsy ran her fingers lightly over its black surface. "My mother plays the piano."

"Your father's told me she's a fine musician. Do you play?"

"I wish," Betsy said. "I stopped playing when I was about sixteen. Recitals scared me."

"Me too," Frank said. "Let me get that tea. Lawton, what for you?"

A stiff drink he wanted to say, but he murmured that tea would be fine too.

Frank brought their drinks over to where they stood by the piano. "It was my mother's," he said. "The fellows who delivered it had quite a time getting it down the hill." He tilted his head toward the sharp grade out front.

"How does one even move a grand piano?" Betsy asked.

"With a lot of grunting, apparently. I couldn't bear to watch—I had to leave the house," Frank laughed.

"Maybe Frank will play something for us after lunch," Lawton said, thinking of the times he'd lain on Frank's white sofa, lost in happiness while Frank played.

"Lunch! Is anyone hungry?" Frank said. "I made oyster stew."

"My favorite!" Betsy exclaimed.

"So your father said."

"Daddy would take me to the Otteray Hotel when I was little. We'd sit on stools at the lunch counter and have big bowls of it with oyster crackers."

"Well, mine isn't going to measure up I'm sure, but let's give it a try."

THINGS were going well, Lawton thought. He didn't see how Betsy couldn't take to Frank. And yet he felt they were tiptoeing across a minefield. At any moment something could be said that would blow up all his hopes for this meeting.

"What are your plans for Christmas, Frank?" Betsy asked over her second bowl of stew. Her face turned red. Lawton knew as soon as the words left her mouth, she was afraid of the answer: that Frank was spending Christmas with him. But Frank explained he was leaving tomorrow to drive to Virginia to spend Christmas with his sister, her husband, and their two children.

Betsy looked at Lawton, a worried expression on her face. She'd made a point of not asking him *his* Christmas plans—just another way of punishing him. He didn't have any plans, except for the dreaded open house on Christmas Eve. Betsy was going to Grand Bee and Lyman's for brunch on Christmas and then to Perry's with Lydia for a five o'clock dinner with Perry's two daughters and their families. Lawton would see his parents at the open house, but on Christmas Day he planned to mope around, missing Frank, missing Betsy, and feeling sorry for himself.

"Maybe it's time for some music," he said, to change the subject.

"Would you play something, Frank?" Betsy rose to clear the table.

"Just leave everything," Frank said.

Betsy and Lawton sat on the white sectional sofa, and Frank adjusted the piano bench.

"Your father and I met at a concert at Furman," he said, smiling at Betsy. "On a cold March night. Someone in the music department invited me to play because they had no one else they could coerce."

"False modesty will get you nowhere," Lawton said.

"All right then," Frank smiled. "Let's see." He paused. "I'll play something I bet you know."

After the last bars of *Moonlight Sonata* had died away, Betsy said, "I know it well. Mother used to play it all the time. I haven't heard her play it lately though. Maybe because she's finally happy."

Frank nodded. "In my profession," he said, "you see a lot of humanity. A lot of it *in extremis*. For me that piece says all that can't be said—at least in words. I play it whenever I need beauty . . . and comfort."

THEY made their departure. Betsy thanked Frank for his hospitality. "Your oyster stew definitely outdoes the Otteray's."

"Please come back sometime," he said. Betsy extended her hand and Frank took it.

They rode down the mountain without speaking. Lawton couldn't read her. Was she mad at him for forcing her to go through an encounter she didn't want? Had she liked Frank? Been won over?

Finally he said, "Did you enjoy it?"

"Yes," she said. "He's . . . lovely."

When they pulled up in front of the house on Crescent

Avenue, the house that used to be their house, Lawton felt a surge of sadness. Happiness came with a steep price.

Betsy turned to him in the car before getting out. "You really are dreading coming to the open house, aren't you?"

Lawton nodded. "I'll stick out like a sore thumb. People will wonder what the hell I'm doing there, and I'll wonder too. But your mother wants me to come, so I am."

"Does Mother know?"

"About Frank and me? No. I have a feeling she'd prefer not to know. Not now, at least. Maybe the time will come. Like you say, she's happy. I don't see the point in spoiling that."

Betsy nodded. "She's in love. And you are too. Just not with someone I'd have expected."

She opened her door and got out of the car.

"And Daddy," she said, leaning back in. "About the open house? Don't worry. I'll protect you."

37

BETSY

BETSY STILL WROTE to Jerome, unsent unread letters, most of which she now penned only in her mind. Her heart held onto him like the shark she'd read about that wouldn't let go of a man's leg, even after it was dead. But she wanted to let go. She was lonely for love.

The problem was how to meet someone who could pry those shark jaws loose. Jenny Meadows, now Jenny Lewis, her best friend in junior high who'd reappeared in her life since Betsy had returned to Greenville, had lined her up with several of her husband Beau's friends: Howard McDermott, a foot too short; Jimmy Callahan, bad breath; Roger Coggeshall, nose picker. She was beginning to think all the good men were taken.

So when her mother told her the O'Brians were bringing their son Tim to the Christmas Eve open house, it was all Betsy could do to keep from rolling her eyes. Her mother immediately said, "Now you be nice to him," meaning, *Give him a chance.* Her mother was, in Betsy's opinion, overly excited about Tim O'Brian, who, she related, was in medical school in Charleston. Betsy remembered him vaguely from junior high: a bratty, pimply, know-it-all who went off to military school in the ninth grade. He hadn't crossed her mind since.

But when he arrived with his parents, Betsy couldn't believe he was the same Tim O'Brian who'd snapped girls' bras from behind. He had on a beautiful camel hair overcoat that matched the camel color of his crew cut. His face had cleared up and matured into male-model perfection. He was five foot eleven, which worked, even with Betsy wearing heels, which she was. Her mother had taken her to Half-Acre Osborne to buy a new cocktail dress with a full white skirt and red velvet bodice, very Christmassy. She'd tortured her hair into ringlets with a curling iron. She and Tim eyed each other with surprise. Betsy, suddenly aflutter, offered to take his coat, resisting the temptation to stroke it. When she ran upstairs to put it in the guest room, she ducked into the bathroom and re-powdered her nose.

Her father poured Tim a drink, adding an extra splash of bourbon. He was getting through the open house better than Betsy had expected, maybe because she'd let him off the hook, maybe because everyone was in a holiday mood, or maybe because he'd fortified himself with a few shots of Old Canadian before he arrived. Betsy had forgiven him for kidnapping her and taking her to meet Frank. She'd liked Frank; she could see why her father might love him. They went together, she thought, better than her father and mother ever did. She knew from experience that love wasn't bound by society's rules. Love was its own kingdom.

She led Tim into the dining room, handing him a crystal salad plate. There was an elaborate spread on the dining room table, festive with a red tablecloth and lighted candles in candelabras: Alma's chicken salad in pastry puffs from Strossner's bakery; shrimp in a silver bowl nestled in crushed ice; Duke's pimento cheese sandwiches Betsy and Alma had decrusted and sliced into finger sandwiches; cheese biscuits with a pecan on each top; salted mixed nuts; iced Christmas cookies; and Alma's three-layer coconut cake on a glass pedestal stand. Alma was there to help with the party, the way she always had when Betsy was growing up. Betsy had grumbled to Alma about her mother's matchmaking while they were getting the food ready. Alma predicted she'd end up marrying Tim and have to eat her words, in addition to too many chicken salad puffs.

Perry was playing Christmas records on the stereo (Daddy's stereo!). When "You're All I Want for Christmas" came on, Betsy felt a Jerome pang. But she turned her attention back to Tim, who was devouring a pimento cheese finger in two bites. She smiled at him. Maybe he could pry open the shark's jaws.

She led him into the den where there was a fire in the fireplace. They sat on the hearth, telling each other about their lives, though Betsy gave him an edited version of hers. She made him laugh, demonstrating her French accent, which had earned her a C. "They must speak that in the South of France," Tim said, and he ripped off a few sentences in perfect French himself, not that Betsy could understand them. He told her how hard medical school was. He was taking anatomy, histology, biochemistry, and some other "ology" Betsy had never heard of. He planned to join his father's dermatology practice. Betsy withheld that his father had treated her face for acne with a sunlamp when she was in junior high.

When he left with his parents, he asked if he could call her. Betsy said yes.

THAT night she wrote to Jerome, telling him she'd met someone, adding that she knew it wouldn't make him jealous because at this point he wouldn't care. She told him how Tim had asked if he could call. She described how strange it was to think of going on a date with someone else, of maybe even falling in love with him. She poured out her conflicted—"stupid"—feelings about "betraying" Jerome, of losing him when in fact she already had. Then she took the letter downstairs and laid it on the dying embers of the fire in the den. Watching it curl and burn into black ash that floated up the chimney, she felt bereft.

GREENVILLE had a two-inch snowfall two days after Christmas. Betsy was awakened by an unusual sound. It was Tim, shoveling or rather scraping the light snow off the driveway. "You can just wait, it'll melt in an hour or two!" Betsy called to him, shivering in the front doorway in her pink robe.

"I insist," he insisted back. "Do you want to go to Capri's tonight and catch a movie?"

"Yes," Betsy said, feeling a thrill she hadn't felt in a long time. "What time?"

Tim rang the doorbell that evening precisely at six. Betsy's mother invited him in, and from upstairs, Betsy heard Perry greeting him heartily, hopefully not overdoing it. Betsy, checking herself for the last time in the hall mirror at the top of the stairs, heard Tim politely thanking her mother for such a nice party and her mother murmuring something. A memory flitted across her brain: Jerome following her up the four flights at her building on Carmine. That world was gone forever, she reminded herself. She turned and started down the stairs, her cheeks flushed with excitement.

Tim, in his camel hair coat, watched her descend with what she could tell was approval. She was wearing a form-fitting white sweater with tiny round pearl buttons down the front, a wide belt that cinched her waist and a pleated navy wool skirt. "Hi," they said self-consciously, while her mother and Perry looked on, grinning too much. Tim helped her on with her coat and said to Lydia, "I'll take good care of her." At least her mother didn't tell Betsy what time to be home. She and Tim walked in silence to his Nash Rambler, blue with a darker blue roof, parked in the newly scraped driveway. He held the door for her, and she folded her skirt and coat into the small car.

They made the smallest of small talk. Had she ever been to Capri's? How long had he had the car? What movie were they going to? Betsy looked out the window at the familiar streets of her hometown. There was something equally familiar about Tim. He was like the boys she had grown up with in Greenville: boys who came from nice families like her own (though as far as she knew, none of them had a homosexual for a father), boys who dressed in khakis and polo shirts and had good teeth. They were, on the whole, likeable boys, sincere, good-hearted boys, boys who grew up to be good family men. Boys who would never leave the South and who distrusted "Yanks." Sunday church-going boys, Clemson fanatics, conservative politically, accepting of the status quo. Such boys were nothing like the inscrutable Jerome. Riding next to the affable Tim, who drove confidently on the ice-slicked streets with one hand while he described in detail the MacGregor Tourney golf clubs he'd gotten for Christmas (the Eye-O-Matic woods, the ceramic-face irons, the Pro Peel steel shafts), she wondered if she had imagined Jerome: a strange feverish dream.

Over pepperoni pizza, Tim told her how awful military school had been—"the worst part was no girls!" He talked happily about his wild days at Clemson, hinting that he'd made up for lost time with girls. Betsy wondered where he'd met all these girls, since Clemson wasn't co-ed. He described how he lived for golf, lamenting that med school had really cut down on his chances to get out on the links. He'd chosen dermatology, not just because of his father's practice, but because it didn't require being on call. He hoped to have a family someday—he loved children, he said, taking a big bite of pizza. Betsy smiled and nodded, and when it was her turn, she told him selectively about her time in New York, entertaining him with stories of the young actors and actresses she'd met at the theatrical agency. When he asked why she'd come home, she hesitated. "I guess I was just homesick."

That night they went to see *We're Not Angels*, with Humphrey Bogart. It was supposed to be a comedy, she gathered. She was relieved it wasn't about some romantic, doomed love affair like *Casablanca*. Jerome blazed through her mind, a shooting star. She focused on Tim sitting beside her, laughing and eating popcorn, enjoying himself. Occasionally he'd turn to look at her and smile. He was nice. He offered her the popcorn, which she'd initially declined. But now she took a big handful.

After he drove her home, they stood awkwardly on her front porch. "I had a great time," Tim said. "I really enjoyed this evening." He looked in her eyes. "Listen, I have to go back to Charleston tomorrow. But I'll be back as soon as I can." He leaned in and kissed her on the cheek.

Under the front porch light, she nodded. "I had a good time too." Her cheek felt tingly where his lips had touched it. When he got to his car, he paused to look back at her and blew her another kiss.

H E R mother was waiting up for her. "How'd it go?" she asked as she followed Betsy into the kitchen. Betsy began rooting around in the icebox for something to eat.

"He's nice," Betsy said when she'd found some chicken salad puffs left over from the party. "He wants to see me again."

"I'm not sure that chicken salad is still good. It sat out a long time," her mother said. "He seems quite nice."

"He is," Betsy said, sitting down at the table in the break-fast room. "And good-looking. Normal. Definitely nice."

It was just that he wasn't Jerome.

"What did you and Perry do?"

Her mother said they'd watched *The Jackie Gleason Show* at his house. Betsy wanted to ask if they'd made out, a lit-tle joke, but she didn't want to be impertinent. Her mother and the balding, rotund Perry were together now practically every night. Betsy hadn't realized how lonely her mother was.

She lay in bed that night wondering if she and Tim would ever have sex. What would that be like? Jerome was her first and only. What would Tim think if he found out she wasn't a virgin? But why would she be? He'd been interested—but a little intimidated she detected—when she talked about New York City. Her hand drifted down between her legs. She con-sidered making love with Jerome or what passed for Jerome now. But she reminded herself she was trying to pry the shark teeth from her heart. She called to mind Tim's handsome face, his tan crew cut, the way he smiled at her as she came down the stairs. The little kiss at the door. Maybe the shark teeth were loosening a bit. Though the rending pain was terrible.

ON January 24, a dozen long-stemmed red roses arrived at the house. The card read "To celebrate our first anniversary!" She and Tim had met a month ago on Christmas Eve. Her mother unwrapped the roses from the clear cellophane and green tissue, exclaiming over each velvety half-opened bud. If Tim had meant to bowl Betsy over, he'd succeeded.

COMING home in the evening from her father's office, Betsy would look first to see if there was a letter not just from Zora but from Tim now on the entryway table. He wrote nearly every day in his big scrawling script, using several pages of notebook paper to write five or six lines, always ending with a sweet or cute endearment: *Can't wait to see you again; I loved you in that white sweater—wear it next time I'm home; Your hair is perfect*—something Betsy had never imagined hearing from anyone, ever. Betsy wrote him right back. She found it easier to talk to Tim in writing than in person. She thought about telling him about the novel she was writing, but it seemed too private. "Writing" Jerome was still a habit she couldn't break, if only in her head. Not a day went by that she didn't think of him.

ON Valentine's Day Tim sent her the biggest red satin, heart-shaped box of Whitman's chocolates she'd ever seen. On the front was a picture of a perky housewife kissing a man in a gray suit on the cheek: "A woman never forgets the man who remembers." Betsy studied this line. In her experience it was more like "A woman always remembers the man who forgets."

H E was finally able to come home for a weekend in April. On Friday night they had dinner with his folks, who had a big brick house on James Street, not unlike the one she'd grown up in on Crescent Avenue; her mother and Mrs. O'Brian had used the same interior decorator. They'd been classmates at Agnes Scott. Luckily Dr. O'Brian didn't seem to remember Betsy from her sunlamp treatments; his own face was rosy and wrinkle-free. They had a daughter, Mary Rose, who was a junior at Greenville High.

She could see where Tim got his niceness: The O'Brians were all nice. "Tim's never brought a girl home before," Mrs. O'Brian confided when Betsy was helping her get the salads ready in the kitchen. Dr. O'Brian, serving from the head of the table, put more fish sticks, mashed potatoes, and green peas on her plate than she could eat.

"Mother said you went to Scott," Mary Rose said politely—nicely—after the blessing. "That's where I want to go. What did you major in?"

"English," Betsy said. She felt she had to add that she'd transferred to Barnard her junior year. There was a puzzled pause at the table.

"Oh that's right!" Mrs. O'Brian exclaimed. "I remember your mother telling me that. Mighty brave of you, going to the big city all by yourself!"

"But why?" Mary Rose asked, incredulous. "Didn't you like Scott?"

Betsy felt on the spot. How to explain. "It wasn't that," she said, as they all looked at her. "It just wasn't right for me." She paused. "It's a wonderful school."

Mrs. O'Brian began recounting stories of how she and Betsy's mother had pulled various pranks on the other girls in their dorm. "Short sheeting was our favorite." She paused to laugh at the memory. "We thought it was hilarious when a girl would get in bed and not be able to stretch her legs out! But our *pièce de résistance* was putting toothpaste in Oreos!"

As soon as they finished eating, Tim said they had to leave in order to make a movie downtown on time. What were they going to see? *On the Waterfront* with Marlon Brando.

"Can I go?" Mary Rose asked.

"Sorry, bunny," Tim said quickly. "Not this time."

"Won't you two stay long enough to have some vanilla ice cream with chocolate sauce and . . . Oreo cookies!" Mrs. O'Brian said. They all grimaced. When Betsy thanked them for a lovely evening, Dr. O'Brian shook her hand warmly. "Tell your mother I'll be calling," Mrs. O'Brian said, giving her a hug.

Betsy and Tim escaped to the Rambler. "They're really nice," Betsy said as they started down Rutherford away from town. "Aren't we going to the movies?" Main Street was the opposite way.

"I thought we might take a drive up Paris Mountain," he said, raising his eyebrows when he looked at her.

No mystery about what he had in mind. "I've always liked driving up Paris Mountain," Betsy said.

He reached over and squeezed her knee.

AT the flat parking spot near the top of the mountain, Tim turned his big body in the little car toward her, put his hand behind her head, and pulled her face over to his. He moved his lips onto hers.

It wasn't at all like Jerome. But why should it be? They kissed and kissed, until she felt bored with kissing. Like they were stuck. She took his hand and put it on her breast. But he quickly removed it. "No," he murmured in her ear. "I don't want to get carried away. I respect you too much, Betsy."

He's a virgin! she realized with a jolt.

38

ALMA

ONE SUNDAY IN May after church, Alma, Huff, and Pretty drove uptown to visit Richland Cemetery. Huff's father had been buried there in 1924. He'd died of TB when Huff was thirteen. Huff had had to drop out of school and take a job dishwashing to help out his mother and two younger siblings. Now he had a job at A.J. Whittenberg's filling station, and along with his yard work, he'd been able to buy a headstone for his father's grave. The three of them stood in front of it in reverent silence. Alma was not ready to be his wife again and maybe never would be. But they were parents together.

It was already so hot Alma's cotton dress was sticking to her like an extra layer of damp skin. It reminded her of how hot— just like today—it had been that sweltering May, seven years ago, when the Willie Earle trial was going on at the courthouse. Tired from the work day at the Chastains, she'd been lying on her bed in the house on Sycamore Street when Huff came in and told her the news: *not guilty*, every single one of them. That memory was seared into her as if by a branding iron.

AFTER they left the cemetery, they began walking along the street above McPherson Park, Greenville's oldest city park. Down below, a creek flowed into a round duck pond encircled by a flat cement lip. On this Sunday afternoon, families seeking relief from the heat were strolling on the paths below. Several little children, still in their church clothes, were throwing crusts of Wonder Bread into the pond, laughing as the ducks scrambled for the bread. While the three of them stood watching from the road above, a miniature green and white train, a replica of the Crescent Alma and Betsy had taken back to Greenville, came around the far side of the pond. Fifteen or so white children were sitting in the seats, a conductor "driving" up front.

"That looks like fun!" Pretty exclaimed. "Can I ride the train, Mama?"

Alma was taken by surprise. Like all the parks, McPherson was whites only, coloreds not allowed. Pretty knew that. Didn't she?

Huff and Alma were silent. How to answer such a question? How to tell your child that she can't ride the children's train in a city park? In her world of home, school, and church, Pretty was just herself, a bright, well-mannered child who was loved and cared for. Her reality was small, confined—mostly protected from discrimination in the outside world. But now she was growing up—and out. Soon she'd become aware of all the Jim Crow "can'ts" she'd have to face.

"That train for white children," Alma said gruffly. "We've got to get on home. They be other trains in your future." She was ashamed of herself.

"You too big to ride no little train," Huff said gently. "I

take you for a ride in the truck when we get home. Where you want to go?"

But Pretty didn't answer. As they started away, she kept looking over her shoulder at the little train rounding the bend by the old stone bridge.

THAT night Bessie and Alma knelt and prayed together as usual. But when Alma went to her room, she couldn't sleep. Her mind was too agitated over what had happened that afternoon at the park. Finally she got up and went into the room where Pretty slept with her great-granny Marie, who was snoring loudly, in fits and starts. How could Pretty sleep through that ruckus! But her daughter was curled on her side, sleeping peacefully, fist tucked under her chin. Love flooded Alma's heart. She had failed her! She'd gone up North to make a better life for her, and instead she'd made a mess of her own life. And now Pretty was facing the same prejudice and discrimination Alma had grown up with.

When she went back to her room, she fell to her knees on the rag rug beside her bed and folded her hands. She pressed her forehead hard against her clasped fists.

"Dear Lord," she whispered. What could she say? She was at a loss. But then as if from a deeper part of herself, words began to come.

"Draw near me, Jesus, and hear my prayer!"

She waited. More words came flooding in.

"Pretty's getting to an age where she's goin' to be hurt. She's goin' to be held back, Jesus." She bit her lip, struggling. Not just words now. She was pleading.

"Help my people, Jesus! We're not free, Lord. Not that different from when we was slaves. White people determined to keep us in chains. You saw what happened today. It happens every day! Some insult. Some wrong! Every day, Lord. Every day."

She stopped to listen; soon enough, the words took charge. "Make my daughter's life better, Jesus! I failed her. But don't You! Bring about the change Huff's always talkin' about. How long must we wait! We been waitin' and waitin', Lord. Give us a sign! You who know the first and the last, the beginning and the end. You who can move mountains, You who can calm the seas. Jesus! Don't let Pretty grow up like I did. I know I turned away from You. But make me strong. Drive the devil out of my heart. I'm here, Lord, on my knees, asking You for help. I know I don't deserve it. But give me a sign! A sign that You are real!" She was trembling. "Yours is the power and the glory, forever and ever. Amen."

THE next morning Pretty didn't mention the little train. She was as cheerful as ever, excited to go to school. They were having a spelling bee that day. Over breakfast Alma gave Pretty words to spell—*thought, people, knee*—and the only one Pretty missed was *knee*. Alma watched her walk down the road with Deely and the other kids toward the new Nicholtown school, a new book in her bag.

Alma put on a cotton shirtwaist to go to work. Another hot May day—May 17, 1954. She stood in the back of the bus on the way to Carolina Blouse, just like always. It was an ordinary day, just like any other. But when she got home from work, there was excitement in the house.

"Guess what!" Pretty met her at the door, a huge grin deepening her dimples. "I'm going to school with white kids next year!"

"What?" Alma said. "Pretty, you tellin' tales!"

She came into the kitchen where Bessie and Marie were listening to the big Philco radio. They raised their eyes to meet Alma's.

"The Supreme Court done ruled," Bessie said. "Colored chilluns can go to white schools now!" Tears filled her eyes. "Thank you, Jesus!" she said, looking up toward the ceiling, lifting her open palms in the air. "Our prayers been answered!"

"What you sayin'?"

"*Brown versus Board of Education*," Pretty said importantly. "Our teacher told us. Next year I can go to a white school!"

What everyone had been awaiting had finally occurred: The Supreme Court had ruled—in favor of school desegregation. On the radio the commentators were discussing how the decision was monumental, historical. Alma was trying to absorb what it meant. *Would mean for the future.*

"I have to run upstairs for a minute," she said.

"Where you going, Mama?" Pretty asked.

"I be right back."

As she went up the stairs, Alma was half-laughing to herself. "All right!" she was muttering. "You showed me! All right then, Lord. Thank you, Jesus!"

Alma took the half-full pint of Jim Beam out of her big black pocketbook. She studied it—so necessary, so beloved. She unscrewed the top and inhaled the sharp scent. "All right then," she said. "Your sheep is done strayin'." In the bathroom she poured the liquor down the sink. She ran water after it until even the smell was gone.

She felt the same strange wind roar through her again that she'd felt at the voter registration office.

Maybe change *was* the Holy Spirit.

Maybe they were one and the same.

AT the end of the month, the family attended Stew and Delores's son Jimmy's graduation ceremony at Sterling. The auditorium was filled with proud families and smiling graduates in the blue and white colors of Sterling High. Principal Beck stood on the stage before the audience and announced, "This is the last segregated class at Sterling High! The Supreme Court has ruled. Integration of public schools is now the law of the land!"

IT would take sixteen more years and an appellate court order before Greenville would integrate its public schools.

39

LAWTON

LAWTON HADN'T SEEN much of Donny Sanders since he'd gotten so involved with Frank. He missed him and felt a little guilty. Donny was one of the two friends he called his own: Donny and John Bolt Culbertson, two very different characters but both good men. He decided to invite Donny over for a drink to meet Frank. Donny showed up in blue eye shadow and mascara. "Helena Rubinstein, darling," he said when Frank complimented him on it. Instead of shaking Frank's proffered hand, he kissed him on both cheeks. "*Mon cheri!*"

He caught them up on the queer gossip around town (not that Frank and Lawton knew any). The *drama*, as Donny called it. He told tales on a group of men who called themselves the Garden Club, some married, some not, middle-aged or older respectable citizens in their straight lives who met privately in homes to socialize. Donny was a good mimic, imitating various members: "Miss Scarlett," "Prissy Poo," "Queen Mary." Frank and Lawton laughed until tears filled their eyes.

Donny told them how since Hurley's had been shut down, he'd had to find other places for some action. In his cups, he described how he cruised places where men had quick and anonymous sex in public bathrooms and parks. Frank and Lawton frowned. "You be careful, my friend," Frank said.

Not long after that, Lawton's phone rang at two in the morning. It was Donny. He was at the police station. He'd met a man in the bathroom at McPherson Park and agreed to get in a car with him. Once he was inside, another officer appeared and slapped handcuffs on him. He was under arrest.

"Ask if he's okay," Frank, who was spending the night, said. He began to get dressed. "Ask if they hurt him."

"I'm okay," Donny told Lawton. "They just drove me around for about a hundred years. I didn't know what they were gonna do, they were having such a good time scaring the shit out of me. Come get me!"

Lawton told Donny he was on his way. Frank wanted to come but Lawton told him no. Too risky. He didn't want Frank associated publicly with Donny. The police might target Frank as a homosexual if he showed up at the jail, even blackmail him. Lawton could pass as Donny's legal counsel.

When he arrived at the police station all was quiet. There was a lone officer half-asleep at the front desk. Lawton had thrown on a suit for the occasion, even though it was going on three o'clock in the morning. He gave his name and said he was Donny's attorney. "I'd like to see my client. I'll need to speak to the arresting officer," he said.

He was shown to an interview room where he waited for fifteen anxious minutes. He was worried sick about Donny and was just about to demand to see him when the door opened. Donny was pushed roughly into the room by the same officer who'd been on duty the night the cab drivers were organizing to go to the Pickens County jail. Lawton recognized his bald head, deeply cleft chin, and a certain shifty slouch he'd had that night and had now.

"Lawton Chastain," he said, not offering his hand. "We've met before." He paused, taking his time. "The night a mob of cabbies convened on Court Street. I'm sure you remember. Your name again?"

"Aikens." He didn't look at Lawton.

"All right, Aikens," Lawton said. "What's going on here?"

"Morals." Aikens raised his chin defiantly. "Vag-lewd."

"What exactly happened?"

"Nothing!" Donny piped up. "I got in his car. He lured me."

"So you entrapped him," Lawton said to Aikens.

"The fag put his hand on my crotch in the john. Said he'd blow me."

"I did not!" an indignant Donny exclaimed. Lawton cast Donny a cork-it look.

"I'm sure we can work something out," he said to Aikens. He let the silence hang there. "The way I see it, you should have been charged with criminal negligence after you let twenty or thirty angry, inebriated cab drivers gather right under the sheriff's window without alerting a soul." He paused and paced a bit, as if giving the matter more thought. "Maybe accessory to a crime? It's not too late. South Carolina has no criminal statute of limitations."

He gave Aikens a severe look. "I don't know. Maybe five to ten years? I don't think a jury would take too kindly to such an egregious abdication of duty." He didn't try to hide his contempt. Aikens was a hoodlum in uniform. He'd set Donny up. He was more than willing to blackmail him or ruin his life by charging him with a sex crime. He'd done nothing to stop a pack of men bent on lynching.

He crossed to where Aikens was sitting. "Stand up," he said. Aikens, startled, stood up slowly, hesitantly. Lawton put his face close to his, smelling his putrid breath. "Now the main thing here," he said in a low snarl, "is that Mr. Sanders' name not appear in the newspaper. It's all just a misunderstanding. A *mistake*. No record, no crime report in the paper. Do I make myself clear?"

Aikens stepped back. He cast Lawton a sullen look.

"You're free to go, faggot," he said to Donny without looking at him. "Now get the hell outta here."

H E and Frank were furious at Donny when Lawton took him back to his apartment. He'd barely scraped out of what could have been a very bad situation. "You have to cut it out," Frank said sternly. "No more cruising, no more anonymous sex. If your name appears in the paper, you'll lose your job. What'll you do then?"

Donny began to cry, mascara running down his cheeks. Lawton put his arm around Donny's small shoulders where he was slumped on the couch. "I'm a horrible person," Donny said. "I'm all the things they say I am. Disgusting. Perverted. Why did God make me this way?"

Lawton told him he and Frank loved him, and God must too, to have made him. After a few sobs and several drinks, Donny began to come around. "I don't even believe in God!" he said. "But wow, Lawton. You sure showed some balls in there!"

A F T E R that Donny reported that he often saw Aikens in his squad car tailing him when he got off work. It was not long before he came by to say goodbye. He was moving back to New Jersey. He had a brother there who would take him in. He thought Harper's would give him a good recommendation. Lawton was sorry to see him go. Life would be a little duller without Donny around.

ONE day that summer when Lawton picked up the phone at the office, the voice at the other end said, "Chas."

Everything about Harry Bumgarten came rushing back: his aristocratic face, his penetrating brown eyes, the way he'd smile at a joke only he got.

"This is quite a surprise," Lawton said. "What's it been? Twenty-five, thirty years?"

"I'm in Inman," Harry said. "My aunt died, and I'm home for the funeral.

"How did you find me?"

Harry's laugh brought him close. "You were hell-bent on becoming a lawyer, why I don't know. I called information in Greenville. *Voila!*"

Lawton's heart was beating wildly. "How long will you be in Inman?"

"I'm leaving on Sunday. I'm thinking I might drive to Greenville on Saturday and meet you for lunch."

Lawton hesitated a moment until the floor came back up to meet his feet. "That would be nice," he said.

HE asked Frank to go with him; he didn't want to see Harry alone. But Frank said it would be best if Lawton and Harry met without him. "It'll change things between you if I'm there," he said. "And this belongs to you."

They met at the same Howard Johnson's where he and

Frank had got their start. Waiting in the restaurant, Lawton was nervous, wondering what seeing Harry again would be like. But when he approached, Lawton wasn't sure it was Harry. He weighed maybe 300 pounds. It took Lawton several minutes to recognize the slender young man he'd known in college in the big man squeezing into the booth opposite him. Harry smiled, squinting his brown eyes, obviously happy to see Lawton. And Lawton was happy to see him. The warmth he'd once felt for Harry was still there—not that all the years hadn't counted—because they had. But there was just something about Harry.

They didn't bother with the menus. They both ordered club sandwiches and iced tea, Lawton's sweet, Harry's plain.

When Lawton had thought about Harry over the years, he'd imagined him as a philosophy professor on the East Coast, maybe at Columbia or even Harvard. He was sure he lived in New York City or Boston. But no, he lived in Key West.

"Key West!" Lawton knew very little about Key West. His impression was that it was not like other places. An image came to mind, of a sleepy tropical island at the end of Route One, full of shrimp boats, gays, and writers. Hemingway had lived in Key West before moving to Cuba, and Tennessee Williams had a house there.

"What happened to philosophy? What about your book?"

Harry shook his head. "I did my time in academe," he said. "But when I came up for tenure . . . Let's just say there were those who assumed I had . . . certain *predilections* . . . not suitable for the tender young men I'd be teaching and advising. I headed for Key West on a lark and never looked back. And you? All these years in Greenville? Married? Children?"

Lawton told him his story. When he got to Frank, Harry's

eyes lit up. "So," he said, "I've wondered . . ."

"It only took me all these years to know what you knew when I was twenty-two."

Harry laughed again. "Better late than never."

"Do you remember how you asked me to run away? You told me I wasn't a sheep and that one day I'd shuck it all off. You hoped to be around to see it."

Harry tilted his head, considering. "I can't say I recall that," he said at last. "Of course I said all kinds of things back then. There's just too many martinis over, under, and through the dam now. So, tell me. Am I seeing it? The real, unshucked you?"

Lawton had to laugh. "This is it," he said. "I believe I've shucked off the sheep skin. I give you credit, Harry." He paused, feeling unexpectedly moved. "It's just so amazing to see you again. How are you? Are you with someone? Are you happy?"

"I've got a few health problems," he shrugged. "Diabetes. No sugar in this ol' boy's double daiquiris. Some bothersome little heart thing. But if I go tomorrow, I've had a wonderful life. I wouldn't change a thing about it." He paused. That grin again. "Well, maybe one thing. That you slammed the door in my face. Or I should say you failed to open the door when I came knocking the next day. Do you remember? And the next. And the next. I wanted to talk to you. I wanted to see you."

"I'm sorry," Lawton said. "I was so naive. And scared."

"But you liked it," Harry said, smiling into Lawton's eyes. "That's not a question."

Lawton smiled. "Yes," he said. "Very much."

They talked for an hour, hardly touching their sandwiches. Lawton felt again that he both knew and loved Harry and that Harry was a stranger. It didn't matter which it was. It was just so good to see him again.

When they parted, they promised to stay in touch, though both knew it wouldn't happen. They'd said all that needed to be said.

40

BETSY

TIM CAME HOME on Labor Day weekend, 1955. They'd been dating a year and a half, but they'd seen each other only on the rare occasions when Tim had a break from medical school. That situation was fine with Betsy. She was busy with work at her father's office and writing her novel, which she still hadn't told Tim about.

On Saturday afternoon Tim played a round of golf at the country club and picked Betsy up early that evening. They drove straight up to Paris Mountain and sat in the car waiting for the sun to sink below the mountains.

"Did you hear about that Negro boy who was murdered by two white men in Mississippi for whistling at a white woman?" Betsy asked. It had been all over the news that week. "He was fourteen years old. He'd come south to visit his uncle and would have gone home to Chicago this weekend."

"No, I haven't," Tim said. "But let's talk about something more pleasant. You wouldn't believe how my game has tanked! I haven't been near a green since Memorial Day. I shanked and sliced, and my ball loved the beach! The boys were nice to let me take a couple of mulligans. Without that I wouldn't have even broken a hundred!"

"The beach?"

"Sand trap," Tim said. "But really, it was so great out there on the course. Perfect temperature, beautiful blue skies, emerald green grass, a beer with the fellas in the club-house afterward . . . and knowing what awaited me when I picked you up." He winked at her. "But enough about me. How was your day?"

Betsy felt chastised. She didn't want to tell him that she'd been preoccupied all day with thoughts of the murdered boy.

"Same-old, same-old," she said at last.

"So, how's work going?" Tim asked, pulling her close, though in the small Nash, that didn't take much.

"I'm learning a lot," she said. "Daddy thinks I should go to law school."

"Do you think that could work with motherhood?"

"I hadn't really thought about it."

"Well, you better start thinking about it," Tim said, begin-ning to nibble her neck. "I can't wait to pump you full of babies."

Betsy laughed, a bit uneasily. She was relieved when he began to kiss her. They could get off the subject of babies. They'd talked a little about marriage, but it was far off. Tim needed to finish medical school and a residency.

WHEN Betsy came down to breakfast on Sunday morning, her mother was sitting at the breakfast room table. "Here," she said. "Read this." She handed Betsy the newspaper.

Halfway down the front page a headline read:

Sheriff Doubts Body is Till's

Tallahatchie County Sheriff H.C. Strider said today he didn't think the body pulled from a river near here was that of Emmett Till. "The whole thing looks like a deal made up by the National Association for the Advancement of Colored People," *the sheriff said.*

In New York, NAACP Executive Secretary Roy Wilkins said, "The sheriff evidently knows nothing about the NAACP. We don't go in for murder."

ANOTHER story described how the services for Emmett Till drew an estimated ten thousand people to the South Side Church in Chicago where his battered body was placed on view.

"It was his mother," Lydia said, "who wanted the casket opened to the public. She wanted people to see what they did to her boy." She pulled her lips in tight. "He'd been badly beaten and shot in the head. The sheriff said his face looked like it might have been struck by an ax." She looked away. "Fourteen years old."

BETSY and Tim had plans to go on a picnic before he had to drive back to Charleston. She determined to shrug off the news about Emmett Till. She put on red peddle-pushers and a sleeveless white blouse tied at the midriff. Tim arrived right at noon. "Ready for a picnic!" he said, rubbing his hands together and grinning at her. "Sure am," Betsy said, though she didn't much feel like a picnic. Tim was wearing Bermuda shorts and knee-high socks with his penny loafers. His hair was wet; he must have just showered. Spontaneously, hoping to change her mood, she gave him a kiss on his cheek, which smelled like perfume from his aftershave. He gave her a hug around the waist. "That's my girl."

They drove to Paris Mountain State Park, which was packed with the holiday crowd. From the trunk, Tim got a picnic basket and a vase of wilting end-of-summer zinnias from his mother's garden. All the picnic tables were taken, but Tim said he knew an area away from the lake where there might not be so many people. Betsy carried the blanket he'd brought and the flowers. They followed a trail about a fourth of a mile into a more private area in a grove of pine trees. It was perfect, Tim declared, but the temperature was at least ninety degrees. Betsy was sweating under her arms. And there were bugs: mosquitoes, chiggers, no-see-ums. Why hadn't she thought to bring repellant? She couldn't help slapping her calf where something was having its own picnic. She didn't mention the bite, determined not to spoil the day with her whining.

Tim spread the blanket on a patch of prickly pine needles and presented the fare from the picnic basket: ham biscuits, egg salad sandwiches his mother had made, potato chips, and warm bottles of Coke. Brownies for dessert. He set the vase of flowers in the middle of the blanket, but the ground underneath was too uneven, and the vase promptly fell over, spilling its water.

"Doesn't matter, "Betsy said, plopping the tortured flowers back in the dry vase and securing it with food containers. "This is wonderful." And it was. Tim was something special. How many men would do this? she asked herself. Yet she felt a little off—as if she should be *feeling* more than she was.

Tim ate heartily but she had little appetite. Maybe she was coming down with something. She hoped he didn't notice, and apparently he didn't. She felt anxious, without knowing why.

"I'm really enjoying rotations," Tim said. "Getting from the classroom to the bedside. Putting into practice all that book-learning on real patients."

"I'm sure you're great," Betsy said. "You're so . . ." She searched for a word. "Nice."

"I feel I'll never catch up on my sleep though." He rolled over on the blanket and put his head in her lap. She stroked his tan hair.

"Ummm," he murmured and immediately fell asleep. Betsy sat without moving, the weight of his head on her legs. It was a heavy head, and he slept with his mouth open, making little snorting sounds. Her legs began to go to sleep, and a mosquito buzzed near his neck. When she slapped at it, he woke with a start.

"Sorry," she said. "I need to stand up. My legs are getting numb." She began gathering the lunch things and putting them in the basket.

When she looked up, she was shocked to see Tim down on one knee. He was holding a ring box, a big grin on his face.

"Come here," he said, and she obeyed, unable to shake off a sense of unreality.

She stood in front of him, wanting to stop him, but she didn't know how.

"Will you marry me, Elizabeth Ann Chastain?"

She was stunned. They'd talked about getting married, but it was always way off in the future. Why did he have to propose now? She'd thought she had more time.

He opened the box and took out a ring.

"It's a family heirloom," he said excitedly. "My grandmother's. See if it fits." He reached for her left hand, which she had curled protectively against her waist. The ring, a big diamond solitaire, went on as if it were made for her. "It's beautiful," she said.

"So will you marry me?" He was looking at her earnestly.

"I thought you wanted to wait until you finished a residency. Like we've talked about." Her mouth was dry.

He was still down on his knee in the pine needles. "I'm getting a cramp," he said, standing up and shaking out his leg. He took her hands in his. "You're the one," he said. "I love you dearly. Will you be mine?"

Tears came to Betsy's eyes. She didn't want to hurt him. She wanted to be who he wanted her to be. He was so . . . nice. He loved her. And marriage had an appeal. Things would be settled. No more turmoil. No more Jerome.

"Yes," she said. "I will."

He gathered her in his arms and gave her the most passionate kiss ever. She did her best to reciprocate, although her arm was squashed between them. Down below, she felt him hard against her pelvis in her pedal pushers. She reached down and touched him, something she'd never done.

"Let's get married at Christmas!" he whispered in her ear. "I can't wait much longer."

"We don't have to wait for this," Betsy murmured against him.

He held her back and looked her in the eye. "No, we do. We have to wait. But only until Christmas."

"You don't mean this coming Christmas!"

"Yes, this Christmas, Bets!" He'd never called her Bets

before. She wanted to scream at him, *No! Don't call me that!*

She pulled away. "You've never mentioned getting married before you did a residency. It's just . . . this coming Christmas?" She was babbling like an idiot. "There'll be so much to do."

"Don't you worry," he said. "I'll take care of everything!"

She rolled her eyes. "I doubt that."

"Oh honey," he said, giving her a big hug. "Our first fight!"

IN September jury selection began in the trial of the two men arrested for the murder of Emmett Till. Since there were no Negro residents of Tallahatchie County registered to vote, none was eligible for jury duty. Twelve white men were selected, men judged "safe" by the sheriff. "It's all over but the shouting," her father said.

Despite his life being threatened, Moses Wright, Emmett's great uncle, took the witness stand, pointed his finger at the two defendants, and accused them of coming to his house and taking Emmett. An eighteen-year-old Negro sharecropper's son, speaking so softly he almost couldn't be heard, testified he saw the green and white pickup truck carrying Till in the last hours of his life. He heard screams coming from the barn where the pickup truck was parked. After his testimony, the prosecutor told the courtroom, "Willie Reed has more nerve than I do."

At the office on September 23, 1955, Betsy and her father awaited a verdict again—just like they had in May 1947.

The jury deliberated only sixty-seven minutes before finding the defendants not guilty. "We wouldn't have taken so long if we hadn't stopped to drink pop," one juror said.

Tim asked her that night on the phone why she sounded so down. Betsy told him because of the verdict.

"What verdict?"

S H E wrote Jerome a real pen-and-paper letter, though one he'd never receive.

I know how you feel about the verdict. I do too. The only good thing is that a lot of people are outraged, Negro and white. Maybe this horror will be a tipping point.

You're thirty-six years old now, Jerome. Maybe you're married. Maybe even a father. I hope you're happy.

I'm engaged to be married myself. To a very nice man named Tim.

I don't want you to become a memory. But it's becoming harder to hold on to you.

I T turned out there was a lot involved in getting married, even for a small home wedding. December 27 was only two months away. Thank goodness her mother and Mrs. O'Brian took over invitations, flowers, music, what kind of cake, and refreshments. Betsy was struggling to finish a draft of her novel, afraid that once she was married, she wouldn't.

At the end of November, she asked Jenny Lewis to be her maid of honor. She wished Zora could be—she was still her best friend. Tim's roommate from Clemson would be his best man. Things were falling into place.

In early December, Zora wrote Betsy about a woman in Montgomery named Rosa Parks who'd refused to give up her seat on a city bus so a white person could have it. She'd been arrested, and now Negro leaders and ministers in town had organized a bus boycott. Zora said the majority of the city's Negro bus riders, herself included, were boycotting the bus system. They were organizing carpools. Negro taxi drivers were charging ten cents, the same price as bus fare.

"This within a hundred days of Emmett Till's murder!"

Zora wrote. "The acquittal is galvanizing Negroes all across the South!"

BETSY bought a simple sleeveless dress with a bolero jacket for the wedding, nothing like the "dream wedding dresses" in *Bride* magazine. Her mother would play the "Bridal Chorus" for her to enter on her father's arm from the kitchen. Alma and Pretty would prepare the party food for the reception. Lydia's pastor would officiate. She and Tim were planning a two-night honeymoon in Asheville at the Grove Park Inn. F. Scott Fitzgerald had stayed there two summers in the thirties while Zelda was in a psychiatric hospital downtown. Betsy hoped she wouldn't end up in the same place.

THE wedding was a week away. Tim would be home tomorrow.

THAT night Betsy dreamed of the jail cell again. Again she saw herself sitting on the hard cot. But this time she stood up and went over to the cell door. It wasn't even locked. She pushed it open and walked out.

She knew what she had to do.

She wrote Tim a letter and left it at his house early the next morning. When he called, he was furious. He accused her of leading him on. She was sorry. Sorry she hurt him. But she couldn't explain how love fails. It dies. It just does.

Now he was heart broke too.

THAT night she wrote to Jerome:

Dear Jerome,

I've tried to keep you with me but I can't. I forgot our night-mare anniversary, the last time we made love. The night you left for good. I forgot you! I go for days now when you don't even cross my mind.

Do those soldiers with phantom pain look at where their leg used to be, and one day it doesn't hurt anymore? It's just a stump?

I don't know.

But I feel free.

THERE was a wedding after all.

Not Betsy and Tim.

Lydia and Perry.

They'd been talking about tying the knot for several months but had wanted to wait until Betsy had her wedding. But now, since so much was already set, they thought, *Why waste a perfectly good wedding?*

They all felt sorry for Tim.

"Daddy," Betsy said, "why didn't you tell me you didn't like him? Why didn't anyone tell me not to marry him? Mother didn't like him—you didn't like him."

"It's not that we didn't like him," her father said. "We just didn't think he was right for you. But we didn't want to interfere."

SHE wrote letters to Tim and the O'Brians, apologizing, saying she hadn't meant to hurt anyone. She called her grandparents and those invited to the wedding and informed them of the change of plans. She calmly explained she'd had a change of heart, and it wouldn't have been fair or kind to go through with marrying Tim.

When the wedding guests arrived, if anyone expected to find Betsy looking upset, embarrassed, or ashamed, they were disappointed.

Betsy couldn't help thinking there was something comical about the whole thing: Lydia in her mother-of-the-bride dress she'd bought for Betsy's wedding; Pretty, instead of Lydia, playing "Here Comes the Bride" as Lydia entered from the kitchen; Grand Bee shaking her head and clucking her tongue the whole time; her grandparents on her father's side looking confused but putting on a brave front; Lawton's eyes shining with tears; Perry so moved by the whole thing he cried, blowing his nose so loudly during the vows that everyone laughed. The groom kissed the bride to applause, and Alma caught Betsy's—or rather Lydia's—bouquet of calla lilies that Lydia tossed her way.

Only once or twice did Betsy's thoughts turn to Tim. He had to be hurting horribly on what he'd expected to be his special day. She was so sorry. She knew how much it hurts when love walks out the door.

She also knew there was no way to call it back when love is gone.

41

LAWTON

IT HAD BEEN painful last Christmas for Lawton and Frank that Frank couldn't attend what they'd expected to be Betsy's wedding. There was no way Lawton could explain to Lydia why he'd invite Frank to such a family affair. But after Lydia's marriage, Frank began pressuring Lawton to move on with his life too. By which he meant Lawton should move in with him on Paris Mountain. He was sick of their living apart. "All this shuttling between our places, hiding that we're together. It's taking a toll."

Frank was on call at the hospital three nights a week and every other weekend. Spending some nights at Lawton's apartment, other nights on Paris Mountain, was not only inconvenient, Frank argued, but detrimental to their relationship.

"I want you here, at home—our home," Frank said. "We're living the only lives we'll ever have, and one day we'll be dead. So we might as well live them the way we want. You inflate how much people will care or judge. As long as we don't broadcast our relationship, as long as we're discreet, we'll be fine."

They were sitting on Frank's white sectional sofa having a cocktail before dinner. The rich smells of *coq au vin* wafted down the three steps from the kitchen into the living room.

"I want that too," Lawton said, not for the first time. He was afraid of what his stalling might mean to them. Maybe Frank would run out of patience. But he'd never completely overcome his shame at being queer, society's bequest to him. Plus he had a major stumbling block.

"Lydia," Frank sighed. "Lydia and Perry, that is. If you tell them you're moving in, they'll figure out about us. About you. Would that be so terrible? Lydia doesn't strike me as someone who would disown you. Look how Betsy took us in stride. Lydia might do the same."

"I don't know about that," Lawton said. "I can't imagine how she'd react."

"You don't have to tell them outright. You don't have to use the 'H' word. Let them figure it out—or not. They may care a lot less than you think." Frank got up to go check on dinner. When he came back, he took off his apron and got down on one knee in front of Lawton. When Frank took his hand, Lawton couldn't help but laugh.

"Please move in with me," Frank said, grinning at his own theatrics. "Be my unlawful, unwedded roommate . . . and lover . . . 'til death do us part."

Lawton felt a shiver of emotion run through him. Looking into Frank's blue eyes, he said solemnly, "I do. I will."

AS it happened, Lydia already knew Frank. She, Lawton, and Frank had been attending informal biracial get-togethers at Gil Rowland's house all summer. Gil and his wife Clay were committed to advancing race relations in Greenville.

Negro and white leaders came to the meetings, along with regular citizens who wanted, as one person put it, "to do the right thing." Pete Hollis, retired superintendent of the Parker School District and a major force for good in town, explained the impetus behind the meetings: "The Negro is down in the ditch, and we either get down in the ditch with him, or we pull him out."

The goal of these gatherings was to promote understanding and goodwill between the races. Defining a goal had been about as far as they'd gotten. The group had no official power or ability to do much to change things. But the consensus was that change would come.

So far the white power structure in Greenville was doing its best to appease Negroes while keeping them firmly in their place. In the meantime, it felt important to get to know each other across racial lines. Of course they had to be discreet. If someone questioned them, they'd tell them they were meeting to study the Bible.

Lawton and Frank always came to the Rowlands' in separate cars. At first Lawton watched Lydia's interactions with Frank at the meetings with trepidation. But he could tell she took to him, easy enough to do. Plus they shared a mutual interest in music. Around Frank, Lydia acted the way she did toward everyone there, white or Negro: friendly, curious, open, a more mature version of the outgoing girl Lawton had married when she was twenty-two. Being apart from him had done her nothing but good.

Perry didn't come to their meetings. He was more conservative than Lydia, more in keeping with most of Greenville, especially doctors. He was a member of the American Medical Association, which was vehemently opposed to a new proposal before Congress. Perry called it socialized medicine; the media referred to it as Medicare. He and Lawton didn't see eye to eye on politics, but Perry was a genial man who loved Lydia. That was good enough for Lawton.

After the wedding last year, Lydia had sold the Crescent Avenue house and moved to Perry's house on Byrd Boulevard. Around the same time, Betsy announced she was moving back to New York. Lawton asked if it was because of the breakup with Tim. Betsy said it had nothing to do with him. She felt bad for Tim, but there was nothing she could do about it. She wanted to be in New York for her writing.

He'd never asked her the specifics about the "boy trouble" that had resulted in Alma bringing her home. It was too painful for her at first, he surmised. But as she was packing to move, he'd asked if she planned to look up the "boy" behind the "boy trouble" when she got to New York.

She stopped folding her sweaters and blouses, holding still at the question. Then, "No, Daddy," she said finally, shaking her head. "No." She tucked more socks and underwear into her suitcase. "It's taken a long time. But I don't miss him anymore." She paused again. "But what I do miss is how much I loved him."

FRANK warned Lawton he was going to get an ulcer if he didn't stop fretting about his Big Announcement—he should go ahead and tell Lydia and Perry he was moving into Frank's. Finally Lawton made up his mind to stop by their house under the pretext of bringing them a bag of fall apples he (and Frank) had gotten in the North Carolina mountains. "Screw your courage to the sticking place, and you'll not fail," Frank teased him. "It does feel like I'm about to murder someone," Lawton lamented.

That evening he stopped by Lydia and Perry's house. Perry offered him a beer, but he said he couldn't stay; he just wanted to drop off some apples. "Keep them in a sealed bag in the icebox," he mumbled nervously, "and they'll last . . . indefinitely."

"Not if they're as good as they look," Perry said, polishing one of them on his pant leg before taking a bite.

It was now or never. Lawton knew he couldn't show his face to Frank if he didn't Announce.

"Say . . ." he began. It was an expression he never used. Lydia looked at him. "I'm moving into Frank Thompson's house on Paris Mountain when my lease expires next month. Such a big house," he said too quickly. "You know, too big for one person."

"Frank from our meetings?" Lydia asked.

"Yes. That Frank."

They were both looking at him now. He saw Perry's expression change; he understood what wasn't being said. "Frank Thompson," Perry mused slowly. Lawton and Lydia looked at him. "Don't much care for his politics. But he's a fine fellow. Excellent doctor too."

Lydia cocked her head like she did when she was absorbing new information.

LAWTON wished them goodnight and made his exit quickly. He drove too fast up Paris Mountain, squealing the tires on the sharp turns. Frank, playing the piano, stopped mid-measure as Lawton came down the stairs into the living room. "Well?"

Lawton threw himself on the white sofa.

"I'll bring you a drink," Frank said. "That bad?"

"I hightailed it out before they had time to react," Lawton said, sitting up to take the glass of white wine from Frank. "Oh my God."

"Good," Frank said. "It's done. You can start moving some of your stuff in this weekend."

WEEKS passed with no word from Lydia. This was not terribly unusual, but her silence unnerved Lawton. The last meeting of the year of the biracial committee was coming up in early November, and he debated whether to go. "Of course you're going, and I'm going too," Frank said. "Pull up your socks, man. Not hearing from her is a good sign. Or no sign at all."

Lydia was late for the meeting, but she gave no indication that all wasn't as usual. She greeted Frank and Lawton from across the living room; the meeting was already underway. The agenda for the night was the need for more recreational areas for Negro teens, but things soon dissolved into people reminiscing about their own teen years. There was laughter, pound cake, and Sanka.

When the meeting broke up, Frank caught up with Lydia outside, motioning to Lawton to join him. They walked her to her car.

"I had to park in the next block, there were so many cars here," she said. "The neighbors must think we're really interested in the Bible!"

Frank laughed, but Lawton was too nervous to muster a chuckle. As Lydia was opening her door, she turned to Lawton. "I've been meaning to call you," she said. "I hope you're planning on coming to Christmas dinner this year. We'd love to have you too, Frank."

"That would be lovely, Lydia," Frank said without hesitation. "I usually go to my sister's in Virginia, but I can go there at Thanksgiving. It'd be nice to stay home for Christmas this year."

"Good! Then it's settled," Lydia said. "I promise to make my famous standing rib roast with Yorkshire pudding."

It took Lawton, stunned as he was by this invitation, a moment to catch the joke. "She doesn't cook," he explained to Frank.

"Don't worry, Frank," Lydia said. "Alma's already promised to come early and cook before going home to her own turkey dinner. Why don't y'all come around noon?"

ON Christmas day, Frank and Lawton, bearing a huge red poinsettia and two bottles of Bordeaux, arrived promptly at noon. Lawton had a new case of nerves, but it helped when Perry greeted them warmly at the door, and Betsy, who'd arrived from New York the day before, came rushing into the entry hall to hug them both. But it was Lydia Lawton was waiting to see. He was still in the dark about what she thought about Frank and him living together. He wasn't sure she understood, and if she did, how she felt about it.

When she came out of the kitchen, she greeted them with smiles, a quick hug for Lawton, and a warm handshake for Frank. "I'm so glad you could make it," she said to him. "And look at that poinsettia! Stunning!"

Perry was examining the labels on the wine bottles. "I'm going to open these beauties so they can breathe," he said. "I'll be right back to fix y'all a drink."

"We'll give this star billing," Lydia said, carrying the poinsettia into the living room and setting it on the coffee table.

Betsy, Frank, and Lawton trailed behind her.

"Look at your beautiful piano," Frank said, going over to it. "I love a Baldwin."

"'America's favorite piano,'" Betsy quipped.

"It was a graduation present from my folks," Lydia said.

"I'd love to hear you play sometime," Frank said.

"Drinks are being served in the den!" Perry called.

"Saved!" Lydia said. "We better not keep Perry waiting. He's been looking forward to serving old-fashioneds all week!"

As Frank and Betsy went ahead of them, Lawton touched Lydia lightly on the arm to hold her back for a moment. "Thank you, Lydia," he began, but he suddenly felt too emotional to continue.

"For inviting Frank? I like Frank." She was silent for a long moment. Then, "I understand now, Lawton," she said, looking into his eyes. "I understand." Another pause. "I can't tell you what a relief it is to finally know . . . why." The smile she gave him held so many things. The lump in his throat grew larger. "Now go see Alma." She gave his arm a little squeeze. "She's waiting on you."

He stood in the hall to blink away tears.

WHEN he went into the kitchen, his mouth watered from the rich smells of roast beef. He snatched a fried onion ring from the green bean casserole sitting on the counter. Alma turned from the open refrigerator and swatted him with her dish towel. "You get away from that," she said.

"Merry Christmas, Alma," Lawton said, grasping her hand in both of his.

"It sure is a merry Christmas with Betsy home!"

"How's Pretty?"

"She keep us hoppin'," Alma said. "Almost eleven going on sixteen!"

"Where have the years gone?" and again his voice clotted with emotion. "Thanks for cooking for us today, Alma."

"Oh I wouldn't miss cooking Miz Chastain's standing rib roast. Otherwise y'all might starve over here."

Lawton laughed. "I want you to meet my friend Frank."

He called to Frank in the den.

"I've heard so much about you," Frank said, shaking her hand. "All good . . . except for the bad parts."

"They's plenty of that!"

Frank reached for one of the fried onions. "You're about to get swatted," Lawton warned.

He told Alma he'd run her home whenever she was ready. "Just like old times," Alma said.

THEY sat in the den having drinks, pimento cheese on crackers, Bessie's bread and butter pickles, and shrimp with cocktail sauce. A fire danced merrily behind its screen. Frank and Betsy bemoaned Stevenson's second defeat in the presidential election and took some good-natured gloating from Perry over Eisenhower's repeat victory. Betsy told about seeing *My Fair Lady* on Broadway, and Perry said he'd just bought a color TV. He turned it on to show them, though nothing was being broadcast in color right then.

While the three of them chatted on the couch, Lydia and Lawton looked across the room at each other. He recognized the high-backed armchair she was sitting in. It was the same chair she'd been sitting in when he told her he wanted a divorce, only now it had been reupholstered in a royal blue material with small red-and-gold *fleurs de lis*. They held each other's gaze. Then Lydia lifted her glass to him. He lifted his in return.

Alma announced that dinner was ready, and they all took their places at the table. As Perry said the blessing, Lawton looked around at his family: Betsy, Frank, Lydia, and even Perry. He had so much to be thankful for.

The day was made all the more special by two other Big Announcements.

Over eggnog and Bessie's fruitcake soaked in rum, Betsy announced to the table that she had an agent for her novel. One of the members of her writing group had provided an introduction. They hardly had time to congratulate her before she warned everyone not to get their hopes up too much. The agent had cautioned her that she might not be able to sell the book. "Tell us what the agent said about your novel!" a beaming Lydia asked. "She said it needs a lot of work," Betsy laughed.

There was one more announcement. It happened quietly, privately, in the kitchen, between Alma and Lydia. It was only when Lydia and Lawton had a moment alone later that Lydia told him: *Alma's going to have a baby!* They stared at each other in amazement. They hadn't seen it coming.

"When?" he asked.

"She's six months along. It's due in March! If it's a boy, they're naming him for Huff's father. And Lawton, guess what they're going to name it if it's a girl?"

"I have no idea."

"They're going to call her Hope."

42

LAWTON

ON NEW YEAR'S Day, 1960, Lawton is in his office in the Chamber of Commerce Building. All is silent except for the heating system kicking on and off. Earlier today he and Frank had a leisurely brunch before Frank got called to the hospital. Lawton didn't mind. This is exactly where he wants to be on this first day of a whole new decade: *The Sixties*. Even the name sounds promising.

He'd called Betsy over at Lydia and Perry's to tell her he'd be at the office this afternoon and to come by. There's something he wants to show her. She's going back to New York tomorrow. He hates to see her go, but she needs to get back to work there. He hasn't had enough time with her over the busy holidays, but he and Frank are already planning a trip to New York in May.

He stands at the window overlooking Court Square. Down below, Main Street is deserted except for a Negro man riding a bike toward Broad Street and an inebriated white couple walking in a not-very-straight line with their arms wrapped around each other. Across the square, the solemn courthouse gazes back at him. At the Poinsett Hotel next door, the guests are no doubt recovering from last night's reveries. A brightly colored party hat blows down the sidewalk and is gone. It's snowing lightly.

Everything here is history, he thinks. From the Cherokees who roamed these parts to the founding of the village on the banks of the Reedy in the 1780s to the mill villages that make Greenville the "Textile Capital of the World," up to this very day. On January 1, 1960, history is still being made—here in Greenville, in South Carolina, and all over the South. Greenville is still being made.

From his desk, he picks up the mimeographed flyer Huff Stone dropped off last week. Handwritten at the top in capital letters it reads:

MARCH TO GREENVILLE AIRPORT THAT DEMOCRACY MAY FLY.

On October 25, Jackie Robinson, Rev. J.S. Hall, and others were threatened with arrest for sitting in the "white" waiting room of the Greenville, South Carolina airport. The Greenville Interdenominational Ministerial Alliance and the Committee of Racial Equality—CORE— along with the state conference of the NAACP and others are calling YOU to a statewide Emancipation Day Protest and MARCH ON GREENVILLE AIRPORT.

January 1, 1960, 12:30 PM. Meet at Springfield Baptist Church, 602 E. McBee Avenue. Remember: democracy depends on you!!!

THERE'S a cheery knock, and Betsy comes in the outer office door. He goes out to greet her. "Hi, Daddy," she says, hanging her coat on the coatrack. "Happy New Year!"

"And to you, honey," he says, giving her a hug.

"My old desk." She runs her hand lightly over it. "And that awful desk chair."

"It's yours if you want it," Lawton says.

"Thanks, Daddy." She gives him a rueful smile.

"Come in my office," he says. "I want to show you something."

He hands her the flyer and waits while she reads it.

"Mother told me about the march," Betsy says. "Huff is going."

"So I've heard. Come here." He motions her over to the window. "I want you to see."

Betsy joins him. All is quiet on Main Street below. The flurries have changed to light sleet. A Yellow Cab drives slowly by the Poinsett. A man with a black umbrella passes in front of the courthouse. When her father doesn't speak, she gives him a questioning look.

"It may look the same out there," he says, still looking out the window. "But it's not." He's silent for so long, she turns to him.

"They're marching in Greenville today, Betsy. And after today, there'll be no turning back."

A shiver runs through her.

It's the past he's seeing—and the future.

43

PRETTY STONE

FOR US IT started with books. Books, note cards, term papers due.

Of course it really started a long time ago, back to when our greats—at least the ones who survived the trip over—got hauled off the boats. The wrongs had been building up for so long in so many ways that books were just a small part of it. But not to us. We wanted books we couldn't get.

I was a sophomore at Sterling High that spring of 1960. The teachers at Sterling weren't just teaching us math and science. Mr. Kilgore and Mrs. Richardson in English, Mrs. Edwards and Mrs. Williams in math, Miss Xanthene Sayles in French. They were teaching us pride and a sense of self-worth. We didn't feel like second-class citizens at Sterling. Our teachers told us we could achieve whatever we wanted, and they didn't accept anything but the best. But out in the world—on the buses, at the lunch counters, in the parks, at the downtown library—we heard a different story.

My friends were mostly juniors and seniors, all of them

on the honor roll. They were ambitious and smart, and they studied hard. They were determined to make something of themselves. I was determined too.

Some of us—Hattie, Dorothy, Benjamin, Virginia, and Robert—were having burgers at the Huddle across from school one day. Ben was telling us how he'd gone to Greenville Senior High, a white school, to take the college entrance exam. He was a brain for sure, and later we'd learn he'd scored in the top 10 percent on that test. He was offered a scholarship to Fisk, and he even had the opportunity to go to Harvard, but it was never clear how that would be paid for. He joined the Air Force after graduation instead.

Ben told us that at first they didn't know if the Negro students would have to take the exam in the basement. But because the college exam people were in charge, not the school officials, they got to take the test in the library along with the white students.

"I couldn't believe how much better their library is than ours!" Ben exclaimed. We listened, nodding our heads. Our school library had mostly donated books and only a few reference books, no *Who's Who in America* or *Encyclopedia Britannica*. The only public library we were allowed to use was the Negro one on East McBee. Mrs. Smith, the librarian there, would try to get us books from the white library downtown, but it would take days. In December, when Jesse Jackson, who'd been our star quarterback, was home on Christmas break from the University of Illinois, he needed a book for a paper. There it was sitting over on the shelf at the white library on North Main. But it would take so long to get it sent over to McBee, it would be too late. He went to the library to try to get the book himself, but they refused to let him in.

For Ben, who was a bookworm—he actually spent recesses reading books—the library at the white high school was a harsh awakening.

"It's just ridiculous that we can't use the downtown library!" Hattie said. "It's not fair! I'm writing a paper for Mrs. Richardson's class, and y'all know she doesn't just give out As. But the material I need is at the downtown library."

Like a lot of us, Hattie had seen her father work overtime at low-paying jobs to provide for his family. Ben's father had died when he was in the third grade, and his mother was raising the four children alone. He said they had running water—if you ran outside to get it. When I was little, I never thought of my family as poor. Mama Bess, Daddy, Delores, all my relatives took good care of me after Mama went up North. I never thought about what we didn't have. It was only when I started taking piano lessons at Miz Chastain's that I saw the kind of fine homes white people have. No colored people had homes anything like that. I began to look around. I saw that some white people lived in houses not much better than ours. But then I realized they had something we didn't have: the right to do, go, and be as they pleased.

"If we want to use the library, it's up to us," Hattie said. "Our parents are too afraid of losing their jobs."

"Or having a cross burned in their yard!" Robert added.

Hattie told us Reverend Hall had chosen the library for our first action, to make a moral case. It wasn't like we'd be trying to eat with white people at a segregated lunch counter. No, the library was for knowledge, and who could object to young people wanting to further their education? Plus our parents paid taxes to support the white library as well as the Negro one.

When she asked who was with her, Robert said, "I'm in." "Me too," Ben said. Others chimed in. "I'll go too," I said, even though at fifteen I was the youngest, and I wasn't even supposed to be at the Huddle until junior year.

"But we'll have to be arrested," Hattie warned, looking to see who flinched. "So the lawyers can take the case to court." She meant Mr. Smith and Mr. Sampson, the Negro lawyers working with the local NAACP.

Arrested! An electric charge ran up my spine. I wondered what Mama would say.

W E knew about Emmett Till and we knew about Rosa Parks. We knew that after a year of the bus boycott in Montgomery, the Supreme Court had ruled that segregation on buses was unconstitutional. We'd watched on TV as the Little Rock Nine, protected by federal troops, were escorted into Little Rock High through a scary mob who called them hateful names and spit on them. We knew about Martin Luther King and about Mahatma Gandhi. We knew about the sit-ins in February at the "whites only" lunch counter at a Woolworth in Greensboro.

Greenville had had its own civil rights demonstration three months earlier, on New Year's Day. After Jackie Robinson was told he had to sit in the airport's colored waiting room, 250 Negroes marched to the airport in protest. They read a proclamation against "the stigma, the inconvenience, and stupidity of racial segregation." They said they would not make a pretense of being satisfied with the crumbs of citizenship while others enjoyed the whole loaf only by right of a white-skinned birth.

That New Year's Day march showed us that we Negroes

in Greenville could take a stand for our rights. All over the South, equality was stirring, and it made us want to do our part. The time was past due. It'd been six years since the Supreme Court ruled in *Brown v. Board of Education*, and still no integration of our schools in sight.

I DIDN'T want to tell Mama that I was involved with students planning a study-in. I knew Daddy would support me. He was a member of the NAACP, and he'd marched to the airport in January. But Mama wouldn't want me getting in trouble. We all figured it was better not to tell our parents what we were up to. They'd probably try to stop us, afraid for us, or the consequences for them. Their generation had been about trying to get along with white people—because they had to. But we weren't like them.

We were living as a family again. Daddy had moved into Stew and Delores'. He and Mama shared her room at the top of the stairs. My baby sister Hope Callista was four and a handful. She was named Hope for the future and Callista for her great-great-grandmother, born to slaves. It was good Mama Bess could help out with Hope. She had two mamas too, just like I did. Both my mamas bossed me, trying to get me to do right. But I figured I was too old now for even one mama. On the night before the study-in at the library, I told Mama I was meeting some girlfriends downtown the next day. She didn't question me. I'd never told her a lie before. But I knew she'd stop me if she knew.

WE all gathered that Saturday afternoon at Springfield Baptist Church. Reverend Hall gave us final instructions: be polite, courteous at all times, don't say or do anything disruptive—and then he led us in prayer. We walked up Main Street to the downtown library. We were all dressed nicely, looking like what we were—young people who'd been raised right. I was excited about what we were about to achieve. We'd integrate the library and actually be able to use it just like anybody. But to tell the truth, it was beyond my imagination at fifteen back in 1960 to think that one day we could do all the things we were prevented from doing because of our race.

At the library, we did exactly as we'd been trained. We were quiet, orderly, didn't cause a commotion of any sort. Some of us went to the book stacks, some to magazine racks, others sat down at tables and read, just like anyone using the library would. Ben told us later he'd tried to read a *Field and Stream* magazine, but he was too worried about the girls in our group and what the repercussions might be for his mother, who was his family's sole breadwinner. I just hoped Mama wouldn't find out where I'd been.

When the police came, they arrested those of us who were sixteen or older. They didn't take me because I was underage. I was sorry I couldn't go to jail, though I was also secretly relieved.

When I came in, Mama, Daddy, Stew, Delores, and Grandma Bess were all gathered around the television. There on the Channel Four news was a story about my friends. The reporter was telling how they'd staged a sit-in at the Greenville library and been arrested. My family was watching in complete silence. Reporters and photographers were gathered around the jail as Mr. Sampson and Reverend Hall ushered the Sterling students out the door, with Mr. Sampson saying, "No statements, there will be no statements." No one had mentioned there would be TV coverage! Mama turned to study me.

"Those fool kids'll just get the McBee library shut down," Stew was saying, shaking his head. "Greenville is never, ever going to allow white folk and Negroes to mingle! They fixing to get our library closed and their heads beat in."

Mama was still eyeing me. I pretended I was watching the news, but my face was burning.

"No reason we can't use the library same as white folks!" Daddy said hotly. "We pay our hard-earned taxes same as the next fellow to keep it open, Stew. Wake up to what's happening. I been in that McBee library. Nothing but white folks' old books. They think that's good enough for niggers I guess." I had never heard Daddy say the word "nigger."

"Pretty, did you have anything to do with this?"

I froze, unsure of whether to tell Mama the truth or lie a little. But I'd never lied to her. Everyone was looking at me, waiting for what I'd say.

"Those are my friends," I said nervously. At least I was too old to be switched. "You know most of them, Mama. Dorris, Dorothy, Ben, Robert. They're good kids." I was finding my nerve.

Everyone was staring at me.

Then Aunt Delores said, "We don't want no trouble. We get along good like we is. Stirring things up will just make it worse."

I didn't say it but I thought to myself, *We already got plenty of trouble. We been living with trouble since slavery and all through Jim Crow. Doing nothing won't change the trouble we already got.*

"I did go to the library with them. I wasn't arrested. Because I'm only fifteen."

"Lord, Lord," Mama Bess said woefully, but I wasn't sure about what. Was it that I might have ended up in the youth detention center, or was it over the whole racial mess coming to a head?

When no one spoke, I said, "I would have been arrested if I could have. We have a right to use the public library. It's not fair!"

Uncle Stew broke in. "Pretty, you got to understand what you up to. Those kids gonna get their folks fired for sure!"

"Okay!" Daddy said. "Okay. Calm down, Stew. No harm been done. Those kids done a good thing. They on the front line. We got to welcome it."

Mama was silent. We met each other's eyes, mine beseeching, hers squinting hard.

Everyone waited. The news moved on to the weather, unseasonably warm with possible showers tomorrow.

Finally Mama spoke. "I don't want you in harm's way, Pretty." She paused for such a long time, I thought she was through. Then, "I saw the way those white folks in Little Rock done those students. We got our own fools here. No telling how white people might do. You got to think of your future, Pretty. Don't go gettin' in trouble that'll mess with that."

But I *was* thinking of my future. That was exactly what I was thinking of—mine and everybody else's.

THE next morning when I came down to breakfast, Mama and them were pouring over the newspaper. There on the front page of the *Greenville News* was the headline, "Seven Negroes Walk into Library Here." I'd seen coverage of the sit-ins in Greensboro in February and in Rock Hill, but it was a shock to see our story right there in our newspaper. Not only that, they'd published all the names, ages, and addresses of those arrested, right there for all to see! Now the Ku Klux Klan would know where they lived.

THAT spring the attorneys for those arrested at the library were preparing a lawsuit to be filed in US District Court. It called for an end to segregation of the Greenville Public Library because the students and other Negroes had been deprived of their rights under the equal protection and due process clauses of the 14th Amendment. One of the five lawyers signing the suit was Thurgood Marshall. Hattie told us the case would take forever. It wouldn't even be filed until late summer. From what I could tell, law was all about waiting. At school we settled down to concentrate on grades and final exams.

BY summer things really started to heat up, and I don't just mean the weather. College students were home, and they wanted in on the action. The Greensboro sit-ins had spread to other cities and towns all over the South. Jesse Jackson came home determined to use the downtown library. He, along with Ben, Dorris, Hattie, and four others, staged a sit-in at that library in July. With Willie T. Smith Jr. and Donald Sampson, the lawyers representing them, they were photographed on the steps of the courthouse, the young men in dark suits and ties, the young women dressed in pretty summer dresses, holding white gloves and carrying Sunday pocketbooks—as if they were headed for church instead of jail. They too were arrested on disorderly conduct charges and released on bail. Now the lawyers preparing the federal lawsuit for the March arrests would be preparing a second one for the July defendants.

ON July 17, led by a young white minister from Atlanta who'd been working with local Negro churches, a group of young people began walking down Main Street. They went in the H.L. Green variety store and took seats at the whites-only lunch counter. They were refused service. They moved to Grant's at Main and Coffee Street, where they were again refused service. Some of the group conducted a brief sit-in at the S.H. Kress store at Main and McBee but left when two police officers ordered them out.

Lunch counter sit-ins had arrived in Greenville.

I HEARD from my friends that when they sat-in at lunch counters, there were no arrests or violence, so I decided to join in. I didn't tell Mama, and she didn't ask. Reverend Hall and the adult leaders at Springfield coached us on how to conduct ourselves. They talked about Gandhi and the principle of nonviolence. No matter what happened, even if we were spit on or knocked off the stools, we weren't to say anything or fight back. They taught us how to fall and how to protect our heads and faces. Hearing what could happen, I was afraid. My mind filled with images of mean white people heckling us, pulling us to the floor, maybe kicking us.

About eleven in the morning on July 21, a bunch of us—ten boys, six girls, and three adults—walked into Kress. When I took my seat on one of the stools at the counter, I expected it to be too hot to sit on. But as soon as I sat down, I didn't feel afraid anymore. Total belief in the righteousness of what we were doing took hold of me. All across the South, Negroes and whites who were on our side were doing the same thing. We did as we'd been told, just looked at the menus we'd taken from the metal stands on the counter. We knew we wouldn't be served.

The manager of Kress roped off the lunch counter area behind us, but we sat on silently, waiting for whatever our leaders told us to do. All the waitresses ignored us except one. She had hair the color of a fox's reddish-brown fur. When I glanced at her, she squinted, looking me right in the eye. Something about that look told me she was for us, as clearly as if she'd spoken. That's when I realized she wasn't free to serve us, even if she wanted to. She'd lose her job if she did. I'd never thought about how whites weren't free either. They were just as bound by Jim Crow as we were, whether they wanted that or not.

The manager busied himself putting little printed "No Trespassing" cards all along the counter in front of us. The city police arrived, but they didn't try to remove us or arrest us. My stomach was clinched so tight, I wondered if it would ever relax. A few whites stood behind the rope, staring at us. We heard some rude comments, but no one touched us.

W E Sterling students and now the college students kept staging sit-ins at the lunch counters—Kress, H.L. Green, Woolworth, and W.T. Grant. The sit-ins always resulted in the lunch counters closing but no arrests. We knew it was just a matter of time before there would be arrests—which was what we wanted, so we could sue—but we didn't know when or where.

On August 9, we staged a sit-in at the S.H. Kress lunch counter just before noon. There were fourteen of us, eight boys and six girls; four of us were under sixteen years old. Though he didn't ask that we be arrested, the manager called the police because we were in violation of a Greenville city ordinance requiring separation of races in restaurants. He would have broken the law himself if he'd served us.

Our leaders had read us this ordinance, one of the Jim Crow laws. It said that it was unlawful for any person owning or managing any kind of eating establishment to furnish meals to white persons and colored persons in the same room unless there were separate facilities. Separate facilities included separate eating utensils and dishes, all of which had to be distinctly marked; there had to be separate tables, counters, or booths, and a distance of at least thirty-five feet between the area where colored and whites were served, and the eating utensils and dishes had to be kept and cleaned separately. As if we had leprosy or something!

The police came and arrested the older students. They were taken to the jail and booked. The four of us who were minors got taken to the youth detention center on North Leach Street. I'd heard from others who had been there that we'd have to call our parents to come get us. When Daddy picked me up, and I told him what had happened, he just laughed. I think he was proud of me, though he wasn't the kind to say so.

"You better tell your Mama," he said. "She gonna find out sooner or later."

I figured she knew what I was up to, at least some of it, but we'd never discussed it. I waited until the others had gone to bed that night. Mama was alone in the parlor, her sewing basket open beside her. She was patching one of Hope's rompers. I stood in the doorway, gathering courage.

"Mama," I began, my voice quavering a little. "I was at a sit-in today. At Kress. The older kids got arrested." I couldn't read her expression. She was looking right at me, and I had to glance away. "I got taken to the youth detention center. Daddy picked me up."

I didn't know what she would say. I waited.

"Come sit here by me, Pretty," she said at last. She set aside her sewing and patted the sofa beside her. When I sat down, I felt like a baby myself, wanting to be held, wanting to cry and be rocked and soothed. All the tension of the day and the last few weeks caught up to me. I swallowed it down as best I could.

"I wanna tell you a story," she said. Her voice changed, like it was coming from a deep well inside. We sat there for so long, I wondered if she was going to continue. Then, "When I was young I had another baby." I was so surprised I stole a quick look at her face. She had such a strange, faraway expression, it frightened me. "I don't mean I birthed him like I did you and Hope. But I loved him like he was my own." She fell silent for several long minutes. "Ever' day I'd go over to his mama's house to hold him. I'd play he was mine. I loved him like he was. I wanted to protect him from any hurt. The way you'll do when you have babies of your own."

I held still, not wanting to break her spell.

"I never told you why I left you and went up North, Pretty. You never asked, and I never knew how to tell you. It broke my heart to leave you. But I had to go." Her voice brimmed with tears. "I don't expect you to understand now. Maybe someday you will. But I just had to go."

Inside I felt an old wound, which I'd buried as best I could. It wasn't as if I hadn't been well-cared-for. Loved. But my mama had left me.

"That baby I loved grew up to be a man. He was arrested for killin' a white cab driver. He probably did. He was drunk and broke." She sighed deeply. "A mob of white men grabbed him out of jail. Took him to the woods, tortured a confession out of him. Left his dead body there like an animal's." Silence again.

"After that I lost my faith. I hated the South. I intended to bring you up North. I wanted to." Another long pause. "But I . . . couldn't. I didn't." Now tears began rolling down her face. She used Hope's romper to sop them.

"What you're doin' . . . these sit-ins. You don't have to hide it from me. I know why you doin' it." Again she stopped, her voice clotted. "It's all part of the same thing," she said slowly. "What they did to that man. What they do to us. The way they try to tell us in every way big and small that we're not as good. Not good enough. It's all part of the same." She turned to me, her voice urgent. "Don't ever let anyone make you feel you're not equal, Pretty. I mean it! Don't let them make you feel less than you are. Because you're as good as anyone. You're better than most!" More tears, mine too. "I worry about you gettin' hurt. But you doin' the right thing. I'm proud of you. You doin' what I couldn't do myself."

ON September 3, 1960, Greenville's library board and its trustees filed an answer in the July suit alleging the plaintiffs entered the Greenville Public Library on North Main Street for the purpose of making a public demonstration designed to create public turmoil. The "public turmoil" we created was to sit quietly at the tables and try to read.

They closed the main library on North Main and the McBee Avenue Negro branch. They asked that the pending lawsuit be dismissed because, with the libraries closed, the issue of integrating them was moot.

The *Greenville Piedmont* published an article with the headline "Greenville Citizens Say Closing of Library is Deplorable." Various white citizens, some of whom spoke on the record, some who didn't want their names used, all found the closing of the libraries "stupid," "ridiculous," "deplorable," and "frightening."

The libraries remained closed for fifteen days. They reopened on September 19, at nine o'clock in the morning. The mayor and the chairman of the library board made a joint statement announcing that the libraries would be open for the benefit of any person "having a legitimate need for libraries and their facilities," but they could not be used for "demonstrations or purposeless assembly for propaganda purposes."

When the doors opened that day, patrons of the formerly all-white Main Street library went about their business. By afternoon, cars filled the parking lot as usual, and people occupied the tables. When the first Negroes came in, no one took any particular notice. Two young Negro students carrying schoolbooks took seats at a table and began to study. Three Negro women came in and checked out books.

I WAS in exams during my first year at Fisk University on May 20, 1963, when the Supreme Court ruled in *Peterson v. City of Greenville*, the lawsuit filed following our lunch counter sit-in at S.H. Kress. The South Carolina Supreme Court had upheld our arrests and convictions for failure to leave the lunch counters. But the United States Supreme Court overturned the state court, holding that our rights had been violated under the Equal Protection Clause of the Fourteenth Amendment. A week later, the Greenville City Council removed all of the city's segregation ordinances from the books. The Peterson victory set a precedent for similar desegregation cases throughout the South.

I WAS so caught up in exams at school, I didn't even learn of the court decision until I came home that summer.

But on a hot June day, Mama, Daddy, Hope, and I went downtown and took our places on stools at the Kress lunch counter.

We ordered hamburgers, apple pie, and sweet tea.

CODA

IN February 1961, Betsy Chastain's novel, *Carolina Quartet,* made a quiet debut. It was eclipsed by another Southern novel published in 1960, *To Kill a Mockingbird.* Betsy graduated from NYU Law School in 1967 and joined the newly-formed Law Center for Constitutional Rights, founded to support implementation of civil rights legislation. She lived in New York City for the rest of her life. She never married.

ON May 20, 1960, after a group of Freedom Riders were attacked by a mob of whites at the bus station in Montgomery, Alabama, Zora Newman joined the civil rights movement. She eventually became director of the Federal Child Development/Head Start program in Birmingham and spent the rest of her life working for social justice.

ON October 1, 1962, James Meredith registered as the first African American student admitted to the University of Mississippi. Riots broke out in which two people were killed and three hundred injured. The Kennedy Administration called in federal troops and nationalized the Mississippi National Guard to quell the riots and ensure Meredith's enrollment.

IN the fall of 1962, the Greenville Chamber of Commerce created an official Biracial Committee. It began intensive meetings on ways to bring about integration peacefully.

ON January 28, 1963, Clemson University, under court order, was quietly integrated when Harvey Gantt became the first African American to be admitted. The University of South Carolina was integrated by three African American students the following September.

ON May 3, 1963, Sheriff "Bull" Connor ordered fire hoses and police dogs to attack demonstrators during a civil rights protest in Birmingham, Alabama.

ON May 27, 1963, after the Supreme Court ruled in *Peterson v. The City of Greenville*, the Greenville City Council, acting on recommendation from the Biracial Committee, repealed all local segregation laws. On June 3, 1963, in conjunction with the committee's carefully arranged agreements with the owners, Blacks and whites were served food and drinks together at eleven restaurants in Greenville.

ON August 28, 1963, at the March on Washington for Jobs and Freedom, Martin Luther King Jr. delivered his "I Have a Dream" speech to a crowd of over two hundred thousand at the Lincoln Memorial.

ON January 23, 1964, rather than integrate the Cleveland Park municipal swimming pool, Greenville created a "sea-quarium" to house six sea lions. The sea lions did not prosper. The pool was eventually filled in to become a rose garden.

ON July 2, 1964, President Lyndon Johnson signed the Civil Rights Act of 1964, prohibiting discrimination of all kinds based on race, color, religion, or national origin. South Carolina Senator Strom Thurmond opposed the civil rights legislation of 1964 and 1965.

ON August 4, 1964, the bodies of civil rights workers James Chaney, 21, Andrew Goodwin, 21, and Michael Schwerner, 24, were recovered from an earthen dam in Neshoba County, Mississippi. They had been arrested by the police on a speeding charge and released to the Ku Klux Klan.

ON August 6, 1965, President Johnson signed the Voting Rights Act of 1965, securing the voting rights of racial minorities guaranteed by the 14th and 15th Amendments.

IN May 1966, Priscilla (Pretty) Stone graduated from Fisk University with a degree in history and a minor in music. She became a high school history and social science teacher and taught in the Greenville public schools for forty years. She married her high school boyfriend, Ray Maybanks. They had two boys, the older of whom went to jail on drug charges. The other became a minister.

IN 1968, Dr. Frank Thompson accepted a position in the Cardiac Care Unit at Johns Hopkins Medical Center. Lawton Chastain retired from his law practice, and he and Frank moved to Baltimore.

ON April 4, 1968, Martin Luther King Jr. was assassinated by James Earl Ray outside his motel room in Memphis, Tennessee.

IN February 1970, sixteen years after *Brown v. Board of Education,* having exhausted all legal means to delay desegregation, and under court order, Greenville, South Carolina, integrated its public schools. Hope Stone was in the eighth grade.

IN 1977, at the age of seventy-four, Lawton died from a coronary thrombosis on his way to have lunch with Frank. Frank continued to visit Betsy several times a year in New York.

IN 1979, Alma Stone died of breast cancer at the age of sixty-six. She lived to see her daughter Hope graduate from the University of South Carolina. Bessie, Pretty, Hope, Huff, Lydia, and Betsy were all heart broke.

IN 1981, Alma's mother Bessie Cannon died of congestive heart failure at the age of ninety.

IN 1982, Betsy Chastain invited Hope Stone to spend the summer with her in New York where she arranged an internship for her at the Law Center for Constitutional Rights. The internship lasted for a year, and the following fall, Hope enrolled at the Howard University School of Law, earning a JD degree in 1986.

IN 1991, when Lee Trammell Jr. was fifty, he learned the facts behind his father's death. He had never heard of Willie Earle until his mother Emylyn, on her deathbed, told him the truth about the lynching and his father's suicide. Lee Jr. had been six at the time of the trial and had repressed any memory of that experience. He had suffered debilitating periods of depression throughout his life. The revelations about his father led him to counseling where he began the long process of healing.

I N 2003, after Strom Thurmond had died at age one hundred, seventy-eight-year-old Essie Mae Washington-Williams revealed that Thurmond had been her white father. Her mother had worked as a maid at the Thurmond home when Strom, age twenty-two, began a sexual relationship with her. She was fifteen or sixteen at the time. Thurmond was known for his strong pro-segregation position throughout his political career.

ON September 8, 2004, in a Capitol Rotunda ceremony, Congressman James E. Clyburn (D-SC) and Senator Fritz Hollings (D-SC) introduced legislation to award Congressional Gold Medals of Honor posthumously to Harry and Eliza Briggs, Reverend Joseph DeLaine, and Levi Pearson, all of Clarendon County, South Carolina. They had instigated the lawsuit that became *Briggs v. Elliott*, one of five cases included in the *Brown v. Board of Education* Supreme Court case which overturned segregated public schools.

IN 2010, the Willie Earle Legacy Committee in Greenville erected two commemorative markers, one at the Greenville County Courthouse and one on Bramlett Road near where Earle was lynched. The Bramlett Road marker was stolen in 2012.

ON the evening of June 17, 2015, a twenty-one-year-old gunman, Dylan Roof, killed nine African Americans who had welcomed him into their Wednesday night Bible study session at Emanuel African Methodist Episcopal Church in Charleston. Roof gave as his rationale, "Well I had to do it because somebody had to do something because, you know, black people are killing white people every day on the streets, and they rape white women, 100 white women a day." A website included a photo of him posing with a Confederate battle flag. He was sentenced to death in January 2017. He remains in a federal prison in Indiana while his case is on appeal.

ON July 6, 2015, following a contentious debate, the South Carolina Senate voted to remove the Confederate flag from the South Carolina State House grounds on a 37-3 vote. On July 9, the House voted 94-20 to remove it. The flag had first been raised at the State House as part of the Civil War Centennial in 1962, as a symbol of the South's "massive resistance" strategy to the civil rights movement.

ON July 10, 2015, in the sweltering noon heat, a crowd estimated at 3,000 gathered to witness the ceremony to remove the flag from the State House dome. On the south side of the grounds, those who opposed the flag spoke of discrimination, racism, and relief that the flag was coming down. On the north side, those who wanted the flag to remain waved Confederate flags, hollered rebel yells, and wore T-shirts saying, "Kiss My Rebel Ass."

Finally, two white-gloved troopers approached the flagpole, turned a crank, and in thirty seconds, the flag was lowered. Most of those in the crowd, white and Black, young and old, cheered.

AND on we go . . .

ACKNOWLEDGMENTS

I'M DEEPLY INDEBTED to Will Gravely, whose nonfiction book, *They Stole Him Out of Jail: South Carolina's Last Lynching Victim*, was published in 2019 by the University of South Carolina Press. Will has been exceedingly generous in sharing his extensive research and knowledge of the Willie Earle case. Thank you, Will!

Great thanks to Ben Downs, Dorothy Franks, and Rose Collins Harris for their stories of participating in the first library "study-in" and the Kress sit-in, which led to *Peterson v. City of Greenville*.

Many Greenvillians were gracious, generous and helpful in the early days of my re-education about the city I'd grown up in but barely knew. Lottie Gibson and Xanthene Norris recounted their personal histories of the Black community in the Jim Crow era. Anna Marie Smith shared stories about her husband, attorney Willie T. Smith Jr., who was a lawyer in many civil rights cases in Greenville in the 1960s. Bettye Fincher was great to drive me around town to show me Black neighborhoods, including where she grew up in the Glen Road area. Special thanks to Marion Mitchell for introducing me to Bettye and being a Greenville historian in her own right. Thank you to Elaine and Joe Norwood, Joe and Sarah Lowery, Diddy Abrams, Maryann Abbott, Manning Culbertson, David Barnett, and A.V. Huff Jr. for telling me about their experiences of Greenville. Judith Bainbridge was generous with her extensive knowledge of Greenville history. Scott Henderson was an invaluable reader, supporter and friend. Sue Inman told me about her student days at Agnes Scott, and Elizabeth Funk filled me in about her time at Barnard. Marion Chandler, South Carolina Department of Archives and History, educated me about voter registration in the fifties. Allan Jenkins, Doug Smith, and Bill Watkins told me about the Greenville they knew when I was growing up. Samuel Miller and the Lunch Bunch entertained me with stories about their Sterling High days. Thanks to you all!

The librarians at the South Carolina Room at the Greenville County Library displayed endless patience with my questions and maintained good cheer as I spun microfilm out of control: Steve Gaily and Rulinda Price.

Furman History Professor Steve O'Neill's articles on race, civil rights, and integration in Greenville deepened my understanding of the past, as did Clemson Professor Keith Morris's article on the integration of the Greenville schools in the Fall 1999 volume of *Upcountry Review*. Furman History Professor Courtney Tolleson's video interview with Reverend James Hall, pastor of Springfield Baptist Church in the 60s, provided me with a firsthand account of the library sit-ins. The excellent article on the march on the airport, photographs, and first-person accounts in *Carologue: A*

Publication of the South Carolina Historical Society, Winter, 1992, greatly added to my knowledge of the early days of the civil rights movement in Greenville. Bill Priestly was generous in giving me his dissertation, *Jackie Robinson and the Civil Rights Movement in Greenville.*

Among the many books that I learned from, two were particularly meaningful and inspiring to me: *The Warmth of Other Suns: The Epic Story of America's Great Migration,* by Isabel Wilkerson; and the paintings of Jacob Lawrence in *The Migration Series* at The Museum of Modern Art.

I'm grateful for writing residencies at Hambidge Center, Clare's Well, and the Rensing Center. Special thanks to Ellen and Evelyn Kochansky at Rensing for their warm hospitality on their beautiful Pickens County land. Warm thanks to Andy Baxter and Cas Spill for my "office" on Dey Street in Key West.

More gratitude than I can ever express goes to Ronit Wagman for her insightful editorial critiques and for her wonderful support and counsel! Many thanks to William Boggess for his incisive comments. Ginger Alden put me back on track when she said, "I want to know what happens to my peeps!" I'm so grateful to readers who struggled through some early (and later) drafts, helping me in ways large and small: Carolyn Holbrook, Mary Junge, Joan Cochran, Welcome Jerde, Gail Hartman, Theresa Quirt, Carol Jean Dunbar, and Randy Sue Coburn. Special gratitude to Jennifer Steele, Carlyle Steele, Rich Chetson, and Pamela Hazlett, who told me they loved the book when I needed to hear it. Hand to heart thanks to Louise Roche, Susan Welch, and Roberta Isleib for always cheering me on, and to my big sister Betty Bates for being there.

Thanks so much to Minneapolis attorney David Koehser for putting my mind to rest about copyright issues.

Thank you to writer Alexander Chee for permission to use a line from his essay "The Autobiography of My Novel" as the epigraph.

I'm indebted to Rebecca West for her brilliant piece of reportage, "Opera in Greenville," which appeared in *The New Yorker* in the June 7, 1947 issue (available online). It opened my eyes to a Greenville I'd never known, and set me on the path to writing *The Empty Cell*.

It's definitely taken a village. If I've left out some villagers, please forgive me. My apologies and thanks to you too!

I've had an A team for my self-publishing efforts: Copy editor Amanda Capps was tireless, professional, intelligent, and a great pleasure to work with. Thank you, Amanda, for doing such a fine job and for caring about the novel. Mary Byers, copy editor, graciously let me draw on her extensive knowledge of publishing. Emily Mahon, cover artist extraordinaire! You created an amazing cover. Thank you. Alan Dino Hebel and Ian Koviak at The Book Designers were a pleasure to work with. Thank you for the beautiful job of the interior design.

My husband Jeff has been a stalwart supporter all the way: the best reader, pumper-upper, editor, husband, and friend I could have. Thank you, Jeff, for always believing in *The Empty Cell* and for bringing me home.

PAULETTE BATES ALDEN is the author of two collections of autobiographical short stories, *Feeding the Eagles* and *Unforgettable*; a memoir, *Crossing the Moon*; and *The Answer to Your Question*, a novel. A former Stegner Fellow at Stanford University, she taught fiction and memoir courses for many years at the University of Minnesota. She now lives in Greenville, South Carolina, where she was born and raised.

If you enjoyed *The Empty Cell*, please let other readers know by posting to your social media, passing the word, and posting reviews on Facebook and Goodreads. Thanks!

For more information and contact:
www.paulettealden.com

ALDEN
2020

1650384

Made in the USA
Columbia, SC
24 September 2020